THE QUARTER QUEEN

THE QUARTER QUEEN

A NOVEL

KAYLA HARDY

BALLANTINE BOOKS
New York

Ballantine Books
An imprint of Random House
A division of Penguin Random House LLC
1745 Broadway, New York, NY 10019
randomhousebooks.com
penguinrandomhouse.com

Copyright © 2026 by Kayla Hardy

Penguin Random House values and supports copyright. Copyright fuels creativity, encourages diverse voices, promotes free speech, and creates a vibrant culture. Thank you for buying an authorized edition of this book and for complying with copyright laws by not reproducing, scanning, or distributing any part of it in any form without permission. You are supporting writers and allowing Penguin Random House to continue to publish books for every reader. Please note that no part of this book may be used or reproduced in any manner for the purpose of training artificial intelligence technologies or systems.

BALLANTINE BOOKS & colophon are registered trademarks of Penguin Random House LLC.

Hardcover ISBN 978-0-593-97676-0
Ebook ISBN 978-0-593-97677-7

Printed in the United States of America

1st Printing

First Edition

BOOK TEAM: Production editor: Jocelyn Kiker • Managing editor: Pam Alders • Production manager: Nathalie Mairena • Copy editor: Laura Dragonette • Proofreaders: Debbie Anderson, Emily Cutler, Julia Henderson

Book design by Alexis Flynn

Adobe Stock illustrations: val_iva (plants, crow, snake), Ghen (stars), theerakit (fleur de lis border)

The authorized representative in the EU for product safety and compliance is Penguin Random House Ireland, Morrison Chambers, 32 Nassau Street, Dublin D02 YH68, Ireland. https://eu-contact.penguin.ie

DEDICATION

For my ancestors, for all the stories they could not tell. And for each and every one of their descendants, for all the stories that they will.

I'll tell you what freedom is to me:
no fear.

—Nina Simone

Freeing yourself was one thing; claiming ownership of that freed self was another.

—Toni Morrison, *Beloved*

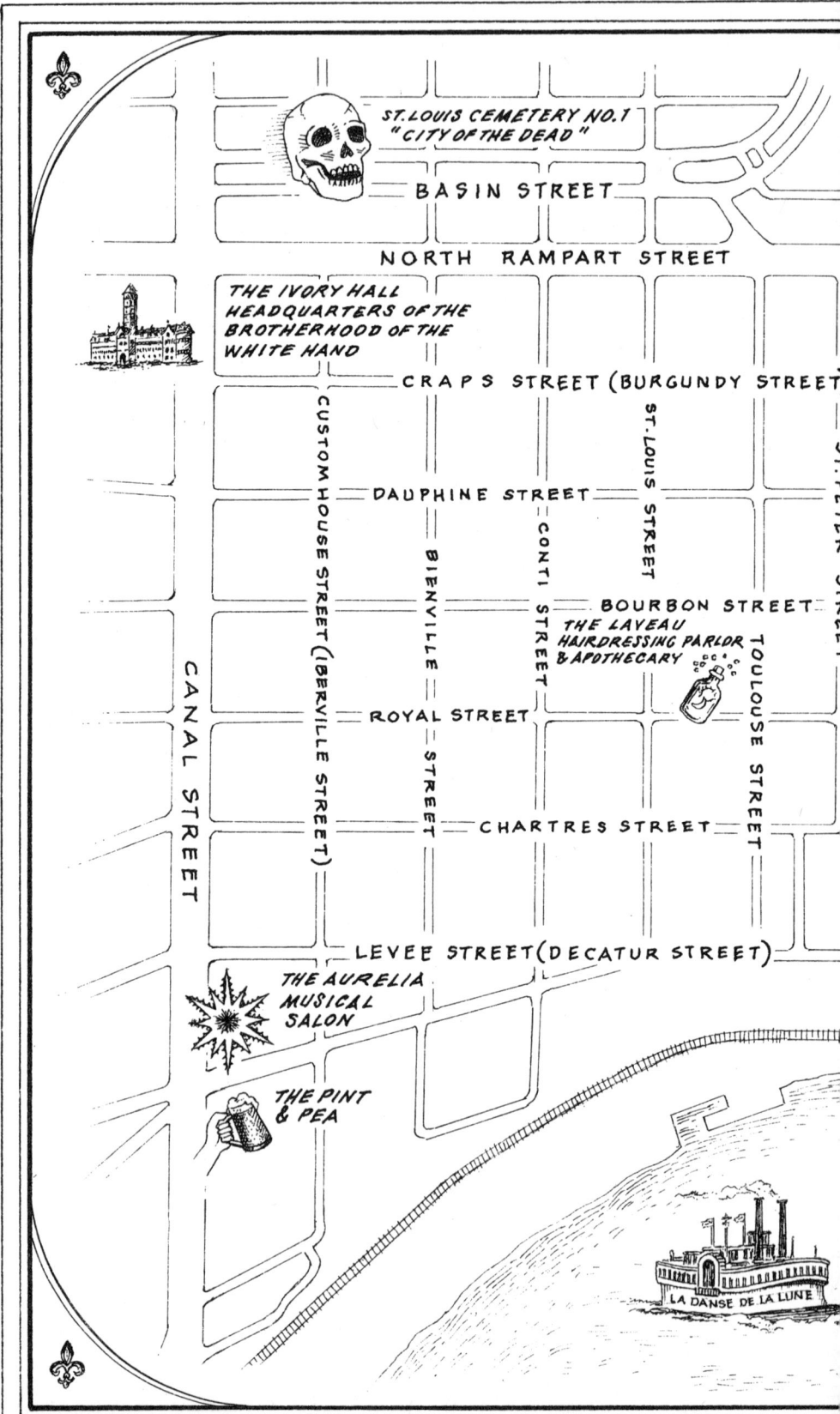

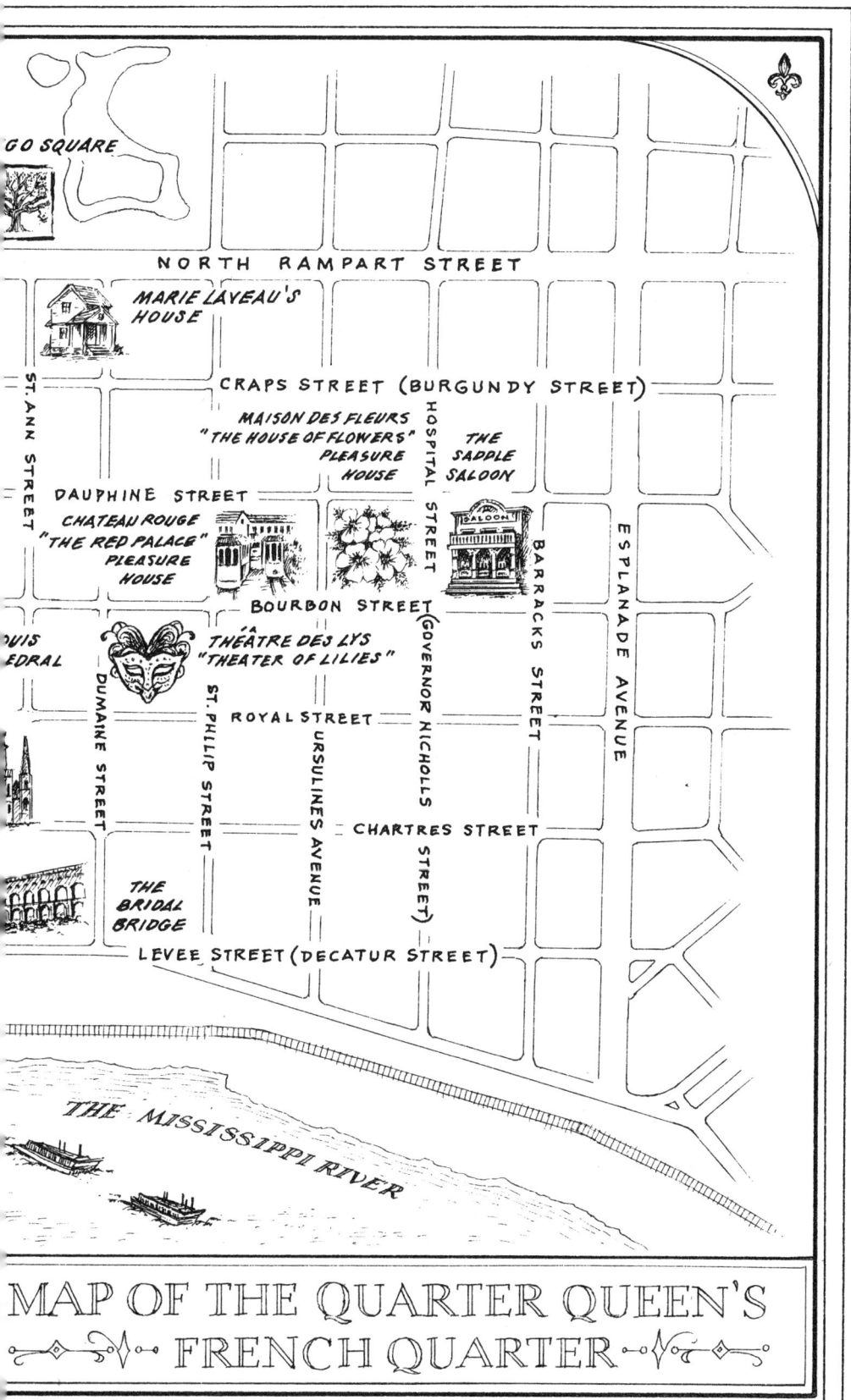

THE QUARTER QUEEN

PROLOGUE

MARIE

New Orleans, February 18, 1846

Marie Laveau had known evil before.

The same could be said for anyone who called New Orleans home. After all, evil could be found commonly enough in the pockets of bartering men, in the turn of an overseer's whip, and in the eyes of clergymen who turned away at the slightest offense. But to practice the art, the magic, the very *essence* of Voodoo was to know darkness as well as one might know their own lover. Being a Voodoo Priestess afforded Marie many gifts, least of all the ability to sense the kind of evil that lived beyond the mortal plane. It was this very evil that came to her one late winter night in Congo Square.

Marie stood before her court, filled with flickering torchlight and dance and song. A handful of her devotees dressed in Voodoo's customary colors of dark violet and gold worked the thrumming crowd, bartering brews and talismans to those seeking remedies for sickness of the body and the heart alike, conducting small rituals to rid customers of mischievous spirits, divining fortunes with tarot cards and tea leaves. The crowd was a motley mix for antebellum New Orleans: slaves out past curfew, free colored people, a few natives, white aristocrats. All come to see the Quarter Queen in her forbidden court. Her trusted acolytes, the scarlet-haired Nan and Ory, beat upon a pair of wooden drums in a pulsing rhythm.

Marie picked through the many watching faces for any sign of her daughter. To her disappointment, there was none. Ree, she knew, was likely drinking her weight in bourbon just a few streets over. Even likelier underneath some pretty boy or biddy. Marie swallowed down a sigh, as she so often did when it came to the matter of her daughter. She'd always been an insolent child, but now, at twenty-four years old, she was as wild and wayward as a mustang. Ree hadn't so much blossomed into womanhood as she did burst through it, her life a drunken string of midnight soirees and silly games. But that was mostly Marie's fault, now, wasn't it? In many ways being a good queen was far easier a task than being a good mother.

Marie felt the crowd's eyes following her, bewitched by her magic. On her head rested her crown: a tignon, the embroidered cloth spun into a knot that was as high and golden as the sun. Her body hummed to the bone with magic, her golden-brown skin glowing. She put a hand to her shoulders, where a heavy serpent rested, twined around her like a vine up an old oak tree, its green-black scales glittering in the torchlight. Her familiar hissed at the crowd of onlookers, many of whom drew back in fright while others leaned in, delighted by the thrill.

"Sosie," Marie cooed, calming the snake. "Enough."

The air in her Quarter had been sour with strange spirits today, and Marie meant to draw them out. Last night she'd dreamed she was standing alone in the middle of the crossroads. But when she'd turned, she'd found Papa Legba, Lord of the Crossroads, red eyes glowing like coals, pointing a gnarled finger to the only path before her: a long road entrenched in smoky darkness, endless to the eye. An omen. An unshakable portend of evil to come. She just had to understand what kind. Now she tapped her heel on the ground three times.

"Un. Deux. Trois. Father. Son. Holy Spirit," Marie chanted.

The crowd followed in an obedient echo. *Un. Deux. Trois.*

"I'm here!" A familiar voice broke the air, halting the music. Marie looked up to find Ree stumbling through the crowd, her dark coils scattered behind her in a wild tangle. Marcel followed, the boy casting a sheepish, apologetic look to Marie over Ree's shoulder. Ever apologizing for her mistakes.

"You're late," Marie said. Her gaze swept over the red flush on her daughter's face, the dewy glaze in her dark eyes. "And drunk."

But Ree only laughed, scarlet lips stretching into a sly smile. "Would you have me any other way, maman?"

Yes, by the saints and loa she would. But there was business that must be attended to, and it was better that her daughter be privy to it. One more lesson to learn, one more instruction she must teach. Casting a final stern look to her daughter, Marie waved her hand, resuming the ritual. The music started up again, the drums finding their rhythm once more.

"We invoke thee. Spirit, come," commanded Marie.

A rush of power, deliciously vibrant, flooded through her, lifting her from the ground, and she began to levitate, gloriously suspended. The air chilled. The crowd collectively held their breath, the drums reaching a thunderous crescendo.

"Spirit, come. Come. *Come!*"

But it was not Spirit who answered her call. There was nothing benevolent about the energy that overcame her. No, this time, something evil had taken her invitation.

It was immediate. Close. Dwelling here in the French Quarter. Here in Congo Square, hiding somewhere in the crowd. The evil called to her, whispered in her ear like a lover's coo. *Come play, Quarter Queen.*

A demon. Its presence should have been no more nuisance than a flea. Many demons called to her, as did spirits and ancestors, and all those in between. It didn't mean she needed to answer. But there was something to this demon's call. Something she could no more ignore than a sailor could resist the call of a siren into violent tide.

The music halted. Then the crowd began to laugh—a horrendously disjointed sound that stretched into one long guttural shriek. An unholy sound that rotted the air itself, pitiless and hollow. It was the demon, hiding amongst the crowd, spreading its influence like a sickness that kept on seeping into any willing flesh. But Marie would not be cowed. Especially not in her own court.

"Come out," Marie ordered the demon. "*Now.*"

Marie's magic flared, and the entire crowd quieted at once.

Ree stepped forward into the middle of the square, her bare feet touching the cool flagstone. She stood eerily still, her face carefully blank. And then with a sickening *crack!* her head snapped backward at an unnatural angle, then forward, dark hair falling over her face. As she tilted her head upward to gaze at her mother, Marie saw a thin smile stretch across her face and a yellow glow set behind her dark eyes, as if they were strangely bejeweled in the flickering torchlight.

The crowd silently watched mother and daughter, the Voodoo Queen and her princess. The demon had taken station in Ree's body. Not quite a possession, but it was taunting her, Marie knew, a blasphemous threat. And the Quarter Queen did not take kindly to threats.

Marie approached the demon. It cocked its head, regarding her with unblinking yellow eyes. "Marie Laveau," the demon sang from Ree's mouth. "Your sinsss call to you, Laveau. Can't you hear them from down below?"

"I hear only you, for the moment, demon."

The demon laughed. "Foolish girl. Silly girl. I know your greatest sin. Don't you remember his name?"

"And what is this man's name?" Marie asked. But she knew. By God, she knew.

With deliberate slowness, the demon said in the Old Tongue, "You know the name well, Marie Laveau. You know it better than your own."

Marie heard the name in her dreams every night. A haunting that would not leave.

The demon opened its mouth, and from it rushed: "*And so it shall be: A Laveau witch's reign will raise hell upon the earth. From its gates, the damned will return. Their king, High Jon, will walk the Quarter once more.*"

The wicked words lodged into her chest like a rusted knife, twisting and twisting.

A feverish murmur passed through the crowd at the mention of that fateful name.

Jon.

The name rang incessantly over and over in her head, a sickening song that would not stop. Demons always lied, but these words tasted of truth. Jon had been many things to Marie. Her teacher, later her lover, and above all else her enemy. He had been the only evil she'd ever feared. The only one she'd ever loved too.

Marie released her hold on the infernal creature, drawing away sharply.

"Begone, demon." Her voice sounded unfamiliar to her, weak. She hated that. Hated that there was a part of her still that could be brought low by him.

"I do not answer to you, witch—"

Oh, but it did. Marie crooked a hand, the motion like turning a doorknob. The demon opened its mouth as if it had been violently pried by unseen hands and emitted a high, keening wail.

Her daughter collapsed. Marie rushed to her and bent low, pressed a handkerchief to Ree's brow. She slowly opened her eyes, which were blessedly dark again, the eyes of her wild and wicked child.

"Maman, what happened . . . ?"

"Hush now." Marie helped Ree to her feet and moved her quickly through the crowd, her mind racing. Everyone was watching. Everyone had heard.

That had been no trick. No lie. Marie knew one thing to be true: Those words had been a *Harbinger*. And soon, everyone would know.

History had a way of repeating no matter how one tried to bury it. Some sins just wouldn't be so easily forgiven, Marie supposed. After all, she knew this better than most. Old sins demanded payment. And she harbored no sin worse than Jon the Conjurer. The whisper of his return had stirred something in her that she'd buried twenty-five years ago. She'd long been rid of him, hadn't she? *Hadn't she?*

Marie waved a hand, and the courtyard gates swung open, iron groaning. She pressed through the swell of onlookers and faithful Voodoos, each one hastily moving out of her way. All except one. A white man in a fine hat stepped into Marie's path, a few of his slaves gathered at his side. An outsider who'd passed through New Orleans on the wrong night, beheld her magic for himself and still couldn't make a lick of sense of it. Marie didn't blame him—no one could. She smiled slowly down at him, her eyes flashing white, the full force of her magic like sudden moonlight. He recoiled like he'd touched hot grease.

The man took his hat from his head in stupefied awe. "What . . . are you?"

A good question, indeed. One she often asked herself in her lowest moments. A widow. A witch. A mother. At times, even a hypocrite. But only one answer mattered tonight.

"To them? But a humble servant to Spirit. But to you and all your wretched kind . . ." The tignon piled atop Marie's head quickly unwound itself like a ribbon, unspooling her hair in a wave of tumbling dark water. In its place shined a golden fleur-de-lis crown, the mark of her sovereignty and shame. ". . . a fucking *queen*."

PART ONE

HEART OF STONE

For it is said that the alchemists have a most forbidden incantation among them, more nefarious than other spells, rituals, and rites of transmutation, the cursed words: Turn your heart to stone. Said with enough intent, and with the right touch of magic, these few words transform hearts and destroy the most stalwart of minds.

—SANITE DEDE, Quarter Queen II, chapter excerpt from her primordial grimoire, *On the Brotherhood of the White Hand and Their Fraternal Order*

CHAPTER ONE

REE

One thing was true as far as Marie Laveau the Second was concerned: If there were rules, you could be sure she would break them. Ree smiled and looked down over the room full of blacks and whites dancing naked under the smoky low light, a sensual melody vibrating in the air from the string band in the corner. Tonight, she was breaking more than a few.

Only a few hours had passed since her mother's ritual in Congo Square, but already she'd begun to sober up. She couldn't quite remember all that had occurred—a flash of Marie's white eyes, the steady rhythm of the drums, whispers among the crowd—but her mother had remained suspiciously tight-lipped about the whole ordeal and had retired early to their shared home on St. Ann Street without another word.

Now Ree watched from her observation balcony, where she had a generous view of Maison des Fleurs's latest stock of courtesans. Marcel rolled dice with Fabrice and Ory at her table. Whiskey-eyed and honey-tongued, Marcel was her second. Fabrice and Ory were cousins, sharply dressed Georgia boys who used their connection to the water loa to run spirits down the bayou. They belonged to her mother's Voodoo circle but, unlike the other members, didn't mind taking orders from Ree if mischief might be found. There were many pleasure houses in the French Quarter, though none like Madame Monet's House of Flowers. As she so often said, she had *a flower for every occasion.*

Loyal patrons liked to call this room *le théâtre*—a favorite for those who liked to watch others take their pleasures. A swirl of sweet incense and smoke slowly rose up into the gallery. Through the haze, Ree caught a glimpse of the festivities below: a throng of glistening bodies intertwined in the most curious positions along the floors and lush cushions, naked flesh writhing in unison, some moving in a hurried frenzy.

"Ree, must you always so shamelessly entertain yourself?"

Ree turned to find Anabelle beside their table, a teasing smile tugging at her lips. Although Anabelle Dupont was always beautiful, Ree had to admit that she looked especially lovely tonight. Scarlet satin, deliciously sheer, draped over the courtesan's sinuous curves, her dark skin glowing like hot coals aflame.

"Too much? I thought so too." Ree waved a hand, and the wild lovemaking and music suddenly stopped, the crowd frozen in place under her thrall. She held them in a trance. The Voodoos at the table paid no mind to Ree's magic. Her magic was not really *hers*, but the work of Simbi Makaya, the magician god, whose cunning could be called upon for the work of divination and illusion. He enjoyed the shift of things, could bend the fabric of the seen to his will. The game of it all. Ree liked games too. So, Simbi Makaya gladly worked through her to satisfy his own whims.

Anabelle took the empty seat beside Ree, casting her eyes toward the naked men and women frozen into precarious positions, no different from puppets on strings. "You know there *are* rules to these sorts of things."

"Yes, and what of them?" Ree mused.

A girl bearing Madame Monet's mark of the red rose about her neck and a scarlet-petaled headdress brought out a tray of sweets, hot chestnuts, golden cuts of cheeses, arranged fruits dusted in sugar and toffee. She eyed the frozen crowd dubiously as she poured more sparkling wine from a porcelain carafe into their emptied cups.

"The queen has gone to great lengths to see these rules set to stone," said Anabelle. "And I'm convinced that you're hell-bent on breaking every single one of them."

"Quite possibly," Ree agreed with a wicked smile. But even she had to concede that there were limits to her magic and to her mother's ever-thinning patience. Ree had been foolish enough to strike a bargain with Marie Laveau, a deal some might say was worse than dealing with the devil. After Ree's latest stunt at the Pint & Pea on Canal Street for all to see, where she'd hexed a group of drunken sailors to strip down to their underclothes as punishment for heckling her, Marie had expressly forbidden her from breaking any more rules publicly. But her mother hadn't said a word about *privately*, had she?

Ree plucked a strawberry from the platter, shimmering and round like a fat ruby, and bit slowly into its sweetness, well aware that Anabelle was watching her. Anabelle tugged at the rose pendant about her neck, the one that all but declared her status as one of the madame's prettiest courtesans. She was without clients tonight, and whatever pleasure she might find in Ree's bed would be of her own choice.

"Careful, princess. Someone might accuse you of sabotage."

"I've been accused of all sorts of indecencies. That would hardly be the first." Ree licked the juices from her teeth. "Nor the last."

Ree leaned in, pressing her mouth against Anabelle's in a coy brush. When they parted, Anabelle bit her lower lip, an improper twinkle in her eye.

"Like in Congo Square?" Anabelle said, a shiver of excitement in her voice. "They said you interrupted your mother's ritual with your own magic."

"Interrupted?" Ree's brow furrowed. She did not remember performing any magic during the ritual. But she'd been coming down from all the bourbon and pipe smoke earlier, and who could be sure what mischief she'd caused?

"They said you spoke with the voice of a demon," said Fabrice. A little younger than Ree, he normally spoke with a monotone indifference, but not now. She could hear the edge of dark excitement in his words. "I didn't know you kept such company, Ree. And to break the queen's rules so . . . publicly? How terribly *indecent* of you."

"The demon spoke of the return of Jon the Conjurer," Marcel whispered.

Before her mother had left, she had made no mention of a *demon*, much less High Jon. And between the copious amounts of whiskey, Ree hadn't thought to ask why she had felt exhausted after the ritual. It hadn't been anything more liquor couldn't fix. Anabelle and Marcel exchanged a glance, and Ree's confusion deepened. Yet more secrets her mother kept from her.

"You should know one thing: My mother's rules are not my own," said Ree finally, brushing the matter aside. "And as far as I'm concerned, she has too many of them. She's a ceaseless prude."

This drew a chuckle all around.

Ory snorted, pink-cheeked from his steadily emptying flask. "And a fucking tyrant, if you ask me. You want to know what I think? I think the whole thing was a sham. Another spectacle. Another bit of useless magic. I know you think you're better than the rest of us, princess, but Marie Laveau used you like another puppet on her string, and she made you dance all the same. Just like the rest of us."

Ree stilled, and her circle grew quiet. *Another puppet on her string.* The words buzzed in her mind. She cocked her head to the side, eyes narrowing. Ory faltered. For he knew that imperious look, the one that so clearly said *Careful, now*. The one she'd learned from her mother.

Ree rose from her seat. Behind her, she heard Anabelle choke a little on her wine. Marcel busied himself with pouring more. Fabrice paled considerably, drawing in a drag from the golden cigarette that shook in his hand. Ory shrank into the wall behind him, as far as the vined drapery would permit. He cast a helpless look at his cousin, but Fabrice kept his eyes low.

"I apologize, Monsieur," Ree began in a cold whisper, "if I gave you the false impression that anything less than absolute reverence for my mother would be tolerated. If anyone is to mock the queen, you'd better be damn sure it will be *me*. Anything else would be, well . . ." Ree's lips twisted cruelly. ". . . treason."

Ree felt the heat of her magic swell behind her eyes, the familiar rush of danger and power mingled into one glorious feeling. She knew her eyes had gone completely white. Ory gulped but couldn't look away. But Ory wasn't seeing her, not really. It was her mother whom he truly feared. Ory was right. Like every other poor soul in the Quarter, Ree was a vessel for Marie Laveau's power. Her mother, the great Quarter Queen. *Marie Laveau,* people whispered at her back. *The woman with the heart of stone.*

"Let him go, Ree," Marcel said quietly, pulling gently at her arm. "You're better than this."

Deep down, she knew. She was making a mockery of her magic, of Voodoo itself. Marcel always kept her little games from going too far. Her heart twisted in her chest. Once, alongside Marcel, Henryk had kept her honest too, their friendship the unlikeliest of possibilities. But that was old history, and it had been before Henryk had left. *No,* a dark voice reminded her. *Before he left you. Before you abandoned him.* Ree let the magic behind her eyes die down, a flame abruptly snuffed.

"I apologize, princess. Profusely! I—I meant no offense," said Ory.

"Of course not. As you were." Ree reached for her wine, sinking back into her seat and utter boredom. The thought of Henryk Broussard had turned her cold and wanting again, as it had done on many an occasion and lonely night.

Ree snapped her fingers. Below them, the crowd unfroze. The heady festivities resumed in a chorus of moans and hurried cries that stretched through the hall like silk unspooled.

Marcel leaned over, nodding toward the frenzied lovemaking below. "Aren't you tired? Tired of wasting your magic on such small games?"

Ree stared into his honeyed eyes for a moment, saw her own reflection in their warm depths. So cruelly apathetic she looked. She stood and shrugged on her traveling cloak. Marcel was right. The truth was, she *had* grown tired of this game. Particularly the game of secrets that her mother was playing. "Come then. Let's go play another."

This time, Ree would make the rules.

She led her circle down the spiral staircase, through the pleasure house's front salon, then outside into the wild music of Bourbon Street and to a waiting carriage. Ory bid farewell, claiming fatigue, and Ree waved him off. Quickly, the rest of them left the French

Quarter and, after some time, ventured deep into the bayou, far enough away from the industrial stink that swathed the city at night and the Church's careful eye, both of which weren't exactly useful conduits for magic.

Finally, they emerged into a small clearing surrounded on all sides by wisps of Spanish moss, the center speckled with various altars and rows of candles. The biggest altar belonged to Damballah, the supreme snake loa of creation. This was the place where her mother had trained her in Voodoo as a child, the place where even Marie had been taught by the Quarter Queen before her. If her mother refused her questions, Ree was still determined to find her answers, even if it meant turning to her own means, her own magic.

Ree lit her candles in a perfect circle around them, their flickering light winking in and out as the wind crept in through the trees. She shivered in the chill of the bayou, always cooler at night, colder still after rain.

"Aram," she called, holding an arm out into the air. A crow darted through the night sky, swooping through mangled branches and fog, then landing on Ree's outstretched arm. Aram ducked his head, eager for her attention. She stroked his coarse feathers, and he nibbled her hand. "What did you see, Aram?"

Aram turned bright gold eyes on her, and a message flashed in her mind's eye. Her mother, standing in Congo Square, speaking with . . . *her*. Ree saw her own eyes flash the cruel yellow of a demon's. The force of Aram's magic was sudden and heavy, filling her mind like a squall of bitter wind as a channeled message passed between them, a single word ringing out: *Harbinger.*

Ree froze. If she had truly performed some kind of dark magic, even by the merits of Voodoo, the likes of a Harbinger were beyond her little games. A Harbinger was the gravest of magical omens. It foretold the worst kinds of misfortunes and disasters, the comings of monsters.

Aram flew off into the darkness. Anabelle placed a hand on her shoulder. "Ree? What's going on?"

The others stood back, angling to hear. Ree shook her head. This was not a public matter. It soon would be, of course, if the Church had this information, further fuel to turn public opinion against Les

Magiques, the predominantly black and colored magical population of New Orleans. The Church wanted eradication of magic. A total clean sweep of the city, a wiping of a plague. She would have to work quickly to find out more before they twisted the Harbinger to their advantage.

"We must begin the ritual," said Ree.

Whatever dark magic she'd performed, the spirits would tell her for a price. Barter was the true currency of a city like New Orleans. Debts and favors flooded the city more than hurricane season ever could, and spirits liked nothing more than to make deals. Ree reached into her satchel and produced a bottle that sloshed with violet liquid, thick and filmy, more like cold morning porridge than a proper potion. "Drink this," Ree commanded her circle.

Anabelle, Marcel, and Fabrice quickly drank. They were Les Magiques, magical-blooded but far less powerful than Ree, making for useful conduits. Although she was High-Blooded like her mother, Ree couldn't summon the spirits without them. In a city such as theirs, blood wasn't just in you—it *made* you. High-Blooded folks held connections to older, stronger bloodlines, powerful magic. The Low-Blooded had seen their magic too mixed up, too muddled to keep its strength.

Ree uncorked a bottle of animal blood and began to pour it into the shape of a veve that meant *invitation* in the Old Tongue. There were many veves in Voodoo, each one inscribed with its own meaning, no different really than the alphabet.

"Now we begin," Ree commanded.

The four of them began the spell, moving easily between Creole and French. The cold that crept into their circle was not the kind common to the bayou. It was the cold of those long dead, of the spirit realm, that dove into the marrow and back up the spine like a bolt of icy lightning. The circle of candles went out in one snap of wind.

Ree squinted through the sudden darkness, her eyes slow to adjust. In a matter of seconds, something had changed. These were not her friends. Ree had summoned only one spirit, but three had come. Much more than she'd bargained for.

Marie Laveau, the first spirit spoke through Fabrice.

"The Second," Ree corrected the spirit. "Marie Laveau the Second, I'll allow. But Ree I prefer."

Insolent, this one. With tongue as sharp as sword. You are your mother's daughter, after all, the second spirit said. The words poured from Marcel's mouth crookedly, like broken bone mended in all the wrong places.

Anabelle smiled at Ree, but that was not Anabelle. The spirit twirled one of Anabelle's braids, marveling at the beauty of its vessel. *You've her face,* the spirit inside of Anabelle remarked offhandedly. *The first Marie Laveau's copy in every way. But there's darkness to you, little girl. Something far, far darker lives within your soul.*

Ree fought to keep her voice level. "I did not entreat you all for pleasantries."

Then make your request known.

"A Harbinger was spoken of in the city. Why?"

We cannot presume to know the reasons of demons. That is outside of our realm, child. Go seek a priest, said the spirit within Marcel.

Ree sneered. Unlike her mother, she had little patience for the Church and the Great Golden Sham they peddled every Sunday morning. "Allow me to be more specific then. What did the Harbinger warn of?"

The spirits glanced among one another. *You like games and riddles, don't you, child?*

Ree's lips quirked. "Who doesn't?"

Fabrice pointed a finger at Ree, and for one split second, the finger looked longer than it should have, gnarled and crooked. *Well, listen close, child of Marie Laveau, for here is a riddle you will not soon forget. The only answer we will tell.*

A voice erupted from Marcel's throat, dark and guttural: *What exists between the crowned sun and fallen moon? That which kisses both dark and light, the living star of eternal bright.*

Her circle spoke in unison:

> Though the land is ruled by the Church's holy trinity,
> We answer with our kin, our vessels of dark divinity.
> And when the holy bring their war of fire,

Set the blood of witches on the burning pyre,
And bind their necks in rosary chain,
so our triad will banish their bloodied reign.
And this, my dear, dear Princess Ree
Is the long-foretold Song of Three.

The spirits faded, leaving behind her circle and a mountain of unanswered questions. Only one matter was clear to her. This was beyond her power.

This was a matter for the Quarter Queen.

CHAPTER TWO

REE

"You should be on your way, princess. Before your mother comes calling."

Ree lay beside Anabelle in bed the next morning. The sun shone over the Quarter's rooftops and through the heavy, petal-embroidered satin drapes that covered the House of Flowers's rosy stained-glass windows. Church bells tolled in the distance, summoning the whole of New Orleans to its feet for the day.

"Don't tell me you're afraid of my mother too," said Ree with a sigh, rolling over to face the fresco-painted ceiling. She studied the rounded backside of a pretty river-sprite bent over in a compromising position, blushing to the roots of her golden hair as some horned god had his way.

"*Everyone* is afraid of your mother." Anabelle pranced from the bed, nimble as a gazelle, her pink heart-shaped necklace rising and falling in between the swell of her breasts, a totem of her favored loa, Erzulie, the sweet-tongued goddess of beauty and love.

Ree swatted Anabelle's bare backside as she passed, then poured herself more mulberry wine from the flagon on the nightstand. Anabelle's bedchamber was on the House of Flowers's third floor and was blessedly quiet, far removed from the sounds of pleasure and debauchery that filled the first and second levels all through the night, even to now.

The fireplace snapped with dying flame. Ree had hardly slept, haunted by the spirits' riddle. It seemed like a prophecy. But it was not like she could ask her friends what they thought—Anabelle, Marcel, and Fabrice had woken from their possession with no memory of the words spoken from their own lips, and Ree had kept the so-called Song of Three to herself. Not until she could talk about it with her mother would she speak of it to anyone else. Whenever Ree asked too many questions, Marie was fond of reciting an expression owed to her mentor, Sanite Dede, the prior Quarter Queen: *There is safety in your secrets. The tongue casts more than spells. The truth can be a more terrible curse than a lie.*

"So, princess. If you spend another night here, what might the good people of New Orleans begin to think of Marie Laveau's noble heir?"

Anabelle meant the question as a harmless tease, but Ree noticed the sourness to her voice, like the first signs of curdling in a cold cup of milk. "Since when have I ever cared what the good people of New Orleans think of me? My reputation is long past sullied."

"It's not *your* reputation that you're truly protecting, now, is it?" Anabelle countered.

Ree pressed her lips into a thin line and said nothing. It was true that lately she'd made herself more at home in the Maison des Fleurs's vine-covered walls than in her own home on St. Ann Street that she shared with her mother. She'd always felt content in the arms of pretty girls and boys, even if it meant running up a tab that she never had the intention of fully paying off. But most recently, that home had started to look like one pretty face—Anabelle. She found the young woman irresistible to a frustrating degree. Anabelle shared Ree's same penchant for mischief, but there was something hidden within its fringes. A lingering sadness that compelled Ree closer.

Ree changed course. "Did you like our little game last night? We could always play again."

Anabelle twirled a dark braid. "You always cheat. You Laveaus have a way of doing that."

"I assure you I don't need to cheat, ma chérie, to make you love me for one night." Ree hesitated, then said, "And is that what you think of my family? Of me? That we cheat?"

Anabelle glanced away. "What else is it? You walk about this city as gens de couleur libre . . ." A hint of bitterness tinged those last words: free people of color. "You Laveau women flitting as you like across the Quarter as free and golden as butterflies. And not because you've bought your freedom from the chains. No, simply because *they* can't even put you in them."

Quiet, Ree considered this. Had Henryk Broussard thought the same of her? Was that why he'd offered to take her away from New Orleans, from her mother, all those years ago, to see who she might be without her status and her magic? *But you didn't go,* a small voice reminded her. *Because you are your mother's daughter.* A flash of regret flickered in her chest, there and gone, a quick sleight of hand.

Ree took a deep swig from her goblet, then another, though she knew she should be spending the morning at least attempting to sober up from the night before. As Anabelle dressed, Ree couldn't help but allow her gaze to linger over her naked backside, on the deep lash marks that trailed her flesh like roads emptied and long forgotten.

The door to Anabelle's bedchamber flew open, breaking the lock. Anabelle squeaked and darted behind her partition screen as Marie Laveau walked in, casting a dubious look about the pleasure chamber. The air was heavily perfumed, sticky with candle wax and waning incense, the walls lined with hedonistic contraptions and paintings of storybook characters in lewd positions.

Ree flashed her mother a sour look. "Maman, you can't just walk in wherever you like, you know."

Judging from the sharp look aimed at Ree, her mother highly disagreed. "Come, we've business in the city." Marie cast a look toward the silk partition where Anabelle was quickly pulling on her robe. "Out. Now."

Half-robed and clutching her gown in her arms, Anabelle scampered from the room.

"Must you insist on ruining all of my fun, Mother?" Ree tossed off the silk sheets, stretching with all the leisure of a cat sunning itself. Marie flicked a finger, and a robe clothed Ree.

"For God's sake, you heedless child, if you insist on lying with whores in the dark of night, at least have the decency to dress yourself by the light of day."

"Oh, I forgot, you're the great Marie Laveau, the ever-pious saint who never sinned a day in her life," Ree retorted with a roll of her eyes. Although she'd only meant to tease, her mother fell silent, dark eyes studying her.

Sometimes, when her mother would stare at her with that faraway look, it was easy to imagine the person Marie Laveau had been before she'd become the Quarter Queen. But there were times when Ree swore that her mother seemed . . . *bewildered* to see her, as if she'd suddenly come face-to-face with her younger self. A self she had no desire to ever, ever recall again.

Even Ree could admit she was Marie's copy in nearly every way. There were differences, of course, little tells. If Marie Laveau the First was the sun, golden-skinned and dark eyes fiercely blazing, then Marie Laveau the Second was the night star. She was darker than her mother in complexion, her brown skin more copper than gold, her eyes darker and more feline, her hair a smoky tangle of unruly curls and coils that shrouded her face in a black veil.

Marie turned on her heel and swept out the door, then paused, her profile crowned in the muted gold light of morning. "Oh, and Ree?"

"Yes, my queen?"

Her mother turned, and the look on her face stopped Ree cold. It was undeniably and completely full of old regret. For that one moment, it was as if she were staring at a different woman. And perhaps she was. "You needn't worry, child," said Marie, her voice strangely quiet. "I've sinned plenty."

Ree followed her mother deeper into the madness of the Quarter day market. The French Quarter had many names: the *Vieux Carré* to the Creoles, the *Quartier* to the Frenchmen and Cajuns, the *hotbox* to the slaves. They had plenty of names for her mother too. The

Quarter Queen, yes. Priestess. And others not so benevolent. Witch. Demoness. Traitor. Ree supposed it was that one that hurt her mother the most—*traitor*. Because, according to her mother, it was also true. Some were bold enough to shout these names at her as she passed, heckling from the safety of their balconies. But Marie paid them no mind and continued past the moneyed men in tall hats who strolled the banquettes, the ladies on their arms who twirled their parasols coquettishly and flicked open their silk fans to gape at the Laveaus.

Though it was late winter, snow would not touch these parts, unlike the states farther upriver. Today the sun was hot and gleaming, and the only sense of chill in the air was one of anticipation for the coming of Mardi Gras, which would soon see the whole of the city in debaucherous chaos. Ree followed her mother beneath black ironwork terraces twisting like cobwebs overhead, where the creole bourgeoisie sipped mugs of steaming chicory coffee and picked at beignets dusted in sugar and jam, trading the day's gossip. Clapboard storefronts and marigold-colored shotgun homes slouched together like drunken friends. Bartering echoed from a maze of merchant stalls, English and French running together into one jumbled note. Any other day, Ree might have stopped and indulged herself in the market's wonders: spices piled into silver trays, spools of silk and damask, crates of goods unknown.

As they walked side by side, Ree waited for the speech on civility and manners she knew was surely coming, but Marie remained silent.

"Rumor has it you were busy last night," Ree finally said.

Marie cast her a sidelong look. "Apparently you were too. Tell me, daughter, do you ever grow tired of spending your nights with canal rats?"

"And you spent the night speaking with a demon. Perhaps I should be the one questioning *you*, Mother."

Marie drew in a sharp breath. "*Ree*. Not everything is the game you make it out to be."

"Sure it is. And I'd wager I had considerably more fun." She paused, then said, "I know what the demon told you. Of the Har—"

The word stuck in her throat, her mother's power flaring.

"Not here" is all she said.

The pressure on her vocal cords relaxed, and Ree rubbed her neck, scowling at her mother. They continued on in silence, leaving the worst of the crowd behind on Bourbon Street, walking farther until they turned onto Royal Street where the market was a bit quieter. Even during the day, the Quarter was a feast for the senses: Enterprising slaves sold their own wares on the side, peddling their stitchwork and calas cakes, and Voodoos plied their trade for a bit of coin—old ladies in rough-spun purple and gold turbans who read fates into the cards, bartered gris-gris bags to hex a wayward husband back home, and sold dried chicken feet as charms of protection. The Voodoos each nodded to Marie as she pressed on, paying silent homage to their Quarter Queen.

"*Change one thing into another, come see a show of magic from the pale hand of a brother!*" shouted a tall, silvery-haired man from a wooden stall to a group of white ladies, who covered their giggling with daintily gloved hands. He made a show of waving his ash-wood staff, which he used to turn a bucket of stale water into sweet wine, then dipped a golden chalice and drank deeply from his handiwork. A member of the Brotherhood of the White Hand, infamous alchemists who practiced the arcane magic of transmutation. Ree wanted to retch at his pompous air.

Never one to be outdone by the Voodoos, the Brotherhood had set up grand stalls along the road draped in their customary colors of dreary black and bone white, where their initiates performed parlor tricks meant to drum up business and steer the poor fools to their headquarters, the illustrious Ivory Hall, which expressly forbid any person of color—magical-blooded or not—from *ever* entering. The Brotherhood's infamous pale handprint was everywhere upon the face of the city, if you knew where to look—in the grand steamboats that carried the wealthy back and forth down the rolling blue of the Mississippi River, in the common household cauldron that could multiply a meal by two. New Orleans gladly welcomed the innovation the Brotherhood's alchemy brought to its markets, so long as it stayed within the narrow limits of what was deemed "safe." But ask any slave in New Orleans for the truth—Brotherhood magic would never be safe for folks like them.

To Ree's surprise, her mother approached the alchemist and looked over his strange arrangement of concoctions set in smoking alembics and cast-iron cauldrons that gurgled and bubbled like the world's worst stew.

"Make your request known," said the alchemist without looking up from stirring a strange green mixture in one of his pots.

"Two coffees." Marie set down a generous heap of coin, although they could order café au lait from the Pint & Pea just one step over on Canal Street. Ree couldn't help but marvel at her mother, who ordered from a rival alchemist no differently than how she might instruct one of her acolytes to fetch a bag of bones for her.

Eyes still trained on his mixture, the alchemist made a motion with his staff. With a flash of black smoke, two tins of water changed into hot coffee right before their eyes. Made the creole way, of course—full of warm sweet milk and earthen chicory.

Only when he passed both cups to Marie, who gave Ree hers with a warning look that said *watch and learn*, did he see the waiting brown hand in front of him. Instantly, his mouth flattened into a sneer. "Marie Laveau," the alchemist said with an air of express distaste. "Bartering with the Brotherhood is illegal to your kind, witch. You might believe your juju magic makes you above the rules, but you ought to do the fair thing and follow them too."

He tapped the wooden signpost hanging overhead with the end of his staff. It read TRANSFORMA, TRANSCENDE, PROGREDERE! Transform, transcend, progress! The alchemical creed of the Brotherhood, stamped on their every invention and muttered by giddy tourists and locals alike. It was a grim reminder to Ree that none of their progress included crossing racial lines.

"*Fair* thing?" Her mother laughed. "You mean the very same rules that dictate you imbecile men use wooden sticks for conduits and swap bodily fluid with a goat, yet you can't share a fountain with a negro man?" The smile vanished from Marie's face, leaving only cold regard. "So, spare me your righteous, pathetic indignation, you half-wit of an alchemist."

His pale cheeks flamed red as he struggled to summon a proper retort, the silence stretching. Ree almost felt bad for the fool—her mother's tongue could curse without ever uttering a single spell.

"There is one more thing. I have a message." Marie took a terse sip of her coffee. "For the Grand Wizard."

All that whiskey the night before *had* admittedly muddled Ree's mind, but she was sober enough now. Had Marie Laveau just propositioned an audience with the Grand Wizard of the Brotherhood? The very same fraternal order that made it their business to shun the magic of Voodoo? And Silas Favreau was no cheap parlor magician. Under his command as the Grand Wizard, the Brotherhood had emerged to the forefront of innovation and commerce, making New Orleans one of the most magically advanced cities in the South, ahead of even the likes of Birmingham and Atlanta. Gaining his audience was no easy thing for anyone, she'd heard.

Yet Marie stood unfazed, lips stretching into that perfect smile Ree knew so well. Now she understood. Her mother *wanted* Ree to see the true nature of Quarter politics at play. Marie reached into her satchel, retrieving a square envelope affixed with her serpentine L-shaped dark violet wax seal.

The alchemist scoffed. "And I'd like to afford a week of Madame Monet's loving in my bed, but tough shit for the both of us. Queen of the Quarter or not, Silas will *never* take a message from the likes of you."

"Won't he?" Marie asked softly. There was the slightest suggestion of danger, the rattle of a snake slowly rising in high grass. "Refuse me. Go on, do it. But I have heard your master has quite the nasty temper. For my kind and for *yours*. Let us see which he hates more: my color or your glaringly predictable incompetence. Hm?"

The alchemist blanched to the roots of his silvery hair. Ree could see him struggle to make the mental calculation. But whatever he weighed in that narrow mind tallied in Marie's favor, because after a tense moment, he silently took the envelope and pocketed it in his dark spangled robes, taking great care not to touch her as he did.

"Merci," said Marie coldly, then turned away, gesturing for Ree to follow.

When they were far enough out of earshot, Ree rounded on her mother. "And what exactly was that?"

"What was necessary."

"Oh, because that clears everything up. You tell me to follow the rules, and there you go breaking them—"

"There is a time for following rules and there is a time for breaking them." Her mother adjusted her golden turban. "Maturity is all about knowing the difference, daughter."

Ree realized their path had taken them to the narrow brick road leading up to St. Louis Cathedral, its high walls and steeples towering in the midday sun. In her youth it had seemed like an enchanted castle ripped from the gold-leafed pages of one of her storybooks, its stucco façade sun-bleached and worn, the noisy clamor of its pealing bells reverberating like thunder beneath her feet. But that was before she'd learned that there was no magic in these hallowed walls, nor in the holy men who dwelled within them. The true magic of New Orleans lived in its people, not in a little book with archaic rules.

Without a word, Marie strode toward the cathedral's front doors. Ree let out a frustrated huff at her mother's retreating back. "Where are you going?"

Marie spared a withering look over her shoulder. "Wait here, and for the love of the saints, stay out of trouble."

"I make no such vow!" Ree called, but her mother had already swept inside the cathedral's giant wooden doors.

Ree needed answers, and she was going to get them. If there was talk of demons and Harbingers, she could be sure that her mother would turn to the one man who would know best on the subject: the priest of the parish, the venerable Father Antoine.

Once she was sure her mother was a safe enough distance away, Ree silently slipped into the cathedral's cool gloom. Her eyes darted around the sanctuary, to the ceiling painted in heavenly clouds and bishops and kings; the little candles that were burning down to their wicks, casting spectral shapes against ruby stained-glass windows; the rows of dark wooded pews where men of science and learned books mingled with the holy and the magical, heads bowed in silent prayer and contemplation.

Every Sunday, in these hallowed halls, Marie Laveau too could be seen consulting her saints. Her dueling faiths as a devout Catholic and a Voodoo Priestess had certainly confused many of her enemies and followers. Other Voodoos had followed in her footsteps and attended mass by day and conducted their own rituals by night. But not Ree. How could she be any good at serving a god she could not see or hear when she was still having trouble serving the Voodoo gods who were as real to her as the ground beneath her feet, the sun in the sky? She didn't know much about the goings-on of religion outside of New Orleans—mostly because she had never stepped foot outside the city—but outsiders who came down on the steamboats were aghast at New Orleans's rampant spiritual mixing, so different from the ways in which Christianity was practiced in the rest of the South. Ree had heard of the white Baptist preachers in Alabama, Georgia, and Mississippi spewing the coming of brimstone and damnation, the separate churches and back rows for blacks and coloreds.

But that was not New Orleans. While Christianity was certainly upheld in the city, woven, in fact, into its very fabric—into the many holidays and observances and festivities—Voodoo had mixed itself into its blood. Curiously, Father Antoine welcomed Voodoos into the fold, much to the dismay of his religious superiors (some even said the Pope himself). Would he still welcome them now, Ree wondered, even with talk of a demonic Harbinger? Since Ree was a child, her mother had sought Père Antoine's council on numerous occasions. Ree had made it something of a game—as she did all things—to eavesdrop on their conversations when the opportunity presented itself. She slipped into a small broom closet adjacent to Antoine's private quarters and pried the old wooden slat away, revealing a small wedge. She peered inside, seeing first her mother, pacing the length of the room, uncharacteristically upset, then Antoine himself. Her mother had said he had been quite fetching once, but now he was a frail old man, tall and thin, with snow-white hair that fell to his collar and a pallid complexion that suggested he hadn't seen the sun in some time.

"Of course I have heard," Antoine was saying. "The discussions of demons are well within my purview."

Marie reeled away from him. "How can you jest about this, Antoine? There has not been a Harbinger spoken in seventy years." A pause. "Surely you know what this must mean."

This drew a grim nod from the priest. "They said the work of the first Holy Inquisition was never finished."

Ree inhaled sharply. Talk of the Inquisition was rare. Not one person of magical blood was eager to summon the terror of its name. The First Holy Inquisition had been before her mother's time, seventy-two years ago, under the order of the Spanish monarchy, who had seized control of New Orleans from the French, keen to see heretics and witches scourged from their newly acquired and very profitable land in the New World, all with the Pope's blessing. They had succeeded too. The first Quarter Queen had been set to flame on a pyre.

"What will the Church's answer be?" Marie demanded. "Antoine, I *must* know."

Father Antoine paused. "There is talk of a tribunal forming."

Ree watched her mother's dark eyebrows draw together, the look of desperate calculation in her eyes. It was not like her mother to be afraid of anything, least of all the Church. "You must delay their coming," Marie said at last. "Antoine, *please*. I would need time to gather protections for my people. For my daughter."

"You overestimate my abilities, dear one. As you always have." A note of fondness in his voice, the barest touch of a smile. "I am but a lowly priest, my child. But for you, I will try. Although it is not the threat of an Inquisition that ails you so, is it, Marie? It is Jon."

There it was again—that name. *Jon.*

"It has always been Jon." Silence stretched between them, and for a moment the only sound that rose up from the quiet was the distant melancholy singing of the nuns preparing for evening mass, the swell of an organ's chords. "I am a fool. A lovesick fool. I thought that I had killed the past. And that whatever had remained of Jon had died along with it."

"And now?"

"Jon taught me better, didn't he?" A bitter laugh escaped from Marie's lips. Her eyes slid toward the far wall, to the space where Ree's face was wedged in the darkness. "Some things never die."

Had her mother seen her? Quickly, Ree slipped out from the closet and back into the street. She knew Jon the Conjurer as the rest of New Orleans knew him—as a dark blight on its history, a would-be Voodoo King of malevolent magic, an old evil that had been thwarted by the powerful Marie Laveau, never to be conjured again. But her mother had spoken of him as if he had been something else . . . something *more*.

"Gather, gather, all around!"

At the corner of Royal Street, Ree joined the crowd in front of the Théâtre des Lys, its high golden walls dwarfing nearby establishments. A show had already started at the base of its grand spiraled steps, where a puppeteer wore a carnival mask made to look like a cheap imitation of the loa Papa Legba. Children sat cross-legged around the stage as stringed shadow puppets danced across an embroidered partition.

"Come ye, hear the tale of this city's bloodied war, and Voodoo Queen Marie Laveau, the witch of lore."

The silhouette of a figure in a long coat and top hat emerged.

"His name was Jon the Conjurer, a man, a witch, and a monster all in one. His darkness swept through the streets, chasing away the sun."

From puppet-Jon's coat, swirling shadows emerged. From the way that the puppeteer so nimbly worked his fingers, Ree almost believed he was using magic to enrich his performance. Perhaps he was.

"From the depths of hell, High Jon called forth the power of the devil. And all the good people of the Quarter bent the knee beneath a king who reveled in misery."

The shadows encased a crowd of puppets cowering with their arms raised in fright. The puppet-crowd sank to their knees.

"But there was one who did stand. A fair creole witch with power beyond man. With all the light of heaven and Voodoo, this witch banished the dark spell, and with one mighty blow, Jon's reign she did quell."

A female puppet in a high turban appeared. She gestured her arms out toward puppet-Jon, and he was unceremoniously flung across the partition and out of sight. On cue, the crowd of onlooking children clapped.

"Hair of raven. Skin of gold. Blood of new. Blood of old. Here be thy queen forevermore, Marie Laveau!"

With a pop of sparkling smoke that made the watching children applaud and laugh, the turban upon the Marie Laveau puppet transfigured into a golden crown. Her hands rose into the air, the war won. The puppet figurines bowed in her shadow. The curtains drew to a sweeping close, the show concluded. Ree watched, unnerved. She'd seen the show dozens of times, and she could no more blame the children for being enraptured with the puppeteer's tall tales than she could blame the city for peddling them. The real Quarter Quarrel was not something her mother liked to discuss. Ree had only just been born then, and she didn't know much beyond the street shows and puppet-fodder for tourists.

The puppeteer was looking her way now. "There she is! There she is! Our Quarter Queen."

Ree shuffled on her feet, slightly embarrassed at the dozens of gazes directed her way. They were seeing her mother, she knew. Not her. "I am not your queen. I'm—"

"Your name is Marie Laveau, is it not?" There was challenge in his voice.

"That is *not* my name." She'd said it before thinking. Marie Laveau was her name, but she didn't *feel* like Marie Laveau—she never had. Nor did she want to. And she was not the Quarter Queen, nor did she ever want to be, despite her mother's hopes.

Ree felt the sudden weight of a hand on her shoulder. She whirled to find her mother staring back at her, her expression unreadable. But Ree saw the way the muscle in her jaw ticked, the tightness at the corners of her eyes. She'd wounded her.

"You would renounce *me*? Your legacy?" Marie asked stiffly.

Ree looked away, both ashamed and triumphant in her insolence. "That's the trouble with you, Mother. You believe those two to be one and the same."

CHAPTER THREE

REE

Her mother didn't say another word to her until they reached the port, the water glistening and blue in the midday sun. At this hour, sailors and dockworkers were busy readying for the next morning's voyage. Ships were docked and tucked away, their sails ballooning in the wind like white sheets stretched and fluttering on linen lines. Beyond them, *La Lune,* one of the city's most prominent party steamboats, glided down the Mississippi, drunken guests waving from the rails, the bright notes of the brass band on board wafting to shore. At night, the beaded lights strung along the sides changed from red to emerald to gold, courtesy of the Brotherhood's alchemy.

Ree hated the port, though she knew her mother's business brought her here on a weekly basis to pick up the incoming supplies for their hairdressing parlor. She could feel a thousand gazes on her, the weight sending a chill down her spine. The city's Les Magiques were under lock and key, sorted according to their magic and employed according to the city's or their masters' needs: the storm-callers and tide-turners as steerers on the sea, even for slave vessels carrying their own kind as cargo; the soil-sowers for their gifts in the field to yield better crops of cotton and cane; the kindlers tasked as cooks, but on some occasions cutthroats too.

The Laveaus could not be so easily classified. While some Les Magiques were bound to a single loa or two, the Laveaus were the conduits for the many and possessed a myriad of powers from the pantheon of loa. But for all their power, the chains still held, slavery still rampant.

There were whispers of rebellion in small pockets in the South, Ree knew. Slaves turning their pitchforks on their masters. Kindler fire sending up whole plantations in smoke until they were nothing but ash in the wind. Those whispers had reached farther south to New Orleans, to its merchants and slavers and planters, who'd begun to fear the worst. The white men who told themselves they'd never allow New Orleans to become Haiti, whose enslaved blacks had won their freedom through revolution. Slaves whispered of Haiti longingly.

I'm gonna get myself on a boat one day, Marcel had said to her when they were children, walking hand in hand down the Bridal Bridge to the port side to watch the steamboats come in from sea. *Sail away from here to Haiti where they live free. All of them.*

Who would ever want to leave a city like New Orleans? Ree had asked, her eyes trained on the rippling blue horizon. *Best place in the world.*

But he'd only looked at her with saddened eyes. *Yeah, for a girl like you.*

Now Ree watched a line of naked bodies chained together emerge from the port's darkness, led by slavers armed with long rifles toward a platform in the middle of the merchant stalls with a sign in front that read AUCTION OF NEGROES AND EXOTICS TO COMMENCE. It made her sick to know that by tomorrow, their prices and descriptions would be printed on the front page of *The Quintessence*, the weekly periodical that detailed the city's most notable comings and goings and gossip.

Ree thought of Anabelle, the hideous marks marring the dark skin of her naked backside, and Marcel, the old burns along his throat and ankles from the heavy manacles meant to manage his magic as he tended his master's fields in the hot sun, the burns that never quite healed right and would reopen and leak and pain him endlessly.

Ree couldn't help it—she looked away. But her mother snatched her by the chin, fingers digging, forcing her gaze to the port.

"Open your eyes, Ree." They were the first words her mother had spoken since the puppet show.

"And if I do? Would seeing this change anything?"

She hadn't meant to sound so cold, so callous. But her sudden concern wouldn't change the cycle of life in New Orleans, as harsh and unjust as it was. In the rest of the South, things were worse, or at least that was what New Orleanian folks liked to say to themselves. At least here some could live free. The Laveaus were a part of that *some*, those faithful, faithful few.

"Have you ever considered that we are free because they are not?"

"Or maybe, they are like that because we are like *this*," Ree spat. Her gaze fell to her arm, the sun-browned skin that was deeper than her mother's but light enough that she could enter those white establishments as she pleased. Anabelle's voice at her ear, sweet and cooing: *You always cheat. You Laveaus have a way of doing that.*

Her mother stared at her, almost in surprise. No matter the topic, the time, the occasion of the day, the issue at hand always returned to one thing and one thing alone: color. It was such a silly thing to be fixated upon, Ree had always thought. But even that thought was a luxury, something she could put from her mind, like a trinket that she'd grown tired of back upon the shelf. But what of the slaves, whose brownness carried the same darkness as quill ink, the deep richness of clove? Could *they* put color from their mind? It was the silly, silly thing that this city had built its wealth upon, that had seen the roads paved and smoothed, had kept the coin passing from one greasy palm to another. Color was the unspoken curse that fell over New Orleans, thick as sea mist, that had seeped its way into every crevice, conversation, and thought. Color was the curse no witch, mystic, sorcerer, priestess, holy man, or even the Quarter Queen— most of *all* the Quarter Queen—had been able to break.

Marie Laveau stood still for a long moment, the wind from the river rolling in toward the port side, lifting the dark curls that framed her impassively set face.

"Come, daughter," her mother finally said, turning back toward the path that led to the Bridal Bridge and, beyond that, the inner heart of the French Quarter. But not before Ree glimpsed something brewing behind those dark eyes, something born of secrets and sadness. "I believe you've learned enough for the day."

By the time they made it to the hair parlor, the sky had turned from blue to lavender as the sun began its descent toward the horizon. The Laveau hairdressing parlor wasn't much, an unfussy little slice of property on the first floor of an old music hall. But it was still prime real estate in the heart of the Quarter, on Royal Street no less, and, most important, it was theirs.

Inside the safety of their own private quarters, Ree figured it would be the perfect time to corner her mother and discuss the matter of the Harbinger and now the threat of an Inquisition. But Marie wordlessly swept into the back room and slammed the door shut behind her, where Ree knew she would stay for hours. She hadn't any clients of her own that day, but she usually pored over the ledgers with a glass of wine, a task that would take her deep into the night. Ree quickly set about her chores to vent her frustration. The sooner she saw to her work here, the sooner perhaps her mother would finally talk to her about what was going on.

She cleaned the old blackened coals from the grate, beat the dust from the heavy drapes and rugs, sorted the pomades from the oils and hair balms, dusted the shelves filled with her mother's latest brews—glowing flasks meant for binding, healing, hexing, and love. Every potion or ritual item had its own feeling to it, its own unique taste. Golden oils for protection, anointing, and a bit of luck; glass vials of sweet incense sticks; Marie's bestselling love potions—philtres d'amour—bottled into red-tinged decanters; holy waters blessed by her mother's prayers and fasting; boxes of skull-shaped candles spelled with intentions; smoky-colored sleeping draughts that made dreams taste as sweet as vanilla; burlap mojo bags tied with string; gemstone-encrusted talismans that twinkled in the candlelight; countless curios. It was a well-known fact in certain circles that the Laveau Salon doubled as an apothecary. Such business Marie did not openly advertise in *The Quintessence*. Why would she, when the world saw fit to come to her?

Ree was halfway through scrubbing the floors with her mother's cleansing solution—a concoction of hot soapy water mixed with white vinegar and sweet orange oil for purging any bad juju, basil and cinnamon for further protection—when the front door suddenly opened. Marcel entered, breathless.

"Ree, I need a favor," he said.

"And I need another whiskey." Ree wrung the rag into the bucket of grayed water and got to her feet, wiping the sweat from her brow with her sleeve. "With ice."

"Ma chérie, please." Oh, she was *darling* now, was she? Marcel was a sweet-talker when he needed to be. She couldn't blame him though—he'd certainly taught her well enough.

"I don't do them for free."

"Not even for friends?"

"*Especially* not for friends." Ree sighed, looked him over. Underneath all that teasing bravado, Marcellus had a jittery edge to him. "What's the ask?"

To Ree's surprise, Marcel's face tightened, a shadow in his eyes. *So, this is serious,* she thought. He was only a year older than her, but sometimes she swore she glimpsed fresh lines in his skin that weren't there before, a weariness a man as young as him should never know. But toiling under a Louisiana sun was unkind work, even more so to slaves shearing sugarcane.

"I can't take another day out there. Not with him. Not like that." Marcel's voice shook, and Ree's heart fell into the pit of her stomach. His overseer, Mr. Tandy, had a reputation for being quick to anger and even quicker to unfurl the whip.

For good measure, Marcel turned and lifted his shirt to reveal his back, a hard collection of muscle born of farmwork and fielding, his skin scarred by lash marks. Right down the center of his back were three new stripes, puckering and red with infection. Ree fought down a gag and nearly turned away to retch. She heard her mother's voice, coldly disapproving. *Open your eyes, Ree.*

"What happened?" Ree finally managed.

"Does it even fucking matter?" Marcel abruptly paused, voice shaking. "I could work for six hours, sweating and pissing myself and shearin' 'til my fingers bled, until I filled up the whole fucking house with stems, but if I missed one piece, Tandy would have my hide. Ain't no point in discussin' what happened. Only that it did." His voice went soft, shaking. "He's going to kill me next time."

She'd met Marcel when she was eight years old, when they were the only two children to successfully complete their initiation rites in the Dreadwood, a grueling trial that had them wandering and fasting in the bayou for three days until the spirits were pleased and they could return home. But Marcel's home had been so different from hers. He'd been born a slave, and while they called the same city home, they lived in two very different worlds. She had lost count of how many times he had come to her like this, his skin hideously raw and red, those whiskey-brown eyes glazed with pain and fever.

A thick spell of silence fell between them. "Did you go to my mother?" Ree finally asked.

"I came to you." He cast a doubtful glance at the door to the back, where Marie had retired in private. "The Quarter Queen has bigger problems."

And Ree didn't. Getting drunk on Bourbon Street and stumbling home in the dark hardly counted as a real problem. And if it were, it was one of her own making.

"What do you need me to do?"

"Just enough of a slap on the ass to get him off my back," said Marcel.

"Poison?"

"Nothing too permanent. Corbin would throw a real good fit if something happened to Tandy. Been with him since his daddy died and left him all those acres."

Monsieur Felix Corbin, the mayor of New Orleans, was better known to the city's magical population as the Collector. Corbin had made a disgusting habit of owning only the very best of the city's Les Magiques, slaves he would organize according to their magic, like sorting salt from sugar, and place proudly on his plantation one by one like golden baubles in a shop window. Like plenty of New Orleanian slave owners, Corbin adhered to the Code Noir, the series of laws and edicts that governed the "proper" treatment of slaves (and by that same token gave ample record of how to properly discipline if those same laws were broken). So, he allowed his slaves their own lives, or at least a shadow of a life. They could venture into town, work as indentures to other guilds and merchants, frequent the Quarter, attend mass or Congo Square. This was, of course, a far more complicated matter for Les Magiques. When a slave held a propensity for magic, their price was considerably higher because they could, conceivably, be exploited in a variety of new and more profitable ways. There weren't many in the city, nor really in the South as a whole. And of the few who made New Orleans their home, even fewer did so free.

"If Corbin ever found out . . . if he ever caught you . . ." Ree shuddered.

"He *won't*. Don't you go worryin', my sweet. I've made it this long with my mischief, haven't I?"

Mischief was one thing, poison was another. And he wasn't just asking her for any poison. He was asking her for *aurum*. He hadn't said it by name, and he didn't need to—everyone knew aurum was as good as rat poison to anyone with magical blood. In smaller doses it was an incredibly effective irritant, immensely painful to be ingested or touched, causing scores of blisters that could sprout up like mushrooms across the flesh, ceaseless retching for days. It was exactly what he needed. Mr. Tandy had a bit of magic in him, enough to keep the rest of the plantation's Les Magiques contained and the fields well toiled, but not nearly enough to be Brotherhood material. The aurum draught, in a half dose, would keep him bedridden for a little over a week with the shakes and a bad fever. Nothing he couldn't overcome with a bit of rest. But a full dose would mean death.

Except, her mother kept her secret stash of aurum in the back. Ree's gaze fell to the door where Marie waited on the other side. She wouldn't be able to get the aurum now, that was for sure.

"Fuck it," Ree said with a sigh. "You'll have to wait 'til she leaves before I can get my hands on some."

"That'll do just fine by me."

Ree waved him off. "Turn around now, let me see to your back."

He stripped out of his ruined shirt, then laid himself facedown on the table. Ree hovered a hand over his ruined flesh. She closed her eyes, reaching out into the dark void of her mind, the place where the loa liked to linger and dwell. The gods could be fickle creatures, invoked only at their own leisure or whims, or by the sheer power of their vessel. If she could connect to Zaka, Lord of Harvest and Earth, she could use the roots and poultices from the apothecary for the healing. But her magic lent itself more easily to Simbi Makaya, god of sorcery and maker of medicine.

Her palm began to glow with a faint violet light as she ran her hand up and down Marcel's back, whispering the invocations her mother had taught her to the sorcerer god. His magic didn't feel like a soft blade of grass in her hand, the coolness of soil against her fingers. It could be said that Simbi Makaya was a secretive loa, and so his magic came in fits and starts; it leapt from her fingertips and onto Marcel's skin with the sharpness of jagged glass. Marcel hissed from the pain but said nothing. When Ree was finished, Marcel's wounds had closed, but the skin had melded together improperly in a clumsy stitch along his spine. It would have to do until he got to a real healer. But if Marcel minded, he didn't say. He hastily pulled his shirt over his head, turning to give Ree that familiar lopsided grin.

But his smile did nothing to calm her. Working with a shifty loa like Simbi Makaya could be a perilous thing for some witches, but it was more than that. What her friend wanted from her was quite possibly far more dangerous. "By the loa, Marcel," Ree said. "I'm warning you if Marie Laveau catches us stealin' from her, then we're gonna need more than poison to get out of this. Won't be enough magic in New Orleans to save us."

Marcel's eyes softened. It was the same way he had looked at her when she emerged from the Dreadwood after her initiation rites, starved and shaking from the cold, only to find herself face-to-face with a boy with whiskey eyes smiling at her like a Cheshire cat. Except this time, it didn't feel like he was saying hello. This time felt a hell of a lot like he was saying goodbye.

Marcel pulled her into a quick embrace. She felt his tears hot against her collar. "Ain't got no need for any more magic," he whispered into the crook of her neck. "No need at all when I got you, Marie Laveau the Second."

⚜

Later, Ree found her mother in the back perched at her long dark maple desk, poring over a large leather-bound book. It was not the parlor's ledger, Ree realized. It was the Quarter Queen's grimoire. Voodoo was still a young magic, born from the mixing of the old ancestral ways of their African ancestors and whatever strange new magic was to be found here in the South. Young enough, in fact, that there had been only two other Quarter Queens before Marie Laveau: her mentor, Sanite Dede, and before her, her sister Saloppe, who had been the first Quarter Queen of New Orleans. The grimoire had been passed down from each queen, and for anyone else to touch it would be a serious violation of their laws. But Ree found herself peering over, her suspicions needling at her. Her mother consulted Sanite's teachings only when things were especially dire. Ree knew she should mind her own business and turn back to her own affairs, but she could not forget what she'd seen. First, Marie sent a message to the Brotherhood. And now this? Something was *very* wrong.

Ree went to the little stove at the back and started a pot of water to boil for tea.

"What are you *really* doing, maman?" Ree sifted through tea leaves and settled on lavender for her nerves.

"Preparing," said her mother without lifting her gaze from the spell book.

"Preparing for what?"

She finally looked up and held Ree's eyes, a battle of emotions on her face. "The worst."

"Will you finally tell me what's happening, maman? Aram showed me that you spoke with a . . . demon. One that *possessed* me. I know about the Harbinger."

Marie snapped the grimoire closed, a plume of dust curling in the air before her. "And what else did that nefarious little bird show you?"

Ree never could understand why her mother hated Aram so. Her mother had Sosie, after all. Was Ree not entitled to her own familiar? Her own power? *Perhaps that is the real trouble,* a little voice insisted in Ree's mind. "That was it. But I petitioned the spirits, and . . ." The kettle whistled. Ree poured her water and stirred in her tea leaves. "They spoke of . . . a Song of Three? Some kind of riddle about a sun, moon, and star, and the Church. A holy war. I couldn't make heads or tails of it. But it sounded like a prophecy."

Ree glanced up to see her mother had gone still, her brown skin suddenly pale. "Put it from mind," Marie said at last. "The spirits play riddles on us for sport and will sooner make fools of us if we allow them the chance."

It was unlike her mother not to say more about spiritual matters, rarer still that Ree actually *wanted* to know more. "Maman," she said quietly. "Are we . . . are we in danger?"

"Ree, my love, we are two black women endeavoring to live free in New Orleans." Marie sighed deeply. "We are always in danger."

CHAPTER FOUR

REE

That night, Ree slipped unseen into the cool dark of the Laveau hairdressing parlor. Although she knew her mother was asleep at home, she couldn't help but hurry through the shadowed space, her only source of light the faint blushing glow of Marie's love potions on the far shelf.

Ree let herself into the back room and began searching through the little chest tucked beneath her mother's maple desk. The brass clasp had been left undone, which meant her mother had every intention of returning to it. Although she had her task for Marcel, Ree couldn't help but remember that unease she'd felt earlier when she'd mentioned the Harbinger to her mother. *The spirits play riddles on us for sport and will sooner make fools of us if we allow them the chance.* But as Ree searched the chest and sifted through Marie's belongings, she knew if she were caught, she could not blame the spirits now for being a fool for a friend. Her mother would blame only her.

Finally, Ree found what she was searching for—a small vial with a gray cork. There was less than an ounce of aurum in the vial, little more than a sprinkle of salt. The aurum itself could be mistaken for powdered pewter but had the strangest touch of gold under the firelight. In New Orleans, the aurum trade was rivaled only by the slave trade, both of which came from the far-off shores of Africa. It was the single greatest irony she knew—that both were stolen from their homeland, and that aurum helped keep it that way.

But Ree's attention had turned from the aurum to something else. She stared at the Quarter Queen's grimoire, carefully tucked beneath a long white gown and a matching white-owl-feathered mask. That book contained power more forbidden than the likes of aurum. Ree tore her eyes away. It was power she had no need of. *Not yet,* a voice sang in her thoughts.

Ree pocketed the aurum and quietly left the parlor. She pulled on her hood as she stepped out into the moonlit streets, careful to navigate the muck and grime that clung to the Quarter's cobbled walkways like clotted honey. Under the cover of nightfall, the city took on its second life. On Bourbon Street, she passed performers dancing in garish masks made to look like the characters of Mardi Gras season—the crowned Carnival King, the mad-eyed Jester who'd gladly play the fool for a coin or two—and many faux mystics: seers in spangled headdresses, necks and arms bedazzled in counterfeit silver, plying their trades on wooden tables covered in weathered tarot cards; false rootworkers who sold bottled dirt masquerading as magical fertilizer to plantation men. But they were not Les Magiques. Not one drop of real magical blood. Ree knew that. The police knew that. But the wide-eyed tourists did not. What did a white lie matter if the coin was real? The police were much obliged to turn away so long as their cut was accounted for.

It was nearly curfew time, and any act of magic in the matter of performance, barter, or spectacle would be illegal and a punishable offense. A row of lawmen circled the road on horseback, nagging a group of black mystics for their freedom papers. Free Les Magiques within New Orleans were exceptionally rare. What owner would want to part with that kind of power under their thumb? *Fools,* Ree thought. *Back roads exist for a reason.* She crossed the road, pulling her hood tight in a ripple of indigo velvet.

She passed a group of giggling girls who—judging from their accents—had come downriver from Alabama, Mobile or possibly Blakeley. They stumbled drunkenly by Ree, their lacy gloved fingers swinging white severed hand trinkets that burned with the silverish glow of alchemical spellfire. The Brotherhood called them Lumen Manus, though everyone else in the Quarter called them for what they were: counterfeit Hands of Glory.

Tourists bought them as souvenirs at the market stalls along Bourbon Street at night instead of the mundane standard fare of lanterns or gas lamps. Ree curled her lip. By principle alone she was above such useless novelties. She had to be. Brotherhood magic wasn't meant for her kind. In a city such as New Orleans, alchemy had never been used to help black hands, only to shackle them.

The pale glow of the Lumen Manus bobbed ahead, ghostly and wafting, casting a gauzy haze over the various shop windows and signposts that swung in the night breeze. Ree followed in their light until she reached the House of Flowers. A sickly-sweet stench swarmed her. Roses blanketed its gallery, threaded along the black scrollwork, enchanted by the madame to grow as big as pumpkins. The roses' razor-sharp thorns kept rowdy and unpaying men from climbing inside for their pleasure and stopped the girls from climbing down and escaping. Ree ducked beneath the flower-laced gallery, stepping onto the wooden banquette and into the pleasure house.

The parlor was unusually sparse tonight, outside of a few courtesans who giggled and ogled Ree over the rims of their golden chalices as she entered. The interior was dim, the lanterns turned low. A grand chandelier hung in the center of the room, fashioned like a multicolored bouquet, its dangling crystals set with orchids and red roses, the brass bars shaped into twisting vines. A faux wisteria tree towered to the ceiling, its long branches like beckoning arms, its purple blossoms floating down into the parlor, where they had been enchanted to fall every hour.

The girl at the desk blushed at the sight of Ree. "Mademoiselle Laveau," she said, sweet as sugared tea, the way Madame Monet had so carefully instructed for treasured patrons. "Anabelle is indisposed for the night."

Ree sighed, plucking a glass of champagne from a gilded tray. "I didn't come for pleasure tonight, Florence." She tried to ignore the bitter pang in her chest at that magical little word. *Indisposed.* Caring for a girl in Anabelle's profession hurt worse than any hex. "I came for business. I have a meeting in the garden."

"Of course, right this way, Mademoiselle Laveau," said Florence.

Ree followed the girl down the hall, past countless doors with placards reading OCCUPÉ where curious noises and sighs could be heard, through a bronzed archway draped in long, waifish threads of gray Spanish moss, and into a private parlor, the part of Madame Monet's house she liked to call "the garden." True to its namesake, every inch of the garden's walls was filled with wallpaper patterned with twisting branches and gaudy red roses, and a floral scent rose from the floorboards, the smell of a spring garden after a soft spell of rain. Ree found that public presence in the garden was blessedly meager, glimpsing only a few moneyed men lingering on the emerald-upholstered canapés scattered about the room, pretty girls in their laps mewling sweet nothings in their ears.

Ree easily found Marcel waiting at a candlelit table facing the street. Although there was a dark pane of glass enchanted to look like it was perpetually misted with rain that separated the garden from the rest of the commotion and clamor of Bourbon Street, you could still hear the music, the cries of revelry and senseless fun. But that was part of the thrill for most patrons: one foot still in the chaos outside, another planted in the pleasures that could be found only in private. By the time Ree seated herself across from Marcel, he was already downing his third scotch, by the look of him.

"You're actually on time," Marcel said. He slid a glass across the table to her.

"Don't try to look so surprised, mon chéri," Ree said as she easily caught the glass and downed the whole of it in one go.

The burn of Madame Monet's scotch was certainly better fare than the clouded lagers they served in dusty flagons at the Pint & Pea. A lovely courtesan glided by in the hall, pink petals spilling from her carnation headdress. She batted thick eyelashes at Ree, who winked at her.

Marcel half turned, slyly considering Ree over the rim of his scotch. "Are you set on bedding all of Monet's whores, Ree?"

"Only the pretty ones."

"And Anabelle? I suppose you are simply *bedding* her too?"

"I suppose that's none of your business."

"You know something? It's fine by me whatever business the two of y'all get up to in your spare time. Don't bother me none. But you need to remember something, Ree. It's still a game in the end."

Why did that sound like a warning? What reason did Marcel have to warn her about a girl like Anabelle?

"Don't worry, I know the rules."

"Do you?" Silence passed between them. For a moment, there was only the sound of the parlor, the tinkle of laughter and glasses, the soft swell of rain that never fell. "Did you know them with Henryk?"

The smirk faded on Ree's lips. "I don't think I like that question."

Marcel's eyes held her, molten brown in the parlor's candlelit darkness. "You forget I know you, Ree. I know how you really felt about Henryk Broussard. However badly that ended. I know it was real. But this thing you got going with Anabelle? Consider this the advice of a friend: You playin' the wrong game with this girl. And it's going to end badly."

"And why is that?"

"You know why, Ree." His mouth quirked into a tight smile. "Because you both been dealt two very, *very* different hands."

Ree said nothing. She reached into her pocket, retrieving the vial of aurum. She passed it to Marcel beneath the table. But when she spoke again, her voice was unusually quiet. "Now you owe me," she said, changing course. "And more than just a few drinks, you bastard."

Marcel grinned. "Forever indebted."

After they concluded their business and stepped out from the House of Flowers's sweet damp and into the street, Ree considered her friend with narrowed eyes one last time. "Be careful, Marcel. Only half a tincture. Not a drop more. And slip it into something he ingests, something that can cover the taste."

"His moonshine?"

"I don't care if the bastard drinks piss. That's his business. You just make sure it's strong enough to cover the taste of aurum."

Marcel's grin deepened, and she could see his plan already

hatching in his thoughts. "You're a good friend, Ree." His voice took on a strange note. "You'll be an even better queen one day."

One day. Those two little words haunted her sometimes. The inevitability of her fate was almost too much to bear most nights. Because she didn't want it. She'd seen what the costs of being queen had done to her mother.

"What if . . . what if I don't want to be queen?" she asked quietly. She could allow herself a moment of weakness with Marcel. He saw past her little games. He saw her.

"I don't think this city will allow folks like us to choose much what we want." He dipped a finger beneath her chin playfully, but his smile didn't reach his eyes. "So, take what you can get, darling."

Marcel turned to go, but Ree stopped him by the arm. "Listen, Marcel. *Not a drop more.* Don't be a fool."

"Don't worry, Ree. I'll be a perfect little saint like you."

Ree chuckled. "No saints," she called after him as he set into a jog down the road.

"And no fucking sinners," he shouted back over his shoulder.

Ree carried those words with her back down Bourbon Street as nightfall deepened over the Quarter and gas lamps flickered to life one by one. *No saints and no sinners.* A common saying among New Orleans's underclass. She couldn't help but think of her mother, infamous for just as many miracles as misdeeds. And what about herself? Would this favor to Marcel be a miracle or, she feared, a misdeed? What if he used more than he needed? It became an annoying refrain she chewed on as she made her way home through the Quarter's mist-laden streets. *What if? What if?*

By the time she turned onto St. Ann, she could see the barest shape of a carriage whisking away. Her mother's private carriage. Curious, Ree approached the front of their house, where there was always a Voodoo acolyte stationed by the door for protection. Tonight, it was Nan standing duty.

"Where is my mother going?" Ree asked.

Nan twisted a scarlet coil with her finger nervously. "She had business. That is all I'm at liberty to say."

"Well, I'm at liberty to make you say more if you don't," Ree snapped.

A talented soil-sower, Nan was a girl all of seventeen who had escaped life on her plantation just the year before. She'd come downriver from Mobile seeking refuge with the Laveaus and had a wicked talent for brewing poisons that Marie Laveau had found useful. She was talented, but she wasn't stupid. Picking a fight with Marie Laveau the Second was a good way to be sent back upriver.

"The Brotherhood," Nan relented.

The Brotherhood? Again? What kind of unholy alliance was her mother stirring up?

Nan shifted uneasily, and Ree crossed her arms. She had a cherubic face, an air about her that made her seem younger than she was. Ree almost felt bad leaning on her so hard. "What else?"

"They spoke of an Inquisitor," Nan burst out then abruptly made a face suggesting she wished she hadn't.

Ree's eyebrows bunched together. "An Inquisitor? Here in the city?"

"Not yet. But they are expecting him."

So, Antoine's talk of a tribunal was true. The Church was already sending an Inquisitor to the city. Inquisitors were witch-hunters, arresting those accused of heresy and blasphemy and interrogating them. Her mother had warned her of their terrible instruments of torture—terrifying contraptions that pulled limbs from their sockets, spikes that would penetrate through the mouth and the anus. Commonly, they set their victims alight on towering pyres of howling flame.

"The Inquisitor. Who is it?"

The girl pressed her lips into a thin, defiant line. She'd already divulged too much.

"Who. Is. It?" Ree said, allowing magic to fill her eyes.

"Inquisitor Broussard," Nan said at last. "Henryk Broussard."

Ree froze in shock, whatever she'd been about to say lost on her tongue.

Henryk Broussard. She hadn't seen him in more than eight long years, ever since he'd left New Orleans. Since she'd refused to join him. An orphan taken in by the nuns of the Ursuline Order, Henryk had been Antoine's ward, a path that she always thought would set him on course to being a priest. Not an Inquisitor.

Ree dashed around to the back of the house, to the barn where the horses rested. She whistled, drawing the attention of Thistle, her mother's favorite mare, who awoke to give Ree a dubious look. Ree pulled her forward by the reins, saddled her up, and trotted her to the street, where Nan was peering after her.

"Not a word," Ree warned Nan from the saddle. And then she was off, riding out of the Quarter, past the city's limits, and into the darkness of unknown roads.

CHAPTER FIVE

REE

The farther Ree rode from the city, the more her unbidden thoughts of Henryk Broussard grew. When Ree was just eight years old, Marie had taken her through the nunnery's sick ward after a plague outbreak to aid the afflicted. There, she'd met a shivering, plague-riddled boy with strange gray eyes, hovering on the cusp of death. She'd coaxed him back to life, and after, Henryk Broussard had become her first friend, and really, if she were being honest with herself—and whiskey tended to have that effect on her—her first love. But she had never admitted that to him. Never had the chance. In the years since, she'd often wondered what had become of him, what path he had set for himself. And now . . . now she knew.

Ree rode onward, following in her mother's trail. The bayou held different magic at night. The cypress trees grew long in the gathering shadows, their branches jutting outward, pointing for her to turn backward with gnarled fingers. She wasn't much of a tracker, having neither the patience nor the talent, but she could still follow her mother's magic well enough. Here, she was beyond the city's rules concerning magic but also their protection. Out this far, there were no lawmen to protect against snatchers and bounty men who were itching to get their hands on wayward Les Magiques.

It was here in the bayou where Ree had first undergone her mother's lessons in preparation for her initiation rites. She'd been eight years old, in dewy-eyed wonder of her mother, the Great Marie Laveau, the beautiful Quarter Queen. Her mother had seemed different during her childhood, larger than life, a goddess descended from the heavens just for her.

On the first night of her initiation training, her mother had poured salt and rose petals in odd crisscrossing shapes, magical runes known as *veves,* each one with its own meaning for a different loa, that Ree could no more name than she could tell apart the stars in the sky.

Voodoo was many things to many folks, but to Ree it was the magic of connection to the loa—the old gods from the old lands. Folks who practiced Voodoo like her mother were conduits for these gods and ancestors, who worked through them viscerally and often violently. Papa Legba, the loa of crossroads, favored her mother, she knew, as did others. Ayizan, wife of Legba and keeper of sacred knowledge and mysteries. Ogoun, god of the forge and fire. Bade, spirit of wind and brother to Sogbo, diviner of lightning. There were more than Ree could count, a pantheon of beings who whispered at her ear, begging for invitation into her body as a willing vessel.

Her mother had warned her the initiation would be painful. In the following weeks, Ree would die many times over, and then she would be born again, in her mother's name, as a Voodoo Priestess. So her training had to be adequate and in many ways more brutal than the ritual itself.

The star-shaped magical veve had burst into flames all around them, and Ree had been flooded with pain and suffering, spiritual visions so vivid she thought she was going mad. Wild whispers had filled her head, the voices too numerous to pick apart. The spirits of her ancestors, her mother told her later.

For many nights, Ree's training had seemed one long, hopeless cycle. She'd walked along the grass barefoot, pouring salt from a jar into the shapes of the veves she'd spent hours hunched over her spell books studying, again and again until her mother was satisfied. Surrounded by unlit candles, Ree and her mother chanted in a mixture of Latin and French until the candles bent to their will and flickered to life. Other times, she and her mother sat back-to-back, cross-legged in the bayou grass in deep spiritual meditation, and Marie would swat her if she cracked an eye open. Marie demonstrated spells with her hand, enchantments meant to bind or harm or manipulate an opponent, which Ree would mimic clumsily. She taught her to channel, to borrow power from the loa while still in control of herself. A handful of dancing fire from Ogoun. A slice of wind from Bade. A lulling kiss deepened by Erzulie's coquettish charm.

Channeling a loa was one thing—but letting one *mount* you? That was the magic of complete and total spiritual surrender.

Mounting was the magic of possession, either by loa or by ancestral spirit, the power of becoming a living conduit for the divine's absolute will. Ree had watched her mother's demonstration in frightful fascination. Deep in this state, her mother glowed, and when she opened her eyes, they were not their usual dark brown, but pure white. Ree was beholding the Quarter Queen in all her terrifying power.

Then, it was her turn.

Her mother described mounting as akin to sailing a ship, albeit on violent waters. Her soul was the ship, and the spirit was the captain. But nothing could prepare Ree for the feeling of full-on possession, which felt more like someone mad had seized control and was steering with no wheel into a storm.

A thousand voices attacked her, some of them pitiful moans, the haunted sounds of souls recounting their greatest pains and sorrows. Others were terrible screams, distorted and stretched in ways beyond her imagination.

Then, something else reached for her. A darkness unknown to even her mother.

Ree had hardly registered her body lifting from the ground, and she felt something hot and wet pool behind her eyelids. At first, she thought it was only tears, but one swipe to her eyes and her hand came away wet with blood. She could barely see her mother below, yelling for her to come down. But the pain ebbed and fell away.

Channeling that dark feeling had begun to feel, well . . . *good.*

Come to me, the dark whispered. The deep, commanding voice of a man. *Let me in.*

"*Ree!*" her mother cried.

Startled, Ree snapped to, tumbling from the sky like a falling star. She landed hard enough to rattle her teeth. A small black bird circled overhead, tracing the air around Ree, cawing in sharp warning. It flew low, landing directly on her shoulder, its claw seizing her skin. It stared at Ree, its golden eyes unblinking. They were not the eyes of a crow, Ree thought. These were the eyes of something ancient. Something she felt she had known before, somehow.

I know you too, those eyes said. *For I am yours.*

Her mother swatted at the bird, driving it away in a flurry. She gathered a trembling Ree into her arms, who stared after the bird in wonder. She knew it would come back for her.

"Maman," said Ree. "I heard a voice."

"Whose voice?"

"*His.*" It hadn't been the first time Ree had heard this voice, this inner darkness. When her mother said nothing, her face carefully barren of any emotion, Ree said, "The things I heard . . . I saw. What am I?"

The voice had told her that she wasn't just the child of Marie Laveau.

It told her she was something else. And meant for so much more.

Her mother had hesitated. Finally, she said, "You are my heir. My body and my soul. We are spirit and flesh. Two and one. Within and without. You are my namesake. You are Marie Laveau." She stood and held out a hand to Ree. "Get up, my love. A queen *never* kneels."

The crunch of bramble underfoot pulled Ree back to the present—she had reached Marie at last in an old fur-trapping camp, where the Cajuns liked to move from time to time to trap the red wolves that roamed these parts. Her mother was sitting around a small fire, her long dark hair loosed from its golden cloth.

She'd know her mother's magic anywhere, of course. Every mystic had a specific scent to their magic. Some sweeter than others, some as pungent as a bulb of garlic or as sour as a bag of lemons. Marie Laveau's magic was sweet as the biggest beignet in New Orleans and hot as the Louisiana sun in the ides of summer.

To her shock, she scented another magic—the bitter, resinous notes of foxglove, the trickster flower. Beside Marie sat an alchemist, his long white hair trailing down his back. And not just any alchemist. Silas Favreau, the Grand Wizard of the Brotherhood of the White Hand.

Once, her mother and the Grand Wizard had been great enemies, though her mother never discussed him. Now the rules meant they never crossed paths, as far as Ree knew. She herself had seen Silas only in passing, caught flashes of his long silvery hair and dark spangled robes as he came and went from his private carriage to the Brotherhood's cloistered halls and to the city's various pleasure houses, heard the drunken praises of Brotherhood fledglings celebrating their leader's latest magical advancement when she visited the alehouses and music houses.

Out of caution, Ree stopped Thistle some distance away from the camp and tied her to a tree.

Footfalls crunched in the underbrush behind her. Ree froze. She had been followed.

But it was already too late.

She was yanked up by the hair and roughly dragged backward, deeper into the damp darkness. A swaying gas lamp was jutted into her face, bright enough that she was blinded. It took one horrifyingly long moment for her vision to adjust, and when it finally did, she saw three grubby faces peering back at her. *Snatchers.*

The truth struck her like a thunderbolt to the chest: They'd come to snatch *her.*

Ree kicked and twisted, but she was outnumbered, and they were much bigger than her.

"We got you now, girl," the snatcher sneered, and before she could say a word, he stuffed a piece of cloth into her mouth. The cloth was sour and stale. She tasted blood, disgustingly wet and coppery in her mouth, perhaps from having bitten down on her own tongue in her shock.

Ree had never met a snatcher before. She'd seen them—terrible, greasy men—at the gambling halls and lower-end music houses. They worked on behalf of the courts—bounty men, one could say. If Les Magiques slaves were caught on the run, the snatchers would drag them back to the courts for a handsome fine. And then there were the *other* stories. Tales about how they liked to find the freed Les Magiques out wandering at night and capture them too and barter them off to slavers without their freedom papers.

"How do we know she's one of them mystics? Could just be a simple colored," said the shortest man of the bunch.

"Here's how," answered the tall one. He jammed a block of aurum against the exposed flesh of her throat. White-hot pain exploded in Ree's body, so vivid she nearly lost consciousness. Ree screamed against the sour cloth they'd stuffed into her mouth, most of it stifled. "See? It only hurt the sin in them. Burn away all the wicked in their blood, don't it?"

If that were true, Ree thought, *you'd be in hellfire.* But men were nothing if not faithful to their own lies.

"Jesus Christ," shouted the third man. He was as stubby as a pig, with cruelly appraising eyes, and he took a long look at Ree, as if seeing her for the first time. "Granger, come look here."

The lamp was shoved back in Ree's face. The men looked her over, taking stock of her face and breasts. For once, Ree was conscious of her provocative dressing, of the bodice that swelled her already ample breasts, the rouge she carefully ran along the apples of her cheeks. All of it made her feel dirty now. One of the men, Granger, swiped out at her. His fingers found purchase against her throat, and she thought for one terrible moment that he might choke her to death. But he only seized her necklace.

"Marie Laveau," he said with a gasp, voice caught between horror and delight. Ree swallowed down bile.

"No. Not the First. This is the Second. The daughter," the stubby one said as a slow smile spread across his lips. Ree heard what he didn't say: *the weaker one.*

In one fell swoop, he fit a collar around her neck, right over her necklace. The aurum burned something awful, and with a pang of horror, Ree realized it was burning her. Her flesh sizzled where the metal made contact. She let out a cry around the rag.

"This? This is the daughter of Marie Laveau?" Granger laughed and spat in her face. "What a crock!"

He knew her by the velvet necklace that was affixed to her neck, where the marking of her surname hung in twin silvery serpents that wound together to make an *L*. She hadn't thought to take her seal off, the one she wore so proudly in the city to announce her status as a Laveau. Oh, the irony. It occurred to her now, facing certain death, that her protesting meant very little. She *did* enjoy the status being her mother's heir afforded her, if even a little. She could admit that now.

Ree spoke muffled words. The men laughed, entertained at her imprisonment. Ree tried again, and Granger shoved his hands into her mouth and yanked out the gag. "What was that, sweetheart?" He leaned in, close enough to kiss her. She could taste the brandy on his breath and for once was sickened by the smell.

"I said," Ree hissed, rage blurring her vision, "fuck you."

Ree slammed her forehead forward as hard as she could into Granger's nose. It made a satisfying crunch, blood spurting down from his nostrils and into his mouth. He yelped. The other two snatchers jumped into motion, but Ree was already primed for the attack.

She smashed her hands together, and the two men collided. It was enough of an impact to knock them breathless. Granger, broken nose hooked oddly, was struggling to breathe through his pain, and he lurched at her. Ree flung out a hand, and Granger was knocked backward, far enough that she could gather her bearings.

"Come to me," Ree murmured. Silence. She tried again in French, panic rising like bile in her throat.

Like any Voodoo Priestess, Ree had access to the spiritual realm, to the ancestors and loa that resided there. But how much access, how many spirits, and which loa would obey was all dependent on her strength, her obedience to the faith. And Marie Laveau the Second was anything but obedient.

One long, horrible moment passed. No answer.

"Venez à moi," Ree tried again. "Come to me."

The men were getting to their feet and loading their guns, which she knew were full of aurum pellets. They readied their collars. Still the spirits were silent. They did not come. With a pang of horror, Ree realized the truth of the moment with sobering clarity: They were not coming to her. No one was coming *for* her.

Now Ree understood her mother's scorn of her defiance. It hadn't been real before. Ree had needed only enough magic to see her own whims satisfied. Never had she needed it to survive, to truly rebel. Until now.

She could try channeling the spirits alone. The last time that she'd dared commune with the spirits directly, she'd used Marcel, Anabelle, and Fabrice as conduits. To offer others as conduits was one thing, but to offer herself as a living vessel? It was what Church folks liked to call a deal with the devil. It very well could be. Her mother had always warned her of practitioners who offered themselves to the loa without proper preparation—poor fools who'd never conditioned their bodies to contain such divinity. At best she could be left blind or crippled, her body destroyed by whatever mischief the loa had done while in it. At worst? Well, sometimes the vessels came back to the mortal realm completely mad, driven insane by entangling with divinity. If they bothered to come back at all.

Ree struggled to stand, gasping through the pain of the aurum collar, which shocked her each time she attempted magic. It was a different kind of pain. It thundered through her body, rumbling her bones. Her veins coursed with fire. Ree gritted her teeth, swallowed down a scream, and tried again to get to her feet.

Ree tried her magic again, but this time as just a thought. A prayer. *Come to me*, she entreated the spirits.

Why? came the voice of the ancestors. *You do not come to us. You do not pray to us. Even now your altar lies empty.*

This was the truth. Ree swallowed down a scream, a mixture of pain and frustration. But truth or not, she didn't have time for sage words, not when she was facing down the barrel of a gun and chains. How were the ancestors any different from her mother? They'd sooner see her brought low and humbled if it meant she would swear fealty to them. Everything was a lesson, even her pain. Hypocrites—the lot of them.

Fuck them. Ree didn't need the ancestors. She didn't need her mother, not truly. She needed only herself. She was done being beholden to anyone or anything—to the city's hollow laws, the sanctimony of the Church, these backwoods witch-hunters, even Voodoo.

She could do this herself, couldn't she? What was Voodoo but another game to be won, another parlor trick she could master on her own with enough practice?

Now, as Ree faced certain death, it was her mother's words that she heard, a vicious whisper in her head: *Get up, my love. A queen never kneels.*

But she was so tired, her body heavy with pain. The aurum had eaten away at the heart of her magic, made it impossible to utter a simple spell, let alone breathe. Even so, it was some small comfort that even if the spirits and ancestors had abandoned her now in her darkest moment, her mother had not.

A hand on her shoulder. This was no fever dream. Ree glanced up and stared directly into the face of her mother, who was wearing an expression she had never seen. Marie's eyes were narrowed, filled with dark, glinting fire, her mouth set low over bared teeth. It was the face of the bayou wolf, full of wild fury.

"Now that"—Granger let out a low whistle—"is the real Marie Laveau."

"In the flesh," Marie countered, her voice a furious whisper, "and the spirit. How terrible for you all."

The snatchers were circling now. Ree caught sight of Silas, who approached from the woods, staff in hand. For one horrible moment Ree thought Silas might flee, or worse yet betray them. But he hadn't. Snatchers wanted white mystics too. They wouldn't enslave them, but they loved burning them on a pyre just as well.

"Y'all gon' make us fucking rich! Can you believe the bounty we'd get for one? But fucking *three*?" the shortest of the bunch said. He hadn't the good sense to be properly scared, delirious as he was with greed.

Silas gestured with his staff at the snatcher, who blanched. "I think your head will make a nice trophy on my wall. What say you, Quarter Queen?" Though the Grand Wizard jested, his voice was low and full of barely contained wrath.

"I detest the Brotherhood. But even they are too good for this filth," said Marie.

"And on that, we can agree." Silas passed her a look. "Let's not make a habit of that."

Granger fired off a shot, but Silas had already struck his staff to the ground in a mighty blow, redirecting the bullet to the ground where it ricocheted, striking Granger in the thigh. He let out a broken yelp.

His mate, the one who'd spit in Ree's face, took an aurum chain and began swinging it wildly like a lasso.

Marie stilled, eyes going flat white. "Do you think you are the first man to try and chain me? Better men have tried and failed."

Marie made a quick hand enchantment, the movement faster than their eyes could catch, the flicker of a conductor guiding an orchestra.

The snatcher with the chain dropped to his knees. He reached out suddenly, blindly, seeing something the rest of them could not. "Get out of my head!" he screamed.

Marie's smile went cold. "Now, why would I do that?"

Lost in the nightmarish vision Marie had trapped him in, he couldn't see what was right in front of him—Silas. The Grand Wizard swung his staff in a half arc, and a gale sent the snatcher flying into the jutted arm of a tree. Impaled.

Ree suddenly looked up, right into Silas Favreau's eyes. They were wrong. Reversed, in a way that made her skin crawl. Black where the whites should be, with a silvery pupil at the center, a lone pinprick of light in the darkness. "Hello again, little witch," he said with an impish smirk. *Hello again.* Strange words, even for an alchemist. Because they'd never met.

The Grand Wizard reached down, offering a pale hand to her. Ree stared at the many silver and moonstone rings that adorned his fingers, the aurum burning her neck all the while, before she reeled back in disgust. "Get the fuck away from me!" she snapped.

Contrary to popular belief, she was not her mother. She'd rather cut off her own arm than work with an organization as vile as the Brotherhood of the White Hand.

The corners of Silas's eyes crinkled in amusement. "Suit yourself, little witch."

A round of aurum bullets shot blindly into the dark toward them. Before Ree could scream, Silas muttered a spell beneath his breath, and a filmy glow encased the three of them.

"Your majesty, if you feel so inclined to conclude this little tiff, that would be especially fucking generous of you," Silas snapped to Marie. His pupils flared, a strange pale light against the inky darkness.

He was spent. Powerful as he was, the Grand Wizard was facing off against pure aurum, and so far, he had managed to stave off the worst of it. But it was in the air now, scattered from the gunfire, putrid to the nose.

"Of course. I just thought you might have wanted to do the honors," Marie replied dryly.

The snatcher with the crooked smile started toward them. He fired into Silas's armor-spell, emerald sparks flying, and little cracks began to appear in the barrier, sizzling where the aurum bullets collided with it.

"Burn in hell, you fucking witch—"

Marie crooked a hand, and the snatcher fell to his knees, his head bent in a motion that it was not designed to do. It was the weight of a thousand souls. What he couldn't see were the tiny ghostly hands seizing him from every angle, the hands of the damned reaching out from the afterlife, forced to do Marie Laveau's bidding. They tore at him, tiny lacerations appearing on his cheeks, forehead, and arms. Marie kept turning her hand until finally, in one vicious *crack!*, the snatcher's neck snapped.

Only one remained. Granger, Ree recalled his fallen comrades calling him. He was still on the ground where his backfired bullet had left him, one bloody hand pressed to his thigh. He couldn't walk, much less run.

"I yield!" he cried. "I fucking yield! Take me in. Take me in to the courts and have me tried. That is the law! That is the proper way!"

Marie looked to Silas. "When will they learn? There's not a thing proper about magic."

Silas laughed, his eyes dangerously narrow and full of black fire. "And I suppose those little chains and collars were just a matter of civility, hm? How *proper* of you, my good man. How decent."

Silas used the toe of his boot to kick the aurum chains away. He jabbed the end of his staff into the collars, tossing them aside. Ree heard a hissing noise and smelled the pungent burn of metal; it was the natural interaction where the magic of the staff touched the aurum.

"There are codes. There are rules," Granger insisted.

Marie looked to Silas. Something darkly kindred passed between their gazes.

Granger turned wild eyes on Ree. "You've heard the stories about these white-haired demons, haven't you, little girl?" His eyes bulged with desperation, searching Ree's for some hint of mercy. "Don't you know what the Brotherhood does to your kind? Far, far worse than we'll ever do—"

Silas tilted his staff and whispered, "*Mutatio.*"

The man's words died on his tongue. Because he didn't have a mouth anymore. In the utterance of one word, the Grand Wizard had transfigured his mouth until there wasn't one at all, only a crooked line sewn together in odd, crisscrossed mounds of flesh. A muffled moaning rang out, the snatcher's words incoherent. And yet Ree heard them all the same, the warning ringing in her head, the crack of a gunshot. *Don't you know what the Brotherhood does to your kind? Far, far worse than we'll ever do.*

Marie crouched over the snatcher and seized him by a handful of hair, cruelly twisting. He let out a panicked moan.

"If this were any other day and you sought to bring harm to any other witch, I might have taken you to court. I might have behaved properly," Marie said in a low voice. "But this is not any other day, and you"—she bent low, pressing her mouth to the poor man's ear. He shivered, and not from the wet cold of the bayou—"did not just attack some common witch."

Ree caught a flash of something silver in her mother's arm. A small blade, one she used for cutting herbs at the parlor. Before Ree could really understand what was happening—the sting of aurum still in her eyes and nose—Marie ran her arm in a low arc, the blade slashing across the man's throat. Blood sprayed out. Marie released the snatcher's body unceremoniously into the dirt. "You attacked my *daughter.*"

And then the collar fell from Ree's throat as her mother ripped it free with her bare hands. She didn't flinch when the aurum burned her fingertips black, nor did she care that she was still covered in the snatcher's blood. Her dark eyes were fixed on Ree, burning with silent anger.

"Maman—"

"Not a word. Not a fucking word until we get home." Marie looked around at the blood strewn across the bayou. The men lying in waste and wreckage. Smelled the gunpowder, the stench of their own flesh charred from the poison in the aurum. "The bodies," Marie said with a sigh, turning to look at Silas. "There will be questions."

"I won't tell if you won't." Silas's nefarious grin was answer enough. His white-blond hair took on an ashen hue in the moonlight, his skin so pale and glowing that it could have been chiseled from moonstone. Drops of red snatcher blood stained his silvery goatee.

Silas muttered an incantation low under his breath, and in a whirl of wind and leaves, the corpses of the snatchers arranged themselves into a pile among broken pieces of dead wood. The Grand Wizard raised his staff high, toward the slice of silvery moon that hung low in the darkness above them, and swung it down in one heavy blow. A bolt of lightning shot down from the sky, striking the pile of snatcher bodies and the dried twigs and sticks he'd gathered for tinder. The bodies caught fire, which soon grew to a full blaze. The three of them stood in uneasy silence, watching the remnants of their enemies turn to ash. A crow cawed from somewhere in the darkness, their only witness.

Ree looked down at her hand. She was still clutching that disgusting rag the snatchers had stuffed into her mouth to swallow her screams. It was all that was left of this bloody ordeal, the last shred of evidence that there had ever been one at all.

She caught her mother's eyes from across the fire. There was anger. And there was pain. She looked less like the fearsome Quarter Queen she knew her to be and more like a mother who'd just endured her worst nightmare.

The fire reeled higher into the night, snapping and hissing. Silas stared into the flames, a rueful smile playing on his lips as those twisting shadows danced over his face. "No saints," the alchemist murmured.

Ree didn't believe in her mother's saints and angels, it was true. But even if she did, she wouldn't dare waste her prayers on the likes of these monsters. She tossed the rag into the flame, watched as it burned down to nothing at all. "And no fucking sinners."

CHAPTER SIX

REE

Ree didn't dare utter a word the whole way home. Her mother watched her, mouth pressed into a flat, displeased line, Silas sitting quietly beside her. Their carriage passed into the city gates, and soon enough they were trundling over the French Quarter's cobbled roads, back into the warmth of torchlight and tinkling laughter that carried down from the tangle of terraces above. Soon, the carriage had turned onto St. Ann, where it rattled to a stop outside of the Laveau home. Their house was a modest cottage once owned by a judge whose ailing son Marie Laveau had brought back from the brink of yellow fever. Now it was Marie's, her name signed to the deed, an ode to her days as a young plague nurse.

The silence stretched between them until Ree couldn't take it anymore. "I'm sorry, I didn't mean—"

"You've done enough." Her mother's tone made it perfectly clear that there would be hell to pay for her insolence, just not in front of an audience.

"Marie," Silas began quietly. "You mustn't be too hard on the child. Better for her to see with her own eyes the violence of bigots than to learn from a book."

"Do not feign innocence, Silas," Marie snapped. "Your kind carry enough bigotry of their own for my people on matters outside of magic. Or did you forget?"

Silas leaned on his great staff, touching a hand to the black stone dragon coiled upon the end, its fanged jaws clenched upon its own tail—the ouroboros, the beast that consumed itself. "How could I, when I have you, my dear queen, for a friend?"

If asked just yesterday, Ree would have never believed that her mother and Silas could be *friends*. But now she wasn't so sure. They'd killed three white men together, burned them down to nothing. That wasn't exactly the business of enemies.

But Marie said nothing, just yanked open the carriage door, gesturing for Ree to quickly get out first, then following and snapping the door to a close behind her. After a moment, the carriage set off down St. Ann before it turned into the Quarter's shadowed alleys.

Ree went inside their home. She knew what people whispered about her mother—that their house's modest exterior was but one more illusion the eternally self-serving witch Marie Laveau had cast upon the city and its people. That it was really a palace, a hidden chateau filled with expensive baubles, cursed objects, and trinkets she'd conned from the men she'd hexed for her own amusement. But there was nothing remotely palatial about their home. Her mother scrubbed the hardwood floors with oil and soap herself, sewed simple lace curtains with her own needle and thread, purchased rugs from enslaved women at the French Market. In the kitchen, Marie kept a tin pot of cinnamon, orange peel, and bay leaves boiling all night and day for luck and protection. Ree smelled it now, that familiar autumnal scent.

The only space Marie Laveau had indulged in was the front parlor, where she'd covered the walls in oil paintings of black folks going about their lives in a variety of ways: A grandmother in a blue cotton skirt and tattered head rag washing her fussing petit-bébé in a wooden wash bucket. A newly married couple gleefully jumping the broom. And Marie's favorite, a mother and her young daughter hand in hand walking down a long stretch of dusty magnolia-lined road, on their way into the sunlit unknown together. *Real people*, she'd told Ree when she was just a little girl. *Real freedom.*

Ree stood in the parlor now, feeling very much like that same little girl about to be scolded.

With a wave of her jeweled hand and just a thought, Marie started a fire in the grate. It was with Ogoun's blessing, of course. The great metalsmith god favored her mother and would gladly lend the fire from his sacred forge for her whims. Sosie came slithering out from beneath the settee, and Marie stooped to pick her up; she wound her way up Marie's arm until she settled comfortably around her shoulders.

"*This is why*," Marie snarled, leveling a ringed finger at her, "I insist on your training. The spirits are not compelled to simply serve you because you ask, little girl. You must serve them too. Prayer. Fasting. Sacrifice. It is a relationship, like any other. One that depends on fairness, upon the utmost equilibrium."

"Because you know all about fairness in relationships, Mother."

"I know better than you. Clearly."

Ree's eyes stayed on Sosie, the way her mother stroked her scales, cradling the snake close like a child at her breast. For some reason, the sight of this made her positively seethe. "Do you? Because every relationship you have, you manipulate to your advantage," she retorted.

"And you'd be wise to do the very same. This city's rules are not made for us, Ree. They never were. Before either you or I were even born, this city had profited from our people's pain, suffering, and forced labor. And I was determined for that to not be our fate. And so, yes, I am guilty of everything that you say. I manipulated. I plotted. I've even killed." Her eyes were cold. "But all of my whims have had ends. And what of yours, hm? What are your reasons, daughter? Simply to spite me?"

Ree froze.

Marie sighed, turned away, and massaged her aching temples. "Like it or not, the safest place for you is this city."

"It is a gilded cage," Ree said, her voice suddenly small, nearly shy.

"Look around, child. Better a gilded cage than a collar." Marie closed her eyes, and Ree knew she was trying to shut out the image of her kneeling in the dirt, a collar bound to her neck. She lay both hands on Ree's shoulders. "The safest place for you is New Orleans, because here, whether you like it or not, you are a Laveau. And that means something. Holds power. But outside of these walls? Your power would be used against you, and you would be forever hunted. Always running. Imagine the kind of power a slaver could wield with a girl like you under their thumb."

Ree shook free from her mother's grasp. "And yet here I am, Mother, right under yours."

It was an awful thing to say. But sometimes her mother could be a truly awful woman.

But was it an awful woman who had saved her life today? Her mother had risked everything, her own life, without so much as blinking an eye. Ree knew she should be grateful, but somehow, standing there with her shoulders squared and facing down Marie Laveau, she felt anything but. She felt . . . resentful.

It was a wound that had always been there, she knew. When she was much younger, it had caused her sorrow. Why couldn't her mother be like the other mothers at church, passing their children sweets and cookies wrapped in wax paper? Why couldn't her mother stay home at night, like the others, to read her a bedtime story? Why did she need to leave by moonlight to gather with her precious followers in Congo Square? What exactly in this godforsaken city pulled her so? What could she love more than her own daughter? In time, as she aged, the answer became crystal clear to Ree: Voodoo.

Marie released a frustrated breath. "When will you be done with this spoiled princess performance and play the part you are meant to? You are my heir, Ree. It is time you behaved as such."

"Oh, maman. You mean your puppet."

"Mind your tongue, little girl."

"No, I don't think I will."

She wasn't a little girl, despite her mother's insistence otherwise. She was the same age, if not a few years older, even, as when her mother had ascended to Queen of the Voodoos.

"You see, I never minded being your puppet as a little girl. Just like a marionette down in the Quarter shows. Their strings pulled by cruel masters. And then I grew up . . ." Ree stared her mother down. ". . . and I began to see your strings too."

"Not another word."

"Oh, I think one more will do just fine. It's your turn to explain yourself—why did you meet with Silas? What is your relationship to the Grand Wizard of the Brotherhood?" Ree was going to be fair about it. She was going to offer her the chance to come clean, to do away with all of her secrets and plots.

A flash of glittering anger in Marie's eyes. But still she said nothing.

"Silence still makes you a liar, *Marie*. But since you are so quiet, perhaps I should tell you that I overheard you with Father Antoine, discussing the Harbinger and the Inquisition. And . . ." She hesitated, then said the name anyway: "*Jon.*"

"Enough!" her mother commanded, vibrant anger radiating from her. The fire flared, smoke filling their small parlor, backlighting her mother in the hearth's orange-gold light, her face twisted first with sorrow, then with fury.

No, it was not Ree's mother staring at her. It was the Quarter Queen, her bone-white eyes, the tignon upon her head coming undone, transfiguring itself into her golden fleur-de-lis crown, her long curls floating about her cheeks like seaweed swaying in black water.

"I am your queen," she spat. "It's high time you acknowledged that."

"You are my *mother*! It's high time you acknowledged that."

And there it was. The real trouble between them.

When her mother spoke again, her voice had grown unusually soft, carrying an unmistakable bitter note. "The ways in which I have failed you as a mother are but small sacrifices to the ways in which I have succeeded as Queen of the Quarter. One day you will understand, when you have taken my place."

"You might fancy yourself a queen, Mother. But you still bend the knee to these white men and the Church like everyone else in this fucking city."

"And you, Ree?" her mother asked, dangerously soft. "Since you know of these things, tell me, daughter—do you know which Inquisitor the Vatican has assigned to hunt us, to hunt *you*?"

Now it was Ree's turn to go quiet. Her mother sneered. "Yes, Henryk Broussard returns to New Orleans. But not as the boy you once loved. No, my sweet daughter." Those white eyes flashed. "As your enemy. So, you see it is you who commits the greatest sin of them all—you put a thing as fickle as love before your own magic."

"Well, maybe, Mother, if you had too, you wouldn't be such . . . such . . . *a pathetically lonely old widow with a heart of fucking stone!*"

The magic behind Marie's eyes abruptly died, her dark eyes empty and impassive. Her mother's face, always so carefully blank. Always so guarded with her armor of piety and virtue. And yet . . . Ree had seen that glimpse of old pain. The kind that gnawed at you with crooked teeth, that bled you dry down to marrow and bone. She was her mother. She was her queen. And she was the *Widow Paris,* the woman whose husband had vanished and never saw fit to return. That was the exact moment that Ree knew she'd gone too far.

Her mother crossed to the door. As she passed, she came to a quiet halt at Ree's shoulder, Sosie reared and hissing in her arms.

"You don't know all that I have done for you, daughter," whispered Marie. There was no anger, Ree realized. Only mournful regret, a shadow of old pain come again. "And for both our sakes, I pray you never will."

Marie swept out of the house without another word.

Ree reclined in a hot bath, her skin raw and stinging after she'd scrubbed off the snatcher stink. Anabelle was perched beside the tub, combing Ree's damp curls away from her face. From below the floorboards of Anabelle's bedchamber came the usual sounds of a New Orleans pleasure house: the mad giggling of courtesans as they flitted about the halls hand in hand, the gruff bickering of men and merchants come to see their business done, the hurried cries of lovers. Tonight, no one would disturb them, least of all Madame Monet, not when Ree had put down enough coin for two nights.

"You know, I have two gifts for you."

Ree sighed. So much had happened—the Harbinger, the snatchers, and news of an impending Inquisition and Henryk—that something as simple and innocent as trading tokens of affection with a lover seemed . . . almost juvenile to her now. "That's kind, Anabelle. But I'm not sure I'm in the m—"

Anabelle tugged the knot that held her silk slip together. It fell from her shoulders, rippling into silken ridges around her feet.

Ree reclined into the lush, steaming waters. "Never mind," she murmured, her breath quickening. "I'll take this gift now."

Later, in bed, Anabelle produced a small velvet box wrapped with a black bow, like the ribbons her mother used to thread Ree's hair with on the slow Sunday mornings before mass.

"You do remember how this works? I am the one who is supposed to pay you," said Ree.

"Hush. This is no payment, Ree. Well, go on. Open it."

Ree slid the bow from the box, revealing a large black flower. It had red veins, dark enough that they appeared swollen with blood. "Not exactly the picture of romance."

"Why have romance when you can have something far rarer? *Freedom.*" Anabelle scooted closer, a strange light in her eyes. Ree did not tell her that last night, she had offered to buy just that on her behalf from her madame. "That there is Conjurer Root. Old folks say it's got the soul of High Jon in it. They say your momma scorched it all from the earth. Well, not *all* of it."

"Then how did you get your hands on it?"

"Suppose the same way I got my hands on you." Anabelle winked. "Magic." She leaned in, pressed her full lips against Ree's, the sweet peck of a butterfly against a rose.

When they finally pulled apart, Ree turned the box over in her hand. "Consider me curious. What would one use Conjurer Root for?"

"Slaves say it's got the old juju in it. From the old land across the sea. Triples your magic. Grants you freedom." Anabelle paused, that strange light in her eyes again. "But then again, you wouldn't much need that, now, would you?"

Ree couldn't ignore the way her chest tightened, the sudden lump in her throat. She wanted to cry. But she couldn't. Not like this, not with her. She accused her mother of having armor for skin, but the truth was she had her own too. She had her fun, her little games. But now? She just wanted to have someone who might understand why she played at all.

Anabelle caressed her arm as if reading her mind. "What were you arguing about this time?"

"It turns out my mother and I have very different visions for my future in New Orleans," Ree said.

Ree could feel Anabelle's hesitation, the way she shifted uncertainly beside her. "What if your future was never meant to be in New Orleans?"

Ree sat up. Her heart had begun to stammer in her chest. "What are you talking about?"

"Run away with me," Anabelle said. "We could leave New Orleans and never look back. Your future—*our* future could be what we make it to be. We would make our own fates, Ree."

Tempting words. *Dangerous* words. It was a bell that couldn't be un-rung. The bell might have been ringing ever since that first night in the House of Flowers's parlor when Anabelle had passed her in precious silks, smelling of jasmine and desire.

"And where would we go?"

"Anywhere but here. Anywhere but this godforsaken city."

"I am a free woman, Anabelle. And you . . ." Ree trailed off, couldn't bring herself to say the words.

The noise Anabelle made was disarmingly sudden, a bitter sound. "I'll tell you what I am—I am *sick* and tired of the way things are. I don't want to accept this sad little life for myself a moment longer."

"This is not a game, Anabelle. We would be breaking every rule—"

"*I am so tired of the fucking rules!*" Anabelle's voice rang out in the quiet of the room, sharp as glass. She hissed in a breath, calming herself. And yet . . . Ree had seen. That perfect mask had slipped, for a moment, revealing the unending pain beneath. Anabelle took her hand. "You were right, Ree. We need to break the rules. Together." A moment of hesitation as she waited, deliberating. "Leave with me."

Ree held her eyes. Anabelle would not offer again. Ree understood this moment for what it was—a moment of brief clarity, a fleeting pause in their little game when they would lay their cards down and bare themselves before each other. If Ree refused her now, they would go on as they were, and in the morning, this moment would be a bad dream.

"Leave with you and be hunted by snatchers." Ree paused. "And my mother."

Anabelle's dark eyes were fixed on Ree's face, unmoving in their conviction. "Your mother will let you go in time."

Would she? How to tell her that Ree had tried to leave once before, on the eve of her sixteenth birthday, almost eight years ago, with someone else who had stolen her heart and had never seen fit to give it back? She'd been a frightened little thing, scared to death of what might become of her during those harrowing spiritual rites that would transform her into a Voodoo Priestess, scared even more of who she might be after. Who would she become in the end? Not a vessel for the gods and the spirits and the ancestors as the laws of Voodoo intended, but just another empty vessel for the great Marie Laveau. Now all she could think of were those bitter words between them tonight, her mother's gaze filled with anguish.

Ree closed her eyes, shutting out that haunting image.

"What do you say?"

"I—" She thought of those snatchers, the blistering heat of the aurum collar fastened around her neck. Those white men and their laughing faces, taunting her from the dark while she cowered on her knees.

Anabelle put a finger to her lips, silencing whatever answer she might have given. "Tomorrow. The Bridal Bridge."

Ree froze. Could she know? No, she decided, this woman could not know of the pain that same fateful place had brought her eight years ago. Because she had never spoken of it. She could not know the pain Ree harbored from her decision to leave Henryk Broussard standing all alone on that bridge, her choice to remain in New Orleans because she hadn't yet learned to sever that invisible, suffocating thread that tied her to her mother. At the time, leaving her mother had felt impossible in a way that it didn't now. Anabelle could not possibly know about that old pain. It was the magic of coincidence and nothing more. Now Ree had learned from her mistakes. Now she might choose her own fate, chart her own path outside of her mother's reign. She felt giddy with delicious possibility. She was scared too. But somehow it was easier to imagine the danger of leaving than to imagine the stifling safety of staying. Because at least when she left, she wouldn't have to face old ghosts.

But Henryk Broussard was more than a ghost. He was the wound on her fickle heart that might never, ever heal.

"When the bells toll at sundown. I'll be there..." Anabelle pressed her lips to Ree's. Ree tasted the salt in her tears. "And I hope you will be too."

CHAPTER SEVEN

REE

Ree carefully left Anabelle sleeping and slipped out of the House of Flowers before dawn. If her mother wasn't going to relinquish the answers Ree so desperately wanted, then she would get them herself. When she reached the hairdressing parlor, she slipped inside and retrieved Sanite's grimoire from the back. By the time she returned home, the sun was just starting to rise, and her mother was still nowhere to be seen. She knew that she shouldn't touch the grimoire, let alone read it. But what did it matter if Ree was really leaving tonight?

Turning the grimoire over in her hands, she shivered. The book called to her. *Sang* to her. There was something dark in it, darker than anything Voodoo had ever shown her. But what did that matter to a girl like her? Something dark lived in Ree too, the very same thing that made the city's gentry quicken down the road when she passed, that startled the nuns and churchgoers to suddenly cross themselves with hurried blessings muttered under their breath.

Ree cast a careful look about her bedchamber, straining to listen for the telltale creak of her mother's footsteps. But the house was quiet. Ree turned back to the book in her hands, running a finger along the twin intertwined *Q*'s stamped in a violet wax seal upon the cover. She opened the spell book, thumbed to the page her mother had left turned at the corner, and began to read:

> It is said that Voodoo is the wellspring from which all magic of life comes forth. But what of death? What might be gained from tampering with life beyond the Veil? The answer to this question was born not here in the new land, but across the sea, in our sister country—Haiti. I have heard whispers that when I banished Jon the Conjurer, it was to these shores that he fled. It was here that he truly began his reign of terror. And for this sin, I alone am responsible.

Ree's eyes fell upon an inky symbol in the center of the page— a small cross erected on a black coffin. She knew the symbol well enough, for it was the veve of death and hung on many a tombstone—it was the mark of Baron Samedi. Lord of Death.

> During the height of Haiti's rebellion, it was said that the renowned general, Toussaint Louverture, sought a means to build his dwindling army. And so he summoned the Lord of Death himself, Baron Samedi. But like other loa such as Legba, Samedi is never one to be summoned without proper offering, lest the summoner suffer terrible consequence. It cannot be known what Toussaint offered Samedi for his power, but from whatever terrible bargain they struck, only one truth remains certain among the many myths that came after: Under Toussaint's command, the raised souls of his dead countrymen and ancestors emerged from the earth . . . and began to walk amongst the living once more. This conduit of dark magic came to be known as one word . . . a word more feared in New Orleans than rebellion itself. Henceforth, this dark magic became known as the unholy re-creation of the undead: the zombi.

Ree traced a finger along the drawings of dark skeletal figures trudging along, one after another, each face more harrowing than the last. The eyes sunken into blackened hollows, the mouths open and gnashing...

> Many years later, with Toussaint long buried, it was said that in the ashes of this war grew a strange flower. Thought to be Toussaint's final gift to his beloved Haiti, this flower became known as Conjurer Root, a conduit rumored to give power over death itself. Those who seek the power of the dead must consume it. But be warned, dear reader. The dead may consume ye first...

Ree closed the spell book, her mind racing. Why would her mother have need of Conjurer Root? Or perhaps it was not Conjurer Root she'd been after at all. Perhaps... she'd only ever sought Jon.

Ree went to the armoire beside her bed and picked up the small velvet box Anabelle had gifted her. She carefully slid off the top and held the Conjurer Root beneath the candlelight. All that forbidden power, the likes of which not even one as formidable as Sanite Dede had wanted to meddle with, right there in her hand. Such a tiny thing. Such a glorious thing. Rumor had it her mother had scorched the earth of all the Conjurer Root she could find after the Quarter Quarrel, had bled the land dry of it, leaving only ash for soil. Now here it was in her hands, the forbidden fruit, plucked from some far-off Eden, hidden even from Marie Laveau.

Just one bite, not a petal more, Anabelle had warned, red lips curving into a lush smile. *Anything more? Well, there would be unintended consequences...*

Just one bite. Ree plucked a black petal from the flower and placed it on her tongue.

Ree stumbled back onto her bed, her body crashing like a boulder onto the mattress, her mind doused in shadow. Her breath hitched, then slowed. Slower, slower, slower...

When Ree woke again, she was standing in the middle of a cotton field, engulfed in a darkness so deep that it consumed her. She didn't recognize this place. No, Ree thought quickly, this *world.* Wherever she was, it was not the New Orleans she knew. It held some of the same wet heat, but not the kind that left a trail of watery kisses down your back. That was the New Orleans Ree knew. No, this dampness was interwoven with darkness, like the entire city had been plunged into the far reaches of black swamp water. If she focused hard enough, she could make out silvery wisps on the horizon. *Spirits.* Coming and going, slipping back and forth through a pale doorway that looked, if she squinted hard enough, more like a flapping piece of silk caught in a ghostly breeze. It looked like . . . a *veil.*

Something squirmed in the dirt beneath Ree's bare feet. She crouched, examined it closely.

A hand emerged from the earth, pushing through root, earthworms, and bone, the hand itself blackened from sun and death. Ree fell back, horrified. The hand clawed out, becoming an arm, the shape of a torso, and finally . . . a man.

Drenched in dirt and root, a man in raven-black dressings towered over Ree. He had the skin of pure midnight, dark and gleaming, with powerful, field-working shoulders. His eyes were golden, bright enough that they gave off their own light, a lantern in the night.

"What are you?" And yet she knew. She knew this man whom she did not know at all. There was something curiously familiar about him, something that drew Ree to him without question. It was the same knowing as when she practiced Voodoo—she needn't know a particular spell or hex; it came to her through seeing, through doing, through channeling the magic from the world she knew and the world beyond.

What was I, is the question. I was chained. But now . . .

He leaned in, golden eyes going flat black. It was the preternatural blackness of eternal night, of a moon that would never fall from the sky.

. . . I am free.

He turned, gesturing to the cotton field that surrounded them in a white halo, where bodies broke through the ground. *Slaves,* Ree thought. Even now, even in death. They were still in their plantation clothes, some still scarred from the whip and the barb, mouths slack from screaming for a justice that never came. They rose, one by one, from the darkness and dirt.

And so are they.

Ree screamed. She was screaming still when she came to, back within the muzzy warmth of her bedchamber, back in the natural world. There were no bloodied cotton plants in her room, no whispering darkness. Ree was on her bed, curled into herself, drenched in sweat and her own fear. She'd been crying, somehow, though she hadn't felt sorrow. At least, not *her* sorrow. She'd felt other sadness gripping at her, a thousand black hands reaching up from the earth and seizing at her, tearing at her, reaching for anything that might recognize their pain. Who had that man been? But she knew.

Ree spoke the only word that came to mind, the name that thrummed in her blood.

"Jon."

The dream haunted Ree the rest of the day, even as she mindlessly tended to customers at their hairdressing parlor and packaged tins of butter balm and love potions and gris-gris into their jars and satchels. Her mother was nowhere to be seen, but it was Friday, and she used the time to prepare alone for rituals to commence at the beginning of the week. Ree knew her mother was due to perform her usual crossroads ritual in the Dreadwood, where she would commune with the loa in private. She wouldn't have the chance to ask her about the grimoire, about the dream, or about Jon. *And,* a small voice reminded her, *you won't be able to tell your own mother goodbye.*

But she knew Marie Laveau would get on well enough without her for a time and would have her hands full with Quarter politics and holding court. Ree wanted nothing to do with the Harbinger, with the Conjurer Root, or with visions of Jon. She would leave with Anabelle tonight and be done with this godforsaken city, just as she should have done eight years ago. She'd missed her chance with Henryk. She wouldn't be so foolish now.

Now the cathedral's bells tolled as Ree stood alone upon the Bridal Bridge, waiting. With each second, she could feel herself growing more nervous. Dusk was falling, and night would soon come. The bridge was a little white stone crossing connected to the long promenade that overlooked the rippling blue expanse of the Mississippi River. It was mostly empty at this hour. The crowds had all but whittled away, gone inside to have supper on the covered patio at Labelle's, where they would eat steaming bowls of crawfish gumbo and golden disks of hot water bread, or to Sweet Kettle, the port-side confectionary that served praline candies tied in petal-pink bows, golden pitchers of clove-spiced lemonade and sweet wine.

Still, she waited. She'd spent the day in a panic, not fully knowing what choice she'd come to, knowing only that staying in New Orleans a moment longer felt suddenly impossible. She'd told her mother as much, hadn't she? *It is a gilded cage.*

And now? She could escape. Once she and Anabelle were far away from the city and found somewhere safe, Ree would ask her exactly where she had gotten the Conjurer Root, how she'd come by such nefarious magic. Ree could hear blaring horns in the distance, those steamboats gliding into harbor; the cry of gulls flying overhead; sailors yelling as they hauled barrels of sugar, cotton bushels, and fresh oysters in from port. But she did not hear any approaching footsteps. She did not hear Anabelle.

Ree stood alone, bracing herself on the iron railing, staring out into the dusky red sky, into nothing at all. The bells tolled again. The hour had changed. How long had she been standing here alone? One hour? Two? Three? The world felt frozen, wrong in a way that it shouldn't. Anabelle was not here. Ree's throat felt raw, itchy. She was going to cry, right here in public. Because now she knew the truth. Anabelle was not coming. She'd been waiting for nothing, nothing at all, just as Henryk had eight years ago.

Unease suddenly prickled up her spine. Had it truly been coincidence that Anabelle picked this exact spot? What was Ree missing? Had Anabelle been mocking her this whole time?

A cry from above startled her. A crow squawked as it circled Ree, drawing a dark ring against a molten sky. It was Aram. And he was trying to *warn* her.

Then she felt it—a twisting pain in her chest. She tasted something too. Something sharp and bitter on her lips. The taste was all earth and root, and something deceptively sweet too, like mulled wine. She'd tasted this before, hadn't she? *Conjurer Root.* But the taste was sharper now. This was Conjurer Root in a dangerously high proportion. It tasted like . . . poison.

A picture flashed in her mind's eye of a woman drinking deeply from a golden cup. And then she was sputtering, spewing ritual wine into the air, gasping wildly for breath . . .

With a pang of horror, Ree realized she was seeing her *mother.*

"Aram!" she called, flinging an arm out toward him.

But he wouldn't come down, which meant he was trying to lead her. Ree took a breath and swallowed down the lump of panic in her throat. She steadied herself, forced her mind clear to channel her thoughts to her familiar.

Show me, Ree told Aram. *Take me to my mother.*

Aram flew low, close enough that she could reach out and touch his wings if she stretched, and Ree kept pace, her skirt catching on bramble. She ran through muck and weeds toward the part of the forested ground that even the moonlight dared not touch. Aram suddenly stopped, circling just on the edge of the path that he would not enter, at least not without Ree's permission. Ree knew this place. Knew it well enough to know that she never wanted to step foot into it again.

The Dreadwood. It was sacred land to the Voodoos in New Orleans, thought to be Papa Legba's first crossroads in the New World. There were many that one might find, but this was the first that Legba had blessed. Tall, spindly trees rose so high into the sky that it seemed the whole of the forest stood on wooden stilts, calling to her, as the trees so often had in the long days since her initiation. Her initiation rites had been brutal, and while she had little else to compare them to, she'd heard her mother's Voodoo acolytes whispering behind her back. All initiations are painful, they'd said. But better pain than torment. *Hell,* they'd murmured. Ree tried hard not to think of those days spent wandering in the forest, so deep in her spiritual fasting that she hadn't had a piece of bread, not one crumb, in days. She subsisted on water and a few herbs she'd boiled over an open flame in a little copper pot she'd fit into the single knapsack she'd been allowed to take. She'd wandered round and round in those dark woods, lost in a fever dream, while the spirits taunted her.

Now Ree didn't think. She ran. Her feet carried her over grass sleek with dew, over twigs and stones and past a variety of creatures that made the Dreadwood their home—imps with molten yellow eyes, boo hags, and spirit-folk that wandered on and on, caught in a labyrinth of memories from a time long gone. One such spirit floated out at her, baring a long, vicious tongue.

"Cross any deeper, child, and I will peel the skin from your bones," the spirit warned.

"Begone from me!" Ree threw out a hand, the action born more of reflex than of any real courage, flinging the spirit back into the mist. Ree kept running, the hem of her cloak snatching in the gnarled fingertips of branches reaching out for her ever closer.

There, the wind whispered. *There is Marie Laveau, after all.*

If it were any other day, Ree wouldn't have had the nerve for that kind of magic. But today was not any other day. Today was the day her mother could very well be dead. Now her magic felt different, sharper, hot against her fingertips and tongue like lightning waiting to strike.

Somewhere high above her, Aram circled. Other crows joined him, cawing, their song broken in places.

Ree screamed. *There.* There was her mother's body, lying still in the wet grass. Ree pressed her ear to her mother's chest. *A heartbeat.* Marie Laveau was alive. Only just so.

Amidst the searing panic, the frenzied stammer of her heartbeat, the scream that scraped from her mouth in a long wail, a terrible thought overcame Ree. It was greedy. Dark. Completely and disgustingly selfish. She had no right to the thought, no right at all. And yet Ree couldn't help but understand the glaring irony of her predicament: She couldn't escape her mother. Not *now.*

Just when Ree had been about to fly away, her mother had made sure to leave her first.

CHAPTER EIGHT

MARIE

Marie awoke between worlds.

One minute she'd been standing in the middle of the Dreadwood, drinking of her ceremonial wine to begin her crossroads ritual, and the next she'd awoken here. She'd seen this place before, only in glimpses, in fragmented dreams. The first time was in a vision after Jacques's disappearance when she'd been bowled over in her grief, feverish and plastered to her bed. The second time had been during the war with Jon, scarcely a glimpse before his banishment. It was different now. She could see it fully: darkness that roiled and pressed in from all sides, as thick as sea mist, and a scattershot of whispers, too numerous to pick apart. She pushed to her feet, heart quickening. She might have thought she was in a bayou of some sort, but no bayou that she had ever seen before had shadow where there should have been water underfoot. It was a world outside of time and all mortal sense.

Because, after all, this was the Veil. *Cursed knowledge*, Sanite Dede had hissed when Marie had dared ask. She hobbled forward. Darkness engulfed her like a night shawl. Despite herself, she shivered.

"Hello, Marie."

Marie turned to see the shimmering outline of a figure approach. There was only one man—no, *being*—that favored a withered cane in one hand and a set of copper scales in the other, with hooded eyes that blazed infernally red as hot coal. Papa Legba, the loa of the crossroads himself. Keeper of keys and opener of all roads. He Who Stands at the Beginning and the End.

Marie drew herself up to her full height, tried to steady her shaking nerves. It was no use. Papa only smiled. He liked the smell of her fear.

When Papa spoke, it was with a slow cadence, a dance of words. "Tell me, Marie Laveau. Why do you trouble yourself with ghosts?"

"Because unlike men, ghosts can't hurt you," Marie said.

"Can't they?"

"Not in the ways that matter." Marie stilled. "Hello, Papa."

He'd visited her in the mortal plane before, once at the start of her initiation, and again after Jacques had died. Both times had been to take measure of her power, as if she were no different from a jewel being appraised for value. For all their endless power, loa were desperately curious about mortal affairs. Why else would they entreat servants and acolytes to their altars? She supposed their prayers and offerings, the deepest secrets of their hearts, were as delicious as freshly wrapped candy. Impossible to resist, delightful to savor on the tongue. But here, deep in his domain, Papa was different, his form much larger, the heat from his gaze as hot as the noonday sun. The Veil was Papa Legba's world, after all.

"You do not ask where you are," he said. "I suppose you already know."

"I know where. I must know why."

Staring at him for too long made her eyes hurt. But Marie held his gaze. Her pride wouldn't allow her much else. Papa smiled—this he knew and liked about her most.

"You know why. You drank of the poison," he said simply.

"I had a vision. It was your voice that I heard, along with the Baron's. So I knew that it must be followed. Without question. I need to know why."

"There was a time when all that you longed for was to enter this realm, priestess. And look at you now, here at last." Papa swept out his arms, copper scales tinkling. "Yet you do not rejoice. Mortals." He sighed. "So fickle of heart. Never pleased."

"I will be pleased when I know why."

"You saw, didn't you?" He smiled. "Last I checked, the gods blessed you with the gift of sight. Not as powerful as your predecessor, Sanite, but blessed all the same. Tell me, priestess, did we waste our power?"

Marie prickled. She was not Sanite, and did not have the strength of her foresight by any measure, but her spirit's eye could see glimpses of the unknown. She had seen but not understood, not completely. The Conjurer Root, mixed into her ritual wine. Conjurer Root, the herb Jon had sewn part of his soul into, his very essence. She'd thought the last of it had been scorched from all of Louisiana. She'd seen herself consume the poison, and flashes of what was to come: her comatose body, the convergence of her enemies crowding for the upper hand, and Ree, her foolishly capricious Ree, forced to rise to the occasion. She had seen a long, dark road open before her, the work of the Lord of the Crossroads and the Lord of Death, and she had known their power was absolute and must be obeyed. She must walk this new road. She had seen no other possibilities, no other recourse, but to drink the poison. To what end, she didn't know.

"Jon," Marie said at last. "This was Jon's doing."

Papa laughed, the force of it strong enough that Marie's curls were flung backward from her face. "Did you think that banishment would stop him?"

"Stop, no. Cage? Yes."

"Foolish child. You left him here, Marie." Papa gestured out to this world of strange shadow and light, where flickers of souls winked in and out like stars. "*Here*. You left him in a place of old magic. Did you not think his own might grow stronger here? Stronger"—he pointed his cane out at her—"than even *yours*?"

Marie froze. There had been so much to consider in those days, in that final moment with Jon, with hardly any time. She'd made the only choice that she could have, didn't she?

"Does my plight amuse you, Papa?"

"Marie, my sweet, I must confess I do find your tiff amusing." In many ways he lived up to his reputation, to his name. *Papa.* He was a seasoned parent, bemused at the squabbling antics of his many offspring. What did he care for the deep fissure between Marie and Jon? He did not see with mortal eyes, nor care for mortal feelings. He did not know the pain that Jon had caused her, the pain she'd caused him in turn. To Papa, they were bickering children. "Jon the Conjurer has you in his grasp."

Marie stilled herself, bracing for the worst. "What . . . does he want?"

"What he has always wanted." He leaned in, hunched over that cane like an old man. But Marie knew better. He was no old man. No man at all, but an old god in need of a new mortal delight. "To teach you a lesson."

Papa led Marie deeper into the Veil. The scales he held in his hand shone in the darkness, the reflection of copper brighter than any lantern. Marie had no inkling of where he was leading her, but fear bubbled deep inside of her, and with every step it threatened to boil over like a potion unwatched. As she walked on, hovering in Papa's massive shadow, she found that her eyes had relaxed some, and more of the Veil revealed itself to her.

It was a world unlike any other, a world of two. A world of two skies: the dark one overhead that glowed with silver moonlight, and the sunlit one beneath her feet. Where there should have been dirt was only golden sky, the clouds passing beneath her toes like schools of fish. This was the world of twilight, of those stranded between life and death. It was a strange thing to do, to fall between worlds as simply as a stone might tumble into the sea, forever lost. Was that what she was now, forever lost?

"That will be up to you, child," said Papa. He'd scried her thoughts so quickly, so easily, her mortal mind leaf-thin to a being such as him. For all her secrets—the pain, the losses so numerous she'd lost count, her envies and fears—she was laid bare before Papa Legba's divinity. And that was what scared her most.

At last, they stopped. Papa pointed out into the darkness, his finger as gnarled and crooked as rotted wood. She knew this place, knew it well. *The Dreadwood.* An ancient place, even in the mortal realm. It held gateway magic, a threshold between realms. It had always been a part of Voodoo—any initiate had to be willing to take their trial in the woods for three days' time. If they survived, the spirit world was pleased. If they did not? Well, the Dreadwood claimed another soul.

"Let us be finished with these games, Papa. I want to go home."

"But my dear, I am showing you the way. That"—he gestured out to the Dreadwood—"is the only way."

It was a lie. It had to be. This was his domain, his kingdom. He was Lord of the Crossroads, keeper of keys. Papa could return her back to the mortal realm if he wished it so.

"When you banished Jon here, did we not strike a bargain?" He stared into Marie's eyes, his gaze red-hot. She felt her cheeks flush with shame. "Did you not think I would come to my own with Jon too?"

So many, many things she had not considered after the Quarter Quarrel. She'd been foolish to think that sending Jon to the Veil was the end of her problems. No, Marie realized, that was only the beginning.

"What were your terms?"

He smiled, pleased. This was the talk all loa revered in the end. The talk of deals and bargains, of flesh and souls to be won and traded. "That if he could bring you here, as you kindly did him, you would undertake my Trial of Spirit."

Trial of Spirit. Once upon a time, Sanite had warned her it would come. It was true.

Sanite had foreseen one final trial, that last rite of her initiation. But then she'd died and Marie had become queen, the matter all but settled. What need did she have for another initiation? She was the Quarter Queen, her throne secure. But Sanite's warning had not been wrong, just far too early. She hadn't said who would deliver this final lesson, only that Marie must learn it. And who better to teach her than Jon? After all, he had always been her best teacher.

"And what did you promise him in return?" she asked.

Papa's eyes flared at her, the fiery glow of iron pulled from the forge. "Silly child. The only thing he's ever wanted all these years: a way back."

Of course. Had she thought the Veil would hold a man like Jon for eternity? She had hoped, foolishly. Desperately. Why, oh why, had she not simply killed him and been done with it?

Because you loved him, her traitorous heart whispered.

Marie found her voice smaller than she would have liked, dwarfed in the shadow of Papa's power. "If I should fail?"

"Then you would remain here, in the twilight, where you would serve me for an eternity."

Marie stared at him, unblinking, even as her heart quivered. "And if I should pass?"

His smile deepened, revealing crooked teeth. "Power beyond mortal comprehension. And I will, of course, return you on home."

"This is the only way?"

"The only way, indeed. Do you accept the terms, Marie Laveau?"

"Yes," Marie said. Something in the air stirred between them, and Marie felt some part of her spirit leave her and join Papa. His scale tipped a little, the deal as good as struck.

"Then you may begin."

Marie jutted her chin higher and walked forward, resolute in her path. *The only way.* Those words followed her, whispered in her ear over and over again. *The only way.* Marie did not dare look back. She couldn't stand to see Papa's smirking face, the veneer of humor she found impossible to read. She would bear this alone, as she had always done in all things. She entered the Dreadwood, the bramble and weeds underfoot snatching at her with cold hands.

Marie peered into the dark wood and gazed upon its true face. The woods were alive. The trees moved, each brush of wind a trembling breath, gnarled branches slowly opening to reveal a long road before her, where Marie was forced to gaze into the dark unknown of her own heart.

Come, the woods whispered. *We have much to show you.*

What could the spirit world show her that she had not already seen? Demons, monsters, and men with faces far more terrible than either—she had seen evils of all kinds, even her own.

The wind picked up. *Come and behold your deepest fears, Marie Laveau.* The trees swayed, laughing at her. *Come and behold the past.*

CHAPTER NINE

REE

In the bayou house, Ree stood over her mother's still body, her dark hair pooled against the pillow. She was pale, so dangerously pale. Was she simply sleeping? Ree couldn't be sure.

A thousand questions. She had no idea how her mother had ended up unconscious in the Dreadwood. In the passing of only one night, her plans had been cast to the wind, as good as dust, so much of her life thrown into doubt. Ree could hardly believe that she had been so ready to leave her, to abandon her own mother to this miserable fate. After one bad fight, she'd been ready to run away, always the insolent child. Ree marveled at her selfishness, the cowardice. What had her mother always told her? *You don't run away from problems, daughter. You run toward them.*

Ree rubbed her temple, her magic spent from getting her mother to safety. All night Ree had paced about the bayou house like a madwoman, overturning chests, ripping through dusty tomes and old scrolls scrawled with ancient spellwork, tossing amulets of jade, moonstone, rippling blue lapis lazuli. She'd seized every trinket, every vial and draught. Surely at least one must hold the answer to her mother's predicament. Surely there was some cure.

Her eyes flitted to the window, where the wind rattled the dusty glass panes, the world outside a faceless dark in the early hours of a slowly encroaching dawn. She waited anxiously for the sounds of Aram's return; she'd sent him to bring Nan the moment she could come. But she heard only the owls crying from their branches as inky shadows crawled along the ceiling and over the walls. The bayou house stood cold without her mother's fiery presence, as if her very lifeblood had kept the place aglow.

The tignon lay on the ground, pooled in a puddle of gold. *Come,* a voice beckoned softly from the dark.

It was a silly thing, but Ree had thought it called to her before as a child, in stolen moments alone. Before she had the sense to know any better, she'd often dressed herself in her mother's silks, swept her curls away from her face in the same elegant knot her mother wore, and piled her head high with a makeshift turban of her own. And she'd pretend she was the Quarter Queen, playing make-believe in the shadow of the true queen's throne. Her mother had warned her the golden cloth was a gift from the loa, that it was the mark of their chosen queen. It would coronate only those the gods themselves deemed worthy. Which Ree would never be.

Her mother stirred. Ree shot to her feet, practically running to her mother's bedside. She snatched her hand in hers.

"Maman? Can you hear me?"

Marie said nothing. Her finger twitched. There was no mistaking it this time. Her mother could hear her, somehow.

"*Maman?*" Ree took her mother's hand in hers, and blackness crowded her vision.

She was no longer in the bayou house. A vast wilderness surrounded her, the darkness swallowing her from all sides. It took Ree a second longer to realize she was channeling. *She* was doing this. A face peered out from the dark, inching closer to her from the shadows. It stared at her so intently, so expectantly, it was as if it had been waiting all along.

Jon the Conjurer.

Jon's mouth stretched into a wicked smile, his eyes glowing like golden fire in the dark as he spoke in a chillingly low voice: *Hello again, Marie.*

Startled, Ree dropped her mother's hand, and Jon the Conjurer's face vanished like smoke dispersing into the dark.

From somewhere outside in the brush, Aram cawed, signaling his return at long last. She heard the front door open, the sound of hurried footsteps as Nan approached, her crown of short reddish coils springing with her every step.

"Princess, you called—" Nan's eyes swept the room, falling to Marie's comatose body. "Oh, saints." Nan immediately dropped to Marie's side, examining her state. "God help us."

But Ree didn't have time for panic, only answers. "How do we cure her?" she demanded.

"She's been hexed," Nan said. Few around these parts were more gifted in rootwork than Nan. That sacred art of magic drawn from the earth's roots and flowers and soil to brew potions and poisons, to conjure protection and cast away harm. Nan laid a hand over Marie's pale one, her own emitting a soft honeyed light, like butterscotch. The smell of her magic perfumed the air—ginger and sweet basil. Nan claimed the voice of Zaka spoke to her, that it was he who mounted her spirit during rituals. Zaka was the patron loa of harvest, whose nourishing power could coax spells from ancient roots and herbs, whose machete could cull poisonous weeds from the land in one mighty swing.

"*Hexed?* Hexed by who?" Ree demanded. She'd first suspected one among her own, naturally. Ory. Fabrice. Nan too. A handful of others. But they didn't have the power nor the cunning needed to pull something like this off.

Nan only remained silent, her lips drawn into a thin line. And Ree knew whatever Zaka whispered at her ear was not pleasant.

"*Tell me!*"

"It is not just a matter of who, but of *what*." Nan sighed. "She consumed poison, Ree."

Ree went still, eyes frozen over her mother's motionless body. She could be a corpse. Marie Laveau counted few people as friends, but there was no shortage of folks she might call enemies lurking in the city. Anyone could have wanted her poisoned and out of the way. The Church. The Brotherhood. Old Voodoo rivals. Ree suppressed a shudder. The possibilities were frightening.

"What *kind* of poison, Nan?"

"Conjurer Root."

Conjurer Root. Ree had consumed it last night, but she was not the one lying in a bed comatose and at the brink of death. Her mother was. And then there was . . . Anabelle. The lovely Anabelle, who'd left her standing there all alone on that bridge like a lovestruck fool while her mother clung to life. It was she who had given Ree the Conjurer Root as a gift, after all, but what on earth could be gained from poisoning her mother with it? A dangerous question with likely a far more dangerous answer, but after Ree handled this business with her mother, she had every intention of finding out.

"I took some too," Ree pointed out. "I wasn't poisoned."

"You did not consume as much as your mother, perhaps. And count yourself lucky, for Conjurer Root holds death magic," said Nan, brow furrowed. "You know who brought this root to New Orleans, don't you?" Ree did know. She had not forgotten Sanite's grimoire, those forbidden accounts of Haiti and those corpses rising from the earth one by one. "*Jon the Conjurer.*"

"What are you saying—"

"After your mother banished Jon, there are some . . . among us who claim to hear his voice still. That his will still lives on. This root is proof of that. Perhaps . . ." She lifted her eyes to Ree's, frightened of her own words. ". . . it is Jon's will now that binds your mother so."

Nan was staring at her strangely. Oh, saints, there was more.

"What is it, Nan?" Ree demanded. But Nan remained quiet, eyes trained on the floor, looking anywhere but at Ree. It was making her nervous, jittery with paranoia.

Nan pulled a paper from her cloak. A copy of *The Quintessence*, dated just this morning, the headline printed in familiar bold, flourished lettering:

NEGRO INSURRECTIONIST TO HANG; MAYOR CORBIN TO ATTEND PROCEEDINGS IN CONGO SQUARE.

Ree froze. Panic, pure and all-consuming, crashed through her in a tidal wave, blood thrumming in her ears. As pressing as her mother's state was, *this* . . . by all the saints . . . this could not wait.

"Stay with my mother," Ree called over her shoulder as she made for the door.

Here she was heeding her mother's advice, even now, even when all hope might be lost. *You don't run away from problems, daughter.*

You run toward them. And run she did—through the door, into the cool damp of the bayou, and toward the danger she knew lay waiting.

By the time Ree reached Congo Square, she was too late.

She saw first the brown bare feet, then the long legs swinging like reeds in the wind, the bare torso corded through with muscle and scars, and the face, deep brown and unsmiling . . .

Marcel.

Ree cupped both hands over her mouth, stifling down the start of a scream. *Gods, no.*

In the space of one second, it all became so clear. She knew. Even with her lack of talent for divination, she could see it all in her mind's eye: All of the aurum stuffed into one tiny vial. The one *she'd* given him. He'd tipped it all into the overseer's drink. It was an easy thing to do, wasn't it? One bad word, one lash too many. Ree had given him the power of a thunderstroke in one tiny little vial. Ree might as well have strung the rope up and hanged him herself. Why had she given him that damned vial? Magic welled up inside her, but she tamped it down with a few shaky breaths. Anger would not do. Not now. News of her mother's absence had surely reached the rest of the Quarter, but to what extent she could not say.

"Serves him right," a white man with long red hair jeered to her left. Ree turned, realizing that he was Brotherhood. "Boy thought he could get bright on one of us. Suppose he got bright enough, didn't he? Getting all the sun he'll ever need now."

The taller alchemist beside him shook his head. "That could be one of us, you know." His eyes slid uneasily among the hungry crowd. "Magic is magic, no two ways about it."

The first alchemist sucked the air through his teeth, the squeak of wet boots in rain, and spit a thick wad of tobacco onto the ground. "That will *never* be one of us."

He caught Ree's gaze and smiled cruelly, his teeth stained dark. She stared back, hatred and defiance burning in her chest. She would remember his face. And one day, if no one else would pay for what was done to Marcel, it would be him, she decided. Someone had to pay.

Ree forced her gaze back to Marcel. She must have just missed his murder. If she had gotten there just moments before, perhaps she still could have saved him.

Done what? a voice whispered in the back of her mind. *Risked starting an uprising against the police? Gotten more Voodoos and innocents killed? Stupid girl.*

Flies were beginning to buzz in the air above, scattering like handfuls of black seeds tossed into the sunlight. Handsome, even in death. He was not gray yet, still deeply sun-browned, eyes closed and unseeing. She wanted to look away, the same way she had always done when the slaves passed by too close and she was too ashamed to meet their narrowed eyes. But this was different. This was no faceless stranger whom she could easily put from mind. This was one of her own, her best friend.

Ree could hear her mother again, the same hot scolding on her tongue. *Open your eyes, Ree.* And so she did. Ree watched Marcel's body swing from the rope, lifeless and limp. They would leave him up 'til nightfall, perhaps even sunup. The lawmen would want the Voodoos to go on about their rituals while one of their brothers swung above them, cold and gray, a warning of what might befall them too if an ounce of magic was misused.

But now someone moved at the center of the square. *Tap. Tap. Tap.* Ree squinted and felt a sharp stab of panic rise in her belly at the sight of the man who strolled from the crowd, brandishing a fine blackthorn cane. It was the mayor of New Orleans.

Felix Corbin was known for his immaculate dress—today's choice was a rich black frock coat with golden buttons, a felt hat with an ostrich feather at the corner that sat atop his straggle of gray-streaked hair, and of course his infamous fleur-de-lis cane, which he twirled back and forth in his hand like a wand.

The weathered skin on his forehead and neck told Ree that Corbin was mid-sixties, and he might have been handsome if not for the unsightly scar that ran the length of the right side of his face. Gossips whispered it was the mark of one of his slaves who turned on him, but Ree knew better. It was an old plague mark, a reminder of a time when disease had laid siege to the city, when the wealthy had something proper to fear at last.

Corbin strode below Marcel's body, pacing like he had all the time in the world. *This,* those laughing eyes promised the crowd, *is mine.* He used his cane to jab at Marcel's corpse, and Marcel swung back and forth in the wind, the rope creaking. Ree swallowed down the surge of rage in her throat, black spots dancing in her vision.

"I like to think that New Orleans is not like the rest of the South," Corbin said, his voice an exaggerated drawl. "We don't torture. We don't maim for fun. We, the people of the good city of New Orleans, live by a single code—that all within our city abide by our God-given rules. But when those rules are broken, well, we answer kind for kind. *Blood for blood.*"

To Ree's surprise, a murmur of agreement started among the crowd. It caught like wildfire, catching on tongues eager to agree at last. Ree had never felt so small, so alone, draped in her cloak. She held her cowl closer. There were no friends here.

Corbin lifted his cane, gesturing out to the crowd as if he were taking aim. "I hereby decree the punishment as fitting and just by the sovereign rules set forth by the Code Noir." Corbin reached into the pocket of his frock coat, producing a scroll of parchment bearing the city's fleur-de-lis seal. He began to read loudly, "Article Twenty-Eight clearly states: *With regard to outrages or acts of violence committed by slaves against free persons, it is our will that they be punished with severity, and even with death, should the case require it.*"

When Corbin spoke again, his voice had grown stronger at the crowd's agreement, like rolling thunder. "This boy practiced Voodoo and used his magic to kill another law-abiding citizen for his own gain. Violent, why yes. Unlawful, I would surely agree. But I am here to tell you today that Marcellus Dumond is guilty of the worst infraction, for his actions represent a sin this city will not ever forgive." Corbin paused, allowing his words to land on every ear with dramatic flair. "*Insurrection.* But I have to wonder, who put these ideas in his pretty little head? Perhaps it was his so-called Quarter Queen, the benevolent Marie Laveau."

The murmur grew into vicious agreement. Haiti's revolution had cast a long, bloodied shadow, even now, some forty years after its end. A revolution New Orleans would not soon forgive, nor forget. Haitian slaves had rejected the Code Noir, that wicked document of governance. Ree shifted, nervously glancing at the faces that told her they were afraid that folks here might do the same.

"So, where is your Quarter Queen? Where is your precious Marie Laveau? Perhaps she owes us all a proper answer," Corbin jeered.

Blood thrummed in Ree's ears, deafening. It was now or never.

She could feel the power thrumming in her veins, the static of lightning and the heat of cauldron-fire, alive in its own way. *No more, priestess,* said the voice in her ear. *You will hide no more.* Ree gritted her teeth and swallowed down the lump of fear in her throat, all the way down to her belly, where it sat like a stone. For just this once, she would have to agree: She would deny what she was no more.

Ree removed her hood and stepped forward to face the crowd unmasked.

Ree drew in a shaking breath and allowed herself to say the words she'd long denied herself. "I am Marie Laveau."

A murmur moved through the crowd, slithering from tongue to tongue like a worm. Ree could feel every eye on her, appraising, as if to some she were a jewel to be prized, to others a bauble to be discarded.

Corbin's eyes fixed upon her, coldly appraising. "Marie Laveau the Second." He smiled, and it struck Ree then that he possessed a face that shouldn't smile at all. "Where is your mother?"

"I—"

A flash of movement at the corner of Ree's eye. It all happened so fast—one moment she was facing the mayor of New Orleans, and the next there was Anabelle, beautiful Anabelle, pressing her way from the whispering crowd. Ree stared, dumbly. She thought for one strangled second that Anabelle was simply walking toward her. But Anabelle was not walking toward Ree. She never would again. She was walking toward Corbin, a glowing hand raised in the air, black sparks flying from her fingertips.

The blast struck Corbin square in the chest, and he went flying across the square, ostrich hat toppling from his head in the wind.

"*No!*" It was a stupid reflex. But Ree felt herself reaching out, steadying Corbin before he could hit the ground. She left her arm extended, still holding him with the weight of her magic, while she turned to face Anabelle, who was sneering at her.

Ree stood frozen. She did not know this face. The voice was at her ear again, laying soft kisses along her neck. *Perhaps you never did.*

"Anabelle?" Ree hated the sound of her voice, so small it was among the growing unrest.

"Let him go, Ree. He deserves this." She was still looking at Corbin, hanging suspended in the air.

"You don't know what you're doing—"

"Don't I? I've known exactly what I've been doing this entire time. Did you?"

Ree's heart gave a sickening lurch. Something about those words. *Did you?* She felt her heart breaking in her chest, splintering right in two, and there was absolutely nothing that she could do about it. "Anabelle . . . what have you done?"

"Everything you Laveaus *wouldn't*," snarled Anabelle. "Some of us prefer the old way. Some of us still remember the way of High Jon."

It all went back to Jon. Had her mother truly rid the world of him? There was no escaping him, she understood now.

Ree moved in a slow circle, keeping Corbin in the air. "If you kill him, harm him in any way, it won't just be you they hurt. They will hurt all of us. You would . . . you would start a rebellion, Anabelle."

Anabelle's lips tipped into a red half-moon. "And that, mon amour"—magic propelled from her in waves—"is entirely the point."

Anabelle let out a cry, and the startling voice of Erzulie, loa of love and protection, screamed through her, an earsplitting sound, the goddess's maternal wrath shaking the very air, rippling right toward Ree. But she bucked against the magic with the sudden force of Bade's wind, and Anabelle's magic bounced from Ree and back across the square. Anabelle was pushed some feet back, her hair windswept behind her, gnashing her teeth from the force of the blow.

Ree gasped. Bade was a loa of justness and scale and longed for balance in all things. What was asked from him, he took in equal measure. The air in her lungs constricted as the hand of the god of wind squeezed for control.

"You can't best me, Anabelle," said Ree, breathless from the seizing force of Bade's magic.

Anabelle was strong, to be sure, but she was not the daughter of Marie Laveau.

"But I bested your mother, didn't I?" asked Anabelle, a toying edge to her voice. "Where is the great Marie Laveau, I wonder? Perhaps enjoying the deep sleep I put her in? Amazing what a little too much Conjurer Root can do."

In that moment, her suspicion confirmed, Ree felt it all flee from her: Whatever sense of restraint she'd been harboring, whatever regard for the Quarter's rules she'd been clinging to, her mother's careful training . . . it all left her, as quickly and cleanly as a stroke of wind. In its place, something else lived and breathed—disbelief, heartbreak. Something else too, mingled with her grief, sharp as knives. Rage.

"You fucking *traitor*!" Ree flung out a hand, calling upon the metalsmithing loa, Ogoun. It was his iron-heavy strength she used now, not fire, to pressure Anabelle back from her, but she dodged the blast.

A bolt of heat zipped past Ree's ear, and she turned to see the taller alchemist had snuck up behind her. He suddenly collapsed to the ground, howling in pain when Anabelle's attack cut right through his hand.

The red-haired alchemist pushed his way through the crowd and raised his staff at an overhanging tree that shaded the square. One of its branches snapped off, sprouting with six more wooden limbs that hung like crooked fingers, re-forming itself until it held the shape of a whittled claw that flew straight for Anabelle.

Ree turned Ogoun's strength on the alchemist now, hissing out her spell, the taste of hot metal on her breath. The man froze, bound at the arms by smoking iron called to form by the metalsmithing loa's forge. He hit the stone with a thud, limbs locked into place.

The truth was she did not know what she meant to do with Anabelle. But there was no way in hell she would allow the Brotherhood to interfere.

The presence of the loa hung heavy in the square, the air thick with the stench of burning metal and something softer, the musk of herbs and incense. Ree understood that, fickle as they could be, the loa rarely liked to clash amongst themselves so viscerally. A fight between vessels was a clash of their divine wills. She imagined the loa considered it a grand waste of magic.

Ree lowered the hand still protecting Corbin to the ground, and he fell back in a heap of black velvet. He was staring at her, blue eyes fanatically wide, as if truly seeing her for the first time. It wasn't a look of anger like she expected, or plain shock. It was a look of *want*. It was the look that had earned him the title of the Collector. The wail of police bells resounded, bouncing along the hollows of the square. The crowd splintered into two, bodies scrambling in all directions.

The world froze.

It was unlike anything Ree had ever felt before—intense, sudden, a shock wave of pressure. It was the mark of old, powerful magic. The spellwork of Simbi Makaya. Lord of sorcery. She had felt his presence before, used his magic for her own, but never like *this*. The vessel commanding Simbi Makaya wielded his sorcery with the blunt force of a sword through steel, cutting through her resolve, compelling her mind to obey the enchantment of his will. *Stay*, the sorcerer loa ordered. And it was so.

For a moment, Ree couldn't move; Simbi Makaya's magic kept her locked in place, pressing in like a shield. And neither could Anabelle—Ree caught her eye from across the square. She stared back, just as startled by the intrusion. So, it was clear—it was the work of another Voodoo. But who?

Ree watched as the police descended. Fabrice, Ory, and a few other Voodoos made their escape, as did the two Brotherhood alchemists, slipping into the chaos of swarming bodies. And then the pressure lifted, and she felt the magic of Simbi Makaya no longer, the pressure on her bones relaxed, his compulsion gone.

A figure stood at the edge of the square, a black woman draped in dark violet silk, a scarf around her mouth. Only her eyes were visible, glowing with the force of her magic, two shining emeralds, even from such a distance. The woman turned away, lost to the crowd, just as Ree heard thundering footsteps behind her, and then someone barked, "Get on the ground! Get on the fucking ground!"

Lawmen had flooded the square, of course. They'd broken city law. Magic was intended to mend bones, to make items anew, but never to harm (officially). And what Ree and Anabelle had done? Ree turned her gaze back up toward the hangman's rope, to Marcel's cold body crowned in the white flare of sunlight. He'd dared only to use a single magic vial for harm. What then would the city make of the commotion they'd caused now, the violent mess two black witches had dared make in public for all to see? Tomorrow, when order had been restored, the mystics hauled off to be tried for their crimes, there would be one word whispered amongst the city officials and bourgeoise, one word emblazoned scandalously across the fronts of morning newspapers, a word more dangerous than any curse even Marie Laveau the First could hope to cast. *Rebellion.*

Ree caught a rush of movement beside her, the flash of metal of a baton. *Crack!* Pain erupted at the crown of her head, her fingers shone with red wetness. Ree's vision blurred as she hit the stone, dimly aware that a man was standing over her. And then—

The unmistakable sear of aurum bound her neck.

The officer let out a whistle, low and full of satisfaction. "I've been waiting a long, long time to put these on a Laveau."

He locked the remainder of the aurum shackles about her hands and feet and set out with her bound to him, dragging her along hot cobblestone that tore her gown and scraped at her back. But even as darkness overtook her, she saw only Marcel's body swinging and heard only those foul words in her mind, playing in dark refrain: *Serves him right.*

When Ree awoke, she was certain of two things: that someone had taken a hammer to her head, and that it was going to take at least two glasses of bourbon to see it mended. Clutching her throbbing skull, Ree sat up and looked around. She was in a cell, to be sure, no bigger than the size of a broom closet.

"I suppose this must be odd to you," a voice taunted from the other side of the cell. Ree squinted into the darkness. Her eyes adjusted at last, her heart jumping. Anabelle. Like Ree, she was shackled by the foot in aurum, her throat bound in a thin circlet. Ree's own shackles were twice the size, the collar around her neck as thick and choking as farm rope. "A Laveau in chains. Who would have thought?"

It took Ree a long moment to answer. In many ways, the time for speaking was long past. Anabelle had said everything Ree needed to know in that square.

Just how long had Anabelle been toying with her? Ree thought back to all those months ago, to that fateful night in the House of Flowers when Anabelle had passed her smelling of jasmine and juniper. Even then. Ree closed her eyes, held back the hot sting of tears. That had not been fate, if there existed such a thing. The only spellwork at hand had been the magic of careful planning.

"Was none of it real?" Ree rasped.

Anabelle lowered her eyes to the floor. "When it needed to be."

"We were never going to leave New Orleans, were we?"

"No." Did she imagine the way Anabelle's throat wobbled? The sound of tears in her voice? "I just needed you—"

"—out of the way," Ree finished, shaking her head. She truly was a fool.

Ree hated that she could still smell her perfume, that heady tangle of jasmine and juniper, even amongst the reek of piss and old flesh. It was useless, even now, to fight the pull Anabelle Dupont had on her. She might be able to pick out Anabelle's scent anywhere: in the madness of the Quarter, amongst all those nameless faces and bodies upon bodies. Her mother had warned her, hadn't she? *So, you see it is you who commits the greatest sin of them all— you put a thing as fickle as love before your own magic.*

"I was going to purchase your freedom," said Ree bitterly.

Anabelle scoffed, jutting her chin. "And *you* would own me instead?"

"Of course not. I would turn you loose. Set you free."

"Merci, Mademoiselle! How generous the Laveaus can be."

"I suppose that's all I ever was to you, right? A Laveau. Cheating my way around town, as you say. Christ, none of that matters now. Marcel is dead." Agony stabbed her heart. Something about saying those words out loud made them more real, more painful. "I suppose you blame me for that too."

Anabelle took a shaking breath. "No, that sin belongs to the city alone."

"And what about your sins, Anabelle?" The stone wall was ice-cold on the torn back of her dress. "You hurt my mother."

"Your mother's time is done. Marie Laveau wasted the throne for her own means. But not Jon." Her voice had changed. It had a note of strangled hope. "Jon will return, and when he does, he will set things right."

That did not sound like the explanation she was owed. That sounded like a warning.

"How?" Ree shook her head, numb. "Just how is he going to *set things right?*"

"Oh, beloved . . ." Anabelle leaned back against the wall, chains rustling, her taunting face partially obscured in shadow. "How you will soon find out."

When Ree woke again, she couldn't be certain how much time had passed. There were no windows in her cell. She'd tried counting the seconds and minutes, but she quickly learned that was an easy way to go mad. She drifted in and out of a dreamless sleep. She'd caught Anabelle watching her, eyes misted over with some unnamed emotion.

Footsteps sounded outside her cell, drawing near. Then came the unmistakable jangle of keys and the molten glow of lamplight.

"Well, well, Laveau," the officer said. "It seems someone took mercy on you. Bought out the rest of your bail."

"Who?"

The officer frowned. "The fucking church, as luck would have it."

He stepped aside, revealing a figure in a long blood-red robe, the hood drawn over a black lacquered mask, frightening in its eerie blankness. It was the mask of an Inquisitor.

Slowly, the Inquisitor pulled the hood down, black gloved hands removing the mask. Ree froze. She stared up at the face she'd seen only in her dreams—her nightmares too. The face of the boy, now a proper man, she'd thought she'd never see again.

"Henryk."

At the sound of his name, Henryk Broussard pierced her with his cold silver gaze.

The years had whittled away the softness of childhood. He was impossibly tall and broad-shouldered, towering in the dark, his square jaw taut and lean. His hair was longer now, falling just above his neck, russet brown in the lamplight. Henryk held the bars with black gloved hands, and she fought the urge to reach for him. Years and years, countless pretty faces filling the space beneath her on her bed, and he was still the most beautiful man she had ever seen.

She should have been thinking of her next words, but Ree was thinking only of that day eight years ago, the day he should have found her waiting on that bridge ready to take his hand. Instead, he found but an empty space where she should have been.

Henryk scanned her face, the metal collar on her neck. Ree supposed even with all the divination in the world at her fingertips, she wouldn't possibly be able to read into the faint tightness at the corners of his eyes, to pry some meaning from the way he pursed his lips at the sight of her. His eyes were the same pale gray, darkening now like storm clouds. For a second, she saw a glimpse of the old pain she'd caused him.

At last, Henryk spoke, the words a pocketknife cutting through her chest into her fickle, fickle heart. "Hello, princess."

PART TWO

NO SAINTS AND NO SINNERS

A man without sin counts himself not a saint but a fraud, and a saint who has sinned for which he has confessed considers himself forgiven. But of the man who does not confess his deepest sins? He must consider himself irrevocably and despairingly haunted.

—Antonio de Sedella, "Père Antoine," from his sacred sermon "The Nature of Man and His Immortal Soul"

CHAPTER TEN

MARIE

Twenty-five years before

Marie bent over a basin of clean water, muttering a spell of mending under her breath, holding off tears. It was funny work, healing. How could she stave off disease with a few magical words, keep her patients from the brink of death and misery, but she couldn't find the strength to pry herself from her own grief?

Marie sponged a woman's sweaty brow and checked her tongue for phlegm; there was none, only the remnants of lentil soup, the only food she could stomach in her condition. Marie knew this woman was horrible, had seen her prancing along the Quarter's streets, her few house slaves in tow, carting her mountain of boutique bags. Marie had wondered if the plague had tempered her some, had given her some dose of humility. She was wrong.

"I know you," the woman rasped suddenly.

Marie didn't doubt that. Plenty of townsfolk knew her. To most, she was "that Voodoo girl," apprentice to the Quarter Queen, Sanite Dede. To others, she was a hairdresser making her coin on Royal Street, a devout woman of faith who never missed a morning mass. Two years ago, she had been a plague nurse facing down buckets of mucus and piling sickbeds, nursing folks back from the maws of yellow fever. Now she found herself a nurse again, but this time, it was a plague of a different kind. Boils that blossomed across the skin like gray mushrooms. Black phlegm. Yellowed eyes where there should have been milky white. This was not yellow fever. Marie fought down a shudder. This was far worse.

Marie placed a cold rag on her patient's brow, hot to the touch. She was staring intently at Marie, the whites of her eyes streaked with yellow. "I know you," she said again.

Marie sighed. It couldn't be helped. "That so?"

The woman smiled, slow and dreamlike, flashing rotting teeth— another symptom of this mysterious plague that must be recorded. Marie made a mental note.

"You are the Widow Paris."

Marie froze. *Jacques.* The tears grew hot against her lashes. Still, Marie held them back. She would not cry in front of this woman.

Her smile deepened. "Yes, yes. You are, aren't you? *The Widow Paris.*" Her voice took on a singsong lilt. "Where did your husband go? Gone he was, like smoke, they say."

They say. People said many things about her. They always had, since she was a girl. Father Antoine had taught her it was her own cross to bear. But then she'd grown up and come to see such talk as the mark of power. After all, people did not waste time speaking of the unremarkable. No, they spoke of those whom they feared.

"*Voodoo,*" she mocked, that same dreamlike smile plastered on her face. "The woman who for all her magic couldn't keep her husband from leaving her."

Marie said nothing. Jacques had questioned her magic too. She could still hear him now, those last fateful words he'd said before he left and disappeared a year ago. *What's the use of having all that power, mon amour, if you don't dare use it for more?*

The woman laughed, scattering spittle. Marie imagined backhanding the woman. Hexing her. Killing her, even. Certainly, she'd killed for less at Sanite Dede's command. But no spell came to her, and all the magic and blood seemed to drain from her veins, leaving her breathless and cold.

The woman's laughter followed Marie through the infirmary, along the rows and rows of white linen cots filled with the writhing and the sick, and out into the murky sunlight of the Quarter. Like a stone pitched over a river's edge, Marie hurled herself out from the chapel, sucking in mouthfuls of late-winter air. The morning brought down a veil of gray mist over the city, and it drifted out upon the Quarter's cobbled streets, a slow-crawling miasma.

All she could think of was Jacques. Sometimes she thought herself a fool for loving him so. They'd scarcely been married a year before he'd gone from her. And before that, she'd known him for only a few months. He was a sailor, a revolutionary whom Sanite had introduced her to during one of her moonlit rituals at Lake Pontchartrain.

The funny thing was, she hardly remembered the sweet days of their marriage. Not when her mind craved only the pain of the nightmare, to relive it each night in the agony of grief and loneliness. That last day. That last goodbye. He'd gone on up to Baton Rouge for business as he always had. Wasn't supposed to be gone for more than three days' time. But three days had come and gone. And Jacques never returned. She didn't know what happened to him. No one did. But one day after he left New Orleans, there had been talk of an attack on Governor Jean-Francis. An insurrection, *The Quintessence* had printed across their front page in large, accusing red lettering the next morning. Someone had tried to stage a rebellion. Although she had never received an official report, and there was no body to bury, no amount of human closure could tell her what she already knew in her soul to be true. Jacques had died that day. She'd felt it, the moment of his death lodging in her chest like a knife, and later, in the long nights after, the sinking weight of his absence when the grief had bled her dry.

If you don't dare use it for more. It was those words that haunted her. The words that kept her faithfully attending confession with Father Antoine, that played endlessly in her head as she silently served Sanite day and night. Because they were true. What good was she doing with her magic? What if she was meant to do more?

"Are you Marie Laveau?" asked a boy in a straw hat.

He was a young white boy, bayou-fed and apple-cheeked. Cajun, no doubt, looking to find work in the city as a runner.

"That depends upon who's asking."

The courier looked her over, nonplussed by her brazenness. "Well, if you are, in fact, Marie Laveau, then you've been summoned."

"By whom?"

He handed the letter over to her, and Marie caught the unmistakable violet wax seal in the shape of the city's official brand, the fleur-de-lis. "By a man I highly suggest you heed."

"Quite politely, you can send my response by mouth. Fuck no."

"You misunderstand, Madame Laveau. This was not a question." He backed away, rightfully sensing Marie's mood darken. "This was an order."

"I do not take orders from men. Even white men."

"I don't imagine you do. But this is no ordinary man." He tipped his hat. "This is the fucking mayor."

Marie's carriage trundled up the long path that led to Chateau Corbin, the road unwinding from its coil like a garden snake readying to strike from the weeds.

Mayor Felix Corbin. The very same mayor that put her people up on platforms to be bartered and sold, like they were not humans but pretty trinkets in a window. The mayor whose father had owned her mother, and her mother before her. The mayor who, until this very moment, it seemed, was quite happy to pretend the likes of Marie Laveau did not exist. Marie bristled. Apparently, he pretended no more. Her eyes moved beyond the house, across the grounds, into the shadowed edges of the fields, where Corbin's stock of slaves toiled in the sopping wet gloom of the sugarcane stalks.

A few were gathered along the garden path, peering at her curiously. When Marie held a slave child's eyes, she ran off—they all did, schools of fish darting through dangerous water. Marie's lips thinned. Her own kind ran from her. She imagined that she was a marvel to them—a freedwoman, in fine enough dress, with hair that didn't need to be hidden under a cap from the sun's lash. Or perhaps she was a specter on two feet, an oddity sorely out of place and time, something that should not exist according to plantation rules but did nonetheless.

Marie stepped from the carriage and was met by a house slave who fell into a deep bow. "Right this way, Madame Laveau."

The moment Marie entered the chateau, she could sense another magic that was not hers. When she turned into the parlor, she knew why. The Brotherhood of the White Hand. Brotherhood spells and curses made her skin prickle and her hair stand on end. As she turned into the hallway that led toward the foyer, she saw only a few house slaves peeking from the back kitchens, eager to catch a glimpse of a Voodoo priestess on the grounds.

Besides the stink of Brotherhood magic, and the buttery aroma of a chicken being boiled in tarragon, thyme, and lemon juices, there was death in this house. She could smell it strongly in the foyer, where it ran like a dark river beneath the floorboards and seeped into the walls. Of course, in any plantation house there was death; one careless mistake, a single glass of sweet tea spilled, a word of frustration uttered under the breath after a long day in the fields—all of that could bring down the deadly wrath of an overseer or master.

The slave led Marie down the hall, stopping in the kitchens to retrieve a bowl of fresh water as Marie had bid. Marie stopped suddenly, having scented another, familiar magic—sage and the sweet smoke of coffee. Out stepped a tall, deeply brown-skinned woman in white skirts, her bosom draped in a lush red that denoted her allegiance to Haiti, her knee-length dark braids held back by two gold flower combs. On her neck she wore the red-and-black beaded pendant of Simbi Makaya, her patron loa.

"Claudette," Marie said with a brisk nod. Staring at Claudette always made her uncomfortable. *She has his eyes.* They were Jacques's eyes, to be sure, emerald green and glittering.

Claudette shuffled a stack of silver-trimmed tarot cards from hand to hand. "You took long enough, Laveau. Have you more important things to do?"

Marie's lips quirked. "As a matter of fact, I do. Speaking with you is just not one of them." Claudette Duvalier was the last person

Marie expected to meet in a plantation house. But today was already proving to be full of surprises.

"Two years since that meek excuse for a wedding, and already you tire me with your uninspired jabs. I shudder to think what my cousin ever saw in you," said Claudette. She'd never approved of Marie as a match for her revolutionary-minded cousin Jacques.

"Then you should return to Haiti," Marie snapped. "Posthaste."

"And miss all the fun? I think not. Sanite sent me to make sure you adhered to Corbin's summons. Come, let us get the matter over with quickly."

A slave escorted Marie and Claudette to the smoking parlor, where an old four-poster bed had been pushed to the back of the room, draped in tattered netting to keep out buzzing mosquitoes.

The slave presented Marie with a little bow. "Master, I've come with the priestess, Madame Laveau."

Claudette hung back in the doorway, keeping to the shadows while Marie strode toward the bed and stopped just shy of its foot, where she could see yellowed toes peeking out from the sheets. Her gaze flickered to the mayor's face: plague-ridden and half starved.

"Marie Laveau." Corbin wheezed a cough. "My family used to own your mother. And your grandmother. Did you know that?"

Yes, she knew that. How could she not, when men like Mayor Corbin could hardly let her forget? White folks who counted themselves planters and masters always had a way of reminding black folks, free or not, of their enslaved bloodlines and kin—no different, she supposed, than rattling off which horses or chickens they kept in stock on their farms. Marie saw as much in a little oil portrait on the far wall where the mayor's father, Marc-Louis Corbin, grinned stupidly in a straw hat, arms slung around his white and mixed-race children, with his house slaves, including Marie's grand-mère, idling in the background, stone-faced.

"What is it that you seek, Monsieur?" Marie asked, her voice cold.

"Isn't it obvious? A cure. A goddamned antidote. If your reputation precedes you, and it does, then I know that you have one, witch."

Marie pressed her lips into a thin line. "You can be sure that I do."

"Give it to me."

"I am a free woman, Monsieur. I do as I please. From where I stand, you're not in the position to be making such demands of a woman like me."

"A woman like you!" He laughed, half mad, his teeth yellowed and stained from his own bile. "What a sassy nigress! Your reputation does precede you." His laughter turned into a fit of coughs. A sudden look of panic filled his waxen face. "Do you want money? Is that what this is about? Money? I've got plenty of money, girl."

Marie scoffed. "I don't want your money."

"Then what *do* you want?"

It was a curious question, indeed. She had no intention of disclosing the answer to a man like Felix Corbin. What she needed was Veil magic. Magic not even Sanite would teach her. *It is expressly forbidden.* Off-limits to even the Quarter Queen. But Sanite had not said it was not *possible.* Marie just needed the right teacher.

"Felix, what I do for you, I do not do for silver or gold." She reached into her pocket, drawing forth a corked vial of black liquid. "I do because I am bidden to. Because these are the rules."

In her work as a plague nurse, sometimes it was better to help patients go gently into the next world, to ease their suffering quickly. So she always carried two vials. One for healing. And one for death.

As she was about to open the vial, a hand seized hers, twisting painfully. Slowly, Claudette shook her head. Of course she had known. Claudette knew Marie's habits, her ways of doing magic. In another life, they might have been sisters. But not this one.

"Remember yourself, Marie! Do you want to see a war?" Claudette hissed into her ear. And then she added, "Not now. Not like this."

Jacques had wanted her to use her magic for more, but she hadn't listened to him. Not when it mattered. Now, in the long year since he'd vanished, the sorrow made her bitter, and sometimes this city made her want to burn it all down, to see what it might become after. New Orleans would be better off without men like Corbin, more diseased than any plague. But then she remembered the smell of the Brotherhood in the house, and she understood. They weren't here to heal him; they were here to make sure that *she* did.

"Take this," Marie said finally with a sigh, drawing forth a second vial of red liquid. The antidote.

Corbin reached for the vial and drained every last drop. "Such magic my father was a plum fool to discard." He watched her, wet blue eyes latching on to her in wonder. "You got that real magic in you, girl. To think, my family could have owned it."

Marie knew men of Corbin's ilk. A speck of magic in his blood. A miserable smidgeon. But not enough that the Brotherhood of the White Hand might want him. They'd closed their doors in his face, turned their backs on him. He was nothing but a Brotherhood reject looking to take magic he couldn't hope to produce himself from others. Now he wanted hers.

Marie offered him a cold smile over her shoulder. "And it never will again."

On the other side of the door, Marie was met with clapping. She swiveled to find two white men leaning against the wall, clearly waiting for her. A small auburn-haired boy lingered behind them, suckling sullenly on his finger.

The older of the two stepped forward. He was well over six feet, and despite looking in the early days of his forties, he had snow-white hair that trailed over his shoulder to his waist. Gailon LeBlanc, Grand Wizard of the Brotherhood of the White Hand.

"My dear Marie, why do you bother with the likes of Voodoo when you're clearly destined for the stage?" He held her gaze, and it was then that she realized his eyes were unnaturally dark—cold and impenetrable as swamp water.

"Bonjour, Grand Wizard."

"Marie Laveau," Gailon said, testing the name on his lips as if tasting a fine wine. "Oh, I've heard much about you."

Marie nodded toward the door, motioning for Claudette to wait for her outside. It would be better for her to handle this little tiff on her own. A woman like Claudette, who'd grown up under Haiti's hard-won sovereignty, had little patience for the likes of the Brotherhood and did not play nice by their rules.

Claudette passed her a final cautious look, then swept out to the carriages.

"I wasn't aware that you discuss the business of blacks and coloreds in your halls," said Marie, feigning hurt, once Claudette had gone. "On account of how we aren't allowed entry."

"Is that your way of asking for an invitation, witch?" the younger of the two said. "Perhaps that could be arranged."

Marie turned to look at him. He was smirking at her, but not cruelly, not like his master. He was closer to her age, with a clean-shaven face, and had the air of a university boy, pompous and self-assured—sadly typical for the Brotherhood of the White Hand's chosen crop. But his hair was reddish-gold, not the snowy white of his master. Which meant he was not ascended, not quite yet. The higher an alchemist rose among the Brotherhood's ranks and the deeper they delved into their mysterious rites, the whiter their hair became—leaving only the most magically formidable with strands of ash. Marie wondered if it was a point of pride for men of the Brotherhood—was their only mission to bleed the color from everything they had the misfortune of touching?

"Let us not be hasty, Silas. The Brotherhood's rules exist for good reason." Gailon's eyes twinkled, as if the three of them were old friends reunited and not enemies sworn to never cross color and magical lines alike.

The child, who could be no more than three, waddled forward, clasping his stubby fingers around Gailon's leg. Gailon tapped his staff once on the ground, and the child fell, hitting the wall behind them. The boy climbed to his feet, wetness in his gray eyes, but he knew better than to say a word. The alchemist had flicked him back as if he were a gnat buzzing in his ear.

So the child is his, Marie discerned. How terrible to have such a monster for a parent. But for all the magic in the world, the gods had never allowed folks to choose their mothers or their fathers. This Marie knew, unfortunately.

"As you wish, Grand Wizard," Silas said, although his blue eyes were trained directly on Marie.

"Supposedly, you are a talented healer, Marie Laveau," said Gailon. "But they say that your queen grows ill, weaker still by the day. Why are you here, on a plantation, healing men like us, when you could be with Sanite, healing her? *Perhaps*"—a strange light touched his eyes, black coal burning in a twinkling flame—"your presence here is merely a sham. I know Voodoo when I see it. Perhaps this is the work of your Quarter Queen?"

He dared call Voodoo dangerous when she'd heard the stories whispered about the Brotherhood of the White Hand—capturing runaway slaves for study and sacrifice all in the name of magical advancement. It was commonly believed among black folks that they transmuted more than lead and gold in those secret halls.

"Perhaps you'd better mind the business that pays you, Grand Wizard," Marie said with a sneer. "And last I checked, that wasn't exactly the business of negroes."

Her eyes flickered to Silas, who lingered just behind Gailon. Did she imagine the twitch of his lips, the shadow of amusement that flickered across his face hummingbird-fast? There was some strange emotion burning in his eyes, something she'd need more than a few moments in a hallway to study. Which Marie decided made this man, whoever he was, far more dangerous than the Grand Wizard.

Without another word, she strode away, their gazes prickling her back like needles.

Sanite Dede was waiting for her.

The bayou house was unusually cold at night, filled with puddles of silver moonlight and the clinking of mortars and pestles, the toiling of potion-brewing and spellwork that couldn't be done by day. The only light came from the sconces along the walls, where tiny candles had been enchanted to glow with violet and gold flame.

Marie and Claudette stepped through the beaded partition and crossed into the throne room. Marie was grateful for the stinging brine of vinegar and lemon that rose from the freshly scoured floorboards, the balm of sage, so different from the stink of death that clung to the chateau. Sanite was on her throne, as always.

"Marie, you've idled much, my child," Sanite Dede drawled. She was knitting, of all things. "Tell me, Marie, what did you learn?"

"Permission to speak freely?" Marie cast her eyes imperceptibly toward the right of the throne, where Claudette stood, hanging on to every word.

Sanite waved a hand, bidding Claudette leave. She cast one last mistrusting green-eyed glare at Marie, the partition's beaded veil rustling as she left. Claudette was not to be privy to Voodoo's inner workings because she was not beholden, per se, to the sacred laws of Sanite's court, not when she already belonged to the court of the old blood. She practiced Vodun—some might say the older, purer form of Voodoo—and served the Haitian Vodun Queen, Cécile Fatiman. She was here purely as a matter of oversight, an ambassador of sorts between their courts.

"Go on, child," Sanite said to Marie.

"Corbin did not just call on me—he called on the Brotherhood too." She paused, thinking on Gailon's spite. "The Grand Wizard made an appearance."

Sanite Dede clicked her tongue. The violet flame cast her in an unflattering light—eyes beadier, the hollows of her cheeks ghostly. "So, Gailon has seen fit to leave his dark hole for once. It makes sense. The mayor cannot heal himself, not from this. Even his own stock of mages could not temper the fever. He would have no choice. But he called on the Voodoos too. Meaning Gailon failed, didn't he? He is no closer to solving this mystery than the rest of us."

"Gailon believes, or at the very least insinuated, that this plague . . . is being perpetrated by *you.*"

Sanite Dede balked. It was not so much an incredible possibility as it was impossible for her to do at her age. Sanite Dede held power, true power. But at eighty-eight years old, she was nearing her end, and her power, for all its vicious glory, was waning.

"The Brotherhood has always fancied themselves thinking men, and yet they still need wooden sticks for conjuring." Sanite's lips curled. "If I wanted to go about killing white folks, don't you think I would have done that? But what good would come from chaos? What would I rule then, but ash and bone?"

But what if you did? What kind of world would rise from the ash? It was the briefest notion, a shooting star across the span of her darkest thoughts, fire-bright until it fell away.

Marie said only what was expected of her. "Of course not."

"Now, on to more pressing business. You've been at the sickbeds for two weeks now, Marie. You've seen firsthand the signs, symptoms. Enough time has passed for your true observation of the plague. Who is really behind this whole matter?"

Wordlessly, Marie went to the oil portrait on the far wall of Papa Legba, holding his copper scales as he stared out, smiling, from a haze of purplish mist. She seized it by the sides with both hands and removed it, revealing dozens of parchment sheets hanging on the wall behind it. All were different sketches, some of veves and old Voodoo marks, others of patients' faces and notable anatomy. Marie had arranged them over the last few weeks in order, then taken them down and hung them again in different patterns.

"This is no simple plague. Not an act of nature nor the will of God. This is punishment."

Marie closed her eyes briefly, thinking back on that lady in the bed, laughing and laughing as she sang her wicked fever song. *The Widow Paris. The woman who for all her magic couldn't keep her husband from leaving her.* She thought of all her other patients too, men and women who on any other day would walk the Quarter banquettes in their top hats and parasols to shield them from the lash of the sun, all those pale faces that blurred together into one face she knew well enough but did not recognize. It was the face of power, of the city's cursed wealth. It was the face of a person who owned another, who did not fancy themselves king or queen, but another kind of royalty that dared rule only in the South. The face of a master.

"All of these people have slaves registered to their names as property. Check the city's ledgers. It's all there. Which makes them all masters of some kind." Marie lifted a sketch from the wall and passed it to Sanite.

"A plague that only befell slave owners?" Sanite clapped her hands. "Perhaps it is true what they say about your god, Marie Laveau. Perhaps he is a merciful god yet."

"Perhaps. But this is not the work of God, my queen. This is Voodoo."

Sanite clicked her tongue, an incredulous little noise, but her eyes had flattened into vicious little lines. "Voodoo? If it is, then it is veiled. Cleverly hidden. A trick."

"And who else in this city could have the power to call such darkness? To possess Voodoo unknown even to the likes of the Quarter Queen? Who else may not rival you in conjuring, but in trickery?"

Sanite gasped. "Jon." She turned away, thinking. "The nerve of him! Just think, a man on the Voodoo throne. He dares not honor the sanctity of exile? Yet again, he spits in the face of Voodoo tradition! What am I saying?" Sanite laughed. "What tradition has a man like Jon the Conjurer ever honored in his blasphemous little life?"

Marie said nothing, instead returning her attention to the wall, to all the evidence of Jon's spellwork. Crafty. Unorthodox. So different from Sanite's careful magic, the magic that she kept bound to Voodoo's traditions and rituals tighter than a Quarter whore's corset. *You could stand to learn from a teacher like that.* Surely, Jon the Conjurer could teach her the forbidden magic she so desperately needed. After all, it was the very reason for his banishment. Marie had never known the full story—why Sanite had forced him from the city. But there were whispers of experiments so gruesome that it made the Brotherhood's own pastimes look tame, of rituals and magic so taboo within New Orleans that the mere mention of it was considered a terrible trespass on its laws. Because Jon the Conjurer had tampered with the magic of death and resurrection—the magic of the zombi. The magic she desperately needed.

After Jacques had been declared dead, Marie, in her desperation, had invoked Papa Legba. He'd come to her at her crossroads ritual in the Dreadwood, a knowing gleam in his wizened red eyes.

She saw him, briefly, a glimmering apparition before her. Few could see the loa so. They much preferred to mount their vessels, to feel and experience the mortal world through the carnal flavor of human senses.

"Your love is gone, done passed on through. I helped him through the doorway myself when the Baron brought him," Papa Legba had said. He spoke of Baron Samedi, Lord of Death.

Marie was crouched in the forest's lone dirt path, her hands clenching and unclenching the bramble beneath her. She kept her eyes low in reverence. "Then you may yet help him back. To me, Papa." She had heard such magic was possible.

Those red eyes had only twinkled with divine knowledge. "Come now, Marie. You don't want that kind of magic. Veil magic comes with a whole lot of consequences, child. I don't think you'd like to pay them."

"I do." She paused. "And I would. Papa, *please.*"

"Then the one you seek is the Conjurer, the one who has bargained himself to death." *High Jon,* thought Marie. The Conjurer who'd challenged the Quarter Queen. "Seek his power, and you may yet return poor Jacques Paris."

Papa Legba began to fade away back to the spirit realm, a grizzled chuckle echoing in the air. "Be careful, child," the loa of the crossroads said as the scales in his hand began to shake wildly. Out of time. Out of balance. *"Some doors just shouldn't be opened."*

Now Marie was certain that the slave-owner plague was Jon's work. He was, after all, what Papa Legba had called him. *The one who has bargained himself to death.*

Sanite squared her shoulders, like a warrior maiden readying for battle. "Well, I will handle Jon."

"Let us hope better than before."

The force of Sanite's backhand was swift, breaking across the hollows of the room like thunder, pain stinging her cheek. "You insolent little girl," Sanite hissed. "Learn your place and show your elders some respect. You might be talented, but you are not queen yet."

Marie licked the blood from her lips, strangely emboldened. "And when I am, you can be sure I will use every ounce of my magic to serve more than my own selfish whims!"

Sanite watched her, silent. Marie should apologize. She should recant. But today was different. She was different, somehow. Something had changed in her. She knew it the moment the woman had dared to speak of Jacques. She felt it the moment she'd nearly killed then saved that sorry excuse for a man from his deathbed. The truth was, maybe she'd been changing all along.

Sanite's face hung low over Marie's. But it was not Sanite's face that was staring into hers, although it was a face Marie had come to know well enough in the time since her initiation. It was the face of the Quarter Queen. Sanite's eyes flared, completely and utterly white, a terrifying picture of spiritual power. The force of her magic was boiling hot, a furnace that roared to life and would gladly take her soul for tinder and coal.

"So long as I am queen, you will hear me, Marie Laveau, and hear me well," Sanite spat. Marie's face flushed, scalded from the intensity of that white-hot gaze. "Never, *ever* challenge me."

Here was the woman who had taken her under her wing when Grand-mère had died when Marie was only twelve years old, leaving her newly orphaned. The same woman who'd taught Marie how to use and control the magic that had frightened her own mother from raising her, who'd generously positioned Marie as her successor to the crown. She was the closest thing she'd had to a proper maman, and she should be grateful for that. But now, in this moment, in the darkest parts of her heart, Marie resented the older priestess. She wouldn't deny it. Some small part of her pitied her too. Sanite's spirit was eternally strong as an ox, but her flesh had failed her. She was old, frailer still by the day. *It won't be long now.*

Marie kept her eyes trained to the floor, swallowing the lump in her throat. "Apologies, my queen."

"Hmph." Sanite turned away, the offense forgiven, her attention already turned toward another pressing matter.

Marie put the portrait back in its place. Everything as it was. The rest of the acolytes were flooding into the room, arms bursting with smoking vials and wicker baskets saddled with mountains of herbs and talismans. Soon, the Quarter Queen would hold court, and the Voodoos would do as they had always done—plot how to live their lives in the shadow of another kingdom. Was that what was waiting for her after Sanite's passing? A kingdom of servants who already served another master, one who kept them locked and chained? *Such small lives,* Marie thought.

Marie turned her gaze back toward the great picture of Papa Legba, the glowing red eyes that seemed to be staring directly at her, silently inviting her into his realm of mist and sky, a cloudy crossroads that only the divine dared walk. *The Veil.*

That old magic would be hers in the end. She would make sure of it.

CHAPTER ELEVEN

REE

Hello, princess.

The blood drained from Ree's face as she stared up at the man she thought she'd never see again. She'd spent the years in his absence stupidly replaying the matter of their separation, striving to see how it had all gone so wrong, trying in vain to remember every detail of his beautiful face. She dreamed of him many nights, some spent sleeping next to Anabelle. She'd imagined their reunion a thousand times. *I'm sorry,* she'd say. *Forgive me, please.*

Ree lurched to her feet and gave in to the urge to reach for him through the bars. "Henryk—"

His black gloved hand caught hers, viper-quick, and twisted it firmly in his grasp. It wasn't painful, but the warning was clear. *Don't come any closer, or the next action will be painful indeed.*

She was aware of Anabelle's eyes on her, but Ree didn't care. Henryk tightened his grip, slipping a coin into her palm. "Don't," he said, the rough burn of his voice sending chills down her spine. His gray eyes flashed as he let her go. "You will address me as High Inquisitor Broussard. Nothing more."

Nothing more. Ree was going to be sick. It was one thing to envision his return, the indifference he might show her—that she deserved. But never in her worst nightmares did she think he would return a witch-hunter.

Ree clutched the small coin behind her back. What could it mean? Why bail her out?

Henryk held her gaze for a second longer before sweeping his eyes over the cell, the aurum shackles that bound both women, the stone stained in the blood of witches long dead. His eyes tightened at the corners, an expression only Ree seemed to notice.

The lantern swayed in the officer's hands. "Sure you don't want the other? She'd fetch a good price up in cotton country, all things considered."

"No," said Henryk. His eyes fell coldly over Anabelle, who had the good sense to recoil back as far as her shackles would allow. "Just the one will do. The other is of no use to me."

And with that, Henryk turned on his heel, disappearing into the dark of the jailhouse's dungeons. A moment later and the door to Ree's cell groaned open.

"Out now, Laveau, before I change my mind," the officer ordered with a scowl.

Ree raised her leg, flashing her shackled ankle through her skirts. "Only if you would be so kind."

The officer grunted at her nerve but made quick work of unshackling her foot. Behind her, Anabelle scoffed. "Still cheating your way around this city, I see. Fucking heathen."

"Same as everyone else," Ree muttered. She kept her eyes forward. She would not turn back, she decided. The past held nothing for her. And that was exactly what Anabelle Dupont was to her—the past.

The officer marched Ree out into the corridor. When they were alone at last, Ree craned her collared neck, and he undid the last of her bindings. They fell to the floor in a loud clatter. Ree flexed her sore fingers, cracked the stiff bones in her neck for good measure. There would be bruises come morning, her skin burned from the traces of the aurum. But she could feel her magic flooding back, and with it some semblance of her old self. She remembered the snatchers, their laughing faces as they chained her. She would never be brought that low again.

Ree raced past the other cells, filled with prisoners lying in their own filth, staring at the leaking ceilings, eyes dull and unseeing. Finally, she burst outside into the blinding sunlight of late afternoon. Ree didn't dare look back. She ran.

Ree ran until her lungs ached, until her already sore body screamed in protest as she plunged herself into the crowd, eager to vanish into the sea of nameless faces of tourists and locals. She ran until red-blue dusk encroached along the rooftops. Night would soon come, and she needed to get to the bayou house to see to her mother. But in light of her arrest, going immediately there felt like a bad idea. What if she was being followed? What if the police were keeping a watchful eye? No one could know why her mother was suddenly gone. Not yet. So Ree changed course, setting off instead for their house on St. Ann, where she would be expected to go. Ree knew she was being paranoid. But better paranoid than stupid. She'd made so many stupid decisions, like reaching for Henryk's hand.

Nearing home, Ree slowed, catching her breath, and held up the coin. It was the mark of the Aurelia, the music hall just down the road. Despite the venom he had shown her in that cell, she knew it was a message to meet there. Her heart twisted at the thought. She and Henryk passed messages to each other as children during communion, Henryk as an altar boy for Father Antoine and Ree as the dutiful daughter at her praying mother's side. She was sure this was a message to meet later, in secret, when no one was watching as they had been in that cell. The smell of the jailhouse still clung to her, the rancid smell of misery and death.

It had smelled like death the day she'd met Henryk Broussard too. The memory came at her fast, transporting her to the dark halls of that sick ward on that fateful day sixteen years ago. Ree hadn't wanted to go, of course. She'd been at her mother's side day and night over the last few weeks, studying herbs and roots, learning how to draw the dizzying, complex shapes of veves that she would need to know to entreat each loa. Her hands had ached from all the sifting and sorting and cutting that rootwork required, and she felt her feet would fall off if her mother made her walk another step.

Her mother had not cared. In the middle of the night, she pulled

Ree by the hand down the darkened hall, where the flames of tiny white candles danced in the rain-lashed windows, casting shadows over rows and rows of bedridden folks, calling hopelessly into the dark for their loved ones—their mothers, their children—or for God. The haunted echoes of the sick made Ree want to cover her ears.

At eight years old, Ree had been old enough to attend her mother's rituals in Congo Square and, according to Marie, learn to use her talents with Voodoo for more than herself. There had been an outbreak of yellow fever again, plague brought downriver on the steamboats. Already *The Quintessence* had reported a handful dead and more to follow. Father Antoine had summoned Marie to stave off what she could, despite the Church's objection to witchcraft. *Folks would take anything—even the devil's magic—to keep themselves alive,* Marie cautioned Ree on the carriage ride over.

They attended to a slave woman, and her mother nodded. The woman would live. Not all would take to her antidote-tonic, she had told Ree. Some magic was not absolute. They saw to a spice merchant next, who complained that his money meant he should not be here, not like this, not with *them*. Ree watched her mother bristle and shake her head, and Ree knew that the man would not live.

And so they went, patient to patient, until they stopped at the bedside of a small boy, a few years older than Ree. He had wine-brown hair and a smattering of sun-dappled freckles on his cheeks. He did not open his eyes when her mother asked, his small chest rising and falling uncertainly. It was as if he were on the verge of a deep sleep, and with each wheezing breath, he drifted farther and farther into the dark.

Her mother went to Father Antoine, gave the barest shake of her head. "The boy will not live. It would be prudent to perform last rites." She was already turning away, preparing to attend to her next patient. She snapped a finger at Ree. "Come, Ree. There is still work to be done."

The boy was a stranger, yet Ree had glimpsed him before, during communion. Something about him called to her, whispered that he was different. Ree placed a hand on his bony chest. It rose shakily beneath her palm, his heartbeat faint. Death was near him. Upon him. She could feel it. See it too, if she concentrated hard enough, swelling around the room in a blanketing black presence that fluttered like a veil. The presence kept away from Ree, hissing at her from afar, as if she were the dangerous thing in the room.

But Ree paid no heed to the darkness.

Death is a doorway you can open and close as you like.

The words came to her unbidden. A man's voice, one from far away in the dark.

She leaned over the boy's bedside and brushed her lips to his, featherlight, the way she had read in her mother's storybooks about dragons and love and spells, the way the magic in her blood told her to. *Come back to me,* she whispered against his lips.

When Ree pulled away, the boy's eyes opened. They were slate gray, not a hint of blue, almost silver in the candlelight. Those strange eyes fell over her face, and she felt the familiar feeling swelling in her chest, the feeling that they had known each other before, that they should know each other now.

"Who are you?" he rasped.

"I'm Ree," she said with a shy smile. "The princess of the Voodoos."

"Well," he said with a smile. "Hello, princess."

Her mother and Father Antoine watched the two of them in plain shock. Death was still here, all around, lingering over the other beds, grasping on to other souls. *But not this one,* Ree thought. *This one is not ready.* She stared at the boy with gray eyes touched with silver. *This one is mine.*

Her mother took her hand and drew her away. "Ree, what happened?"

"Death is but a doorway," said Ree unthinkingly.

Her mother stood frozen, pale and tight-lipped. "What did you say?"

Death is but a doorway. Those were not her words but the words her magic whispered in her ear. Sometimes her magic had no voice at all, it was just her own intuition, and sometimes the voices of the loa spoke to her, the ancestors too. Other times her magic had the deep, raspy voice of a man who was neither god nor spirit but powerful all the same. And he told her things only she could do and how to go about them.

Now Ree remembered that dark feeling of death, the cold draft of its lingering presence. And she still remembered that kiss, so innocent, so simple it had seemed at the time. Henryk had recovered quickly, and they had been inseparable after that night. How had she and Henryk drifted so far from where they'd begun?

But she didn't have time for such questions, not when she turned the street corner and the sight of her home came into view, tiny and white, the windows shuttered. Ree slipped inside. In the parlor, the painted faces in her mother's beloved portraits glared accusingly, reminding her of the last moment they'd shared in this room. They'd said ugly things to each other. But had they said the truth? Bits and pieces of it, Ree supposed. But never enough. Not nearly enough. And her mother had warned her about Henryk's return. *Not as the boy you once loved. No, my sweet daughter. As your enemy.*

Ree held out her hand, pointing to the barren hearth, allowing Ogoun's power to channel through her. Today the loa were kind, and the fire god's magic leapt from her fingertips, igniting the coals. And then it hit her—the unmistakable bitter scent of foxglove.

"Hello, little witch," a voice spoke from the shadows.

Ree whirled to see a man stepping into the light of the fire, drawing back the hood of his long black velvet robe trimmed in silver and white crescent moons and stars.

"Silas," she hissed.

"I suppose we are on the basis of first names now, aren't we?" Silas let a suggestive silence follow, the flames bathing his white hair in orange and red. "Considering I saved your life."

"My mother saved my life."

"And where is she?" The Grand Wizard took a slow look around the parlor, marveling in its rustic charm, the simple furnishings. "Where exactly is Marie Laveau?"

"What do you want?"

He held out an arm, and his staff whooshed past Ree, lifting her hair, and into his waiting hand. His eyes held firm on hers. "Where is your mother, young witch?"

"She—"

He tutted at her, slowly circling, the strange black stone dragon atop his staff staring at her with twin glittering gemstone eyes. A faint vibration in the air made her skin crawl. "Something tells me your next words will be a lie. Let's not waste each other's time. I know that your mother sleeps in the bayou, hexed by some nefarious magic."

The room tilted upside down. How? How could he know? Anabelle had betrayed her, yes. But she'd attributed this betrayal to Jon the Conjurer's return, to Voodoo. She couldn't see how the Brotherhood fit into all of this.

"And how do you know that?" she finally asked. She could have lied—she *should* have lied—but she needed to understand what exactly she was missing.

"I have my means. You see, in the past your mother needed my magic—"

"She would never need your magic."

But Silas remained undeterred by her insistence, his eyes silently taunting, *Didn't she?* "*Never* say never, little witch. She did, in fact, need my magic. And when she used that magic, it created a . . ." He waved a hand, as if trying to find the most appropriate term. ". . . tether between us."

"You *surveilled* my mother?" It was preposterous to think anyone could have been keeping watch on someone as powerful as her mother. But Silas was powerful too. Ree did not know the limits his strange alchemy might reach.

"The Brotherhood surveils all matters of magical importance. Even the magic of your kind when it suits our ends. Now would be one such time. The Vatican will spare no resource to see a second Holy Inquisition in the city. You'd do well to gather allies, daughter of Marie Laveau. And quickly."

"Are you proposing an alliance? Between *us*?"

"You and I will be as I was with your dear mother . . ." His lips quirked. "Friends of a sort."

"I will never work with the Brotherhood," she snarled. "Never."

"No?" He lifted a silvery brow. "I think you will, little witch. You will find the dangers in this city require concessions to survive them."

"I can handle a little danger."

His eyes fell to her neck, to the ugly burns the aurum collar had left. "Yes, quite well by the looks of it. I have heard that you enjoy games. But tell me, do you know the *rules* this time? I'll tell you a secret, little witch: I've another piece on the board. And I intend to use it to my full advantage. You should know one thing about me—I don't lose." The dragon's eyes twinkled, the vibration in the air sending a shiver through her. "I play to fucking win."

"We're done here." Ree nodded toward the door. "Get out."

"Very well," the alchemist replied curtly. *For now*, those strange eyes promised. Silas drew on his black velvet hood, and as he passed he murmured, "*Mutatio.*" Immediately there was an odd cooling sensation along her neck. In the gilded looking glass against the wall, she saw that the skin was healed, the burns perfectly mended, almost as if they had never been there at all.

Ree turned to face Silas, but he was gone. She cursed. The Brotherhood of the White Hand knew about her mother. And now? She had no idea what they might do next.

She held the coin from the Aurelia in her hand, the gold glinting in the firelight. Silas had cautioned her to find allies. Although she detested the Brotherhood and all that it stood for, she couldn't help but think that the alchemist might have been right. The game was changing right before her eyes, and she needed allies, and *fast*. Was she foolish to hope Henryk might become one of them, instead of her enemy?

Ree started toward the door. She'd been dealt a new hand, it was true.

And she'd be damned if she didn't play it.

Ree sat at her preferred table in the back of the darkened parlor. The lights in the Aurelia burned low tonight. She cast her gaze about the room, anticipation and nerves squirming in her gut. Like the windows outside, the ceiling had been enchanted to look like the night sky—an inky vastness swaddled in a web of silvery constellations, as if the stars themselves had been woven into the dark canvas. It was her favorite music hall in all of New Orleans. Feathered dancers in shining silver and black silks danced across a stage, swaying their hips back and forth to the brass band that struck up a tune in the back. Lithe acrobats dangled from silvery cords suspended from the constellation ceiling, spinning on and on in a dizzying blur. Ree ran a hand through her curls, still damp from the bath she'd taken to rinse away the putrid stink of the jailhouse. Try as she might, there was no washing away that terrible memory.

Ree stirred the piece of lavender in her drink, what the pretty barmaid had called *le royale,* named for its rich purple coloring. It was normally her favorite. The music was the best in all the Quarter. One song could usually drown out whatever sorrows the drinks wouldn't. But not tonight. The loss of her mother, Marcel, Anabelle . . . the moment the officer had unlocked those burning shackles from her skin, Ree had run like a coward, escaping the horrors of the day. Marcel's empty face, backlit in the harsh sunlight, buzzing with black flies. Anabelle's mouth twisting cruelly at her. Her mother's body, unmoving. Sitting in that darkened cell, collared with aurum for the second time, the sting of the metal burning into the skin of her throat, had changed her. Scared her. Maybe this wasn't just a game, not the way Silas made it out to be. This was real.

And Henryk. His eyes meeting hers in the dark, only coldness in their depths.

The tune ended, another starting up in its place. This one an old folk song she hadn't heard since she was a child, a favorite of her mother's. Ree took a long drink from her glass, savoring the burn against the back of her throat to distract from the burning in her eyes.

Henryk Broussard slid into the seat across from her.

He was no longer in his Inquisitor uniform but dressed down in simple linen. The long-sleeved shirt he'd chosen was well suited to his frame—clean and deliberate, the dark folds clinging to his broad shoulders, dipping at the chest to reveal a garnet-flecked crucifix hanging from his neck.

His lips quirked as he crossed his gloved hands. "Hello, Ree."

The sound of her name on his tongue flipped her stomach. That same sense of familiarity and ease that made her heart ache. The gruff burn of his voice. After all these years, he sounded the same. His accent had slipped. But it was still the voice she remembered, beautifully Cajun.

She stifled a pang in her chest. That they could be sitting here now, like this, as if they were simply old friends, seemed like the cruelest joke of all.

"Henryk," she said stiffly. "You look well. I suppose holy work agrees with some of us, at least. Welcome back to New Orleans. Back to us heathens."

Ree snatched a glass of bourbon from a passing tray and slid it across the table. Henryk caught it with one hand and took an indifferent drink, eyes locked onto hers.

Now properly face-to-face, she could see that at twenty-eight years old his features had refined themselves into perfect place. He was . . . embarrassingly handsome. His hair was longer than she remembered, combed away from his face, still the same deep ruddy brown, the color of communion wine. Part of it curled into his eyes, the same piercing gray, as bright and pale as quicksilver under certain light. His skin was paler than hers but still held the same touch of gold, the permanent mark of an unforgiving Louisiana sun. Needless to say, Madame Monet's girls would have gladly bedded him for no coin at all.

"I know why you chose this place."

"Of course you do." His expression hardened. "How could you forget?"

Ree's face stung. She hadn't—it would be impossible to forget her pain, to forget his. "But I don't know why you called me here *now.*"

"Don't lie to me. It's too early for that, princess. And to think"—he leaned in, gray eyes bright with bitter regard for her—"we haven't even gotten to the work of confession."

So, he'd come to torture her then. Just not in the way she'd thought. The Inquisitor had come to draw a different kind of truth out of her. *His.* And it was one that couldn't be pried with instruments of agony or holy rituals. Despite the venom in his words, his eyes did not lie. He might feign disinterest, but she saw a glimpse of hurt beneath it all. And she deserved it, didn't she? He was purposely digging at her, prying out a truth that had nothing to do with the Harbinger. And somehow that made it worse. How to tell him that she couldn't leave?

Eight years ago, they'd met in the Aurelia on a Sunday night, at this very table. And it was here that Henryk Broussard had asked her to run away with him. She remembered it like it was only yesterday, the way her heart leapt into her throat, the light in his eyes when she agreed.

That old wound between them, finally torn open at the seams. The one neither could admit was bleeding all over them.

She wavered, then said, "Just tell me what you want."

"I am told you were friends with the prisoner they hanged in Congo Square," Henryk said. Ree closed her eyes, shutting out the image of Marcel's swinging corpse. She gripped the glass hard enough she might break it. "I am also told you started a very public and very nasty magical disturbance. You've been busy. After today's events, I would say you might need that drink after all."

"It was Marcel. Did they tell you *that*?" If he was not moved by the sight of her in chains, then perhaps he would be by the knowledge that one of their oldest friends was now dead.

He puffed out a surprised breath and leaned back, sadness in his eyes. "No," he said quietly. "They didn't. Marcel was supposed to leave this place. Out of all of us, he was the one who was supposed to make it out."

And yet he hadn't. Ree could taste his dream of Haiti on her tongue. The smell of wind and sea and the dancing freedom of rituals by moonlight and sunlit day. No need for secrecy. If she closed her eyes, Ree could still feel some piece of Marcel here with them. He'd loved the Aurelia—the shining silver constellations that drifted across the ceiling, the bright spell of music that played on a carousel, the theater of it all. Every bit of it felt hollow now. The magic was lost.

"He told me he was going to run away once. Risk it all. But he didn't." His voice twisted, heavy with an accusation he did not say. Not directly. "Because he loved you."

Because he loved you. Hot tears stung at Ree's eyes. Marcel, the only proper brother she'd ever had, stayed in this godforsaken city because of her? Everyone who had ever loved her ended up hurt or worse, it seemed.

Henryk finished his drink, set it down on the table with a loud *clink*. She felt the mood shift, their pleasantries finished. Behind him, a dancer tossed glistening beads into the crowd, showed her naked breasts to a gaping man, kissed another on the mouth.

"Now, where is your mother? Where is Marie Laveau?"

Despite the ache of tears pressing at her throat, Ree found the will to keep her voice level. "The Quarter Queen has more important business to attend to than sharing whiskeys." Empty posturing on her part, but she didn't need her mother's secret in the hands of two enemies today. One was enough.

"More important than checking on her beloved daughter? If memory serves, Marie Laveau was fiercely protective of you. To a fault. *Controlling,* I believe you always called her."

"Is this why you went through all of that trouble to send me a message, Henryk? To torture ourselves with the past?"

"No." *Yes.* That same tightness at the corners of his eyes. "When news of a Harbinger reached the Vatican, I was sent to inspect these claims. You do understand the grave significance of a Harbinger, don't you? A demonic prophecy means that your city is likely under the siege of evil. And that evil is Jon the Conjurer."

"The only siege this city is currently under is a plague of wealthy white men with whips and collars."

"Fair enough. But when demons foretell the second coming of one of New Orleans's greatest enemies, then I fear you may be wrong. This city may very well be in need of a second Holy Inquisition."

"Why ask to meet here? Why not leave me in jail?"

"Because in the jail, you would become the property of the city and fall under their jurisdiction. Unfortunately for you, if there is going to be a formal inquiry into the Harbinger, the Church cannot allow that."

So her freedom was a matter of bureaucracy then. Nothing more and nothing less.

"And now that you have me?" She took a lingering drink, painfully aware of the way his eyes flitted to her mouth, the splash of whiskey that wetted her lips. "Are you going to torture me now? Make me confess?"

"Do not be so eager for punishment, Marie Laveau the Second. It will come to us all in due time." He sighed, as if it all couldn't be helped. "I am forbidden from formally interrogating you until seven days have passed since my arrival. I suppose you've got God's favor, princess."

"And why the hell not?"

"Maybe you should ask Father Antoine. He always did have a painfully soft spot for Marie Laveau."

She recalled her mother's frantic plea to the priest: *You must delay their coming. Antoine,* please. *I would need time to gather protections for my people. For my daughter.*

And so he had, in a way. Ree had admittedly never cared for the priest, but it was possible that he did not share her indifference. She had one week. A week to find a way out of this entire ordeal. A week to save her mother.

"Of all the things to become, you chose the enemy."

"I think you made it clear I was that to you already, Ree."

It was her turn for anger now. Her voice rose, shaking with every word. "I never considered you an enemy. I—"

"You what?" he asked.

I loved you. "So this is revenge then. That's it."

"No, princess. And if it were, it wouldn't be against *you.*"

Her brows drew together in confusion. Something about those words troubled her. *And if it were, it wouldn't be against* you. Who then?

Before she could ask what he meant, the air shifted. Ree looked up to see someone standing over her.

"I saw you at the hanging earlier, witch." A man, big as an ox, with a suntan that strongly suggested he was just another drunken sailor. His smile reminded her of that alchemist who'd mocked Marcel. "I'm thinking maybe it should have been your black ass hanging from a rope right alongside him. You and that n—"

Henryk slammed the man facedown against the wooden table, rattling their drinks.

Ree gaped. One of the dancers wending around the floor froze, snapping her feathery fan across her face, aghast. But Henryk didn't seem to notice. He'd seized the man by both of his arms and twisted them painfully behind his back in a viselike hold.

"Stop. You can't . . . you can't do this." The sailor's glassy eyes filled with tears.

"And why not?" In the parlor's silvery light, Henryk's face was different. Cruelly alive in a way she had never seen before.

"But you're a priest!" the man sputtered helplessly. He'd seen the dark dress, the crucifix at his neck. Ree could not blame him. It was an easy mistake to make. A foolish one too.

Henryk's smile was cold. "I'm no priest." He pulled the man's arm tighter, contorting the bone oddly. "I can pray for you, if you like. Pray that this arm heals correctly. But I promise you by the time I'm finished with you"—Ree heard a sickening snap—"*it won't.*"

The man shrieked. Hot tears streamed down the sides of his face and into his mouth. People were watching now.

But Ree understood. He was a witch-hunter. And he was right. He was no priest, no Father Antoine. The Church had seen him educated in a manner of ways that had nothing to do with saints and prayers. Inquisitions were nasty work. He would need to know the very specific art of torture—how to break exact points in the bones and joints, how to draw confessions from flesh by touching only the mind. The work of an Inquisitor lived in the dark threshold between suffering and sanity.

"Apologize to the lady," Henryk snarled at the man's ear. But the man kept blubbering, the pain too much. Henryk shoved the other arm, breaking it too. "Now."

"I'm sorry!" He gasped. "I'm sorry—I'm sorry—I'm sorry—"

"Enough," Ree said quietly. No matter the circumstances, she'd seen enough pain and misery for one day. And really, it wasn't the man who was bothering her now. It was Henryk. Because this was not the Henryk she remembered.

"You broke my arms!" The man sobbed, red-faced and swollen from the tears.

"Be glad that's all I did," Henryk said, and let him go. "Now leave."

The man stumbled off, in quick search of a healer, no doubt. Henryk turned cold gray eyes back on Ree. If he could reduce this man to a blubbering mess in a matter of seconds, she could only imagine what he did to witches.

His eyes were coolly appraising. Just who was this Henryk standing before her? He was a mystery to her—a stranger whose face she'd somehow always known.

Ree sipped from her drink. She realized her hand was shaking a little. "So, you take offense to my magic but not color?"

"No, I think I'll leave that bit to the Brotherhood."

"How noble of you, Inquisitor."

Henryk didn't say a word, his gray eyes watching her in silence. Her mother had warned her about the work of Inquisitors. They were hunters, skilled interrogators who played with their prey up until the moment of death. This might have been a harmless drink between . . . strangers. She might have a week to hold him off before she was dragged into confession. But there was no mistaking that tonight was only the first of many interrogations to come.

Henryk straightened his crucifix. "I bid you good night, princess." He gave her one last once-over, but she couldn't read him. "But we're not done here. Far from it."

Henryk turned to leave. He was threatening her; there were no two ways about it. And yet . . . she couldn't think about any of that. The truth was, all she could think about was the day she'd left him standing all alone on that bridge.

In a burst of wild desperation, Ree shot out a hand, catching him by the wrist. "Did you come back to hurt me, Henryk? To make me pay for what I did to you?"

Henryk went very still, his eyes going flat. "I didn't come back to New Orleans for an apology, Ree. And despite what you may think, I didn't come back for *you*. Not in the way you think."

Ree sat frozen in her seat, face stinging with hurt. She supposed she deserved worse, but hearing him say those words cut deeply. "You won't forgive me, will you?" she said quietly. She took a deep, steadying breath.

How to tell him that she had loved him, but that, despite all their differences, she had loved her mother more?

There was a moment of hesitation, a moment in which she thought like a fool that he might oblige her. But then he snatched his hand from hers. "I thought you were listening, princess." His voice lowered, full of venom. "I'm not a priest."

He quickly turned and left, disappearing into the night.

CHAPTER TWELVE

MARIE

"You'd do well to be on your best behavior tonight, Marie." Sanite pulled the laces of Marie's corset tighter, cinching her breath.

"But of course, my queen," replied Marie. She was facing the looking glass in Sanite's bedchamber while the older woman tied the last of her corset's bindings.

Marie turned her gaze to Sanite's four-poster bed, where countless frilly gowns lay strewn in waiting—a golden one poured over the side of the bed like melted butterscotch, another with violets and wildflowers sewn along the bosom. Sanite had ordered only the best for her apprentice, but none were to Marie's liking. Instead, she'd chosen a gown of white silk taffeta with a delicate neckline trimmed in silver. Sanite had pursed her lips at Marie's choice but said nothing, appeased that Marie had agreed to attend the gala in her stead without much of a fight.

Marie turned placid eyes to the mirror, then froze at the sight of her reflection gowned in white. It was her wedding day to Jacques all over again. Marie swallowed the surge of mourning that swelled in her throat at the thought of her lost beloved. Sanite would never understand her tears. None of them would.

"Aren't you the picture of beauty?" Sanite Dede watched Marie in the looking glass, satisfied at her hard work. If all eyes couldn't be on Sanite tonight, then she'd just as gladly have them on Marie instead. "That is power too, Marie." She clicked her teeth. "If only you'd understand how to wield it."

Marie caught her eyes in the mirror. "Would you have me wield it on Jon?"

"Dear child, I'd have you wield it on a fucking pissant if it meant gaining the advantage." Marie turned to the older woman, a smirk on her lips. Well, no one could accuse Sanite Dede of being a subtle queen. "But tonight, I would rather you, as my beloved apprentice, deliver him a message on my behalf: You are to tell him to leave this city at once, or risk my retribution. And this time, banishment will not be an option. Do you understand?"

Sanite handed her the final component of her costume—an owl-shaped mask the same silvery-white of her gown, with large feathers at the corners of the eyes. As Marie reached for it, the older priestess's hands curled around hers, digging in sharp like talons. "Do you understand?" she repeated firmly. "They do not call him the trickster for naught. What Jon lacks in pure magic, he makes up for with cunning. Keep your guard up, Marie."

Sanite could not know that Marie had her own purposes for seeking out Jon tonight. He would show her the magic Sanite would not, the possibility that lay beyond death's door. She would open the Veil. And she would come to know what had befallen Jacques, at last, and bring him back to her. And maybe then she could find her own peace.

"You needn't worry, my queen . . ." Marie slid the mask perfectly into place. "For it is never down."

Though she would never admit it, a tremor of trepidation raced through her.

Marie had met Jon the Conjurer once before. She had been scarcely ten years old, capricious for her age but dutiful. Obedient. Always one to follow the rules.

"Fetch more water," Grand-mère had all but snarled over her shoulder. She didn't mean to sound so vicious, Marie had told herself. The work of a midwife was hard, often thankless work, even harder when the man who bought your services was accustomed to getting them for free. Mayor Corbin used to own Grand-mère before she bought her freedom papers and he was forced to turn her loose with a stroke of his quill. But the mayor still called on her from time to time when her rootwork was needed. That day had been one such time. One of his slaves had gone into labor a month early, and the labor had already run the course of a day, yet no baby had been born. She'd brought Marie along with her too. But Marie didn't much like Grand-mère's line of work—the buckets of blood, the sticky afterbirth, the screams that tore the air. She didn't want to see. But that didn't matter to an old woman like Grand-mère, who would sooner claw Marie's eyes open herself. *Open your eyes, Marie. See what your freedom gifts you.*

So, Marie did as she was told and fetched the water. As she made her way down the hill from the well, across the patches of blueberries underfoot, and back to the slave quarters, she heard a noise above her. Like someone calling her name faintly on the wind. She looked up. A circle of black birds darted through the orange twilight.

The crows were calling to her.

Marie followed, sloshing water from the tin pail in her hands, moving twisting branches out of her way until she came to a clearing where a carriage house sat in the distance, smoke curling from the chimney out into the sleepy dusk.

A man was chained to a wooden stake in the middle of the field. A flogging pole, Grand-mère had told her one day. Where they punished those slaves foolish enough to break the rules.

Marie slowly approached. The smell hit her first. The sharp tang of snakeroot mixed with something darker and much, much older. It was the smell of his magic. The closer she got, the more she could see the bruises and gashes that marred his beautiful midnight skin. A cotton-white shirt hung off him, all but tattered to shreds. Bile ran down the front.

Three crows landed on the wooden points of the flogging pole, peering down at her with unblinking dark eyes. Like they were keeping watch over him.

His eyes were closed as if he were sleeping before his overseer returned. *He ought to drink*, Marie had thought. If the wounds didn't kill him, a Louisiana sun sure might.

She brought the pail to his sun-parched lips, forced them to part . . .

The man's eyes flew open, finding hers immediately, as if he had known she was there all the while. As if he'd been expecting her.

She stopped dead in her tracks. His eyes were strangely golden, a color she couldn't say was common for folks around these parts, even a place as strange as New Orleans.

She had heard that this was the mark of those exceptionally powerful. High-Blooded. It was true. There were few among Les Magiques whose blood was not yet diluted. That was still pure in heritage, in magic from the old land. *You can tell by the eyes,* Grand-mère liked to say after she lit the altars at night. *Tell how much magic a man got in his blood.*

He stared at her, as if his breath had been caught on his tongue. She stared back, frozen, terrified at the thought of what he'd endured. It was all too much. Marie started to cry. She didn't know why, but she couldn't stop it. Those chains rattled. And suddenly his hand was on her cheek, thumbing away a hot tear.

"Do not cry for me." His calloused hand cradled her cheek. She felt a spark pass between their flesh, a heart-pulsing feeling of her magic recognizing his. "Cry for them."

"Why?"

"Because the gods listen, Marie Laveau." She didn't recall ever telling this strangely beautiful man her name. "And let me tell you a secret. They do not only listen," he said with a twinkle in his eyes. "They *punish.*"

It was all he could do to lift a bruised hand, chains rattling as he gestured toward the sky. Three crows were cawing above her, moving in a vicious black ring over the sun.

Their song was angry, Marie thought to herself. *This song of three.*

Marie arrived late at Chateau Corbin, the church bells tolling just past sundown. The sky flushed a deep purple as dusk deepened overhead and the shadows grew long. By the time Marie entered the courtyard, the gala was well under way, which meant almost everyone was too drunk to realize she'd come at all. The recent onslaught of plagues had seen the streets of New Orleans emptied and barren of life. But not tonight. The wicked fun of Mardi Gras was not a spell so easily broken, not even by the likes of Jon.

A sparkling fog filled the courtyard, swirling at their feet. It was the simple work of a tide-turner, who'd no doubt been instructed to enchant the air with mist to fight the heat. Flickering torchlight illuminated scores of colorfully masked faces. Some bore the shape of fairy-folk, with glittering stones and silken flowers wreathed around the eyes, others of grotesque horned gods.

Marie searched the crowd, finding no sight of her intended target. She knew the Brotherhood to be skulking about, no doubt on guard against any Voodoo mischief. Every planter and master was on edge, worried that their own stock of slaves might be spreading the sickness. Sanite Dede had been the only colored Les Magiques invited, and she'd of course sent Marie in her place.

A moist heat clung to the air, mingling with the sticky sweetness of magnolia trees that towered over the cobbled courtyard. Girls tossed petals and beads for luck from a terrace above; a flurry of gold and violet cascaded down into a laughing crowd below.

Marie could feel eyes on her. She adjusted her owl mask, taking some comfort behind the white-feathered disguise. At every turn there was another jeering face, another glittering mask. She made her way through the city's bourgeoisie, pink-cheeked and tipsy as they engorged themselves on fat slices of king cake—big morsels of sweet blood-red loafs that dribbled from their laughing mouths. Gilded goblets of wine and honeyed mead sloshed in their hands.

A rumbling laugh caught Marie's attention. She turned to find Mayor Felix Corbin the glowing picture of health, almost as if he hadn't been one breath away from dying of Jon's plague only days ago. Marie plucked a glass of wine from a passing tray, wordlessly slipping through the muzzy haze of cigar smoke and merrymaking.

"Bonjour, Felix," said Marie. "You seem to be on the mend."

"Marie Laveau," Felix said with a slow smile. He had on a dashing mask of copper and gold. "I suppose I have you to thank for this small miracle."

"What else are *friends* for?" Marie held his gaze until he looked away. As she had hoped, he had not so easily forgotten the debt he owed her for saving his life.

Mayor Corbin blanched a little at the memory. He leaned in, plucking a dark curl from Marie's shoulder. "Such pretty hair! What a pity you wear it veiled."

That colored women had once been forced to keep their hair covered while strolling the streets of New Orleans during daylight hours was common knowledge. Although the days of Spain's control of New Orleans were long gone, Marie still wore her hair this way in the ritual of tradition. "Such were once the rules, Mayor. Surely you need no reminding?"

He lifted his copper-and-gold mask, flashing the side of his face that Jon's plague had eaten away at. "Could you—"

"I couldn't. Such magic is beyond my reach."

She very well could. Marie knew what he wanted—what they all did. To have that ugly reminder of Jon's power wiped from the skin, from the city's memory, as if the whole ordeal had never happened. How curious it was that a man who publicly flogged the backs of his slaves, created ghastly scars in dark flesh without a second thought, wanted a single scar gone.

Corbin frowned, his eyes lingering bitterly over her. "I doubt very much anything is beyond your reach, even your queen's rules. Some might say you saved my life to bend them in your favor."

"I was only doing as I was bid, Monsieur." Under Sanite's careful rule, her Voodoo had limits. There were certain expectations for her power to keep the peace. And healing him of his scar was simply not one of them.

"You do not fool me, witch. You may wear a mask, but I have glimpsed the face that lies beneath it. Do you want to know what I think?" He leaned in, his voice a warm breath at her ear. For all the honey in his voice, Marie heard the venom too. "I think you are far worse than that wretched Voodoo Queen of yours."

"And why is that?"

Corbin pulled away. "Because at least Sanite serves her people. But *you?*" His eyes flicked over Marie, silently appraising. "You, Marie Laveau, serve only yourself. And that's a trait I quite admire, actually." Those eyes brightened with interest. "Send Sanite my regards, Madame Laveau."

"Of course," said Marie. She bowed her head, dipping low into the expected curtsey.

Felix pulled his mask back down and excused himself to entertain Governor Jean-Francis, who'd just arrived from Baton Rouge, two golden-cheeked courtesans hanging on his arm, a cloud of simpering fools in his wake.

The air rippled, like the wingbeat of a bird had flown over her. She was overcome with the familiar smell of snakeroot and something older and unnamable. It was the smell of ancient magic, viscerally divine, as if the gods themselves had stepped foot into the mortal plane. By the time Marie raised her eyes again, someone else entirely was standing before her.

He was a tall man, powerfully built, with dark skin that gleamed in the lantern light, smooth as a blackbird's wing. A gentleman's top hat sat upon his head, and a black feathered crow mask obscured most of his face, except for his eyes, which were bright gold, the piercing eyes of a hawk. Marie knew exactly who he was.

The orchestra began a new song. Lovely. Mournful. The kind of number that swept you along in the gentle swell of its waves, each lambent note begging you to follow it to its very end.

"Get up, love," Jon the Conjurer said, a hint of a laugh in his voice. "A queen never kneels."

Jon was different than he had been that fateful day ten years ago, when he had been chained to the flogging post. The man before her was no slave. He held himself tall, dignified, reeking of self-assured power. His eyes were as she remembered: keen, almond-shaped, molten like the liquid gold the alchemists sought. His hair was full of beautiful dark coils, longer than she remembered. His right ear bore a curious little piercing, an amber crescent moon.

"Hello again, Jon," she finally said.

"Marie Laveau." He spoke her name softly, like a spell, his gaze raking over her. "Shall we have this dance?"

He offered his hand. Marie stared at it, acutely aware that a man like Jon did not offer himself so freely, even for a dance. She had to remind herself this was the man who'd nearly undone her queen, who was supposed to be the strongest of them.

Marie hesitated, cheeks burning as Jon waited patiently for her next move. She had nothing to fear, really, Marie reminded herself. This was the game Sanite had asked her to play, after all. And what danger was Jon the Conjurer to her? If it was the throne he was after again, he could have it once Marie got what she wanted from him.

Marie placed her hand in his warm, strong grip. He pulled her into a dance, and they fell into easy step, familiar with each other in a way that startled her. His hand lightly caressed her lower back, and she shivered. Dappled starlight shone above them, winking in and out as they glided across the mist-covered cobblestone.

"You make for a vision in white, Marie. Tell me, did you choose the color in remembrance of the day you married your husband"—his eyes fell over Marie's white owl costume—"or in mourning for the day he *died?*"

Marie's mouth quirked into a wry smile. He hadn't intended to wound her, she realized. He was testing her. "Both."

"Did you like my invitation?" he asked, a touch of dark mirth in his voice. "I confess I made a bit of a mess trying to reach you."

"I would prefer if you had not killed men to get my attention." Her eyes slowly found his, the gold searing her just as intensely as the first time she had met him. Her heartbeat quickened.

His hand was on her cheek again. Marie did not shrink away from his touch. How long had it been since a man had touched her? Since anyone had? It was lonely work, the work of Voodoo. Jon knew this best.

"They were no innocents, priestess," Jon said softly. It was as if he could read her thoughts, as if he too were remembering that day they stood in the dusk together beneath the crows. "You know what they are. What they do to us. And you do not care?"

She cared. Those men had been masters in every sense of the word. They owned folks because they could. But there were some free colored Creoles who owned their own people too. Would Jon kill them as well? She stared into his eyes and saw cold resolve. *Yes. Yes, he would if it came down to it.*

"You've made things considerably difficult for the Voodoos, Jon. Sanite Dede is not happy with your handiwork."

"When is that old crone ever happy with anyone?" This drew a laugh from Marie, and he stared down at her, eyes twinkling.

"I confess, even after everything . . . she is fond of you. Why do you think you still yet breathe in her city?"

"*Her* city? If this were truly her city, do you think our kind would walk about collared and heeled like fucking dogs begging for scraps?" Anger deepened his voice now. Magic vibrated from him, emanating along his skin in cold waves.

Marie grew silent. Jon spun her in a twirl, and she fell into his chest, against the hard, corded muscle beneath his shirt. Marie blinked, gathering her senses about her. She had one mission. One task to be done. Nothing more. "Sanite wants you gone by dawn."

"And you?" Jon asked, drawing near enough that they might kiss, his lips a breath from hers. "What do you want, Marie?"

He was watching her closely, a glimmer of mischief in his dark eyes. Another test. "Things you couldn't possibly give me," she said at last. "Not yet."

"I could give you power beyond your limits, priestess. Show you magic older than this land"—his gaze flickered to her lips, then back up to her eyes—"and pleasures you've not dared imagine."

A shiver down her belly, between her thighs. "Tempting words, I confess," Marie breathed at last.

"Words have power, Marie. Cut a man's arm off and he'll use the other to steal. But cut off the tongue? He'll be left without a proper sword to defend himself," Jon said with an impish smile.

"Sword?" Marie's eyebrows drew together in mock confusion. "You speak as if this is a battle and not a dance."

"A battle, no." He stilled, their dance done. "But *war*?" He leaned in close, lips brushing her ear. "War I will have, and war I will win."

A scream tore through the sky. Another. And another. Marie turned, shocked to see men and women on the ground, writhing in agony, blood and black bile spurting from their mouths. A gentleman standing next to Marie dropped his goblet, splattering wine down his front. He clutched at his throat, clawing at his own skin as if it were a collar, eyes bulging.

Marie whirled to Jon, who was watching the man as if trying to work out a particularly vexing puzzle. "Jon! What have you done?"

"Only what I must." Jon was smiling now, and Marie was reminded of Corbin's words, his saccharine voice at her ear. *You may wear a mask, but I have glimpsed the face that lies beneath it.* This was not the face of a trickster, some parlor charlatan, or a lowly shape-shifter. Those were only the stories Jon *wanted* them to believe. This was the face of the fallen, of the devil himself. And in his eyes burned the intensity of a single word: *revenge*.

"I will bring this city to its knees, Marie Laveau," he continued. "And I want you standing at my side."

A shivering thrill passed through her at his invitation. Warm. Unbidden. In many ways the Quarter Queen dismissed her. But not him. With those few words, he'd invited her to be his equal.

A little black bird circled above him, cawing as it arced across the sky, wheeling through the moon's silver light. Screams tore through the courtyard now, rippling into a vicious chorus. People were dying all around her, tipping right over like fragile baubles Jon had gleefully pushed from their shelves. Cold terror permeated the air.

Marie found Jon's gaze. He tipped his hat at her, and in the next breath, he ruptured into a flurry of screaming black birds—every bit of him breaking away into a hundred fluttering wings that lashed the air, then shot skyward in a trail of darkness.

Marie stood frozen. Sanite had sent her here to make peace with Jon. Not war. But she could see now there would be no peace with Jon returned. Surely it would be only a matter of minutes before the tide turned against her and all the Voodoos. This was exactly what Jon wanted. The city in a mindless terror, and the Voodoos caught in between, ready for the taking. But that would be only the beginning.

Marie hurriedly scanned the crowd. There were some already still as stone over the cobbled ground, too far gone for help, and others writhing in invisible agony, wildly gasping. A mixture of blood and wine splattered from their mouths. But of course—she could have guessed.

"The wine!" she cried. "It's been *spelled*!"

A woman beside her hastily dropped her glass, the shards scattering at her feet. A rumble of panic seized the party. Mayor Corbin was being whisked away by a flock of Brotherhood alchemists he'd paid for additional guard.

There was no way Marie could heal everyone on her own. She'd need more time for preparation, more potions than she could make in just a few spare minutes.

Marie turned her eyes back to the man clawing at his own throat. He writhed and bucked on the blood-splattered stone, as useless as a worm beneath her feet. In a few seconds he would die if she did nothing.

Then do nothing. Let him die. Let them all die.

Jon was right; there were no innocents here tonight. And yet . . . Sanite had not sent her here to cause more chaos, only to find the source of it. And indeed, she had. This had been a mission of peace, nothing more. If she let this man die, what fresh horrors would await the Voodoos come morning? What would the papers say? The city-goers with their aurum rifles and pitchforks and collars and chains at the ready . . .

Marie knelt beside the man. His wild eyes found hers, reeling from the panic of Jon's hex.

His hand flew up to Marie's face, cradling her cheek with clammy fingers, smearing a bright red handprint. "Merci, priestess. Merci!" His brows drew together, confused, when Marie made no move to assist him. "Help me! *Please!*"

Marie opened her mouth, readying a healing incantation on her tongue, then remembered that day ten years ago again: Jon's beaten and lashed body chained to that post, arms stretched like some sort of messiah, the heat of those golden eyes on her, challenging her, coaxing her. Those circling black birds overhead, the scream of their crow-song in her head. What had he said about the gods? *They punish.*

"No," Marie said softly, surprised at the grim resolution she had come to. How easy it was. She pushed that bloody hand from her cheek. "I cannot."

She could. She could heal him now, suck the poison from his veins. But she would not. She was done serving selfish men. She was done serving this city. *Let them bear the mark of their sins.* Because death had marked them. Marie cast her gaze toward the darkening sky, where the black birds circled the moon, singing. Death was coming.

⚜

Drenched in blood and bile, Marie hurried down the garden path that led away from Chateau Corbin's inner courtyard, eager to put the night's horrors behind her.

"'Tis a real pity. All that magic, Laveau, and you could not spare a drop."

Marie whirled to find Silas Favreau leaning against a stone fountain that was spewing water from a marbled goblet. He held a chalice of wine to his own lips and drank deeply from it.

"Wait! That's—"

"Do not fret. It is not poisoned." His dark blue eyes danced behind a silver viper mask. "I checked."

"How curious that you did not check the rest an hour ago."

"Who says I didn't?" The alchemist's lips twisted in a sneer. "You misunderstand the Brotherhood's aims, priestess. And here I thought you an exceptionally quick study."

Irritation spiked her blood. She was in no mood to humor the likes of the Brotherhood any longer. "Out with it, alchemist."

"It is true what they say. You are as formidable as you are lovely."

"Careful, now, Silas. We wouldn't want any of your kind to hear you bestow such flatteries on the enemy."

"There is no harm in speaking the truth, witch." He leaned in, dark eyes glittering. "Only in acting on it."

"You're playing a dangerous game. Keep away from me. I want no part of it."

"As you wish." He finished the last of his drink. His long hair fell about his collar in ruddy gold waves. "Oh, and Marie? If tonight is any indication of the coming days, your friend Jon poses a threat to us all. The Brotherhood might be willing to overlook certain . . . *differences* to accommodate a mutual goal."

"Are you proposing an alliance, alchemist?"

"Do try to have some patience, priestess." The alchemist strode down the garden path, spangled robes billowing in the night air. "Everything in due time."

Everything in due time. Marie couldn't help but mull over the alchemist's cryptic words as she made her way to the carriage that would take her from the city and back to the wilderness. By the time she reached the bayou house, Marie found Sanite outside amongst the whispering dark of the trees. She was facing the sky, crowned in the white flare of moonlight. And that was a good thing, for she did not see the bloodstains slashed across Marie's ruined gown, her matted hair, the red handprint across her cheek.

As Marie approached, the older woman's fingers curled around her gnarled walking stick, her displeasure clear. "You took long enough."

"I had to be sure. I needed time to observe him."

"And? What does Jon the Conjurer want?"

What you dare not do. What none of us have ever done. "He doesn't want the throne, Sanite. His ambitions lie far past that." Marie hesitated. "He wants war."

"And you, Marie? Tell me, after observing Jon's power, what exactly is it that you want, my dear child?"

A test. This was a test. She could not tell Sanite that she wanted Jon's magic for her own, because it was forbidden—*he* was forbidden. "I do not know what happened to Jacques. No one does. But I know what he wanted, for me and my magic. He wanted it to be for something more." Marie hesitated. "Like Jon."

"You are tempting the devil. You don't want Jon's war. You simply want the magic he could give you. And I warned you repeatedly, little girl, about the magic you seek. Veil magic is expressly forbidden. Even to one such as I."

"But it is *possible*," Marie said. She couldn't smother the note of hope in her voice, a piece of tinder caught aflame now that she'd dared speak the words aloud.

"Many things are possible with the help of a man like Jon. But there are costs."

"And I will gladly pay them."

Marie did not bother hiding her ambitions from Sanite any longer. What did it matter? Sanite was dying. Her death was imminent, and soon Marie's reign would be upon them all. This they both knew. They were beyond lies and games now.

Though her eyes were failing her now, Sanite Dede had the gift of vision. What she lacked in the art of channeling or pure might, she made up for with her talents as a seer. It was this talent, Marie supposed, that made her such an exceptional queen. To see her enemies' moves well before they'd conjured them up, to peer into the realm of possibilities and see the shape of things not yet formed. That was power.

Sanite Dede turned to face Marie at last. Her eyes were completely white, glowing with all the sovereignty of the Quarter Queen. Fear flared in Marie's belly. Because Sanite was seeing her with the eyes of a true seer. When she spoke again, Marie knew that these were the words of *prophecy.*

"You will look, Marie Laveau . . ." The light from Sanite's eyes faded, and Marie startled to see they were full of unshed tears for her. ". . . and you will never find."

CHAPTER THIRTEEN

REE

Someone tapped at the window as Ree ran a damp cloth over her mother's feverish brow. Her heart leapt, nervous that yet another intruder had discovered her mother's secret. But it was only Aram, who'd brought a sprig of lemon balm tucked into his beak. Ree pried the glass up, and Aram flew in, landing on Ree's shoulder, where he liked to perch after his travels.

"Silly bird," she cooed, stroking the soft feathers along his neck. He turned his head, proudly showing off the bright green herb. He was always bringing her gifts, but this she knew was for Marie. Lemon balm could be used to bring down fevers. They sold bags of it at the apothecary from time to time.

But not even Aram's arrival could brighten her mood. How could it, when so much else blighted her mind? Henryk's arrival in the city; circling for answers she didn't have; and then the matter of Silas, cryptic and toying, who somehow knew about Marie's condition, which, with one look at the sickly sheen on her skin, had only grown worse in the span of one night.

Sosie was curled at the foot of Marie's bed, watching Ree with piercing eyes as she worked over her mother. She knew the snake didn't trust her. That was fine. She never had. But ever since Marie had fallen into her sleep, the two of them had struck an uneasy alliance of sorts.

Nan entered the chamber, armed with a pitcher of cold water and fresh linen to replace what Ree had used. "Has there been no change?" she asked quietly, refilling the wooden bowl with water. Aram fluttered over, politely dropped in the sprig of lemon balm, then flew back to Ree.

"She's worse somehow," said Ree. "Whatever she's experiencing . . . it's taking a toll on her."

"How long can she go on like this?"

Ree's heart beat in a jittery rhythm. She did not want to think of the worst, of what might become of her mother in a few days' time, what might become of *her* when she was gone. "I am . . . not sure. But it cannot be much longer."

A few days. A few days was all she had to save her mother.

"Ree, forgive me, but we need to turn our minds to what comes next." Nan's voice drifted, and Ree knew where this conversation was heading—into dangerous territory. "The Voodoos cannot be without a queen. The others are getting nervous. First, news of a Harbinger spreads, and now Marie has not been sighted. We need to think—"

"You *need* to stop," Ree snapped. "Not another fucking word, Nan. Fetch more water, and this time be quicker about it."

Nan lowered herself into a stiff bow, then promptly made herself scarce. Ree sighed, rubbing a hand along her pounding temple. She shouldn't have been so coarse with the girl, but she didn't need obvious reminders of how dire their situation was. Nonetheless, Nan spoke the truth, one she hadn't ever let herself consider. The Quarter could not be without a queen. Not for long. The Voodoos needed a leader; without one, the city would gladly take control, and what would be left of them then?

Ree turned her eyes back to her mother. If not for the slow rise and fall of her chest, Ree might have already mistaken her for dead. She remembered grasping her mother's hand, her mind suddenly flooded with an image of Jon. Was it possible she was seeing what her mother had seen—what she had *wanted* her to? Perhaps Marie had been trying to tell her something; perhaps she was still trying to now.

Ree went to the side of the bed and took her mother's hand in hers. She felt the pull of Marie Laveau's magic drawing her in, taking root inside of her thoughts. Dozens of images flickered inside her mind's eye, flashes from another time, another place, a scattering of sounds, bits of words and phrases she could hardly catch. *Her mother at a younger Mayor Corbin's bedside, holding a vial. A brown-skinned woman named Claudette beside her with eyes of deep emerald. Her mother gowned in white, like one of the mourning widows. Marie kneeling, staring up at a golden-eyed man who gazed down at her in hushed wonder. A bloody handprint across her cheek. Cold white eyes glowing out from the dark.*

Ree opened her eyes, the images and sounds vanishing. None of it made sense. But it would. It must. There was one image she recognized. The woman with the emerald eyes. She had seen those same eyes staring at her that day in Congo Square, when she'd stopped Anabelle from killing Corbin. The eyes had been glowing then, full of old magic.

Claudette Duvalier.

Ree had heard her name traded among the Voodoos, but never had she met the woman. *L'Enchanteresse,* some called her. She was proudly Haitian, as many were in New Orleans, and had brought older magic across the ocean with her. Although she was no friend to the Laveaus, she was the only person from her mother's past who was left in the city. Which meant she might be the only person in all of New Orleans who could help her. Ree turned to Aram, who was perched on the golden brass knob of the bedpost, fluttering his feathers at her expectantly, as if to say, *I can help you.*

Ree held out an arm, and he flew to land on her wrist. She showed him with her mind's eye the same image of Claudette she'd received from Marie, and at once the little blackbird cawed.

"Show me," murmured Ree.

With a ruffle of his black feathers, Aram took flight back through the open window and out into the bayou. She followed him for some time, and it was after sundown when Ree finally turned onto

Canal Street. It was less a common street, Ree supposed, and more a crossroads of sorts, one that separated the rest of New Orleans from the inner cloisters of the French Quarter. Ree could feel the boundary of Marie Laveau's magic, the invisible tug of her wards, as she walked along the road. The Quarter Queen's magic ran stronger, truer, in the heart of the Quarter. Less so outside of it.

The street itself ran in a long spine down to the riverside, but not narrow and twisting like the rest of the Quarter. It was enormously wide, each side swaddled in stately retail: Countless regal emporiums and dressmakers advertised their wares in big, glittering letters. Hotels shot up from the ground like weeds, flanked by charming coffeehouses and banks with gilded doors guarded by men in caps and gloves. Horse-drawn streetcars raced down the middle, as did grand carriages and noisy marching parades that went on at all times of the day, folks waving their handkerchiefs and dancing in step. Here the signposts changed every few minutes from French to English, alchemically transforming, all the better to accommodate those uptown folks who didn't speak a lick of "bayou talk."

Ree followed Aram, stopping only when he suddenly swooped over her head and landed on top of a creaking wooden sign; its placard read THE PINT & PEA.

It was a small cherry-pink alehouse with green shutters crouched low beneath a sagging gallery, bordered on one side by the Aurelia and on the other by a hatmaker whose shop had long since closed for the evening. Ree stared at Aram. *Really?* She could not see a woman like Claudette Duvalier taking up in an establishment like the Pint & Pea. But Aram only fluttered his wings, his yellow eyes seeming to say, *Go on, now.*

Still huffing from the long walk, Ree went inside and was met with the usual evening crowd—sailors and dockworkers looking for a quick meal, regulars sharing the day's gossip. The Pint & Pea had none of the fuss of the other refined pubs along Royal Street, nor the loud charm of the alehouses that lined Bourbon, like the Saddle Saloon (which Ree much preferred). It was a place of mismatched odds and ends—patrons lounged on quilted chairs stuffed with tattered cushions, the floor a patchwork of secondhand rugs arranged in a riot of color, the air mingled with the garlicky bite of simmering red beans and trapped humidity.

An old creole trumpet player sat by the door, a toothpick lodged into the side of his mouth. The song he played made Ree's eyes prickle with tears. Because it had been one of Marcel's favorites. Ree flipped a coin at the musician. He caught it, tipped his hat, sputtered out a "Thank you, kindly," then promptly changed the tune.

Ree made her way through the slew of splintered tables pushed ungraciously into the middle of the room, where folks drank coffees stirred with dark spoonfuls of chicory and chocolate. A fire danced merrily in a crooked stone hearth at the back; a large shaggy gray dog dozed loudly in its warmth.

Miss Hattie-Jean ran the bar, same as she did every night, a flowered apron tied around her front, a rag on her shoulder. A tiny teacup of a woman, she hummed along to the music, her molasses-brown pin curls bobbing up and down as she worked the counter. Every word she spoke was dipped in honey—overly saccharine and thick. "Got the best gumbo in town. A sight better than Labelle's," she was telling a man who clutched his clouded pint, teetering woozily in his chair.

It wasn't—but that was beside the point. There was no arguing with a woman like Hattie-Jean.

"I got the best pig feet in the whole Quarter," Hattie-Jean went on as she served another round.

She didn't. But what the Pint & Pea lacked in taste, it made up for in portions: bowls of spiced greens as big as wagon wheels, and pints of lager and moonshine poured as deep as trenches.

"Aw hell!" she exclaimed when Ree dropped into a seat at the edge of the bar. "I don't like y'all Laveaus up in here. Not one bit." She flicked her eyes at Ree disdainfully. "'Specially you. At least your momma follows the rules when it suits her."

Ree couldn't blame her—she'd caused enough trouble to last Hattie-Jean through the year. But Hattie-Jean didn't bother to ask Ree for her order, just went to pouring her a dark red lager into an oversized murky pint glass until it sloshed. "Get on with your drink and get the hell out."

She plopped the drink down on the counter in front of Ree, who picked it up, turning it over in the dust mote–ridden air. The pint's glass was as cloudy as sea mist.

"Not before I get what I came for. I need to meet with Claudette Duvalier." Ree felt the pull of the older witch's magic, now that she knew what to look for. "The one they call *L'Enchanteresse*."

Miss Hattie-Jean kept her eyes on the wooden counter, shining circles into it with her rag. "No can do."

"And why the hell not?"

"Because don't no enchantresses live up in here. Only witch here is *you*. And I want you gone. You hear me?"

It was a lie. For whatever reason, Claudette was not like Marie Laveau. Whatever power she wielded she much preferred to do from the dark of the shadows.

"Get me Claudette Duvalier *now*, or I will make a scene." Ree leaned in, eyes flashing. She found her gaze in the mirror along the back of the bar. Eyes as white as bone. "I promise you I'll make enough trouble they'll have this place shuttered for a week. You want that, Hattie-Jean?"

Miss Hattie-Jean recoiled at the sight of Ree's eyes, the mark of her mother's magic. Ree was only posturing. Just a few days ago, she might have thrown a similar tantrum to get her way. Now such a bargain brought her no pleasure. But she was running out of options.

Ree went to take a sip of her lager, silently calculating how far she would have to take this whole ordeal. Suddenly, a jeweled hand shot out and snatched the drink from Ree's hand.

Ree looked up into the face of Claudette Duvalier.

She was a tad older than her mother, with smooth brown skin, long dark braids trailing to her hips, fox eyes, and full lips painted a deep mauve. "I heard you were looking for me," said L'Enchanteresse. She downed the rest of Ree's drink in one go, finishing with a smirk. "Careful what you summon, little Laveau. It just might come calling back."

Claudette's gaze dropped to the *L* pendant on her throat, and Ree heard the spirits whisper in her ear, the soft tickle of a feather. *Careful. Careful.* This woman was powerful, her bloodline old and well kept. L'Enchanteresse was already moving to the back staircase. Her invitation hung thick in the room like an unspoken spell for Ree to follow.

She would not ask twice.

Claudette showed Ree into the upper parlor. The room was dim and moist, the air thick with trapped heat that rose from the alehouse below. Rows of makeshift iron cots filled the room, the beds lined tidily from wall to wall. On them rested a slew of black folks: some wore tattered shirts sticky with sweat and unwash; mothers cradled crying babies close; children absently tossed dice; others picked through bowls of sun-ripened fruit. Runaways, if Ree had to guess.

Ree glanced down, feeling something pawing at her leg. It was the dog from downstairs. A loping, shaggy thing, it had followed them up and was now pacing attentively at Ree's side.

"Down, Petey! Get on!" Claudette snapped at the dog. But Petey remained, undeterred by his mistress's foul mood. He galloped over to one of the children, who offered a piece of banana.

"What is this place?" Ree asked.

"Think of it as a tunnel of sorts," explained Claudette as she walked. "Those who'd like to leave this godforsaken city pass through here on their way to Haiti. It takes more than a few pretty spells to get this many folks free passage."

". . . I had no idea this existed." She would have never guessed such a place would be sitting just above the ordinary likes of the Pint & Pea, least of all hiding in plain sight in the Quarter. This was surprising to say the least. And very much illegal.

"Of course you didn't. You're a Laveau," she muttered curtly. "I detest this fucking city down to its cursed bones. But someone has to do something." The implication was clear: Marie Laveau did nothing. And if she did, it was surely not enough.

At Ree's stricken expression, something in the older witch's face quietly relented. "Sorry about your friend—the boy with the pretty eyes. I quite liked him. He was dedicated to the cause. Real fire in his bones, that one."

Ree's brow furrowed. "*Marcel?* Dedicated to the cause?" At last she understood. "He helped you get these people to Haiti, didn't he? But he never told me—"

Claudette shrugged, cutting Ree off. "Maybe you never asked."

She led Ree past a sprawling map of Haiti unfurled over a long table, the parchment frayed at the corners. Sea-blue strokes curved along the coastline, its cities marked in red and violet swirling ink—to the northern coast was Cap-Haïtien; to the south was Jacmel, wreathed in green mountainous ridges; and at its heart was Port-au-Prince, the crowned jewel, the seat of revolution and power.

Claudette showed Ree into a back room where an altar to Simbi Makaya still smoked. She stood over a worktable spread with tarot cards and a heap of herbs: lemon balm that was cut and sifted, talc, sprigs of wormwood. She picked up a cigarette from a dish, lit it with a spell, and used a mortar and pestle to crush the herbs to grit.

"Speak your piece and begone. You've caused enough trouble for us all."

"You were there that day in Congo Square," Ree said. "I saw you."

"I knew I would regret getting involved in your messy little tiff."

"Then why did you?"

Claudette looked up from her work, pestle still in hand. She didn't seem angry, only vexed. "Presumptuous, aren't we?" She sighed. "Sanite wouldn't have wanted the other Voodoos hurt because of some sniveling little brat. Old woman been dead and still a fucking thorn in my side. *Shit.*"

"How noble of you."

"You have your mother's tongue. Tell me, how fares it living in Marie Laveau's shadow?" Claudette made a tutting sound with her teeth as she turned back to the work of crushing her herbs. "Marie Laveau the Second, but never the First."

"You say that to wound me. It doesn't. I never set out to be my mother."

"Spare me your questions, you little brat, and leave." She waved a jeweled hand. "I don't need the stink of your pity of a mutiny catching on to me."

"I can't leave. Not without answers for my mother." Ree hesitated. "She's in trouble, Claudette."

The pestle stilled in the older witch's hand. She slowly looked up at Ree, her green eyes alight. "What kind of trouble, per se?"

"Jon the Conjurer."

"Yes, the conjurer of old," Claudette said, lips pursed. "I am familiar with his power. The question is, are *you*, child?"

Ree reached into the satchel on her arm and pulled out the crushed dark blossoms of Conjurer Root. The forbidden fruit her mother had set the earth ablaze to destroy.

Claudette followed her gaze. "So, it is true. Jon is returning. Those flowers are from Haiti, child. They bring the magic of revolution and death. When Jon consumed them, he tied his soul to Baron Samedi, Lord of Death. He struck a bargain." She stilled. "Have you consumed it?"

". . . Yes."

"Then you've made yourself a willing conduit to Jon." She paused as if about to say something else but thinking better of it. "And so has your mother."

"But I did not become like my mother. I'm not comatose. I didn't—"

"Because you are *not* like your mother!" Claudette snapped. "Not fully. Not completely. Your blood is well suited to Conjurer Root. To death magic." She stopped herself from saying more. "Go home, little Laveau. And if you want my advice: Pack your things and leave the city at once. From the talk I hear, things are going to hell quickly, in a matter of days. An Inquisitor walks among us."

Oh, that Ree knew well enough. "My mother needs me."

She balked. "Listen to me. Marie Laveau needs no one. Save yourself, little girl. While you still can. Now go, before I force you out."

"What is it you aren't telling me?"

Claudette stared at her for a long moment, green eyes blazing with contemplation. "You have always known you were different, didn't you?" she whispered at last. "Wicked, they call you." Her eyes flickered over Ree. "But I suppose no more wicked than your holy mother. At least you keep no mask."

"I have no need. People know what I am well enough."

At this, Claudette smiled. Begrudgingly. But a smile, nonetheless.

"The question is, do *you*?" She let the question hang between them, a suggestion that made Ree nervous. She took a long inhale from her cigarette, then stamped out the rest of it in the dish. "Your mother was a liar."

She could be at times. They all could.

"She lied to me too," Ree said. "But she was still our Quarter Queen. Which means"—Ree held her dark gaze—"we have a duty to protect her. Both of us. Which is why I am here. I can't feel her anymore. I can't channel her fully. It's like our connection is ... *dying.*"

"Do you know the true reason why you cannot fully channel your mother without interference?" Claudette waited, and Ree shook her head. "Because the connection to your father is only getting stronger."

Father.

"Yes, child. The wicked conjurer is your father," Claudette said. "There's another influence over you, Marie Laveau the Second. Deep down, you've always known, haven't you? Surely, you must have felt it? That dark thing living inside of you, the one your mother always tried to stamp back down."

Haven't you? What did the nuns whisper at her back? *Marie Laveau the Second, the wicked, wicked daughter.* But now she knew. It was Jon's wickedness they saw when the city gazed upon her. Jon's wickedness they remembered.

And yet, her mother had never told her. She'd shared everything else with Ree, every spell, every parlor trick, every long-lost ritual. She divulged to her the secrets of the gods, the other women Baron Samedi had taken and bedded outside of his wife, Maman Brigitte. The scores of children born from these little dalliances. The deals Papa Legba might easily bestow upon those he favored, the swift punishment that would damn those he did not. Marie had shared the fickle whims of the loa with her daughter, each secret sin. But never her own. No, she'd kept those stowed away inside, and if she had any heart left, Ree supposed, she'd guard that too. Her fierce mother, revered queen, Voodoo Priestess, and hypocrite.

"The truth is, I cannot help you. If Marie is consumed with Conjurer Root, then she is tied up with the likes of death magic beyond my abilities. Beyond *everyone's*. There are stories, whispers that say

Marie Laveau banished Jon to the first realm of the dead, to the Veil. If your mother consumed Conjurer Root, then Jon must be using it to hold part of Marie's soul there with him as well. And the only two people to have successfully practiced Veil magic in New Orleans are Marie"—she took a stilted breath—"and Jon."

"Then how do I learn it?" asked Ree.

"By turning to the past, of course," said Claudette. "If you harbor any hope of saving Marie, then you best learn the forbidden magic Jon taught her. And you must learn it quickly."

Ree unfolded her hand, staring down at the strange, dark little flower. She didn't know the muddied history between her mother and Jon, only the bits and pieces she'd seen from her mother's mind. But now she knew that the only way forward was to go backward in time, that the answers she sought could be found only in Marie's veiled past. Answers her mother had kept so carefully hidden all these years.

But one thing was for certain. She would stop at nothing to learn the truth.

CHAPTER FOURTEEN

MARIE

Less than a week had passed since Mardi Gras, the spelled wine, and already scores of men had died. The plague ships were becoming full, as they had during the terror yellow fever had set upon the city some years before. The bodies were piling up, the crematories were working overtime, and the whole city billowed with black smoke as if the sky rained ash. It was all the work of Voodoo. The strangest kind, one she had never practiced herself, but it mattered not. Jon was one of them.

"We are under attack, Marie." Sanite Dede sat on her throne, peering into a basin of water in her lap. "I will not have a war at the end of my reign."

Marie stood before her, readying herself to hear her latest marching orders. "What would you have me do, my queen?"

"Stamp it out now, before the flames become too large to quell. They believe us responsible for these plagues." Sanite lifted her gaze from her scrying, a certain sharpness in her eyes. The water had been collected from Lake Pontchartrain near La Sirene's shrine and consecrated in her name. She was Sanite's patron goddess, whose venerable blessing made the Quarter Queen's foresight strong.

"We are."

"*We?* Jon is not one of us." Sanite spat on the ground, fury alight on her face.

"Isn't he?" Marie thought of his voice, the delicious thrill that had traveled through her body when she'd heard his declaration. *I will bring this city to its knees, Marie Laveau. And I want you standing at my side.* Whatever Jon had planned for New Orleans would mean war for them all, a risk Sanite Dede thought too great.

"You've a soft spot for him." Sanite pursed her lips, her gaze souring. "Well, you certainly wouldn't be the first. You need to make him see reason, Marie."

No, Marie thought. *It is you who needs to see reason.*

Sanite cocked her head to the side, peering down at her closely. It was the look that always made Marie's skin crawl. Those filmy eyes had a way of seeing through her as easily as if she were that bowl of water in Sanite's withered hands.

"Unless, of course, *you* agree with him, Marie. Tell me, do you agree with his methods too, the kind of terrible magic he is willing to unleash upon us all? The very same kind, need I remind you, that puts us all at risk for torture and death?" Sanite leaned forward, golden bangles on her wrist rattling as she did. "You were not alive during the First Inquisition. You did not see the carnage, the absolute terror, as these old eyes have."

Marie did not need to. It was not often that Sanite spoke of the First Holy Inquisition, nor of what horrors had been wrought upon their kind. But when she did, she made sure to spare no detail, not one bloody memory. They'd burned the first Quarter Queen, Saloppe, on a pyre, left her to wither slowly like a boar on a spittle for all to see.

"His magic . . . it is of a different kind of Voodoo," said Marie. "It is not more powerful than my own. But it is *craftier.* And I believe that makes it all the more dangerous, does it not? We'd do well to keep him close."

"Close?" Sanite Dede mused, a hint of dark laughter in her words. "He cannot be brought to heel like some dog. A man like Jon will never be chained again. Heed me well, Marie: Whatever leash you may think you have on his neck, you will soon find on your own."

⚜

Marie took her seat inside the confessional and crossed herself. She knew Father Antoine was on the other side of the latticed divide, could smell the scent of his anointing oil and the myrrh he'd used to bless himself.

"Hello, Marie." A moment of silence from his side as the priest crossed himself. "How long has it been since your last confession?"

A week, Marie wanted to say but did not. A week since Jon had returned to New Orleans and wrought a gaping hole in the city, in her life. *And in your heart, priestess,* a little voice said. "Too long," Marie answered finally. She knew the words, knew them well, but today they did not come easily to her. Today they tasted bitter in her mouth. "Forgive me, Father, for I have sinned."

"And for what sins are you confessing?"

Marie wanted to laugh. Oh, there were plenty. What had Jacques accused her of? Selfishness. Harboring such great magic for herself, being unwilling to use it to break the rules that kept their kind down. Murder and cunning plots on behalf of her queen. Numerous others. But only one sin remained on her mind, seared into every thought.

"I have . . . coveted another."

"And whom have you coveted, Marie?"

"Jon."

A beat of silence. "Tales of the Conjurer's return have reached even this weary one's ears. Be that as it may, how did this come to be?"

"Sanite adheres to the rules, Antoine. Even if it means that nothing will change. And Jon? He will break every single one, but with him . . . everything would change."

"Is that what *you* want?"

She did not speak of the Veil, nor of her intention of bringing Jacques back from the dead. Those sins she could not confess, not to Antoine, least of all to herself. "I find that I still love him. My husband. Jacques. And yet . . . I find I may have tempted another into my heart. One whom I have no right to covet."

"Marie," Antoine said quietly. "Jacques Paris may never return, my dear child. But that does not mean that your heart holds him any less."

Tears stung Marie's eyes. The truth was, sometimes speaking with Antoine brought her more peace than the prayers to her saints. And sometimes, just sometimes, she thought it might be his forgiveness she was seeking more than God's.

"For your penance, you are to say three Hail Marys, and I want you to sit with yourself, Marie. Examine your own heart. The heart is a fickle creature to us all. It can be full of evil, truly wicked things. But love is not one of them. Do you understand?"

Marie wiped the tears from her eyes, nodding. "Yes."

"And Marie?"

Silence stretched for a long moment. She sensed these next words were not the words of her priest, but the gentle words of the father she'd never had.

"We all sin, dear child. Some of us more than others. None of us is above temptation," Father Antoine said quietly. "But no matter how sweet the fruit, it poisons us all the same. Be careful with him, Marie."

Be careful with him. Marie was still mulling over Antoine's words when she stepped out from the cathedral. The roads were mostly vacant, apart from a handful of sailors stumbling drunkenly back to their inns and boarding rooms. Above her, the sky waned to a deep gray. Black smoke billowed from the crematories, expelling the fumes of the dead into the air. This was Jon's work, Marie told herself. Folks were too scared to wander alone now, nervous that they might meet some Voodoo hex in broad daylight.

There were signs too—official mandates warning of earlier curfews and fines and fees for those who did not abide. One read BY SUNDOWN NEGROES AND COLOREDS TO THEIR ROOMS. LEST THEY MEET THE HANGMAN'S DOOM. Another one hung above her on a streetlamp, parchment flapping in a gust of warm wind: MAGICKS MUST BE MANAGED.

Did the Brotherhood of the White Hand face such trivialities? She had it on good authority that Gailon and his lot could be pettier than even Sanite Dede and had a bad habit of transfiguring those who ran debts with the guild—turning men into toads, whores into one-eyed crones, and whatever else struck their fancies.

A cold wind swept into the road. Marie glanced up—one by one the streetlamps extinguished themselves like candles snuffed out, plunging the path ahead into darkness.

Three alchemists stepped into her path. They all bore the same milky-white hair, marking their status as the Brotherhood's ascended, those who'd climbed its higher ranks. And if there were any doubt, there was the Brotherhood's mark on their cloaks, a moonstone brooch in the shape of that infamous pale handprint.

"I imagine," started the tallest of the three, "that these new rules make you feel safe, don't they?" His attention turned, briefly, to the signpost warning of curfew for Les Magiques. "So why aren't you following them?"

Marie held herself still. She would not be so easily cowed, especially by lesser mages. "Rules have never made my kind feel safe."

This drew a laugh from the tall one, their leader. "Gailon said you had more sass than a house slave on a holiday. You delight me, Marie Laveau. Which is why it will pain me to do *this.*" He drew a black wand from the blue folds of his cloak and pointed it directly at her. "*Mutatio.*"

At the alchemist's command, a pile of ropes meant for tethering horses uncoiled into six great snakes, slithering toward her, hissing at her from the shadows.

Marie narrowed her eyes and called upon the strength of Ogoun. God of metalsmithing and the sacred forge, his flame could eat through the skies in one breath. *Great Ogoun,* Marie prayed. *Lend me the flames from your forge.*

It was quiet, but then came a sound like heavy iron chains, the hiss and pop of fire rising, the sounds of Ogoun tending his swords over his searing forge. His mighty voice in her ear, fervently mocking. *Marie Laveau. My altars have gone unlit too long. A lesser god might take offense. But a good priestess knows to only light the candle, should you find yourself in darkness. Let it be so, child.*

Marie drew in a great breath and blew it out, releasing a cloud of orange-gold flame from her mouth. Ogoun's flames devoured the tangle of snakes at her feet, disintegrating them in one sweep. All three alchemists pointed their wands in the air, holding a warding spell together. But Marie was satisfied to see that, despite their shield, the hems of their cloaks were charred, the ground around their feet scorched to dust.

Marie sneered, enlivened with rage now. Ogoun's power fed on such emotions, and she could feel it thrumming in her veins like drum-song, a white-hot pain that made it hard for her to keep conscious. But she did. She would kill them all for daring to attack her. She would scorch their bones to dust and scatter their ashes upon the Brotherhood's halls in retribution.

But Ogoun's power was leaving her. Her next realization hurt worse than the blistering agony of summoning his sacred fire: She simply wasn't strong enough to contain him. She heard the god of fire's voice in her ear, speaking a searing promise: *Do not take so long to light my candles, priestess. Lest I burn your flesh as tribute instead.* If she were in a better mood, she might have laughed at his fickleness. But Ogoun was like all loa, swift in their rewards, so petty in their vengeances. It was a wonder she served them at all.

Exhausted, Marie flung out a hand, and the smallest of the alchemists flew back into the alley wall, then hit the ground, unconscious. The last two rounded on her, sending bright sparks from the tips of their wands.

"You are more powerful than Gailon warned," said the tallest. "But this was never a battle of wills, witch."

With a swish of their cloaks, the two alchemists vanished, leaving their third brother behind. He couldn't return to the Brotherhood's halls if he wanted to. As far as Gailon was concerned, he'd been bested by lesser ilk. And that was as good a death sentence as any.

Gailon.

Had she really offended the Grand Wizard so when she'd mended Felix Corbin all those days ago? No, Marie thought quickly, thinking back to the night of Mardi Gras. This was no petty revenge. Gailon was seeking a foothold over Sanite. And what better time to usurp power than when public goodwill for the Voodoos was so thin? Attacking Sanite would prove difficult. The old woman's paranoia meant she rarely left the bayou without a guard, her time in the

Quarter only for rituals on Sunday nights. But Marie? She was easier prey.

The bells of the St. Louis Cathedral were tolling now, thundering across the sky. Over and over again. It was a signal meant only to be used when Les Magiques were causing unrest.

At last, Marie understood. It was a signal meant for *her.* The Brotherhood had not intended to kill her. No, they intended worse. To have her arrested, then publicly charged. Hanged before all the city as warning of what would happen to any Voodoo who might follow in her footsteps.

A bright stab of pain at the side of her neck. Marie clasped a hand to the wound, and it came back covered in blood and something else. A thick, dark gold substance, strangely alchemical. *Venom.* Horror flooded her. She'd been bitten. On the ground, a yellow-and-black serpent reeled back, hissing, scaled head raised, its eyes bright with a preternatural yellow glow, the glow of alchemy. She'd missed one. The serpent slithered on and away. But the burn of its bite remained. Marie could feel it slowly spreading in her blood like a smear . . .

No, thought Marie. She could not flee in time, drained as she was. *Reckless,* Sanite Dede would have spat. *Why conjure one as powerful as Ogoun? A lesser spirit would have done just as well. Your pride hinders your magic as always, Marie.*

Marie steadied herself upon a railing, struggling to breathe. At the end of the road, men on horseback approached. Snatchers by the looks of them, ready to collect their bounties. A trap. The whole thing had been a fucking trap.

Suddenly a crow cawed above her and landed on the post across from her, staring at her, its gaze dark and unblinking. Jon stepped from the shadows, as if he had been there all the while. His gaze swept over her haggard form, narrowing when he noticed the glowing embers still licking the ravaged road, remnants of Ogoun's breath, and the oozing wound at her neck.

Her vision darkened. "Jon . . ." She didn't have the strength to say much more. What would Sanite think? What would the others say if they knew she was with him?

But the bells still tolled. Her enemies pressed closer. She did not have long.

The poison made her unsteady on her feet, and the world was spinning until the whole of it seemed upside down, and she was falling—

Jon caught her, pressing her close into the circle of his arms, a great crow enfolding her in its wings.

"You can't . . . you can't . . ." She wasn't sure. She couldn't remember the rules anymore.

"Come now, love. I can," he said, lips turning into a wicked smile. "And I *will*."

Marie closed her eyes and felt the soft caress of Jon's breath as he whispered a spell into her ear. A soft fluttering sound surrounded them from all sides, the wingbeat of a hundred birds.

And then they were gone.

Marie awoke—screaming.

Fire consumed her blood. She seized and bucked wildly. Strong hands immediately grasped her, holding her to the ground.

"If you want to live, do not move," a gruff voice ordered. Marie cast a wild look about her. Darkness hedged her vision from all sides. A face loomed over hers, blurry in the shadow. Jon. His eyes glowed, more golden than she had ever seen them, bright enough that they gave off their own light.

And then the pain returned—harsher than before, a wave of agony that rocked her insides. She screamed, and Jon quickly pressed something bitter into her mouth, a piece of willow bark.

He was moving over her, doing something she could not see. She heard the rattling of utensils, the slosh of water in a basin. "Bite down when it feels like too much."

Then his lips were upon her throat, feather-soft, and there was only fire, more pain than she had ever felt in her life, as he sucked the poison from her wound.

Marie tossed her head back, gasping and writhing as the pain worked itself from her insides. She bit down, hard enough that it felt as if she might snap the bark in two. But it remained whole, as tough as leather. She bit the bark again and again, until all she could concentrate on was the deep aching in her teeth. The room was a dizzying blur. Shadows danced along the walls, mocking her pain. She was spinning, and there was laughter, maddening laughter. Was it her? Was she the one laughing, making such vexing noises?

She saw strange dark shapes moving toward her, smelling of rotting flesh. Demons, she thought. But no, they were not fallen ones. They were a wholly different kind of creature, something not quite alive. *Twisting, undead things. Dragging themselves from the long, darkened depths of a shadowed corridor toward her...*

Jon lifted his mouth from her throat, and she heard the *ting* of the serpent's venom hitting the basin somewhere beside him as he spat out the poison, bit by bit.

"I'm sorry," Jon whispered. One hand was beneath the curve of her breast, flat against her belly, as he held her writhing body still. And on and on it went, that same *ting* and his hurried whispers of *I'm sorry...I'm sorry*... until she thought she might go mad.

She drifted after that. When she awoke again, she was drenched in sweat and wrapped in a heavy blanket, the colorful patterns not like any she had seen in New Orleans. She had heard slaves talk of such designs in Africa, but never had she seen the swirling shapes and glistening colors for herself. A fire burned in a small hearth. The whole room smelled too sweet. Chamomile, she recognized. For healing.

"Those are from my tribe," said Jon. He was sitting across from her, feeding the flame pieces of chopped wood. So he'd caught her looking. He turned to her and grinned, the corners of his eyes creasing pleasantly. "I am the last of my kind. My wife . . . my children . . . I weave what I can remember."

His wife. Her heart sank down to her belly, cold like a stone. Children too. *I am the last of my kind.* It occurred to her that this was a man who'd lost everything. And yet here he was, sitting before her, willingly telling her about it. She had forgotten. Jon was not like her. Depending on whom you asked and why, Marie was either a colored girl or a black woman light enough that she scarcely had to think of the roots of her bloodline. Creole in every sense that mattered—a person of the new blood born in the new land. So many slaves shared her same story. But not Jon—he had come directly from the old land, young as he was. She could sense it in his magic—a beating song that ran through his veins, strong and steady, unblemished and true.

Marie sat up and looked around. They were in a wooden shack, the walls hung with dried herbs: bundles of marjoram, garlic cloves, prickly bells of thistle. Bits of silver moonlight shone through cracks in the ceiling, the bayou wind rattling the wooden planks like old bones. "And what tribe is that?"

Her gaze landed on canvases leaning against the far wall, some still drying, others splattered in dried paint slashes. A white-capped shoreline. Towering grass soaked in the blood of sunset. Laughing children in luminous pattern work. A Voodoo King. A conjurer of legend. Her queen's bitter enemy. And a talented artist. Jon the Conjurer, a man of many surprises.

"None that you might know." He hadn't meant it as insult, but Marie's face stung. She hated not knowing. Perhaps that was why she was drawn to him so: the possibilities twinkling in those mischievous eyes, that knowledge still as yet unknown to her.

"Then tell me," Marie implored.

"Is that a command or a question?"

"I'll leave that to your imagination. I hear it is quite creative."

"Sanite Dede has been speaking far too kindly of me then."

Marie's smile faltered. "Before . . . when you . . . when I . . ." She hesitated, remembering the soft press of his lips against her throat, that briefest moment of pleasure and relief amidst the madness. ". . . I saw things."

Jon stirred a bubbling cauldron over the fire. "Of course you did. You were close to death, Marie. You were moving closer to the Veil. There is a magic that lives between life and death, a crossroads few can open."

Marie's mind turned to the moment Jon had saved her, the way he'd transported them away in a blast of air, the turn of a blackbird's wings. "And the spell you used to take us away?"

She didn't hide her curiosity about his magic. And he didn't ask her to, as so many others might.

"That was a road opener spell."

"That was not like any road opener spell I've ever seen."

Road openers were rituals to Papa Legba meant to open paths to better alignment or luck, to clear spiritual blockages. But he'd pushed beyond her understanding of Voodoo traditions. Jon hadn't just entreated the spirits to open the paths before him. He had *forced* it, bent time and space to his will. It was unlike any magic she had ever seen or tasted. And by the loa, she wanted more.

"Then perhaps you've had the wrong teacher, love." He winked at her, and Marie flushed. "You would be surprised what you can accomplish, if only you'd dare break a few rules."

Jon offered nothing else after this, working instead in silence. He ladled hot water into a tin canister. Marie's nose was suddenly met with the soothing smell of fresh coffee. Her stomach turned. She was hungry too. Jon poured the coffee into cups and passed her one. Marie quickly downed it, not minding that she'd scorched her tongue and throat; channeling the fire god had already left her insides seared. Jon passed her a biscuit tin with crumbled ashcake inside. She ate it greedily, not stopping until she'd had the crumbs too. She looked up, suddenly embarrassed.

Jon laughed. "Go on, now. Don't worry, there's more." He passed her another tin, this one filled with chocolate wafers and tea biscuits wrapped in wax paper. They were stale and tasteless, but she ate them anyway, ravenous. All the while she watched Jon. And he watched her.

Jon always seemed more myth than man to her. Even now. But in the warm glow of the firelight, he didn't seem the threat the others made him out to be. She heard what they called him—High Jon, Dr. Jon, Jon the Conjurer. A healer, the slaves whispered down at Congo Square. A conjurer with dark power. But his power didn't seem so dark to her now, did it? *It brought you back to life.*

Properly unmasked, he was what Sanite Dede liked to call "pleasing of the flesh," handsome in a way that not many men in New Orleans were. His features were strong, fiercely chiseled like those of the heroes from the old legends Grand-mère had read to her by the light of the bayou's moon. When he turned to smile at her, that little crescent moon piercing at his ear glinted wickedly.

When she felt full, Marie reached for more coffee. As she did, the blanket fell from her shoulders, revealing her cotton slip. When she'd been sleeping, he must have undressed her from her muslin gown, leaving her in only her undergarments. Marie stilled. Only Jacques had seen her like this. He'd been her husband, after all, the only man she'd ever lain with. Jon averted his gaze as Marie pulled the blankets tighter, flushed at her own modesty.

She'd caught him looking. Those golden eyes flickered unabashedly to her lips, then lifted to her eyes. She realized then that they were the soft brown of sweet tea now, that in his effort to save her she'd drained him of his powers. "You are curious, aren't you? About my magic?" he asked softly.

So, she'd not been the only one trying to read faces and thoughts. Jon could take one look at her and know the secrets of her heart, even the darkest ones she'd kept hidden. A moment of panic seized her. Could he know the darkest of them all, the secret that she'd kept closer than any other? She watched his face. Yes, she decided. Yes, he might know that too.

"Yes. And you will teach me," she said.

"Teach you what, Marie?"

"Veil magic."

He did not recoil as Sanite did. He did not even move. Jon sat as still as stone, gazing upon her with calculating eyes. "Do you know what you are asking?"

"Yes."

"And why do you need Veil magic, Marie Laveau?" A glimmer of teasing in his voice. He was testing her, testing the limits of their trust.

"Why else"—Marie held his eyes, forcing herself to speak the truth for once—"if not for love?"

"You should understand one thing: Death is but a doorway. And trouble comes to those who open it."

She needed to open that door, to see Jacques returned to her at last. The costs did not matter to her. Only a fool who had never tasted grief should think there was more to lose. When she had lost Jacques, she had lost herself. And she'd already lost her mother, and then Grand-mère. What should she fear now? Not death. She sought only to bend it to her will.

"I understand," said Marie quietly.

Jon's eyes told her that she didn't. That she might never completely grasp the costs. But he rose to his feet, offering his hand. "Good. Then your first lesson starts now."

They stood barefoot in the bayou, the grass cool between their toes. The magic was better this way; the earth would reach from its roots toward their feet and speak its spells into their bones. Her grand-mère had taught her this kind of magic, wild and full of dirt and flowers and roots. The kind of magic free from Sanite's careful rules and silly edicts.

A small black crow darted out from the brush and landed on his shoulder. "Hello, Aram," he cooed to the bird. The crow watched Marie closely. She had the sense that it did not trust her one bit. "I will not coddle you as Sanite does," Jon said when he turned back to her. "But I will not lie to you either. The only illusions you will find with me will be in spells, not in our words."

Marie thought back to her marriage with Jacques. Hindsight had made their days seem rosier, easier than they'd really been. She was sure Jacques had loved her. But her magic? It was never enough. Jacques was Haitian by birth and had inherited its revolution in his blood. But his magic hadn't come close to Marie's. He'd always pestered her to think of how she might stretch herself for more, to be more than she already was.

"I will have the truth only, Jon."

"And the truth you will have," said Jon. "Now, let us begin."

Jon began to walk in a circle, murmuring under his breath. As he did, veves scorched themselves into the grass, as if he'd taken a white-hot brand and seared them by hand into the earth's face.

Marie had never seen such markings. They were exceptionally old, older than Voodoo itself. "What are you doing?"

"Wards," Jon answered, still intently focused on his spellwork. "All the better to quiet the noise." He looked up and grinned. "We wouldn't want anyone to hear your screams, now, would we?"

Jon's eyes darkened, the black of pitch. And before Marie could react, she was on the ground, doubling over in agony. A cry ripped out of her as pain shot across her skin, stabbing her all over. She looked up at Jon through watery eyes. "Make it stop. *Please.*"

He shook his head. "That was only an illusion, Marie." In an instant the pain ceased. Marie remained on her knees, panting. She could breathe again. "Lesson one—never leave yourself unprotected. Even from those you love."

Marie froze. Is that what she had done with Jacques? Left herself unprotected in his absence? The thought made her sick.

Jon's eyes were steady on hers. "Sanite has taught you rituals, no? Let me tell you a secret, love. *They take too long.* In the coming days, you will need to defend yourself in the moment. There may be no time for such rituals. Your magic requires immediacy, Marie. You need to learn to conjure like this—" He snapped his fingers, releasing a crackling charge of cold green light.

Marie blinked, dumbfounded. He'd seen what she'd attempted with Ogoun, how summoning him had nearly consumed her. But now, standing before her with that smug smile, he made it all seem so easy.

"And as for pain . . ." His smile went cold. "Pain can be so very useful."

"You hurt me." Marie said it before thinking, startled by her own weakness.

His look was unflinching. "And I will hurt you again if it makes you stronger."

Marie thought back to the blistering pain along her skin that she had felt only a few seconds ago. He'd channeled his own pain into the illusion. The realization left her breathless. Just what kind of torture had Jon the Conjurer endured? That day when she was ten and had found him on the flogging post must have been only a bitter taste. The Man with a Thousand Lives, the slaves called him in whispers—a thousand lives' worth of pain.

Jon clicked his teeth, disappointed. "Your illusion casting needs work. If you are to open the Veil, you will be facing Legba directly. None is better at trickery than him. You must be ready for anything. Look at you now, so guarded. So cold. Your emotions are your weapons, Marie. They can be channeled to make illusions stronger. Rage can turn a priest mad. Lust can make a man bed a girl with the face of a goat. Anything can be real so long as the emotion can be felt. Do you understand?"

Marie remained still, afraid to answer. She'd made a terrible, terrible mistake. Perhaps Sanite had been right about Jon all along. Perhaps he really was the devil in the flesh.

Jon strode toward her and snatched her chin in his hands, forcing her to meet his eyes. They were completely black, so far away from the silvery-white glow of the Quarter Queen's true power. "Do you understand, Marie?"

She nodded, eyes closed. When she opened them, it was not Jon who stood before her but . . . Jacques. Marie stumbled away from him. "*No.*"

"Hello, Marie," said Jacques.

"Jacques?" Her voice trembled. It was him. The same golden-brown skin, the gentle wave of his hair, the light green of his eyes.

Jacques smiled warmly at her. "Come now, my love. We've been apart long enough. Wouldn't you agree?"

Marie flung herself into the circle of his arms. Jacques held her close, stroking the small of her back. Oh, how she had ached for his touch. In those first days, she'd cursed the gods and the saints for leaving her without him. But now she thanked them. She would light a thousand candles upon their altars, and on Sundays she would kneel before God and say her prayers. Because they had finally been answered—her husband was home. Marie pressed her lips to Jacques's, welcoming his sweet kiss.

She cupped his face, pulling him to her. His mouth crushed hers, hand tangling in her hair, tilting her head up so he could plunge his tongue inside, deliciously slick against hers. He devoured her with a hunger sinuous and dark. Pleasure blistered her skin, the kiss more intense than she had ever shared with her beloved. He swallowed her moan.

But it was not Jacques that she tasted. No, she tasted cigar smoke, and something else. Something bitter. Vervain. The herb to calm the mind, to better cast *illusions*.

Marie screamed, leaping away. The illusion fizzled before her eyes, and it was Jon staring at her now, his eyes flinted amber, not her husband's gentle green.

"You bastard!" Marie hissed, her face flaming. "You had no right. No fucking right—"

"You said you wanted me to teach you. And now you scorn the lesson."

Marie froze. He was right. If she had any hope of opening the Veil, she would face far worse, wouldn't she? She had to be ready, even if it meant baring her soul to a man like Jon. Slowly, she nodded.

Jon grinned. "We go again."

Marie closed her eyes. When she opened them again, there was her husband, smiling at her. She knew it was an illusion, she did. But this spell was stronger than any she'd ever felt, stronger even than Sanite's. In the distance, someone was screaming loudly. Why wouldn't they stop? In a surge of horror, Marie realized the screams were her own.

"Get out of my fucking head!"

Jacques stood over her, sneering all the while. He turned his head to the side, amused by her agony. "Now, why would I do that?"

Marie gritted her teeth, forcing herself to see past the illusion. It felt real only because of the pain, she thought. If pain could make an illusion stronger, then it could dispel it too. She thought suddenly of the pain losing Jacques had wrought on her, the whispers of *Widow Paris* at her back, the snickers of jealous biddies who were happy to see her brought so low. She thought back to even before that, to the pain of losing her grand-mère to yellow fever. And then the very first pain . . . the pain of losing her own mother. The woman who had taken one look at Marie's magic and abandoned her on sight. Marie dredged up the pain of her earliest memories like pulling a stone from the dark of a well. When she opened her eyes, it was Jon staring at her now. Not Jacques.

Marie climbed to her feet, glowing with victory. Jon stood across from her, panting from the force of his own spell. The one *she'd* backfired onto him. Just what had he seen in his own terrible vision? Then she remembered his words, filled with the ache of painful memories conjured again. *I am the last of my kind. My wife ... my children ...*

It mattered not, Marie decided. Because in time she would know all.

"Now . . ." Jon smiled through the pain, dark eyes full of wonder. "Now you are learning."

CHAPTER FIFTEEN

REE

Ree was in her mother's dream. Or, her mother was in *hers*. She couldn't be sure anymore. It was as if her mother's eyes had become her own. She saw cryptic flashes, shining in and out like bright pops of light: her mother facing down sneering alchemists, venom from the snake's fangs, fire in her blood. Ree twisted and writhed, screaming into the oblivion for some sense of relief. But no one answered. She felt herself falling and falling until the darkness of sleep overcame her.

When she woke again, the pain had receded, and she was moving down a long dark corridor, drifting quietly as if the air itself carried her bare feet across the cold stone. The corridor stretched before her, the darkness pooling around her as thick as tar. But she could see something moving at the end of the hall, pale as a ghost. It was a long tattered white veil. The veil drifted, as if stirred by a stroke of wind, revealing a tall black door.

And someone was knocking from the other side.

The pounding got louder and louder, a maddening sound that made Ree smash her hands over her ears and squeeze her eyes shut tight. *Open your eyes.* Her mother's voice. Always her mother's voice.

When Ree opened her eyes again, she had moved—she was

standing directly in front of that great black door. The knocking had ceased. The corridor hung empty, filled with blessed silence. And then the white veil parted before her, as if in invitation.

Come closer, Marie Laveau, a voice sang from the other side, *and right your mother's wrongs.*

Slowly, Ree parted the silken veil further and pressed her ear to the door. It shuddered, and she heard the wailing of a thousand ancestors, their voices carrying as one. *We are many,* they called from the other side, *and we are coming.*

Ree woke with a strangled cry, casting a wild glance about the room. There were no more terrible whispers calling from the shadows, and the only veil that dared move now was the curtain hanging over the terrace door, drifting with the early morning draft. Two pretty redheads lay on either side of her, fast asleep. She'd been channeling her mother. After finding Claudette at the Pint & Pea and learning the truth of her father, Ree had felt a shift in her mother's condition. An unseen desperate tug that beckoned her closer. It was Marie—calling to Ree from the Veil to channel her. But Ree had little experience with this kind of magic. She needed a teacher, someone to guide her the way Jon had guided Marie. But Claudette Duvalier had flatly refused, leaving her with only the cryptic instruction that channeling was best done when she was asleep, when her spirit was closer to the loa.

But she couldn't think about that, not when someone was loudly knocking at her door. Miffed, Ree shoved the arm draped over her bosom aside and got to her feet. A silken robe flew into her waiting hand, and she threw it on, quickly tying it into a clumsy knot. By the time she reached the door, a hand was already turning the doorknob.

Ree yanked the door open, a hex already on her lips. "Oh, for fuck's sake—"

Henryk waited on the other side, a dark velvet cloak drawn over his face, auburn strands in his eyes. But of course he'd done his best to slip in unseen. What business did a holy man have in a pleasure house at this hour? A flicker of impatience crossed his face.

"We must speak." At Ree's protest, he cut his gray eyes at her. *"Now."*

Ree snapped her fingers, and the lovely courtesans of the Chateau Rouge were already scampering from the room, ducking past Ree and Henryk without a backward glance. The courtesans of the Quarter's infamous Red Palace were known not just for their flaming hair, but for their talents in discretion.

Henryk's gaze swept the room, taking in the rumpled silken sheets, the emptied wineglasses strewn over the armoire and table in rigid silence. When he finally spoke, his voice was so carefully even. *Too* even. "Do you always pay for your fun?"

"I paid Monsieur LaCroix for the room and the dinner," she corrected with an impish smile. "The whores were simply a gift."

Henryk's lips quirked. Was it stifled bemusement? A hint of the old Cajun boy who used to humor her games and advances? "I see."

"What do you want, Inquisitor?" Despite her own smile, Ree was in no mood for Quarter politics. She'd been expecting that he might find her again. He had warned her of as much. But he did not look as if he was going to drag her in for questioning. The look on his face told her other troubles concerned him.

"When you intervened that day in the square, you set a new game in motion," said Henryk, the gruff burn of his voice catching her off guard. She'd missed it. "Corbin saw you, saw what you could do for him. I don't think you understand what you've done: You made yourself useful to the most dangerous man in New Orleans. You've caught the eyes of the wolf. Next will be his teeth. I wonder, what does your mother think of this?"

It was a tactic to draw the truth from her, but she would confess to nothing.

"Thank you for the warning, but us Laveaus can handle ourselves."

"Did you handle your little tiff in Congo Square?"

Her lips pursed into a sour line at the thought of that particular chaos. Only two days had passed since, but already so much had happened. "I've not forgotten."

"Well, neither has the Church. Or"—he sighed—"Felix Corbin. They've reached an agreement of sorts, a public response that suits both of their agendas."

Ree bent over the armoire to grab her brush, intentionally flashing a good deal of flesh as she did. When she turned around, gazing at him over her shoulder in a half-lidded expression, she watched with some pleasure as his eyes immediately shifted to the floor, then back to her.

"Do you understand what this means?"

Ree raked the brush through her curls, satisfied with the way the Inquisitor followed her every action, his gaze lingering on the spill of her cleavage when she turned just so.

By the loa, what was she doing? Toying with him? Was she trying to drive them both mad? She told herself it was easier like this, to keep herself removed from him as best she could, to treat him the same as every other pretty boy and girl she'd had her fun with. Except Henryk Broussard was not like the others, never had been to her. *Tell him.* But she couldn't; her pride would not allow her that. So instead, she settled on saying, "No, but I have the strangest feeling you'll enlighten me."

"They want a witch to answer for this, Ree," explained Henryk. His face contorted, almost cruelly. "Both the Church and Corbin have decided they can't simply abide such a show of magic. They fear it would make them look weak. And they've . . . well, they've called for an execution."

Ree's lips curled. "They are weak." The Vatican could peddle their myths on another street corner for all she liked, so long as they left the Voodoos to their own lot.

"After the Quarter Quarrel, they won't allow another one." He went quiet, pensive almost. "You've quite the parentage. You should know it has made you a target."

Ree went very still. She hoped her face betrayed nothing. She'd hardly had a moment to herself to process these new revelations in her life—Marie's secrecy, Jon's reputation, and her place in all of their twisted history. The last thing she needed was to give the Church some sign of weakness.

"Your mother had a very telling relationship with her most famous enemy," Henryk continued. "One that intrigued the Vatican. It was a long-held position that you might be the daughter of the one they call Jon the Conjurer. Your bloodline makes you the bigger threat to the Vatican. The bigger—"

He stopped himself short, but there the word was, hanging between them unspoken. *Enemy.* "The only payment this city has ever demanded is blood. So play your games and have your fun, princess, so long as you understand, the city will demand a witch's blood spilled before next dawn." He moved to the door, their business done. "But they can't spill what is already gone."

This warning was not for her. It was for Anabelle. She couldn't understand in the slightest why he was telling her this now, why he could possibly want to spare a witch from a fate his faction so easily doomed witches to. If he was warning her, there was only so much he could say, she knew. But what he could not tell her in words, he spoke with his eyes. She knew what she must do.

"Why are you telling me this?"

Henryk's eyes held hers, silently willing her to understand. He hesitated. "I can't forget what you did for me."

She'd saved his life, pulled him back from the doom of yellow fever, even when her own mother had thought him beyond saving. And how? How had she done that? It was with her father's magic, she knew now. Magic her mother had denied her and kept secret.

Ree knew that she shouldn't—shouldn't ask, shouldn't even think of the possibility—but she couldn't help herself. She was selfish. "And what of me? I don't suppose you are willing to spare me in the end, Inquisitor?" questioned Ree, her voice cold. Her eyes turned toward the window, to the city that sang with music and spells, where dawn would wash the day anew.

Henryk stopped. And just like that, she watched him falter, saw the moment a crack had worked its way across the stoic lines of his handsome face.

For a moment, the room fell away. It was just the two of them. So many words unspoken. So many feelings kept carefully guarded. It might have hurt her less to know that he was furious with her. He'd be right to be. But it was his indifference that wounded her the most. She was just too stubborn a woman to dare tell him about her regrets. And would he listen, truly? She was not sixteen anymore. And he was no longer a simple parish boy.

Ree reached for the decanter beside the hairbrush and stiffly poured herself a drink, the sweet wine pooling in her glass, shining like a ruby. She brought it to her lips and drank, the taste flat and cloying. Hollow. What was wrong with her? But she knew. It was *him*. Ever since Henryk Broussard had returned to New Orleans, she'd felt herself become unmoored, slowly coming undone at the seams, bit by bit.

"Did you become an Inquisitor because of me? Because I . . . did not go with you?" she said after a while. She didn't know exactly why she asked, only that in that moment it seemed like she should.

He grunted, a bitter noise that twisted her chest. "You think too highly of yourself."

The Inquisitor's hand stilled on the door before he slowly turned to face her again. There was conflict brewing beneath the mask of perfect restraint he wore so well, a flash of longing, a moment of searing ache she'd become acquainted with in the long years since their final goodbye. After all, she knew that face well.

Because it was her own.

It was the one she'd masked beneath her games and lovemaking and petty ways.

"We fooled ourselves once, Ree. In the end, we both became what fate always intended. And the sad thing is . . ." Slowly, Henryk's gray eyes met hers. There was some unnamed emotion in them. Some feeling she swore she'd seen before, long ago. "We were never going to be able to run away from that," he murmured finally, and left.

The drink shook in Ree's hand, and she stared down at it, stunned, silently relishing the cool weight of the crystal against her skin.

She hurled it against the mirror, fracturing the glass, dark wine seeping into the cracks.

Her reflection splintered into a thousand different faces: the witch, the failing daughter, the lovesick fool. Different masks, she told herself. There was only one problem now.

None of them quite fit anymore.

The sun was just beginning to set over Congo Square, a dark purplish-blue light creeping through the dark horizon like a vein.

Henryk Broussard stood before a wooden stake, a woman shackled to it. She bucked against her bindings, rustling the aurum chains, a hood covering her head. But Ree would know her anywhere. Anabelle. A small crowd had gathered for the bloody spectacle to come.

Upon an overlooking terrace, Ree positioned herself for a better view. Her mother owned the room above the little café below, one of the handful of safe houses she kept about the city. Her name was not on the deed, of course, but the name of a man she'd long spelled under her command should the need arise. Ree had thought her mother's tactics paranoid, but now, as she gazed upon the High Inquisitor below, she felt herself grateful for her mother's farsighted strategy.

Other Les Magiques had taken great measures to put as much distance between themselves and Congo Square as they could. But not Ree. She needed to set things right.

Beside her, a redheaded alchemist was shaking on his knees, his hands bound behind his back. She crouched down, trailed her scarlet-painted fingernails along his back like a spider, deeply enjoying every quiver that racked his body.

He bucked against her, wild with panic. But there was nothing he could do. She'd thought to save some aurum from the vial she'd given Marcel. It had been easy enough to slip into this alchemist's drink. And now that last little bit was inside his belly, spreading in his veins.

"Shhh," she cooed against his ear. "*Serves him right.* You remember those words, don't you, love?"

The stricken look on his face told her that he very much did. She saw grim flashes of Marcel swinging from that rope. It brought her some pleasure to know he was seeing it too. The alchemist was trembling. She hadn't bothered to get his name. She didn't need it, and he wasn't worth the trouble. By her mother's saints, she'd managed to snatch him from the floor of some alehouse without being spotted and had dragged his sorry ass up two flights of stairs. She didn't need his crying. What she *needed* to do was concentrate. The kind of magic she needed to work was fickle. It was what Marie Laveau might call reckless magic.

Ree slid a gold-tipped knife from the pocket of her satchel and cut crisscross into the alchemist's back, quick, so the poor fool wouldn't feel a thing, but he bucked and moaned, slobbering all over the rag she'd stuffed into his mouth. Ree ignored him and returned to her spell. She'd done this spell before, a variation of a road opener incantation, though it had been, like many other times, to suit her own whims. Pluck a few cards from a man's hands, swap them out for others, gain a few coins. She figured a man couldn't be much different.

Legba, she invoked. *Lord of the Crossroads. The gatekeeper to all paths.*

Silence. The wind changed direction. Her dark curls fell to one side of her neck. And then a cold whisper at her ear. *Hello, priestess.*

Ree could smell the warm spice of rum on his breath, the syrupy sweetness of hot pralines. Papa Legba was fond of her mother, she knew. He'd come to Ree in flashes and spurts before and seemed to like her mischief well enough. It made her wonder what he saw in her mother, her endless virtue.

Open the path before me, Ree silently prayed.

The wind whispered coldly, *Whatever for?*

Ree kept her eyes closed, forcing herself to concentrate. The alchemist was rocking back and forth, making ugly groaning sounds. *To spare one of your own,* she said.

You dare to use your magic for more than yourself, child? Papa made a sound of startled amusement. A tickle of laughter at her ear. *As you wish.*

Henryk circled the pyre, pouring oil upon the logs arranged at its base.

Ree glanced down. The alchemist was crying fat, ugly tears that she was certain his own Grand Wizard would have little patience for. Silas would not take kindly to her mishandling one of his own. Trouble for another day.

Henryk faced Anabelle, quivering on the stake. In one sweep of his gloved hands, he removed the cover from her head, revealing her tear-streaked face. He removed the old cloth stuffed into her mouth.

"I've done nothing wrong! I've done nothing," Anabelle sobbed.

Henryk remained unmoved, face like chiseled marble, carefully blank. "You were caught practicing magic outside of your sanctioned time and place. You are directly linked to a magical insurrection that left innocent people dead." His lips twisted. "So, you've done plenty wrong."

Henryk brushed a dark coil from Anabelle's cheek. She recoiled, eyes bright with fear. Perhaps Ree was wrong. He might still have some compassion in him yet.

She knew that she should be focused on Anabelle, on seeing this task done so that she could return to the work of saving her mother. But her heart shattered at the sight of Henryk preparing a witch to burn, mechanical and rote in his manner, as if all the feeling had been bled from him. How easily he could do this to a young woman who'd never chosen her magic, or her station in life. *And how easily he might do this to me.*

Had he forgotten that he'd grown up friends with a witch, and that it was a witch who'd brought him back from the cusp of death? Was becoming an Inquisitor some sick revenge for leaving him alone on that bridge, the same as Anabelle had done to her? Beautiful as he'd grown to be, he was unrecognizable to her. In his cruelty, he'd become a terrible kind of monster. She found herself doubting everything. Maybe she was mistaken. Maybe he'd never tried to warn her about Anabelle. And maybe, just maybe, the monster might want her next.

Father Antoine hobbled from the crowd, dressed in his black friar robes, the heavy crucifix at his neck catching the fading sunlight. He made a solemn cross in the air before Anabelle, speaking quietly, performing her last rites.

But Anabelle would not need them. Not today. Not ever, if Ree had her way.

Henryk lowered the torch upon the kindle. Anabelle went slack in shock, the fire hissing as it took on the logs and caught to roaring flame.

Ree cast her eyes on the space in Congo Square she'd traced with the matching veve that she'd marked the alchemist with. *Now,* she murmured to the air.

In the passing of one breath, Anabelle was screaming, a sound that tore the air, and in the next, she was gone before the fire could touch her. There was a *pop!*, and in her place the alchemist appeared. Another *pop!*, and a shaking Anabelle landed beside Ree. The crowd gasped.

"Ree—" Anabelle sobbed, but Ree put a finger to her lips.

Onlookers crossed themselves, followed by cries of witchcraft, of devilry afoot.

The wind shifted. *Perhaps your mother was right about you.* Papa Legba laughed, a sound that sent a cold shiver down her back. His voice was preternaturally deep, eerily resonant—everywhere all at once. *You are learning yet, Marie Laveau.* And then he was gone.

The fire ate quickly along the alchemist's feet first, traveling higher and higher. His screams came rippling from his throat, wild and undone. Henryk stood back in shock, but there was nothing to be done. The fire consumed the alchemist whole.

Anabelle stared up at Ree in shock. Ree's heart stammered in her chest at the sight of the fresh bruises along Anabelle's dark skin, the charred marks where the aurum had burned her. Her arms were still bound, thankfully in rope. Ree cut it with the knife and waited for the moment Anabelle might strike her, might lash out like she did in Congo Square some days ago. But she did nothing, tears pouring down her cheeks. She flung her arms around Ree and wept. Ree pulled her trembling body close, at a loss for words.

"*I'm sorry,*" Anabelle sobbed into the crook of Ree's neck.

But there was no time for apologies, not when the air itself burned, thick with the rancid odor of curdling flesh. Black smoke rose from the flames, past the cottages and gallery houses, rising into the darkened sky. Ree saw Henryk's eyes dart around the square, then higher, to the buildings with a vantage, before finally landing on her.

The Inquisitor, shrouded in harsh, swirling smoke, stood still. Gray eyes locked onto hers.

And for that one moment, she saw someone else standing in his place. The face of the man he might have been. Or maybe, perhaps, who he truly was deep down.

The moment passed as quickly as it had come. Henryk's face hardened over, cool stone sealing itself into place. He'd seen her, it was true. But it was too late.

For the space of just one heartbeat, she'd seen him too.

Ree retreated inside, pulling Anabelle with her.

The sun was setting as Ree led Anabelle out the back of the building. She'd thought to cover them both in old muslin caps and thick wool dresses that swallowed the shape of their bodies. They disappeared into the thick of the crowd that overtook the street. Folks passed them by on their way home for evening supper, not one sparing them a single glance. Purple twilight filled the sky. It would soon be dark.

By the time they reached the bayou house, the moon shone silver. Nan was waiting around back, holding Thistle by the reins. To Ree's surprise, Claudette was there too, leaning against a tree, emerald eyes glittering. After learning the truth of her father, Ree hadn't thought that L'Enchanteresse would leave her uptown house to get mixed up in her problems. When Ree and Anabelle approached, Nan wordlessly bowed. *I am not your Quarter Queen,* Ree wanted to say. *I never will be.*

Their queen was in the house, lying as still as a statue while hexed poison worked its way through her blood. She was running out of time. But right now Ree's problem was the one at hand, the one staring her in the face with bloodshot eyes.

"Ree—"

"Go," Ree said, her voice gruff.

"We could—"

Anabelle reached for Ree, but she caught her hand and twisted it cruelly away. "We could not."

"But I—"

"Do not say it," Ree hissed. "Don't you dare."

Anabelle held back her tears. Ree watched her face, that same beautiful face that just days ago made her heart leap into her throat. She'd wanted more, and she'd been a fool.

"I will save my mother," Ree said. "And when she returns, who do you think she will punish first? You committed treason against the Quarter Queen."

Anabelle blanched. "I had good reason!"

She did. And it did not matter. Ree could understand it, this sin. But she would not forgive.

It was better this way, Ree told herself. Marie Laveau would be out for blood. This way, she would be spared any more pain. They all would.

Ree nodded toward the horse. "Go now. Get away from this saint-forsaken city." She held the tears from her eyes. "And never, ever return."

Far away, in the city, the church bells were tolling. Anabelle took Ree's hand one last time. Ree felt a strange wind cross her face and lift her curls into the night. Legba was laughing. Maybe all of the loa were. Maybe they enjoyed seeing what a fool her heart had turned her into. But Ree couldn't bring herself to care, not in this moment. She tried to see in Anabelle's face all the things they could not say, that they would never say to each other again. Ree tried to understand how they'd gotten here, how they'd hurt each other so deeply, so carelessly, but in the end, she could not. She let her hand go.

And then Anabelle was saddled and off, riding away into the damp dark, down roads unknown. Ree watched her go and muscled the tears from her eyes.

"You did a kind thing."

Ree turned to see Claudette at her side. There was an unexpected softness in her face, the face that Ree had only ever seen taut and toying, the cruel perfection of a jewel.

"Then why doesn't it feel like it?" Ree's voice caught.

"Because the kindest thing you could do for her was also one of the most painful things you could do for yourself." Quietly, she said, "It is not what Marie would have done. Perhaps I was wrong about you, child. Perhaps you will not be the queen your mother was. Perhaps"—Claudette turned her eyes to the long road ahead—"you will be different."

Ree choked back a bitter laugh. She was really no different from Anabelle Dupont; they'd committed sins, caused enough pain with their games. They just played by different rules. And that was the thing, wasn't it? Sins were never forgiven in a city like New Orleans, not truly.

In the end, someone always paid.

CHAPTER SIXTEEN

MARIE

Marie clung to her side of the rowboat, searching the faceless dark. As their boat sailed along, mist rose from the black waters below in silvery folds, swallowing everything in its path in slow, greedy gulps. Everything but her fear.

Truth be told, the moment they'd pushed off from the wharf, Marie had felt a seed of dread growing in her belly, a feeling that now quietly blossomed into the unshakable panic that they were, in fact, going the *wrong* way. But if Jon shared her fear, he didn't feel inclined to say. He sat beside her, his legs languidly crossed, dressed in a sharp black suit and matching frock coat, a gentleman's top hat perched on his head.

He studied her with that self-assured tilt of a grin that made another, darker feeling grow inside of her. Marie caught his eye, then quickly glanced away, embarrassed at how easily he made her flush, the way her heart fluttered fast as a canary. Three weeks had passed since she'd started her lessons with the Conjurer. Always strictly by midnight. Always alone. But tonight was different. The hour wasn't quite midnight, and they were far from alone now.

They were joined by the tide-turner Nonc Croc—Uncle Croc, as the Cajun boatmen knew to call him—who was kneeling at the stern, one hand holding a small brass harmonica to his mouth while he played a few woeful notes, the other plunged into the inky water, his fingers guiding their boat along with his magical coaxing. The old man had strange, wintry blue eyes set into the weathered lines of his brown face, and he wore a braided cord of hemp around his neck that dangled with jagged seashells, pearl fragments, and carved driftwood beads, each piece an offering to the water loa all tide-turners served—La Sirene, the devastatingly beautiful silver-tailed goddess, and Agwe, loa of the ocean, patron of fishermen and sailors.

Marie tugged at the long black-latticed veil over her face. The veil's thin fabric did nothing to keep the water's spray from her cheeks, the subtle hiss from La Sirene that something was amiss in her waters. Through its netting she glimpsed the moon in a gauzy blur, glowing and full, a lone white eye peering down at them from a starless sky. Although Jon hadn't explained himself when he handed her the long black gown and matching veil, Marie found something painfully familiar about the cool silk that clung to her, forming a strange second skin that felt heavier than it should. They were mourning garments, the costume one might expect of a grief-stricken widow. It was a part she had played before, after all.

As Nonc Croc steered them away from the Quarter, red and green and gold lights shone in the distance, cutting through the fog like flames dancing on their wicks. As their rowboat drew nearer, Marie could hear music, and if she strained hard enough, she could make out the barest traces of other sounds beneath those bright notes. A peal of maddening laughter. The dull echo of what might have been a scream in the dark.

"Where are we going, Jon? Is this supposed to be another lesson?" demanded Marie. She hadn't meant to sound so wary, but she found his silence made her more uneasy than the shadowy waters that surrounded them.

"No lessons," said Jon as his gaze slid toward her. For a moment, that spark of mirth dimmed, a golden candle snuffed out. He was utterly serious. "Only a story. And you, my lovely student, will decide how it ends."

Jon's voice was low and rhythmic as he began to speak over the rolling fog.

"They say the ancient Greeks had many a god stranger than ours, *hungrier* than ours," began Jon. "When a band of slaves ran away into the wilderness, they stumbled upon a tall man dancing right over a bed of ivy and bloodied animal skins, the glittering white bone of a bull's head pulled over his face. The slaves froze, seeing too late that this was no man at all. At least no *mortal* one. He was the one they called the mad god Dionysus, lord of ritual and theater. The mad god was eager for a show." His gaze found Marie's, held it steadfast in the dark, his eyes bright as torches. "And one does not refuse the gods."

Nonc Croc stopped playing. Even he was listening. The only sound that remained was the soft creaking of their boat as it cut across the river's face.

"'*Fear not, mortals,*'" continued Jon, "Dionysus declared as he rose to meet them at once, arms wide open as if they were very old friends reunited at last. '*For I am as gracious as the gods come. I seek only to be entertained.*' Overjoyed to be embraced so easily by the divine, the men desperately entreated Dionysus to lift their chains. And free them he did."

The story sprang from his tongue like a dark spell, conjured before them in the air like smoke. But Marie heard something else simmering beneath his words, something crueler. Jon wasn't just telling a story of violence. He was remembering one. "One man let out a bloodcurdling howl, a sound that could wake the dead. Another grew teeth as long as a wolf's fangs. One by one, the men shredded the clothes from their bodies and tore the chains from their feet and hands. As free as Dionysus had promised. But when Dionysus held up his mirror, laughing all the while, they saw only their own reflections as they were. As *men*. Confused, they looked amongst themselves, seeing only yellow-eyed beasts, deformed beyond all recognition. Driven mad, the men ripped one another limb from limb as Dionysus eagerly clapped along, pleased at last."

Marie suppressed a shiver. What an odd story, and what terrible gods the Greeks served. "So, what were they in the end? Beasts or men?"

Jon considered her question in silence. For a moment, his expression was dark, frustratingly unreadable. Then it was gone, and the corners of his eyes crinkled pleasantly as his lips crooked into that wry grin she'd come to relish. "Who could say? Suppose it's just as well, 'cause the truth is, love, folks are what they believe they are."

Jon's story made it easy to imagine that Nonc Croc was not a tide-turner at all, that the mist-laden Mississippi River had transfigured into the dour, shuddering waters of the River Styx, that her guide was now the silent ferryman who carried them across the threshold of the living into the barren dark of the underworld. But it was not the shores of the underworld their rowboat slowly approached.

It was a steamboat.

They called her *La Danse de la Lune*—*La Lune*, as she was known to most in the city. She was the boat that glided down the river by day but whose magic truly danced only at night. It was less a steamboat, Marie had heard, and more a glorious theater cast adrift, a nest of decadence so wild that not even the likes of the French Quarter could contain her.

Her body rose silently from the still black waters like a great-bellied beast, glistening and wide. The steamboat's three decks were gracefully layered, each tier encircled by golden railings strung with spherical ornaments that burned with a strange alchemical light, the color pulsing between red, green, and gold. Twin smokestacks jutted from the crown, gently breathing ashen plumes against the night. At the prow was the figurehead of a maiden in a wreathed headdress angled out over the dark water, a carving of the moon in her hands. The moon glowed a dark, smoldering red, and she held it tenderly to her chest, as if cradling her own bleeding heart.

They reached the rear of the steamboat, where the paddle wheel turned noiselessly, lapping at the bluish-black water beneath. Nonc Croc's fingers glided through the air, and a strip of the river rose, as if being conducted. It churned and spun, forming itself into a foaming staircase to the steamboat's second deck. He waved them on. "Get on, now. Only goin' to wait 'til half past the hour. Not a second more, y'all hear?" When Jon cast him a look, the tide-turner blanched, his grin turning lopsided. "No trouble, Conjurer-man. No trouble at all."

Nonc Croc started back up on his harmonica. Marie heard it still even after she ascended the churning staircase onto the steamboat's second deck, the notes chasing her from the roiling mist. At the last step, Jon hoisted her onto the steamboat's second landing. Marie gripped the golden railing, then slowly lifted her eyes to Jon's waiting face.

In one perfect movement, he slid on a mask: a dark, sleek thing shaped into the taut lines of a panther's face. Marie felt the veil gently lift from her face, acutely aware of Jon's eyes on her. He allowed his gaze to linger for a moment longer, then slowly pulled the veil back down. He offered his arm, and together they made their way across the barren deck. There was a dim pulse of music on the wind that grew louder and louder as they approached a set of gold-plated doors guarded by a bald white man draped in a deep wine-colored garment that folded over his shoulder.

As they neared, Jon suddenly squeezed Marie's hand, the barest of touches. Lightning coursed through her. "You should know one thing," he whispered under his breath. She saw the tawny glint of his eyes behind the panther mask, the only tell that it was him at all. "The moment we cross that threshold, we will be in . . . *different* territory. Our magic will not be highest here. Remember that."

Marie remained silent, unsure of what to make of this warning. Though she could not be certain of the occasion of their visit, she was quite sure they were on a steamboat full of rich folks, not one riddled with monsters and enemies. What need would they have for Voodoo tonight?

At the door, the man bowed his head a little, acknowledging their presence. The bronze-leafed circlet on his brow shone against the boat's dangling lights. When he spoke, it was with the leaden inflection of an actor made to say their lines until all manner of feeling had been dulled down to nothing at all. "What spills first on the altar of gods in gift? A chalice to toast, or the blade that tears flesh and bone in rift?"

"Wine before blood," Jon answered at once.

The doorman's eyes were steady on Jon, then slowly flicked to Marie, silently gauging. Then his lips lifted into something like a smile but not quite. "Welcome, revelers. May your thirst be quenched, your appetites sated at last." He stepped aside like a curtain being drawn back just as the golden doors swung open. And with that, Marie and Jon stepped inside.

Marie was met with a sight that left her breathless with confusion. In the spectacle before her, she saw none of the old French or Spanish influence that ran through the French Quarter. This was something older, stranger.

It was as if they'd stepped into a different world, a different time altogether.

La Lune's entrance hall had been transformed into a temple of some kind, the air choked with sweet, swirling incense, sweat, and something unmistakably metallic. Something alchemical. But there was no Brotherhood here, only the city's elite dressed in garish Grecian costume. Musicians plucked on harps and lyres, their strings like shining threads. Men passed her draped in white and bright red, their heads encircled in gleaming laurels, halos wrought in gold. The women in black were veiled widows, like herself, and the red-cheeked maidens were almost entirely nude, their sweat-glistened flesh wreathed in holly and hyacinth that coiled over their arms and breasts. They were maenads, those mad-eyed worshippers of Dionysus, the horned god of Jon's tale.

Jon guided Marie through the crowd, beneath pillars of white marble twisted with ivy, his hand pressed upon her lower back, the part where the folds of her black gown revealed a tantalizing square of flesh. Strange as this place was, she felt assured at Jon's side in a way she had never felt before. *Not even with Jacques.* The dark thought rose from within her. The truth was, least of all with him. She had always felt fragile at her husband's side, even when she knew her magic was stronger than his, than that of most in New Orleans, and he had never failed to remind her in a thousand small ways. But not with Jon. At his side, she felt . . . his equal.

Marie could not help but admire the opulence around her: Men in jarringly angular panther-shaped masks, white-faced bulls, horned stags—beasts favored by the mad god. They danced and drank wine as she had never seen before—too dark, thick as syrup, heavily spiced with a scent that stung the air. Fat grapes and olives piled high and glistening as pyramids, fire burning in golden dishes. But something seemed wrong about it, like she was watching a mirage take hold, and the people moved in a stilted sort of rhythm, their smiles too wooden, their endless laughter crackling the smoked air. She couldn't help but feel Jon's story in the rowboat had been no mere myth.

The widows veiled in black watched her. As Jon led her on through the crowd, their eyes all seemed to be fixed on Marie, as if they could sense her kindred grief. Although her own veil hid her face well, Marie could not help but think of what they must be whispering amongst themselves: *There goes the Widow Paris.* Women watched Jon too, their eyes hungrily latching on to him. Disguised or not, Jon the Conjurer moved like a man with power—real power—and that drew women in like a honey trap. Marie's tongue burned, the words she suddenly wanted to say trapped inside her, hot grease against her throat. Envy would do her no good. It was a sin she had no right to, none at all. And yet . . . Marie bristled. She wanted to be through with this task, with these strange people and whatever business Jon thought he might have in a wild place such as this.

As if sensing her mood, Jon leaned over, his whisper a cool breath at her ear. A shiver coursed through her. "You're beautiful when you're impatient, Marie. But you'll still have to wait, my dark sun."

At the back of the hall was a marble fountain shaped into stone-white nymphs, their gaping mouths spewing waterfalls of bubbling dark wine. Behind it, a man stood guard in front of a towering black door marked with a chain of pulsing sigils that ran in strange, concentric patterns. Truth be told, Marie might have mistaken the man for a ghost or a haint. Cherry-red circles were painted on the apples of his cheeks, the rest of his face covered in chalky powder, the theatrical pomp of a stage actor.

When they approached, he leaned in close, red cheekbones jutted high as he spoke the words barring their passage in a dreamy lilt: "What follows the flesh when the soul is long gone? What comes to the front when the man in the mirror sings no song?"

From behind the door came a swelled roaring, the great and terrible shudder of a beast opening its maw. Just what was waiting behind that door? "Beast after body," answered Jon.

Marie silently turned the words over in her mind. *Wine before blood. Beast after body.* The phrase hung thickly in the air, a spell complete, a dark ritual coming to a close.

For a moment, she was sure that he would turn them away. Then a smile broke across his face, quick as lightning, stretching from ear to ear. "Magnifique! Y'all best hurry on now," the doorman urged, that smile still frozen into factitious cheer. "Show 'bout to start."

He led them through the door and down a staircase that spiraled so deep into the boat that it seemed to lead to nothing at all. Marie reached for the banister that ran along its length, but the moment she touched it, she quickly withdrew her hand. The metal quivered beneath her fingertips, alive and writhing like a wet-bellied thing.

She held firm to Jon's hand as they descended. Down and down they went, the walls growing tighter, closer, the music from above waning with every step as they wound deeper into the steamboat's shadowed innards. Marie had been sure there was only one deck beneath them, so why then did the steps lead so deep? She was sure the staircase should have ended two turns down. The walls tremored every few seconds, as if something were slowly worming its way through them. She was beginning to think there was something deeply unnatural about this place. Something very *wrong*.

When they descended to the bottom deck, their guide led them down a tight passageway hissing with steam, then into a private viewing box that sat high above rows and rows of seats filled with chanting people—widows sheathed behind their veils, maidens, and golden-leafed men—some banging their fists, others hooting and howling, their eyes excitedly trained on a pit carved into the center of the room. Except the pit was dressed to be more of a stage—covered in a flowing red velvet curtain that was pulled to a close. If she didn't know any better, she might have believed they were in an opera house in the Quarter. But this was not the Quarter. And this place, she knew at last, was no opera house. It was more of a colosseum. Which shouldn't be possible. This place was larger than any steamboat could conceivably contain, even one as abundant as *La Lune*. There was magic at work here.

"What is this place?" asked Marie.

Jon's gaze was trained on the pit below. "I would say it was hell. But I hear even a realm such as that has rules. There are no rules here." Then he turned, considered her from behind the sharp, pointed lines of his panther mask. His voice was flat. Final. "Only misery."

Frantic chanting overtook the crowd. The sound was deafening. They raised their Hands of Glory in the dark, a sea of silver flames dancing in open white palms. She'd scented something metallic and alchemical on the steamboat's second deck. And now she knew why. Because they were here.

The Brotherhood of the White Hand.

She counted at least a dozen of them—the alchemists in their hooded robes drawn over their sallow faces. A man in the front row with long white hair suddenly stood, turning to address the crowd. It was Gailon. She recognized him immediately—because he was one of the few in the entire chamber who did not conceal his face. No mask. No covering. And why should he? In Marie's opinion, the Grand Wizard was the special kind of idiot who relished in the notoriety. He wanted everyone to know—to *see*—the results of his work. He stood, draped in the Brotherhood's colors: a long black robe that flowed out around him like rippling dark water, trimmed in glowing white sigils. The moonstone brooch at his chest shone in the shifting torchlight, the mark of the pale hand.

The alchemist lifted his white staff, then slammed it on the floor, sending a shock wave of power throughout the chamber, hushing the crowd at once.

And then the curtain rose.

Ten black men were chained together in a line. Emaciated down to bones. Their faces deeply swollen from fresh bruising. They were slaves. Quite possibly runaways. It was true, runaways were often dealt the worst blows by their masters, anything to weaken the resolve of anyone who might harbor similar notions of escape.

Marie's chest constricted. This was not going to be a show, not one she would ever pay to see. This was going to be punishment. Public. And if the chanting crowd was any indication—unspeakably brutal.

Gailon's voice thundered out to the crowd, his words cracking the air like a lash.

"*Transforma!*"

The first man let out a screech.

His arm split cleanly open—bone bulging, bits of pink fleshy muscle exposed and writhing as it reconfigured itself into a new shape at the alchemist's behest. The rest of the slaves watched in wild fear, shaking and trembling. The smallest of the ten wet himself. Marie's eyes shifted through the crowd, searching for an ounce of disgust, some sense of reason. But the crowd only watched, breathlessly enchanted.

"Transcende!"

The horde of robed alchemists answered in one hollow voice, echoing Gailon's words back to him. This wasn't cheering. This was decree. Marie gripped the railing, her gut clenching, fear and rage twisting her insides with a cold fist as a single realization struck her. The Brotherhood had not simply boarded the steamboat like the rest. They were not guests to this cursed sport, bloodthirsty spectators seeking to be entertained. They *ruled* it.

The man was bowled on the ground now, screaming and hollering as his bones broke and mended all at once, his arms extending out until they merged into a crooked winged shape. Marie didn't know much about the laws of alchemy. But she was sure of one thing—that it should never be used on people. It was for objects—for stones and metals and the like. And for elements of the natural world—fire, wind, water, earth. But not people. Never people.

Marie glanced at Jon. His eyes remained unflinchingly fixed on the spectacle. But she saw the way his jaw tightened, the hard set of his lips when the black man screamed out for mercy.

"Progredere!"

Feathers erupted from his skin, raised on horrible end. His jaw broke, unhinged and hanging, until it stretched itself into a hooked beak. His wings spread wide, his eyes bright, molten green. He let out a long, broken cry, a horrible sound that ripped from his beak and out into the chamber. The transformation was complete. Marie stared, breathless and shaking, at what the man had become. But he was not a man anymore. Not fully. The beast had come and taken his place. Marie was reminded of Jon's story on the rowboat. *Suppose it's just as well, 'cause the truth is, love, folks are what they believe they are.*

Wild cheering erupted.

Marie's eyes fell to the seat beside Gailon's, to the face she'd know anywhere. Felix Corbin. Front and center, the mayor of New Orleans grinning like a fool. Of course he was here. He was as much to blame as the Brotherhood for this madness. He would want the runaways publicly punished, even more so if their debasement lined his pockets with more coin.

Transforma, transcende, progredere! Transform, transcend, progress! The Brotherhood of the White Hand's sacred creed. She'd seen it all over the city, plastered on the shining placards that advertised their latest miracles and advancements. But this was not advancement. This was ungodly. Unnatural.

Tears stung Marie's eyes. She felt Jon shift beside her. "Do you see now? This is their altar, Marie," he whispered. "And the body is the only sacrifice."

Down the line the Grand Wizard went. Coldly repeating those words—*transforma, transcende, progredere*—until each man had been changed at last into Gailon's new image. Monstrous half beasts. A chimera—only the face of the man remained, his mouth slackened in agony, his body changed into that of a golden lion, a goat's head rising from its back, and a long-tongued serpent at the tail, swaying from side to side. A horribly grotesque merging of beasts. Another with the stretched, distended wings of a bat. A half man, half wolf. The sound of flesh tearing, bone re-forming in brutally quick succession.

Gailon tapped his staff again, and the chains fell from the beasts, hitting the ground in a resounding *clank*. The crowd surged, eager for more. It took her a second too long to realize what was happening—they were going to force them to fight to the death. Marie watched from behind her veil, wishing she could slap her hands over her ears to somehow forget the screams that scraped along their tongues, the bulge of their eyes as the lifeblood drained from their veins and across the polished stone. The more blood that spilled, the louder the crowd grew. All those cries. Gnashing teeth and wild eyes. Ravenous for more. An earsplitting throb that thrummed inside her ears, tunneling down into her bones until it could go no further.

When it was finished, the only ones who remained were the man who had first changed into the birdlike creature and another who paced the stage on all fours, more wolf than man.

Marie's stomach twisted. She was wrong. This was not some kind of crude blood sport at all. This was a perverse ritual being done in the open, permitted by a hundred waging hands. A flicker of movement caught Marie's eye. It was the wolf creature. He was only a small boy, she realized. His mouth was slack, left open to a deadened scream, a profusion of blood and bile leaked down his ruined face. Through the crowd, his eyes found Jon's. Those eyes, wide and streaked, begging for mercy. Jon stared back, his mouth clenched in silent fury. Marie felt her stomach lurching toward her throat—she was going to be sick.

The curtain snapped to a close, the show done.

Marie shot to her feet and hurried back out the way they'd come. She heard Jon's footsteps behind her. She snatched the veil from her face, whirled to face him in the empty corridor. "You brought me to this cursed place to watch *this*?!"

Jon's eyes flashed from behind the panther mask. "Not to watch. Never to watch, love. To *change*."

"I don't understand—"

"I received a message yesterday, Marie. *Wine before blood, beast after body.* Only those words were scrawled on the paper, along with the location to this boat and twenty names. Twenty names of runaway slaves sought by the city of New Orleans. The message was clear. Someone *wanted* us to find this place, Marie. To stop this madness. And that's what I—what *we* intend to do—"

"Monsieur and Madame. May I help you?" a voice called from behind them.

Jon and Marie whirled to face the doorman from before, a tray of wine in hand. "Wine for the lovers?" he asked pleasantly, offering up a sweet-smelling flute to Jon.

Marie realized that he had mistaken them for a pair of giddy paramours looking to find a safe place to take their pleasure in the dark. Surely, they were not the first folks to want to do so aboard this vessel, among the countless debaucheries and sins it encouraged. She should have been relieved, but the thought only made her sicker. It was not that some small part of her did not want that. Saints, she did. But she did not want that here. Not like *this*.

But Jon only grinned, a twinkle in his eye. "Certainly." He took the wine, drained the whole of it in one fluid tilt.

Then he drove the glass into the side of the man's throat.

Marie watched, frozen, as Jon twisted the glass sharply until blood sprayed the air. Marie was reminded of the bubbling fountain on the steamboat's second deck, the stone nymphs who frothed dark wine from their screaming mouths. His body crumpled to the floor. Jon made a flicking gesture with two fingers, and the man's corpse slid away from their path, his flaccid limbs making a wet squelching sound across the wood.

Jon pulled the panther mask from his face, quickly casting it aside into the dark. They were past games now. His real work had begun. Jon pulled her through the darkness, through another door, and they stepped into a holding pen scattered with cages. Inside were the rest of the runaways, who had not yet been transformed. One of the men shook at the bars, his eyes red-rimmed and pleading.

"Conjurer!" His gaze flitted to Marie, eyes widening when he recognized her. "Madame Laveau! Save us! Don't leave us here! Look at us, goddamn you!"

Jon kept walking. It was as if he didn't hear them. When Marie gripped his arm, he cast her a sidelong look. *We will come back for them.* They hurried along through another door, this one leading to the stage, where the curtain was still mercifully closed. By the time Jon and Marie emerged fully onto the platform, she could hear the crowd booing, calling for more bloodshed.

Only two of the men remained, if she could call them that. The boy who had become the wolf. And the first man, his dark brown arms stretched into long, distended-veined wings. The rest were scattered across the stage floor, a mess of blood-soaked clothing, torn ligaments. The air was thick with the stench of alchemy and rancid flesh.

From somewhere above them, she heard the tapping of Gailon's staff, the signal to continue with the show. The curtain would soon rise again. They had minutes, possibly seconds, before they would be discovered. And what then? Would they take on the whole of the crowd, the Brotherhood of the White Hand?

The winged man crawled to them, smearing blood across the shining wood. He looked to Marie like a fallen angel groveling at the feet of the Lord. "Conjurer," he said in a gasp. There was relief in his voice, a note of strangled hope. "Kill me," he moaned. "*Please.*"

Marie stood frozen, shaking. "Jon, no! You can't . . . you can't just . . ." Her eyes swept over the disfigured corpses on the ground. The long, bloodied smears. "There must be a way . . ."

But even as she spoke the words, she knew there was not. Because if there was, Jon the Conjurer would have done it. He was stronger than her, his magic older than even the Quarter Queen's. She understood now the hope she'd heard in the man's voice had not been for survival. It had been for rest.

"*Jon,*" Marie pleaded.

But Jon kept his eyes on the man crawling toward him. "Lock the main entrance, Marie. And lock it now." When she didn't move, he snarled, "I said lock the door *now,* Marie!"

Marie held up a hand, silently called out to Legba. Through the loa of crossroads's power, she felt along the darkness of the chamber, the air hissing and curling as her magic searched along its edges. Jon was right. This place did resist their magic. The Brotherhood's magic was too strong here, the alchemy resolute. It had steeped and hardened into diamond, nearly unbreakable. The door resisted her, bucking wildly against Papa Legba's pull, but she heard the shudder of the lock sliding into place at last, the final click of the latch.

Now Jon turned to the men, golden eyes burning with some unnamed emotion. The boy was crouched on all fours, whimpering as a hurt dog might, too frightened to approach closer. But the winged man was at Jon's feet now, his rasping breath shaking the whole of his transmuted body. Jon bent low and reached out, held the man's deformed cheek in his palm. In that moment, he seemed less the famous High Jon the Conjurer. He was a lone priest charged to perform the last rites of contrition for a dying man.

"You will be avenged," Jon promised softly. Tears leaked from the man's bright eyes, down his cheek, and into Jon's palm. A tender smile touched Jon's lips, an offering of one last small comfort. "And then you may finally rest, brother."

Jon snatched his hand away, the motion cutting the air like a sword. And at once, both men's necks snapped out of place in a sickening *crack* that made Marie flinch. They dropped to the floor and did not move again. Marie stared down at the corpses, her head throbbing. But Jon was not finished yet.

"*Rise*," he commanded the air.

One by one, the bodies on the ground began to stir. The eerie snapping of bones forcing themselves back into place, limbs twitching, as the creatures righted themselves. They rose again, not dead, and yet not fully alive either. In their eyes glowed a strange purplish light, a cold flame that should never burn.

"Jon? What is this?"

But, saints, she knew. This was the magic that lived beyond the Veil. This was death. And they were zombi. The undead circled around Jon, ready to heed their Conjurer. The hair on Marie's arms stood on end as she watched the zombi gather around him, awaiting his command. Another stench filled the air, stronger even than the smell of death. It was spilled rum, the ash from a burning cigarette, the cool darkness of grave soil.

Jon's head suddenly snapped backward. He remained that way—frozen, his face directed upward—as if someone had pulled him by an invisible string.

"Jon?" But he was not Jon.

The loa were here. But he was not simply channeling one of the divines. He had been mounted—fully. His head snapped back into place. When he lifted his face to hers, Marie saw that white powder had been smeared across his cheeks in the shape of a skeleton. His eyes black as pitch. In that moment, Jon was no more.

He was Baron Samedi now.

Jon's lips twisted as he tipped his top hat at her. "Marie Laveau. Hello, chère."

He Who Holds Lordship over Death. There were other Barons, but Samedi was the head of the death gods, their supreme. Marie stood motionless before the loa of death. She felt herself within his cold grasp, her throat packed with ash and soil, unable to speak.

The Baron did not entreat her for words, nor excuses. He demanded only that she listen and listen well.

The death god stepped toward Marie, the floorboards creaking beneath his ancient weight. He wore Jon's body easily, a well-tailored suit that fit him just right.

"You keep thinking you can float on between two sides. Back and forth. Back and forth," the Baron drawled, making a crawling motion with his fingers in the air. "But you ain't gonna be able to do that much longer, little girl. War is a'comin'. Choose now, and choose good," the loa ordered, all mirth vanished from his voice. "Or *we* will choose for you, witch."

He would not ask again. This was her only warning.

And then he laughed, a dark, full-throated sound that could crack the sky in half. Jon snapped back to himself, gasping, his eyes light and shining again.

Marie stared at him. He had *let* it happen. He had welcomed Baron Samedi into his soul fully, completely, because he had wanted her to take his terrible heed. She understood now that this was not Jon's will; he was but a pawn in a much larger game. They both were.

But there was no time. In a snap of air, the curtain rose with a flourish.

For a moment, no one dared move. A breathless hush fell over the crowd staring down at the stage, a thousand eyes trying to comprehend what their dull minds could not.

Jon lifted a finger, pointing into the crowd at all those frozen faces. *Go, have your fill.*

Slowly, the dead began to walk again.

A woman screamed. Then another, until panic exploded like glass, the air crowded with shrieking terror. People surged toward the entrance. But the door was locked. Marie should know. She had locked it. Marie flexed her fingers, still feeling the heat from Legba's power. She watched as the theater dissolved into a frenzy of silk and carnage.

The zombi fell upon the crowd, moving with feral resolve. Their groaning mouths sank fervently into the flesh of the spectators, skin and bone torn in eager handfuls. A redheaded woman in ivy was dragged down by her vines, sinking to the floor, where she was wildly feasted upon by the reanimated chimera-man. Another spectator went streaking by Marie, his throat rendered completely open. Blood painted the air. Still Marie would not open the door.

She saw Corbin frozen in their midst. His eyes swept from Jon slowly to Marie. She smiled back, delighted by his fear. *I know you've broken your own rules,* her smile said. *Your rules mean nothing now.* An alchemist suddenly appeared at his side, seized him by the arm, and in a flash of pewter smoke they vanished from the room. *Cowards. Let them run.*

Gailon remained, surrounded by a handful of his men. His dark eyes were fixed on Jon with the fascination of a man watching a play conclude its final act. "Jon the Conjurer. You dare violate the natural order of things by playing with the dead?" The alchemist spoke as if he were a thing to be dissected, a specimen in his white-gloved hand.

Slowly, Jon descended the steps, putting himself directly in front of Marie, between her and Gailon. "No more than you dare desecrate the living, alchemist. They were people. *My* people."

"People?" Gailon sneered. He held up a hand, as if in correction. "*Three-fifths* a person." A toying gleam touched his eyes. "If that."

Jon spat upon the ground, teeth bared. *Your truth, but never mine. I spit you out like poison.*

Chaos still reigned around them all. The zombi fed with wild abandon. But Jon did not seem to notice. The Grand Wizard had his full attention now. "The infamous Brotherhood of the White Hand." Jon's voice dripped with mockery and musing. He held out a hand, beckoning the alchemist to dance. "Come with it then."

One of the alchemists lunged forward. Jon turned to him, eyes narrowed, and Marie felt the chill of death in the air, the subtle shift as it seized upon the alchemist, who froze in place, trembling. He touched a pale hand to his cheek and let out a horrified whine when his hand came back sticky and wet, flesh clinging to his fingers. Flesh. Slowly, skin began to slough from the alchemist's face, and beneath that, muscle peeled from bone.

He is rotting from the inside out.

Marie stared, unable to tear her eyes away from the frightening image of skin falling from place as easily as butter slid from a dish, the horrible gut-turning stench of rot as the alchemist crumbled into nothing at all. A second alchemist cried out, lifting his staff, white hair rippling behind him in a fury as he advanced toward Jon. He too froze midair, screeching wildly as his skin withered and curled from his skull like singed parchment, then peeled, dropping in wet clumps until he wasted down to nothing.

One by one, Jon turned his gaze on them, the eyes of the Baron of Death, the pitiless gaze of oblivion. And each alchemist ruptured where they stood, skin bursting open, innards and blood flying into the air, spraying the faces of the wailing women and men who were still trying desperately to escape the carnage. With a single look, the Conjurer had painted the air in a shower of blood and bone shards, drifting robes falling to the ground in emptied heaps. To have such control, such unrefined power from the loa, it was beyond anything Marie had ever seen, beyond even the likes of Sanite's power. And even then, she had a selfish thought. *This is the kind of power you seek. It may yet be yours.*

Marie could feel Baron Samedi's power radiating from him, curling at his feet like unseen smoke. Jon stalked toward Gailon, advancing with furious intent. He had the all-consuming fire of the loa in his bones, and the flames demanded blood.

Jon would not be stopped.

Gailon stood frozen, his eyes darting about the chamber, tallying the bloodshed. She had not known the Grand Wizard to be a man easily frightened. He was bested. Judging by the pinched expression on Gailon's face, he knew it too. This was not a fight he would so easily win with the Conjurer, not even in his own territory. Gailon settled his gaze over Jon, his dark eyes glittering with silent contempt, his teeth grit down into a snarl.

"Kill him! Do not let him leave this place alive," the Grand Wizard spat. And in a turn of his dark robes, he was gone.

A prickle crawled its way down Marie's spine. She turned but was already too late.

One of Gailon's alchemists loomed over her, mid-strike, white hair hissing out from his enraged face in a magical static. Marie prepared herself for the blow, a defensive spell caught in her throat, then felt the air freeze as something faster moved through it, cutting the darkness in the space of one breath. The alchemist stilled, eyes wrenched wide as his flesh was rendered completely open in one terrible *crack!*

Marie stared numbly at Jon's hand, lodged inside the dark, gaping cavity of the man's chest from behind. He wrenched it back in a wet, splintering thrust, the alchemist left to fall in a dull *thud* at his feet.

Still trembling, Marie slowly lifted her gaze—Jon stared at her, his eyes flat black. She flinched, recoiling back from him. She hadn't meant to. He had saved her, after all. But it wasn't Jon that frightened her so. It was the power that worked through him—raw and unbidden, something ancient and horribly divine that watched her right back.

"Take the others and run," Jon grunted. And when she didn't dare move, she felt his power reach for her, shaking the very air she breathed. "I said *run, Marie!*"

Marie remained a breath longer, eyes locked onto his. Then she ran.

Out she went, down the stage and into the darkness of the holding room. In a twist of her hand, the locks bent, the cages released. The men did not take much convincing, and they stumbled behind her. Marie could hear each of their trembling breaths in her ear, violent thunder that broke the quiet, as they burst out into the darkened corridor and made their way toward the great winding staircase. Heavy footfalls joined theirs. Brotherhood.

"Go!" Marie nodded toward the door. She would stay, hold them off. Just long enough that they could make their way out onto the second deck, then to Nonc Croc and his boat. The men ran through the door, didn't dare to look back. Marie turned, saw two alchemists appear from the dark, glowing staffs aimed at her.

Marie didn't wait. She opened her mouth, and Ogoun's power flowed from her in one searing breath, flames springing from her throat and across the floorboards in a violent surge. The air rippled with heat, burning the alchemists until they twisted in the flame and fell into a screeching heap.

Smoke curled from Marie's mouth. Every spell stole a piece of her; such was the cost of Voodoo. Every bit of magic worked some part of the soul, and only so much could be cast at one time. But here? Trapped in this alchemical void, the cost was double. The magic moved through her, slow and heavy as lead, the loa out of reach. It made the realization of Jon's power all the more frightening.

She ran, staggering up the last of the steps, and hurled herself through the door. She emerged gasping and wild-eyed onto the steamboat's upper deck. But the upper deck was not as she remembered. The large entrance hall was gone. She was standing in a long corridor, the walls cramped and pressing in. Heavy pipes hissed steam down from the ceiling in curling breaths, their iron-slick bodies winding through the dark like coiling intestines. Sticky heat rose from the floorboards, clouding the path ahead. Terrible noises sprang out at her: the clanging of chains and pipes, the whittled echo of a distant scream chasing the dark. Only a dim redness pulsed overhead, a throbbing vein of light.

Marie swallowed, the horrible realization slowly becoming real: She had not gone up.

She had gone *down*.

The truth was like cold ice down her back: Marie was inside the bowels of the steamboat. Hot steam crowded in from all sides, suffocating her. The walls breathed and constricted, womb-like, slick with dripping wetness. A flicker of movement stirred in the darkness ahead.

Someone was standing at the end of the hall.

A woman with long dark hair. She stood as still as stone. Until, very slowly, she turned her head. Like Marie, the woman wore a long black veil over her face that trailed to the floor. Steam blew in, lifting the veil, revealing the half-moon smile slowly curving across her lips. And then—

Marie froze.

"*Maman?*"

There was no mistaking it. It was Marguerite Darcantrel.

With that placid smile still frozen on her lips, Marguerite turned the corner, veil trailing like smoke. She walked until she was swallowed into the gathering darkness. Marie didn't move at first. How could she? Every muscle in her body screamed in protest, every instinct in her mind warning her to turn back. But she followed anyway, lurching forward down the tight corridor. She turned the corner, expecting to find her mother there, waiting ...

Marie emerged into the next hallway and took a breathless look around. Marguerite had gone. Just as she had when Marie was a girl. And Marie was filled with that same hopeless yearning, the pit in her stomach widening with ache. Her mother had left her again. But of course she had. Marie slapped a hand to her cheek. Because none of this was real.

Marie looked up, a prickling feeling crawling down her back. She had not emerged into a different hallway. She faced the same door marked with the same concentric circles.

Saints, she was back where she started.

"No," Marie murmured. "*No ... no ... no ...*"

She took off running. Down the same corridor, taking the same turn. Time bent. Forward. Backward. The awful truth dawning on her with each hurried step: *She was running on a loop.* There was dark, terrible magic at work. She could feel it, clutching her in its clawed grasp. It had no intention of letting her go. Still Marie ran, determined to find a way out of this maze, the endless dark. Steam drifted around her, parting like a curtain to reveal other rooms, other terrors ...

A woman in a bull mask riding gleefully astride a golden-skinned man, her pale skin glistening, the neckline of her gown half-clawed down to expose her breasts. Up and down she went, wild with violent desire. Up and down ...

The steamboat was calling to her, revealing itself in layers.

... men and women drinking and drinking from a spewing red fountain with their hands, sloshing thick wine between their fingers until red slopped down their fronts. And still they had not had their fill ...

A song started, the silence broken. Marie recognized it—it was the song the musicians had played on the steamboat's upper deck. Except it wasn't quite the same. The melody was mangled and twisted, the notes whirling on a carousel that spun backward. It was mocking her.

...men and women inside the room dancing. Faster. And faster. Their bodies crashing into one another with violent force as the song swelled, swallowing their cries of pleasure and laughter. They began to move in such tight formation that they seemed to Marie's frazzled mind to have fused together into one pulsing mass. The thing raised its arms, too many all at once, clawing out together for her to join them...

Marie screamed, wrenching herself away from whatever darkness pulled her in. This wasn't real. She knew that. By the saints and all that was holy, she knew that. This was alchemy. And here in this strange place, alchemy reigned supreme. It transfigured bodies into monsters, molded space and time into malleable clay. Had she thought that she had truly understood the limits their alchemy might reach?

Marie kept running even when the unbearable smell of something ashen and long decayed—sulfur?—stung her nose. There was no path, only more twisting shapes and shadows and screaming. The rasping red glow flickered in and out as if someone were lighting a candle, then promptly snuffing it out. Was this hell?

A silken whisper at her ear: *This is you. You've done this to yourself, Marie.*

She had been abandoned. Twice now by her own mother. By the loa. But no, she wasn't being abandoned—it was far worse than that. She was being *spat* out. Same as Jon had openly done before Gailon, no different from Father Antoine's words ringing down at her from his pulpit, more warning than sermon: *So then because thou art lukewarm, and neither cold nor hot, I will spew thee out of My mouth.*

Both Jacques and Jon had warned her. As had God. And now the Baron of Death himself. In her selfishness, she had not chosen a side, only her own. And she supposed it was divine judgment that she should be left here now, utterly alone. Marie staggered through the darkness, desperate to be free of this hellish cage.

The boiler room. The air swollen with steam, tinged with the glowing red embers of burning coal. Dark-robed figures crouched before an open furnace, its insides red like a belly split open down the middle. They fed it strange offerings ... dark limbs ... and stones ... teeth.

Behind the furnace, the dark, shadowed shape of a long-horned thing, growing larger with each sacrifice, fat and grossly protruding from its offerings. The thing stood, and it kept on rising, stretching, looming larger than any natural room could contain, than the entire steamboat could hold, until the shape of it seemed to swallow the darkness whole ...

Marie stumbled back with a cry.

This was not the work of some distant Greek deity, not at all the work of the horned god Dionysus conjured from myth. Marie understood at last the blatant truth of the whole of the steamboat: Every decadent arrangement, every act and drop of wine had been a performance meant to mask something much more malevolent that lived within its dark heart.

This place was an altar to something truly evil. Demonic.

She could feel it. Something infernal breathed within that room, something alive, powerful and ancient, and so very wrong.

The robed figures snapped their heads up to her, turning as one. They stood. And slowly started toward her—

Marie turned and ran. Her mouth open and soundless, weighed with a silent scream that wouldn't come. Thundering footfalls behind her. The dark thing was close. It would soon have her.

"Legba!" Marie called. "Papa!" she cried, hot tears blinding her as she stumbled forward.

Then she felt it. The subtle curve of the air, the cool breath of the loa of the crossroads as he passed over the threshold into the land of the living. *There,* Papa Legba whispered. *Turn there.* Crying with relief, Marie did as she was told. She turned, the hallway twisting into—

A dead end.

There was no door this time. Only an empty wall. No exit. No way out. The footfalls grew closer.

Marie screamed. Why would Legba lead her here? Was this amusement for him? Was she nothing more than a puppet that could be worked on a string like those poor men on the stage? Was this simply a game for the gods to see how far her mind could bend before it broke? Marie clutched at the walls, but her hands came back wet, slippery with something dark and warm like blood.

"Goddamn you! You left me! *You all fucking left me!*" She gasped, desperately frantic. "There's no way out," she whispered, half sobbing. Blind panic seized her. Her hands dug into her hair, grasping at her scalp, dragging down the sides of her face, smearing the blood. "There's no fucking way out!"

Marie screamed. For the men who had been enslaved and mutilated and killed for sport. For the loa. For her saints, for God. Jon. Her mother. The echo of her terror circled the dark until she felt the entire presence of the steamboat screaming back at her.

Behind her, a presence.

Marie whirled to face a figure stepping out from the coiling mist. Black-robed, a pointed hood concealing its face. The flickering red lights stuttered in and out overhead, a mad heartbeat hammering in the dark. It approached her slowly, as if floating.

Marie shrank back against the wall. Her first, frenzied thought was that it was a demon, something infernal conjured from the boiler room that had found her at last. But it was not.

Silas.

The alchemist neared her, and she could see as he grew closer the way the snow-white ends of his hair made a determined climb toward the ruddy-gold roots, eating away at what was left of his natural color bit by bit. A dark, inky ring spread out from the center of his irises, slowly overtaking what was left of the blue. A sickness slowly spreading.

Marie was shaking when he stopped in front of her. Reaching out slowly for her.

Marie slapped him—hard. "You monster! All of you! *Fucking monsters!*"

Silas watched her in silence for a moment. If he was angry, his face betrayed nothing. Then, so softly she almost missed it, he murmured, "Wine before blood, beast after body."

Marie stared blankly at the alchemist, not comprehending at first. ". . . It was you." He had slipped Jon that message. He had wanted them to find this place. "Why?"

"It is not for you to know yet." The alchemist turned to the wall behind Marie. "*Mutatio.*" The steamboat resisted, hissing like a snake. "*Aperi,*" he pressed on, coaxing the beast to obey. No, not coaxing. Demanding. "*Aperi.*"

Finally, a shape worked itself into the steamboat's cursed metal, the sound like breaking bone. A door appeared, etched with glowing symbols she couldn't decipher.

Slowly, it opened.

When Silas spoke again, his voice was a cold rasp. "Go now, Marie. Go and never return to this place."

Marie would not return to this hell, even if the loa demanded it. But she understood all the same. He would not be here next time. And the beast would not release her from its maw. The next time, it would make sure to swallow her whole. Still shaking, Marie started toward the door.

"Marie."

She turned, pausing at the glowing threshold.

"You were wrong," said Silas. He pulled the black hood over his face, taking a step back into the roiling shadow. "There is always a way out."

And then he was gone. Marie turned toward the door and passed through, stepping right into—

Chaos.

Marie emerged onto the higher deck at last surrounded by wind and terror. People streaked by in half-ruined costumes, screaming for help. Some had already sailed off on rowboats, escaping back toward the Quarter. With no rowboats left, the remaining guests flung themselves into the river. Anything but to face the chaos. Farther out on the dark water she saw Nonc Croc and the runaway men, their little rowboat seized by Gailon and his alchemists, who'd entrapped the vessel in a swirling vortex of water. Nonc Croc was not a strong enough tide-turner to withstand such an assault *and* navigate them to safety. They would die.

"*No,*" said Marie. Power coursed through her, vibrant and strong. She was not under the pull of this vessel anymore. And she would not be cowed again.

Marie flung out both arms wide as the power of three loa entered her body, coursing in opposite directions. On one end was the torrential pull of Agwe and La Sirene. On the other came Bade, his searing wind cutting through the noise of her mind. It was painful to contain one loa. It was agony to contain a trinity. *More,* the loa urged. *Use us. Use us all, child.*

Marie lifted from the ground and screamed. With one hand, she held back the alchemists, lashing wind pressing down on them, and with the other, she used the river to push Nonc Croc out of harm's way. Gailon and his men were flung to one side of the boat, a rippling funnel of wind barring them from advancing. Marie used the rest of her power to push Nonc Croc's boat along the dark water and away from *La Lune*'s long shadow. Just a little farther and . . .

Marie's nose bled. Her limbs seized, contorting from the pressure of the loa bearing down on her. Her lungs filled with the weight of deep water. She could not contain all three at once. They were going to tear her clean in two.

Finally, the rowboat broke free. It floated off into the dark, sinking into the mist.

Marie exhaled—a sound of relief, a hushed prayer. She dropped back down onto the boat's deck, barely able to hold herself up against the rail. From the far side of the boat, she saw the Brotherhood running toward her, staffs raised and glowing. A hand seized Marie by the arm—

It was Jon. The sharp lines of his face sagged from exhaustion, depleted from the cost of his magic. But still his eyes blazed, hellbent as he always was on seeing his way through the dark. Here was a man who would not break. Not now, Marie decided. Not ever.

"Shhh, I got you now," the Conjurer soothed against her ear.

Jon nodded toward the water, his message clear. They needed to go. Now.

Together they jumped, free-falling through the dark and down into the lapping black water below. When Marie broke the surface, gasping, Jon pulled her close. Even through the pain and the stench of alchemy, she was overcome with the smell of him, the bitter ancient magic that wrapped itself around him, an impenetrable armor. It was wrapped around her too now.

"Don't let me go," she begged, clinging to him, dizzy from the fall.

His eyes twinkled, the only light she needed in the dark. "Only a fool would."

Arms clasped around each other, they swam away into the night, leaving the wreckage behind.

By the time they reached land again, the stars had turned in the sky, and the first hours of morning were not far off. Trembling from exhaustion and sopping wet, Marie collapsed. Jon staggered to her, then slumped onto the ground beside her, his chest heaving. Strong as he was, she could see the night had left its mark upon him too. He might be unbreakable, but even the Conjurer was not without scars.

For a moment, there was silence. They lay side by side, chests heaving, too drenched and tired for words. Only the thrum of cicada-song, the soft turn of the river against the wind.

"Why did you take me there?" She hadn't meant to sound so accusing, but the horror of that wretched place had seeped into her, poison she desperately wanted out.

Jon turned to her. The look on his face told her he'd been expecting this. "I showed you the truth of that place—of this entire city. You cannot control monsters, Marie. They will devour as they please. And they will never have their fill. You heard the Baron, love. No two ways about it now. You either choose or—"

"Or what? Or what, Jon?"

His smile tipped at the corners, tinged in sadness. "You don't want it to come to that, Marie." *Trust me,* his eyes promised. "Do you understand now what I must do? I'm not going to break this city. It already did that on its own. But I am going to bring it to heel. To new order. The loa will have their war, Marie, whether you like it or not. Do you understand now?"

She realized that Jon had wanted to save her from herself as much as he wanted to save those men. This entire ordeal had been a lesson. And he would not teach it again.

"If your war comes to pass, my life would be over, in a way," murmured Marie, her voice so small.

She hated herself in that moment. Every selfish thought, every privilege, every single comfort her cloistered life in the Quarter had afforded her now seemed like poison in her mouth. So very bitter on her tongue. And yet she'd said the words anyway. *No lies*, they had promised.

He reached for her, his dark hand upon her cheek. She leaned in. It was strange. She didn't know how starved she had been for touch, for *his* touch. But Jon's smile only deepened, as if he knew something she did not. "Or maybe it would truly begin."

And before he could say another word, Marie quickly pulled Jon to her and laid a searing kiss on his lips. His hands were immediately upon her, tangled in her hair, roving across her back, pulling her to him. When they finally pulled away, she snatched him back, parting his mouth greedily again with her tongue. She wanted more.

She wanted *him*.

Jon tasted coffee-sweet, of old magic forbidden to her, of deliciously strange, unknown spells. Was this the taste of true freedom? Was this what Jacques had wanted for her all along—to dare to use her magic for *more*? To dare to be something more than her own selfish ambitions had ever allowed her. And Jon the Conjurer had showed her how. He would show her *more*.

Jon began to speak, but Marie held a finger to his lips. "Careful, now," she said. "Some spells just shouldn't be broken."

Later, they found each other in the darkness of his bayou house.

Marie wrapped her arms around Jon, pulling him viciously to her. Her back hit the wall, twisted wreaths of dried basil and heather tumbling into a mess upon the floor. But Jon did not seem to mind. His eyes were fixed only upon hers, burning amber in the shadow. Marie pulled him into another kiss, felt his tongue trace her lower lip, then dip into her mouth, pushing for entry. The rough underside of Jon's hand worked its way along her dress, dipping beneath it to hurriedly push it up around her waist. Desire scorched her veins, burning away all other feeling.

The walls shook again, shuddering from the force of Marie's body, and she wondered if his little bayou house had any hope of withstanding the night. Glass potion decanters on the shelves behind them fell loose, splintering across the floor into smoking puddles. Marie laughed against his smirking mouth, then quickly pushed him away. She flitted over to the bed against the far wall. It was a sad little thing, so different from her gilded accommodations in the Quarter—each side surrounded in tattered mosquito netting. But she did not care.

She wanted to forget the torture of that steamboat, to burn it from her memory. And if she could not? She wanted something else from the night that might replace it. She wanted Jon. Here. Now. Like this. But she couldn't be rid of another feeling slowly gnawing at her from the inside. The gods wanted her to choose a side. For so long there had only ever been her side, alone. It was why she had sought Jon the Conjurer in the first place.

But tonight had changed that. Something had shifted inside of her in that terrible colosseum. She'd felt it. And whatever resolve she'd had left had completely shattered inside its hideous inner sanctum. Was Jon still simply a means to an end? Or was he the new path her heart might take? She had thought that she needed a teacher to give her forbidden magic, but she hadn't bargained that he might become more to her. That it might not even be the magic that was forbidden between them. It was *this*—this dark feeling of desire. But it was also the warmth of his hand on hers as they drew the veves into the ground, the weight of his golden eyes on hers when they caught each other looking. He saw her, and she felt perfect in his gaze. Whole in a way she had never been. Never felt. They'd been careful with each other before. Careful to not cross this line.

But there was nothing careful between them now.

Jon came up behind her, snaking dark arms around her torso, then roving greedily over the neckline of her gown, the swell of her breasts. He squeezed lightly as he dipped his head down to plant a trail of kisses along her collarbone, sucking beneath her ear. Marie leaned into him, into that deliciously searing feeling slowly traveling down her flesh toward her center. Had it ever been like this with Jacques? The thought should have soiled everything—but it didn't. Because with Jacques, lovemaking had been sweet but always expected. It had never been like *this*. Forbidden.

"They still call you the Widow," he whispered, tickling her ear. "Tell me, if your husband is gone, then why do you still wear his ring?"

Marie froze, and all thoughts of forbidden pleasure vanished in one cold second. He was testing her. Even now. Even like this. On her right hand, the small gold band glinted upon her ring finger. It was not like her other talismans—this ring that Jacques had placed upon her hand the day of their marriage held no real magic. Only the magic of a few words—a promise. *I will never leave, nor forsake you.* It was what they'd vowed to each other that day, standing under the crown of purple wisteria in her grand-mère's garden before Father Antoine's watchful eye. Before God's. But words were spells, weren't they? And now . . . now her being with Jon had broken it.

"You have no right to ask me that, Jon."

"I have every right, Marie."

Marie took the ring from her finger, placing it carefully on the oak nightstand beside the bed, where it would wait for her until morning. She stood facing the window, the glass that gleamed silver in the moonlight, and slowly tugged at the shoulder straps of her gown until it fell around her ankles in a pool of ribbon and lace. She lifted her gaze to the window and caught his eyes in the glass slowly appraising her naked body. She knew that look—one of soft worship, of hushed wonder before the altar of a goddess who'd shown herself for the first time. It was the look of reverence all loa liked when they mounted the body of one of their faithful vessels, when the power of their divinity flowed through them with the violent surge of the ocean. And now Jon had lavished this worship onto her, and it gave her a heady sense of power that not even the divine could give her. She wanted this. She wanted *him.*

Marie turned slowly, her fall of dark hair concealing part of her face—and she was glad for it. It might shroud that flicker of guilt she felt needling in her chest. But there was another feeling slowly building inside her now, a spark kindling to greater flame each second she spent alone with this man. She could want both, could she not? Even if she could have only one in the end. But she didn't want to think of Jacques now, nor of the terrors of *La Lune.*

She pulled him into a slow kiss, relishing the taste of him, the hint of wonder and magic unknown to her. This man contained multitudes and mysteries. There was still so much he might teach her. So much they might accomplish together. Tonight had shown her that. But it was colored by the horror of that steamboat, the hideous stench of profanity that lurked in its depths.

"Make me forget tonight," she murmured against the curve of his mouth. "*Please.*"

"No, there will be no forgetting, love. You will remember tonight." A hint of mischief glinted in his eyes beneath the pain. "*Always.*"

"Another lesson?"

"*Always,*" he murmured again.

With a wave of her hand, Jon fell back against the bed, beneath the weight of her magic. He watched her, something like shock flitting across his face as Marie ripped the clothes from him until he was completely bare before her—every taut line of muscle across his dark flesh, every raised scar lashed across his chest.

"You are mistaken, Jonathan. This is a lesson, yes," Marie warned in a hushed breath as she lowered herself upon him. "But it is *you* who will learn tonight."

His lips pressed along the crook of her neck, trailing down and down until his tongue had traced wicked patterns along one of her breasts. Marie leaned forward suddenly, her body arching with heat, and pinched her teeth into the side of his neck, stifling her cries. Such desire she had never felt before with Jacques. It shamed her to admit that to herself. But the feeling of Jon, the utter abandon she felt in his arms, could not be a normal thing. There was something else at work here, some other golden thread of magic that bound them together at last.

His hands moved down to her hips, digging into the damp flesh as he hurried her forward. And then they were in her hair, the wild, wild hair that fell over them both like a dark wedding veil, a veil of mourning.

Marie felt the world shift beneath her, a subtle realigning of the divine. A new path had opened before her in the sultry darkness of this room, before them both. As their bodies hurriedly joined together, so did their magic, intertwined in ways she could not yet know. Jon made a noise of dark pleasure beneath her, the gold of his eyes steady on her, its magic giving off their own faint, pulsing heat in the dark. It felt ordained in a way that her own marriage had not, a coupling of old and new magic threading itself together into the shape of something new.

It felt like fate.

CHAPTER SEVENTEEN

REE

So, they had been in love.
This was Ree's first thought when she came to in the bayou house, a sweaty mess on the floor beside her mother's bed. She needn't be near her to channel, although the proximity helped to deepen her connection. The channeling was stronger now, as if it had a life of its own, as if her mother was the one forcing her to see. And see what exactly? That she had told another lie? It was clear that Jon the Conjurer was not just the enemy Marie had made him out to be.

Of course, she knew her mother must have felt *something* for the Conjurer if Ree was the result of their coupling. But it was more than that. Her mother had loved him. She'd felt as much. And, if the images of the past were any indication, he had loved her too, once upon a time. Just how had they gone to war?

Ree wanted to press on with her channeling, to go deeper this time, but with one look at her mother's waxen face, she knew it would be too much too soon.

But you are playing a dangerous game, little Laveau, Claudette had warned after the ordeal with Anabelle had ended and they'd found themselves in the bayou house, standing over her mother's body. *The more you draw on your mother's mind, the more life force you take from her body.*

Under Claudette's guiding hand, she'd learned how to reach deeper into her mother's mind, to carefully pry through the dark of her thoughts. Now Claudette entered the room, a warm cup of tea in hand. She passed it to Ree, who drank it quickly. It tasted of lavender and rose hips. Protection and strength.

"And what did you see this time?"

"My mother and Jon." She met Claudette's gaze. "And . . . the Brotherhood. What they did to those people . . ."

Ree shut her eyes to those horrible visions. Bone shattering and re-forming. Bodies contorting wildly to raucous laughter. She'd never known *La Lune* to harbor such evil. But then again, she'd never thought to look. What other evils lay beneath the Quarter's grandeur, its spell of illusion? And there was the matter of Silas. He'd slipped that code to Jon and had opened that door for Marie. But for the life of her, she couldn't understand why.

Claudette balked. "So you've seen what the Brotherhood of the White Hand is truly capable of. I say good! With each new invention they pretend advances the city's cause, no one thinks to wonder the price. Fucking imbeciles."

The pieces of Marie's past were beginning to form into a clearer shape for Ree. She could see now, perhaps, why Marie might have aligned herself with the Conjurer, why she might have had little other choice in the matter. But what she couldn't understand was how they'd become such bitter enemies in the end. Not yet.

Outside, Ree heard music coming their way from the surrounding wilderness. Her heart twisted as she realized that she was late, today of all days. Today was the day they mourned Marcel, when they would commend his spirit on to the next world. She wasn't ready to say goodbye to him, to the part of herself that had loved him. Already so much had changed in her world since his death, already so much loss.

"Go," said Claudette, nodding toward the door. "They will be expecting you there. Not me. Do not worry, I will keep watch over your mother."

Ree nodded, then made her way to the door.

"Oh, and little Laveau?" She sponged at Marie's damp brow. "Do try not to cause any more trouble for yourself. You don't need any more eyes on you."

But that was exactly what she felt now, a thousand eyes on her as she walked amongst her mother's Voodoo court. They carried Marcel's body deeper into the bayou, where the moss trees hung above them, their spindly arms tangled together in cobwebs that blotted out the fading sun. With so much suspicion toward their kind now, he could not be laid to rest in the city, where they might make a mockery of his corpse, swinging him from a rope, or chaining his body to a pole where passersby might spit and piss on his withering bones.

Ree watched from the back of the procession, eyes trained on the wicker box holding Marcel's body as it was carried along on the shoulders of stone-faced men, her mother's devoted followers. *But are they devoted to me?* It was a thought she could not escape. Ree was not their chosen Voodoo Queen. After all, Marie Laveau was not dead—not yet. But by now everyone knew she had disappeared. A new queen would need to be named. *And soon.*

Ree was dressed in her best mourning white, her hair braided away from her face, her cheeks and lips bare of their usual dark red rouge. For all their tears and sorrows, funerals were celebrations of another kind in New Orleans. But Ree could not summon an ounce of revelry.

Marcel. Her friend, her unspoken brother. Teasing and rash, he'd liked her games and had endured her terrible moods with nothing more than a laugh and a drink. Oh, by the saints, why in the hell had she given him that aurum? Why couldn't she have passed that task on to her mother, who could turn a man away with only her eyes?

At last, they found their way to a small, blue-grassed meadow, basil and fennel abundant underfoot. This was consecrated land that her mother had cleansed and blessed in the name of Baron Samedi, supreme god of death, father of those long passed from this world. His altar sat empty, a great stone carved to appear like a hand breaking soil, reaching from the ground. The acolytes laid

Marcel's body down in front of the stone altar, waiting for Ree's command.

"Light the pyre and fill the altars," Ree ordered.

The others did as they were told, but Ree noticed a flicker of hesitation in the air, and she worried it would soon catch to flame and spread quickly among them. Queen she was not, but she was still her mother's heir, and that counted for something. It had to.

Her skin prickled. She was being watched.

Henryk stood to the back of the procession, the horse he had rode in on some yards away. He hadn't said a word to her, and he hadn't needed to. Not when she knew why he was here. After the debacle in Congo Square, it was her understanding that all Voodoo and ceremonies would need to be under supervision. And it would seem the High Inquisitor had made it his business to do just that. But she wondered if it was more than that. Was the part of Henryk who had loved Marcel still alive in the shell of the man she saw before her now? And if he was . . .

Ree tried her best to put the thought from her mind. But still it rang, haunting her. *Is that part still in love with you?*

A hand squeezed Ree by the shoulder. She turned to find Father Antoine at her side. His lined face bore deep, timeworn grooves, but his light blue eyes were as bright as ever beneath a pair of bushy gray eyebrows.

"Responsibility suits you, Marie," Father Antoine said simply.

He was using her birth name—her Catholic name—to grate her nerves, she supposed. "I do not keep your faith. So you needn't have ventured out this far, old man."

The priest was harmless—kind, studious, and certainly generous to the poor and needy. Père Antoine let his parish believe how they wanted and seemed to keep the Vatican at arm's length. Until now.

His eyes crinkled at the corners. "No, but I liked to. And besides, your well-being is still of concern to me. You *were* baptized Catholic, you know." So, he *was* teasing her.

"That was my mother's choice." *As all other things in my life were.*

Soon the pyre smoked, the air clouded with bittersweet poppy to bring rest, rosemary for remembrance. Her mother used to say that if you looked closely, you might see Baron Samedi in the smoke, his skeletal face forming in the silver wisps. But Baron Samedi did not come, and Ree was glad for it. She was in no mood to entertain the loa, especially one such as Baron Samedi, who would call for dance and song as tribute, for laughter instead of tears. The Voodoos poured the god of death's favored rum along his altar, lit cigars wrapped in wax paper, scattered coffee grounds into his stone hand.

Henryk was questioning Ory now. He took down careful annotation of what he said in a leather book. She wanted to scream at him, to curse his name loudly for everyone to hear. How could he stand there and pretend as if Marcel had never meant anything to him, as if *she* had never meant anything to him at all? It was easier before to distract herself with a bit of whiskey and lovemaking, but there was no distraction from *this*—the cold fury lacing its way up her spine and through her blood.

Antoine followed Ree's gaze, his eyes softening. "I'm afraid Inquisitor Broussard believes, as most of my peers do, that magic must be . . . managed."

But had he always believed that? Had he simply hidden his prejudices from her when they were children? What had she been to him exactly in those quiet, loving moments? And why had he asked her so desperately to leave that night eight years ago? But the answers hardly seemed to matter now, not when she could feel Marcel's spirit drifting further and further away. What had become of his dreams of freedom? Those beautiful dreams of Haiti? Where might all those hopes and dreams go now?

"You'll forgive me if I don't share your sympathies," Ree said. "That sense of *management* usually ends with a witch up on the end of a pike."

"No." The imploring sound of his voice surprised her. "Forgive *him*, young priestess. His mother was killed by the magical-blooded. Now Inquisitor Broussard believes this is the only way to spare others from that pain. Belief can be a fickle thing."

Ree stilled. She had never known how Henryk Broussard had become an orphan, only that he didn't remember much about his life before he was sent to live with the rest of the children with the

Ursuline nuns at the convent. But if his mother had been killed by those with magical blood? Well, that kind of hate didn't die easy.

"And what about me, Father?" Ree asked finally. "Did he always hate me?"

But Father Antoine's eyes only twinkled. "We are not always the sum of our beliefs, young Marie. Listen to me, I believe the boy you cared for is still in there. You saved his life, brought him back from the edge of darkness. You made him believe in more once. Maybe not in magic itself. But in *you*." His line of sight moved to the pyre. "And you may yet do it again."

When he left, Ree approached the pyre. They hadn't yet transferred Marcel's body to the flames. She closed her eyes as she silently paid her final respects to her friend. *Oh, Marcel. You fool.* Hot tears stung her eyes. *What I'd give to see you again.*

It had been a quick thought, a selfish thought, one she had no right to. Marcel had other friends, other family. But she was so alone now. Without her mother. Without Anabelle. And now without him too.

Ree felt a familiar pull, the lightness beneath her feet, the shiver down her spine as a voice whispered, *Is it so?* It was the same dark voice of a man she'd heard as a child, the voice she'd heard in the sick ward while staring at a pale, bedridden Henryk Broussard, the voice she now knew belonged to Jon the Conjurer. Her father. *Death is but a doorway*, Jon sang. *Open it, daughter. Open it further and see what you may find.*

Then she felt the oddest sensation, like plunging into ice water, the magic flowing through her, surer, stronger than any magic she had ever felt. She reached for it, that spark of power living inside of her, the one she had always known had been waiting, patiently dormant. And it felt . . . well, it felt *good*. It was life and it was death, and it was the pale dusk that lingered in between. It was power like she had never tasted.

Thump. Thump. Thump.

Ree glanced down. But she was too late. The wooden lid to Marcel's coffin burst forth, throwing itself open. And before she could utter a single word, a grayed hand was already emerging from the box. And then another, until a man—no, a *corpse* hauled itself from the coffin and onto its feet. It straightened its body in odd, crooked movements, each one preceded by a sickening *snap*.

A scream erupted behind her. It was Nan, she recognized. Others too.

Ree was rooted to the ground, frozen in place. The blood drained from her face, her heart hammering wildly against her chest.

Marcel took an uncertain step toward her. But it was not Marcel, was it? Marcel was dead. Two days hanged. His soul was gone from this plane and on to the next. What then was walking toward her? But she knew. He was not human any longer, not even a corpse.

He was a zombi now.

Creatures of old folktales. They were the undead, the unholy resurrected, damned to walk the earth barren of soul, hungering for life and flesh. The portion of Voodoo forbidden in New Orleans. The same magic that had overthrown Haiti during those long years of revolution. It was the terrifying magic she'd glimpsed Jon wielding aboard *La Lune*—the awakening of the dead.

A thin, grueling moan came from his cracked lips. As the zombi neared, she could see violet light burning in his irises, a strange cold fire. When she'd consumed the Conjurer Root, she'd seen the undead rising from the earth. Had that been some sort of premonition?

"Marcel . . . ?"

He was coming straight for her. Each step wooden, an unnatural contortion of limbs. Ree felt suddenly very dizzy, her head ringing. Still, she couldn't move, couldn't bring herself to utter a single spell. And what magic would she call upon? Her mother had never prepared her for *this*.

People ran by her, screaming. Even among the Voodoos, this was not the magic they had expected. She caught Father Antoine's eye from across the crowd. Not horrified like the rest. Worry churned in those eyes. Eyes that were old enough to have beheld the bloody work of the First Holy Inquisition, to have seen before the result of such magic, the dark path where it would surely lead again.

"*Move!*"

Ree felt a whoosh—then was flung to the ground.

Henryk shot in front of her, and in one thrust, he sent the zombi back into the flames of the pyre. That thin, groaning sound stretched out into the dusky air, a sound of utter pain that gnawed through Ree's chest and right into her heart. Tearfully, she watched that dead thing twist and twist upon the roaring fire until it burned down to ash and became nothing at all right before her eyes.

Numbly, Ree struggled to her feet. The world was spinning in a maddening blur. Smoke filled the clearing, blanketing everything in its path. She couldn't tell up from down; nothing made sense.

Through the twisting red flames, Henryk was staring at her, coldly appraising.

His face had changed again—as if he'd come to some grim resolve. It was, Ree recognized with a stab of fear, the face of a hunter. Her eyes dropped to the fire, to the last of Marcel withering away. Then Ree realized—*she* had done this, performed this forbidden magic. The Harbinger was slowly but surely coming true.

And so it shall be: A Laveau witch's reign will raise hell upon the earth. From its gates, the damned will return.

Ree slowly met Henryk's gaze through the fire.

This was her sin. And the Inquisitor had realized it too.

CHAPTER EIGHTEEN

MARIE

Magic had changed Jon's face again, this time into the shape of a monster she'd thought herself rid of many, many years ago.

It was the face of the one who had left her first, whose absence had marked her soul with a terrible brand of loneliness. Her mother. When Jon's face had changed again and taken on the shape of Marguerite Darcantrel, she couldn't bear it. Flashes of her mother's face came back to her—that eerie smile from behind that long black veil, the shape of her sinking into the shadows. Would she ever be free of that terrible night on the steamboat? *La Lune* might never let her go.

"Enough!" Marie snapped. "I said enough!"

She crashed her own magic into the illusion, smashing it in the moonlight, bits of silver floating away in the bayou wind and into the ragweed and trees. Marie was on her knees, panting. Although Jon held nothing back in their lessons, she found this one to be particularly cruel, worse even than when he had pretended to be Jacques.

"What do you fear, Marie?" asked Jon quietly.

He knelt beside her, lifting her chin so that she was gazing into his eyes. So very gentle he had become with her in these last few blessed weeks, so gentle those golden eyes had been when she was gazing down at them in the dark, astride him.

"Tell me, what do you fear, Marie?" he repeated. "Those fears will be made manifest when you open the door to death if you do not learn to conquer them now. The loa do not respect any show of weakness. You cannot demand them to change the course of death if you haven't conquered your own life."

His words circled in her head, a maddening riot of sound. *What do you fear, Marie?* But he knew. He had seen inside her mind, had made himself privy to the dark thoughts and fears she kept hidden away. The steamboat had seen inside of her too, hadn't it? It had gazed into the dark of her heart. And it had wanted more.

"I thought . . . I thought I wasn't afraid of that monster anymore," said Marie finally.

"That wasn't the face of a monster, love." His hands moved to her shoulder, slowly caressing the bare skin where the sleeve of her dress had slipped.

Oh, yes it was, a different kind of monster altogether. "It was my mother."

"Ah," said Jon. His grip on her shoulder tightened. "The curse of family."

Sometimes it did feel like Marie's family had been cursed. Marie was the first in her family to have been born free. Both her mother and her grandmother had not been so fortunate. Grand-mère had bought her freedom, of course, toiled off her debt in the sun until Corbin's father had turned her free. Didn't know what he had in her bloodline, because if he had, he would never have let her go so easily. Her mother had a tryst with a mulatto freedman, Charles Laveau, and birthed Marie shortly after. Because her mother was newly freed, so was she. It was the one good thing her mother had given her—freedom.

"She left me, Jon," said Marie finally. "She left because I was too much, much more than she bargained for. My grandmother didn't have *this* strength of magic. My mother didn't either. So she had no reason to believe her daughter might. But I did. And I . . . couldn't control it."

Marie was barely five when her mother had left her with Grand-mère. Said she wasn't right for motherhood, didn't have the *knack* for it, as if it were simply a card trick you could learn on a street corner. Truth was, she'd been afraid of Marie, of the strange happenings around her, the magic in her eyes, the spirits that whispered from every dark room. She let her go. Went to chase her freedom. Marie had sworn if she was ever to be a mother, she would not do the same.

And so, Marie had learned to hide herself, to make her magic smaller. To make herself smaller. But that did not help, did it? People still laughed at her, whispered about her behind her back during mass and in the dusty roads of the corner markets, jeered at her on the street. *Such a strange, strange girl,* they'd sneered. And then, years later, Grand-mère had passed on, leaving Marie with no one to guide her, to shape this strange magic.

There were tears in her eyes, perhaps even tears in his eyes too. He cupped her cheek, slowly thumbing away the wetness from her skin. "It is not your fault, Marie Laveau. The ancestors bless their magic accordingly to those who can handle the burden of their divinity. To those who are worthy."

Was she worthy? Her own mother and grandmother had not thought so. Her magic was something to be snuffed out like a candle burning too brightly. Later, when she'd married Jacques at eighteen, she'd struggled to meet his expectations of her. To make herself larger than she was, to use her magic for more. And when he had disappeared, had vanished so easily from her life, she felt that wound reopen. Yet again, someone she had loved had gone and left her alone.

"And so very often"—his golden eyes dimmed—"that magic can feel like a curse. This I know all too well, love."

Jon straightened to his full height. He held out a hand to Marie, waiting.

"The Veil is the twilight, the final crossroads. There are many doors to death, but it is the first." Jon stared at her for a long moment, his look strange. It was as if he were trying to see within her, looking for the trap that surely lay beneath. "Are you sure that you want to learn to open it, Marie Laveau?"

Marie stared at his hand, thinking. Was she sure of anything at this point? She told herself that she'd started this because she wanted—no, needed—to have Jacques returned to her.

But that had been before. Now things had . . . changed. With Jon. With her. She didn't just want Jacques—she wanted Jon too. She was selfish. She was every terrible thing people called her behind her back. *Maybe it is not Jacques that you want back, not truly. You want what you have never had. You want love, Marie. Devotion. The communion of souls. You want it all.*

Marie stared at the Conjurer, heart stammering. Did she have that now? Maybe she need not open the door to her past to find those things again. *Maybe,* a small voice reminded her, *they are here with you now. With him.*

"Yes," said Marie at last, as she took his hand. "Teach me."

Hours later, when Jon had finished his lesson, he'd made a fire and cooked trout for them over a spittle. Marie sat tucked against his chest while they watched the flame hiss into the night.

"Why did you learn such magic?" She cast her eyes up at him, trying to imagine who Jon might have been before all of his pain. So much of him was still a mystery to her.

The fire breathed between them. Finally, Jon said, "There was an attack on my village. Slavers dragged me from the shores, from my family, and into the sea. I was sold to the highest bidder, brought here."

A flash in her mind's eye: *A young man dragged along white-foamed shores, thick silver-gold chains dragging him by the neck. More chains . . . and white-capped fields of cotton so pale they glistened like melting snow beneath an impossibly hot sun . . . countless lashes against a young man's back, each turn of the whip forcing the flesh apart like teeth . . .*

"To Corbin?"

"No. He came after. When I returned to New Orleans again." Jon shifted away from Marie, and she was forced to sit up, watching as he stared absently into the flame. "When I was first captured, it took me some months, but I managed to escape. I sailed back home. Only there was no more *home*. There was only ash on the wind. Decay everywhere I looked. Later a fisherman from another village told me that my wife slit her own throat. She didn't want to—*couldn't*—live in a world with chains." He closed his eyes. And when he opened them again, she saw that his face had changed. He looked more human than Marie had ever seen him. That bright, endless magic about him had waned. "My children . . . three sons . . . and a daughter . . . had been scattered. They were young, too young to be left alone. Later, I was able to piece together the knowledge that my sons had all died in the belly of a ship. Cold and alone. Starvation, a woman who had been captured with them told me in Haiti. They never made it to shore." He stopped for a moment, his throat wobbling with choked emotion. Marie took his hand. "Only my daughter remained. By the time I found her in the sickbed of some village doctor, disease had already taken root. I was a great healer. I was the best. But I was late. I was too late, Marie. The fever made her loose of tongue. She told me she had dreamed that a man in a tall dark hat whispered in her ear that I might have another. A *daughter.* A silly story, I remember laughing, even as I wept. And I realized, holding her cold body in my arms, that even if that were the truth, it was a dream I couldn't afford to have."

"Jon—"

He held up a hand. She understood. The story was like a spell that demanded to be finished once started.

"When I went to bury her that night, who should appear at her graveside but a man in a tall, tall dark hat? And this strange man with eyes of coal offered me a deal—that if I learned his magic of death, I could use it to avenge those like me. But there were costs to his magic, he warned. Sacrifices. He said I would feel this pain once more, but only once more. 'We must be willing to sacrifice the few to save the many,' Baron Samedi whispered in my ear." His eyes were full of wrath. "And I listened."

Silence. The fire had smoked down to almost nothing. Cold bayou wind stirred between them now. Jon stared into the coals and ash, into its nothingness. "This war requires an army, Marie. Baron Samedi intends to give us one."

There had been rumors. Stories of why Jon had been banished by Sanite. Talk Marie had never allowed herself to indulge because she had been afraid.

"Do you intend to raise zombi, Jon?"

She was a hypocrite for asking. But she must know. What she had intended for Jacques was to bring him back, even if it meant he was undead. She had heard such magic was possible. Why not then, for love? What could be the harm in raising one zombi? But many? Marie let his hand go. Maybe, she thought, some doors were better left closed.

Jon slowly turned to her, golden eyes full of unshed tears, and fury like she had never seen, and sorrow, endless sorrow that no man should ever endure. "Our people toiled in this land, sowing their blood, their pain into it. What do you think happens to pain like that? Where does it go? *It always comes back.*"

She could see now—fully—what it had done to him. All that pain and wrath twisted into one unnamable feeling that burrowed within his very bones, sinking into the dark waters of his heart. *Where does it go? It always comes back.*

He placed a soft kiss on her knuckles. She was reminded then of the hissing alchemical snake that the Brotherhood had transfigured, whose golden eyes had looked deeply into her own before it had struck out and bit her. That look had been a warning from a hidden enemy, she realized, one last chance to turn and run. But she didn't. She couldn't.

She was in love.

"I need you, Marie. This world needs you." Jon's lips found hers, and she tasted that bittersweet, unnamable feeling for her own. "And together, we may make a new one."

CHAPTER NINETEEN

REE

After Marcel's funeral, Ree felt like she was trapped in a fever dream she had no idea how to wake from. Screams twisted in the air. Henryk's accusing stare pierced her through the fire. She'd forced herself to slip into the turmoiled crowd, running through bramble and muck until she reached the bayou house, where she barricaded the door, shuttering herself from the chaos.

Hiding would do no good against the Inquisitor. The Inquisition would surely come now. The raising of the undead was cardinal sin, blatant blasphemy. Ree was uncertain of her next steps, but she had the sinking feeling she'd just damned herself, that her newfound magic had set into motion some terrible machination. Her mother's memories had only further confused her. Marie had sought the power of the Veil for herself, had been conflicted between her dead beloved and her love for Jon. History had gotten Jon the Conjurer's story wrong. He was no menace, hardly the worst player in all of New Orleans.

From what she could see, her father's "war" had been a rebellion. Her mother was closer than ever to learning the secret of the Veil. Which meant Ree was closer than ever to learning how to bring her back. She need only channel her a bit further, push a bit further . . .

But the Veil's power was taking its toll on her mother's body. She was thinner than she had been three days ago, and gray hairs had begun to sprout along her hairline where there had been none before. Being among the dead for so long was literally draining her. Ree knew she did not have much longer.

Earlier in the bayou house, Aram fluttered to her shoulder, a piece of rolled parchment tied to his leg. She unfurled the note and quickly read the scrawled handwriting. Father Antoine wanted to meet with her. Of course he did. He had seen with his own eyes her strange new power. But better him than the Inquisition.

"If you go to him now, there is not much protection he could provide," Claudette had said. "But it might do your reputation well to be seen communing with a holy man."

"What would you have me do?"

But L'Enchanteresse had only shrugged. "Go to him. See if you might be able to work the fondness he has for your mother for yourself. Perhaps he will speak on your behalf with the Inquisitor and hold him off long enough to see your mother returned."

"And then?"

"Do not worry about after," Claudette had chided. "Go to him while you still have the upper hand in this mess."

Now, as Ree walked Royal Street alone, she wondered if she'd ever had the upper hand at all. Darkness had fallen, but the city was still alive, a dizzying whirl of color and lights that never slept. There was cheer in the air, in the music that drifted from the various parlors and coffeehouses, and in the windows of the shops that had begun to hang their gold and violet tinsel in preparation for Mardi Gras. She passed almsgiving priests who handed out loaves of stale bread to beggars and left warnings to not indulge in the sin the holiday encouraged, as Lent would soon be upon them.

Ree walked into St. Louis Cathedral's cool, damp interior, past the city folks who'd come for evening mass, allowing her feet to take her to the door of Antoine's private chambers. She knocked once, but there was no answer. The door was unlocked. Inside, Antonio de Sedella's chamber was sparse—a candle burning in a small copper dish, a desk piled with letters and tomes, the familiar white marble bust of the Holy Virgin cradling an infant Christ, a reading chair pushed beside a fire that crackled behind the grate, smelling gently of pine.

The door shut behind her.

"Have a seat, Marie Laveau the Second."

Before Ree could answer, someone had shoved her into the chair by the fire. But she'd know that rough scrape of a voice anywhere. She'd heard it too often in her dreams, whispering huskily in her ear, or in nightmares that kept her turning in her bed, his voice full of venom.

Henryk stepped out from the shadowed corner. He wore a long, hooded blood-red robe and a pitch-black lacquered mask, the shape of it terrifying in its utter blankness. Ree stared, wide-eyed. It was the kind of mask Inquisitors wore before questioning. Before torture.

Henryk Broussard had come to question her at last.

He stepped farther into the firelight and away from the shadows where he'd been waiting for her to come. Like a moth sucked into hideous flame, she'd walked right into a trap.

"Henryk—"

Silver cords shot out from the chair, wrapping tightly around her arms, banding all the way down to her wrists, bolting her in place. They burned into her skin, a gnawing pain that could only be aurum. But it was also, strangely, the work of magic too. Not Voodoo. But it was magic, to be sure. That the Church was willing to use magic in its efforts to root out those with magical blood should not have surprised her on matter of principle, only irony. But this problem was hardly her biggest. Her most pressing problem at the moment was more than six feet tall and staring down at her from behind a black mask, its lines listless and cold. The picture of silent terror.

"What is this?" she demanded.

But she knew, didn't she? This was the long-overdue interrogation, the one she'd known was coming ever since she gazed up at him through the bars of that miserable little jail cell. He'd come back for *this*, and the High Inquisitor would not be kept waiting any longer.

Her time was up.

"As it turns out, the Brotherhood's inventions can prove quite useful," Henryk explained. "They supposedly use these little novelties on their subjects in their laboratories. I wouldn't struggle if I were you. Only makes things more painful."

You would hurt me? she wanted to ask. But of course he would. She'd told herself he kept himself from harming her maybe out of old sentiment, maybe because it had simply not come to that. But it was Antoine's doing that had kept her safe from him. And even that goodwill had gone. She tried to keep herself from thinking of the stories of torture she'd heard Inquisitions wrought on their victims: *Stretching contraptions meant to pull limbs in directions they expressly weren't made to go. Brutal bullwhips set with spikes shaped like gnarled teeth. Countless and nameless horrors that might be had in dark rooms.*

"An Inquisitor who dares to use magic?" She was stalling, her eyes searching the room for some means of escape. But there was none. He had her cornered at last. "How very heretical of you. What might the Church think of this?"

"You will find that my aim diverges from the Church's when it suits me."

The Inquisitor seized the chair tucked behind the desk and dragged it with deliberate slowness across the floor, the dull scrape making the fine hair along Ree's arms stand on end.

"I have a game for us to play," he said finally as he positioned the chair in front of hers. "We both know how much you love those. It's the one where you finally tell me the truth. And I mean every bit of it." Henryk took a seat, facing her directly, then pulled a small black book from his robes. "According to an eyewitness account, under demonic influence, you spoke the words of the Harbinger at your mother's midnight ritual in Congo Square. I will repeat the words as I have them here: *And so it shall be: A Laveau witch's reign will raise hell upon the earth. From its gates, the damned will return. Their king, High Jon, will walk the Quarter once more.* Is this true?"

"If you believe what's written down in your little book, then yes."

"Don't"—he snapped the book closed—"lie to me."

"I think all we've been doing is lying to each other."

He leaned forward with frightening speed, his arms pressed on either side of her chair. Ree stared into the black mask, the face that was not a face at all but the horrible visage of a red-cloaked demon. "Out of respect for our friendship when we were children, I have tried to be patient with you, witch. But you are out of time. You created the living undead before the public. Do you not think word has already spread around the city? Do you not think every friar, every priest and nun has written to the Vatican of your accused heresy?"

"I do not care what the Vatican thinks." Capture made her bold. Or maybe it was the fear snaking its way through her belly.

"Oh, but you should. You see, because of your little stunt, the Church has sent a Tribunal of Inquisitors across the sea. They come to New Orleans as we speak. And these are not kind men."

"Do you believe yourself a kind man, Henryk?"

"Do you admit to committing necromancy, Marie Laveau the Second?"

"We do not call it necromancy in our culture. So, I cannot call my magic a name I do not accept from a religion I do not believe in." She was bluffing, but it was buying her only meager time. "But if I did, surely you must know that it was that same power that brought you back from the cusp of death too."

It wasn't quite the same. Henryk hadn't been dead yet, not fully. But he'd been slipping into its dark folds, and she'd found a way to reel him back to the land of the living.

"Maybe," Ree said quietly, "you should write that down in your little book too, and give *that* to the Vatican."

"There may yet be a way for both of us to get what we want."

Ree hesitated before asking, "And how might we do that?"

A minute passed, then another. He stared at her from the gaunt holes of the black lacquered mask, and she found it terrifying she had no idea what he may be thinking. And then he did something she did not expect him to do.

Henryk knelt in front of her, then slowly took the mask off.

His face was before hers, so close they might kiss. Close enough that she could smell the soap on his skin, the almond oil in his hair, see the lighter flecks of flinty color around the center of his irises. It was hard to look at him and not see the boy he had been, the boy she had once so innocently loved. He was Henryk again. Her Henryk, if she could call him that. Or maybe this was another one of his tactics to pry information from her at any cost.

"Give me your mother," he said coldly. "The Harbinger names a Laveau witch. When the tribunal arrives, we can attribute whatever magic you performed to your mother's influence. They would question you for a time. But you would be let go with your life intact. This is the only move you have left, Ree."

He is trying to spare you. Because he cares about you, a voice said. But then reality set in, cold and unforgiving. No, he cared for his position, to sew up the bleeding before she caused any more damage. And if he did care, if some small part of him had revived some warmth of feeling for her, then it was surely not enough. Not nearly enough.

"And my mother? What would become of her?" But she knew. She would meet a fiery end on a stake. "They would kill her."

"Better her than you, Ree."

Oh, she was Ree now, was she? She had not been Ree to him in many years. She was simply a witch in his way, another heretic he could do away with.

When Ree said nothing, she could tell something in him changed. For a moment the room was silent, and they could hear only the hushed singing of the nuns in the sanctuary, their voices wafting eerily into the space between them. A dark cloud passed over his features, and what she saw before her now was a face more frightening than the black mask.

"Do you want to know what will happen to you when they take you?" he asked softly. Her heart struck a jagged rhythm. "You will be arrested and held in darkness. This will go on for a day, two, or ten. You will not know because there will be no light. No windows. Only you and the darkness you have brought upon yourself. And then they will come for you. They will undress you, force you naked in a room full of wonderfully inventive contraptions. And they will torture you with them. All manner. All means. And then, finally, because your body cannot handle the pain, you will confess. But by then it will be too late, and you will have begged for death."

The Inquisitor's words took frightening shape before her like a heinous Quarter puppet show. By the loa, she *was* terrified. And yet she forced herself to speak anyway. "And will you be the one to torture me, Henryk?"

Something in his eyes softened, and she knew it was not a part of their game. It was the human part of him rising to the surface, clawing to get out. And it did not matter, she understood at last. This was who he was now. "I would hope not," he answered, his voice taking on a strange note. And then that tender glimpse vanished, his face cool stone before hers. "Where is your mother? Where is Marie Laveau?"

Ree remained silent. The bindings tightened around her arms, squeezing painfully. The chair was alive, sentient with alchemy. It squeezed her flesh until she saw black spots dance in her vision. And still she did not answer.

"I'm going to ask you one more time: *Where. Is. Marie. Laveau?*"

"Away from the likes of you fucking hypocrites!" she spat.

"Do you want to know why I knew you weren't coming that day on that bridge, Ree? Because of *her*. It was always her. The great Marie Laveau. More titan than mother. Her influence is so tangled up in you, you don't even know where you begin and where she ends."

"Stop it."

His eyes flashed, cold steel that cut right through her, down to the quick. "But it's the truth, isn't it? Even if you despised her control. Even if you longed for your own choices. Even as Marie sought to maneuver every aspect of your life for you, you could never leave her, could you?" Was this the Inquisitor talking? Or was this Henryk Broussard, the quiet altar boy she'd saved with a kiss?

"Because she is my mother, Henryk. And I love her."

"Perhaps you need to learn to love yourself more." *You could have loved me more,* his eyes said. Or perhaps she was still a lovesick fool, imagining things that were not there. Things that had never been.

The door swung open, and Father Antoine stepped through. The alarm on his face was more emotion than Ree had ever glimpsed in the old priest, more than she'd ever thought he might feel for someone like her, a heathen and a heretic. "What in God's name have you done? Enough! Henryk, enough! Let the girl go!"

Henryk rose to his feet. Antoine moved past him to Ree and quickly undid her bindings. He helped Ree to stand, her legs uncertain beneath her. She panted, weak with relief. The aurum had made her dizzy and depleted her magic. When she looked up, Henryk had paused in the doorway, only his profile facing her, a single cold gray eye peering down at her, alchemical and all-seeing.

"You should have let me die that day, Ree," he murmured, a strange husk to his voice. Some hint of old emotion. "I am the same as Marcel, in a way. An undead thing of a different kind. You didn't bring back a man. You brought back a monster."

Ree stared at him, quiet. Although he'd meant this little interrogation to pry truths from her, at last she'd pried one from him. This was the truth. Or maybe it didn't have to be.

"No. You're *wrong*," Ree said, voice soft. "I brought you back because you were worth saving." *And even after everything, you are worth saving now.*

Father Antoine stepped in front of Ree, his lined face set into one of grave seriousness. "I bid you leave her be, Inquisitor, and go from here!"

"Good." Henryk slid that horrid black mask back into place. "We're finished."

He disappeared into the shadowed halls. When Antoine released her, Ree was shaking. Fire burned in her throat, a knot that ached and trembled. She'd held herself together as much as she could before Henryk's best efforts to break her, but she knew some part of it had worked. Some part of her had broken after all.

"There, there, child. It's all right."

"No!" Ree wrenched herself away from him. None of this was all right. It might never be again.

She would not stoop so low as to be consoled by some guilt-ridden holy man. Antoine and his empty sermons and benedictions. Well, he was no more than a fraud on a street corner running a con like the rest. How could her mother not see him for what he was? Or maybe she was a hypocrite too. Maybe the goodness her mother believed Antoine held was the same as the goodness she'd glimpsed in Henryk, the goodness she hoped might still be there deep down. But now, after this?

She hadn't realized that tears had been building in her all along, stuck to the back of her throat. "Do you agree with this, Antoine? You claim to love my mother."

"I do," he said quietly. "I love Marie like one of my own."

"Do you want to know what I think? I think you are a goddamned hypocrite! An old man who feels sorry for himself that he chose the wrong side, but you're too weak to change it."

"*You* must change it, Marie Laveau the Second. You must be a catalyst for change as I believed your mother might be. You must have Marie's faith, child."

Marie's faith? What good would that do her? There was no saving grace in this city, and if there were, God hadn't seen fit to spare it on the likes of her.

"Whatever has happened to him, whatever dark thing he has become . . . just know that I don't blame him, not completely. I blame *you*. That faith you speak of? That corrupted him into what he is now. Tell me, will God forgive you for that in the end, old man?"

Furious, she felt the magic flood behind her eyes, the face of Voodoo that terrified so many others. But not Antoine. He was not terrified, only silent. Always so pathetically silent.

"Let us see where all of that contrition is now," she spat.

Ree pushed past him. She was done with this. She needed to find Marie Laveau's memory of her Veil magic, the final piece of this wretched puzzle. For her mother's sake, and for her own.

CHAPTER TWENTY

MARIE

Marie and Jon stood hand in hand before a towering white mausoleum. There were many others like this one; the cemetery was filled with them now. Every moneyed man desired one, a final resting place that said *Look, see the weight of my silver.* The thought almost made Marie laugh. Silver would do them no good where they were going.

Marie pulled her cloak tighter against the chill of night. Even during the day, in the bristling heat, St. Louis Cemetery could be an exceptionally cold place. The city of the dead. The spirits grew restless on this land, eager to speak their riddles, their curses. One such spoke to Marie now. *Priestess,* a voice hummed in her ear. *Hypocrite,* said another. Marie ignored them.

Jon moved a hand in the air, and the mausoleum slowly opened, the ground trembling. He motioned for Marie to follow him inside. But as they stepped into the darkness, Marie saw it was empty. There was no casket.

"What is this place?"

"This was to be my final resting place." His lips turned into a wicked grin. "My tomb. When I first challenged Sanite for her rule, she did not take well to my threats. The venerable Quarter Queen built this place as a warning: that if I should challenge her, she would kill me where I stood. But I learned to embrace my reputation among the Voodoos, and I grew to like it a little." He shrugged. "Turns out the dead aren't such bad company after all."

Dark flowers twisted along the stone walls. Marie plucked one from the darkness, held it in her hand. It pulsed with power, dark red veins running along the petals.

"Conjurer Root," Jon explained. "Think of it as a key. Not a door." He plucked the flower from Marie's hand, twisted its strange dark blossoms softly between his fingers as if he were admiring a treasured pet. "The root is a conduit to the Lord of Death. Baron Samedi. Those that have its power may resurrect the dead through the Baron. But his magic comes at a cost, and resurrecting life through this means may very well drain your own. By this magic alone, I would not be able to raise an army of zombi, not on my own. My life force is not yet strong enough."

"Which is why you learned Veil magic."

"Yes. If Conjurer Root is the key, then think of the Veil as the door to death, the first realm of the afterlife, the first gateway. There are seven, but that is magic you need not know. Not *now*." His eyes glittered, enlivened by their secrets.

"But you will teach me Veil magic?"

"It remains the only way. You are not suited to Conjurer Root, Marie. The Baron does not make a pact with every soul who seeks his power. You've too much light, my dark sun." He closed his eyes. "Too much goodness in you for his liking. Taking Conjurer Root would only hurt you more than help. You would need to entreat Legba instead. He favors you some."

She could sense that there was more. He turned to face her, but she could see something in him had changed. He looked less like the dark Conjurer of lore but rather like a man, humbly baring himself before her.

"I'm going to ask you something now, Marie, and I want you to answer honestly. Once I give you this power, it will be yours to wield. But I need to know."

"You are going to make me choose."

She had always known it would come to this. The minute she'd told him why she needed Veil magic in the first place, he'd known her heart had belonged to another. But that hadn't stopped her from sharing his bed. His heart. She had thought that their lessons might not turn into something more, that she could keep herself safe from this strange man. She'd been warned to be careful with him, but he'd never been warned to be careful with her, had he? Every moment spent together, every kind word, every longing glance, had stolen her away from that one little word, *careful,* until she was his, and he hers.

"Are you going to use the power of the Veil for Jacques Paris, or . . ." His eyes, molten amber, held hers, steady in the dark. "For the loa? For me?"

Silence stretched between them. If she chose Jacques as she had always intended, she would have her way. She would have accomplished her own whims just as she had set out to do. But she would lose Jon. And losing Jon now, after everything . . . that seemed the worst kind of pain. Worse than losing her husband. Baron Samedi himself had warned her this choice was coming, hadn't he? That the loa would decide for her, if she could not. But she would.

"For you," she whispered. "I think . . . always for you, Jon."

She knew it was the truth the moment she said it. She felt as if she had betrayed Jacques, and maybe she had a thousand times over in Jon's bed. But hadn't everyone told her to let him go, to let his ghost finally, *finally* rest? Perhaps she could now. Perhaps in choosing Jon, she was choosing herself, to love without consequence, without pain. Maybe now she could be done with being the *Widow Paris.* She could simply be Marie Laveau, and that would be enough.

He kissed her, and she tasted something different, something bitter. *Something is wrong,* Marie thought. But when they pulled apart, he led her by the hand to the wall farthest from the entrance to the tomb. It was too dark to see much of anything, but he guided her hand to the space in the middle.

"There is no going back," said Jon. "You will learn this magic through touch. And you should know many have been driven mad by its power."

A steep price to pay to learn the art of manipulating magic that belonged only to the gods. And now she understood why he had fortified her so. Why she had endured so many long moonlit lessons screaming and crying as he pried into her mind and conjured old demons. He'd been preparing her.

"Are you ready?" he asked.

Marie nodded. She touched a hand to the wall. Glowing white light snaked from her palm out into a winding pattern over the wall. It was the veve of the Lord of the Crossroads, the keeper of the first gateway. Papa Legba. He Who Stands at the Beginning and the End. But the mark changed shape, turning into something she had never seen before, older magic than she had ever known, until it formed a symbol written in the Old Tongue. *Open.*

Bitter cold swept into the tomb, into *her*. The voices of the dead whispered, louder and louder until they were crying out for release, a wretched wailing that made her quiver. But she could not give it to them.

Marie pried her hand back from the wall. It was as if it didn't want to let her go. As if in that single space of a breath, death itself had held her hand. Marie was shaking, but Jon soothed her, wrapping her in his embrace, wiping the tears from her eyes.

"It is done," he murmured against her ear.

When they parted, she saw the white light had crawled across the entire face of the wall, revealing a mural it had been too dark to see before. Marie could see now there was a painting of three figures, old and fading, the color bleeding from it. Shock tore through her.

She was staring directly at herself.

Marie was painted in expert brushstrokes, her wild coils falling in dark ribbons around her face, a glowing sun symbol at the center of her forehead. And to her left was Jon, a crescent moon upon his brow. And there was another, one who looked almost identical to herself, a copper star painted at the center of her brow, a mischievous light in her eyes.

"What is this?" Marie breathed.

"The old slave folk call it the Song of Three. When the first Quarter Queen, Saloppe, was burned at the pyre in the Inquisition, she spoke of a horrendous future: The Church would one day return to New Orleans, and it would wage a war upon those like us. But that is not the will of the loa. So, they convened to make their own trinity." Jon gestured toward the strange mural. "The sun, the moon, and the star that hangs between. The Song of Three."

Marie stared, her mind turning back to the whispered stories of the Holy Inquisition, of the torture and darkness black folks and Les Magiques had endured. And if this Song of Three was true, would they endure it again? Surely it would not come to that. Destiny could be changed, entire futures rewritten.

"You are with child, Marie." There was a softness to his voice, perhaps even a tremble of fear. "*Our* child."

Marie tore her eyes from the young girl's face to look at Jon. "A daughter?"

"Yes. A daughter." His face bore the same old pain she'd glimpsed by the fire the night he'd told her about his origins, a tightness at his eyes that she could not yet understand.

Fear and joy filled her heart. Hadn't she felt the earth move at their coupling, the invisible needle of fate threading one line between herself and Jon, tying them to some invisible force? It was some relief to know she had not simply imagined that divine feeling inside herself, for now she knew it was her child. *Their* child.

With Jacques, the children would not come. Was it the gods themselves who held them back from her? Was it because of this? Was her path always meant to lead to Jon?

Marie smiled, a hand going to her belly. It was not yet round, not yet firm, but it would be. *Soon.* She could be done with her pain at last. For now, she had what she had always needed, what she hadn't thought to want for herself until now. She had a family.

Marie hurried to evening mass, feeling as if her joy carried her down the road. The great blessing of a child. But something else was brewing beneath the surface, some other dark feeling. She'd felt it in their kiss, tasted as much on his tongue. She hadn't been able to shake the feeling that he had told her only a piece of the truth, not the whole of it. It was that word that bothered her most: *Inquisition.*

That the first Quarter Queen had foretold of their coupling, of their child, on the stake troubled her. It was a violent prophecy born in the pain of twisting flames, a tormented purgatory between life and death. Jon was hiding something. She'd tasted lies on his tongue. *No lies,* they had promised each other.

Marie turned her eyes to the cathedral. And who better to seek the truth from than one who had seen the horrors of the First Holy Inquisition himself?

Marie hurriedly crossed the flagstone, careful to keep her hood drawn. She ran. Just as she always did when she was scared. She ran to Antoine, same as she had as a child, to the church, into the arms of her saints and angels. He could help her make sense of this.

Father Antoine's chambers were guarded by two stone archangels: the sword-bearing Michael and his brother Raphael, who bore a long spear in hand. Voices drifted from the shadows. Marie stopped, concealing herself just behind a pillar. There were two men speaking in hushed voices. It was Father Antoine and... Marie's heart stuttered—*Silas.*

Marie stared, finding it hard to believe this was the same quietly commanding alchemist she'd glimpsed in the flickering darkness of the steamboat's belly. What stood before her now was a wretched thing hollowed out by the turn of his own alchemy. His face was pale, all color drawn from him.

"Silas, you mustn't be afraid," Father Antoine was saying. "Your soul will endure this trial." The priest laid a hand on the wizard's shoulder, but Silas recoiled.

"*Soul?*" Silas gave a half laugh, a bitter edge to the sound. All humor vanished from his voice. "Tell me, Father, what *soul?*"

Silas had a strange, faraway look in his eyes, no different from when Sanite scried into the future. But he was not seeing the future, Marie understood. It was the dark of the past.

"Nothing can take what God has given," Antoine said. "Not even from the likes of a wretch like you."

Nothing can take what God has given. Antoine had told her the same, many years before.

Marie had been six years old, sitting in Sunday school with the rest of the girls in her class, when she'd first seen the face of a demon. The parish's priests and nuns could be a prickly bunch, especially when they had to endure "the Voodoo girl." When Marie would pass them in the cathedral halls, they would whisper so that she could hear: *What a strange girl. What an odd child, Marie Laveau.*

Marie always knew she was different; she hardly needed the whispers of holy men to know that. Still, it hurt. Her grand-mère had always cautioned her that the bright thing that lived inside her, that ran through her blood, could be a dark thing as well. That her magic could be poisoned by the words of others if she allowed. So Marie kept her magic hidden, said her prayers, and hardened her heart. But still, they knew.

Marie had taken a piece of charcoal and began tracing. Out of the corner of her eye, a tall, oddly skeletal thing sat at the desk beside hers, next to Ginny Boudreaux, a girl who liked to put wads of honey in Marie's hair when she wasn't looking. It had its hands crossed politely like the rest of the girls who faced Father Antoine as he lectured on about the Book of Psalms. But there was nothing polite about this . . . creature, only a foul darkness that lingered in the room and began to creep into the magic Marie kept hidden away in her heart.

Marie kept tracing but now mumbled a string of prayers under her breath. She remembered Grand-mère's warnings, to always guard her magic from those who wished to poison it. But the creature didn't want to simply poison it—he wanted to *take* it. That's what he'd told her anyway, in a language Marie had never heard before but understood all the same. The creature was hissing, warning her of all the foul things he would do to her once she finally ceased her prayers.

Finally, the church bell tolled, signaling the end of the lesson and the beginning of midday mass. The class emptied, and the rest of the girls clamored on, all except for Marie, who remained at her desk, determined to finish her picture. She knew it was important for her to do so, though she couldn't say exactly why.

Father Antoine stood above her, peering down over his copper spectacles. He looked first at Marie, who remained bent over her task, her fall of dark hair obscuring her work, then to the picture itself.

"Marie?" Father Antoine crouched to her height. He was as tall and spindly as a scarecrow but with eyes as warm as the hot cocoa and chicory Grand-mère made for Marie each morning. *Those are kind eyes,* Marie had found herself thinking. And there were so few to be found in New Orleans. "Marie, did you hear the bells?"

"No, I heard a voice." Marie lifted the picture and showed it to the good priest.

He stared for a moment, those kind eyes going dark, seeing some deeper meaning that she could not. Then he took the page from her, eyes roving over the hideous face, the charred skin, the red eyes that sparkled like rubies from hollow sockets, the long forked tongue that hung from a lipless mouth.

"Do you know what this creature is, Marie Laveau?" asked the priest calmly. Behind him, the creature began to laugh.

"An angel." Marie stuck her tongue out, mimicking the creature. "Not all angels are beautiful."

"Very true, my child. Very true indeed." He said nothing else but took her quietly by the hand and led her to the headmaster's study in the western high tower, hurrying through the torch-lit corridors and then out across cold flagstone. When they had entered the headmaster's quarters, Marie feared she might be expelled. What would Grand-mère think? She couldn't afford to pay for Marie's schooling elsewhere, and who else would take a colored girl, free or not, in their classroom?

Father Antoine pulled a large book from a locked chest at the very back of the room. When he brought it before Marie and showed her a collection of horrid faces, she suddenly understood this wasn't a meeting to expel her from the Church. This was an invitation to go deeper.

"Is this the one that you drew, child?" he asked, tapping the face of the very same creature Marie had glimpsed in the classroom.

Marie nodded.

"And how did you come to see it?"

"It was sitting beside me." Marie thought hard. "Well, actually, beside Ginny, but close enough that I could hear it whispering to me."

"I see." He closed the book, scattering amber dust from its crinkled folds. "You were correct, child. That creature you saw was an angel. In the genesis of its form. But now it is of the fallen, and we call these creatures demons."

Marie considered this explanation. The demon, in its strange language, had announced itself an angel upon arrival. Marie had thought it slightly strange but could sense some truth in its words. She supposed hearing a half-truth was a bit like seeing a color that possessed no name. You knew it was there, could see it clearly, yet hadn't the sense or the knowledge to give it a proper name. She supposed demons lied the same way—twisting their lies into truths so intricately that it was impossible to pick one from the other, to know which from which, so that their words took on a new form entirely, impossible to name.

Father Antoine uncorked a vial of blessed oil from his shelf and made a cross over Marie's forehead. The oil was warm against her skin, the first brushes of spring sunlight. "That was no ordinary demon, Marie," said Father Antoine quietly. "That was a demon of an exceptionally high demonic house. He serves the arch-demon of violent subjugation, Moloch. *The Lord of Chains.*"

The demon had told her that too. It had whispered of the Lord of Chains, whose shackles held an ironclad stronghold over all of New Orleans, whose misery and contempt poisoned the air of every auction block, who fed from the pain that lived in the writhing darkness of every slave ship's shadowed belly.

"The demon you saw today was called the *Snatcher of Gifts*. Often sent as an emissary to stop a thing before it can truly begin. To snatch an innocent at the bud of its power before it can grow. And let me tell you something, child: You've a very special gift, young Marie. Many will mock you, spit at you, try to stamp it out and steal it for their own. But no man, no demon, and no *angel*"—the corners of his eyes creased pleasantly—"can take what God has given." He stared down at Marie as if seeing her properly for the first time. "You are a very special child, Marie Laveau. Do you know what that makes you, truly?"

"What?" Marie asked quietly. *Monster,* the demon whispered in her ear. He was here with them now.

"An ally," Father Antoine said. "An exceptional ally to God. And in these coming days, the Vatican will need friends from all places, those high and low. You will help me save the Church."

"Save the Church from what, Father?" asked Marie. The demon was laughing, a high keening. *Liar,* the demon taunted from over Antoine's shoulder. *Liar. Liar. Liar.*

But Father Antoine's face was filled with such conviction that Marie couldn't help but steal some for herself. *"From itself."*

Now Antoine kept his eyes steady on the alchemist, as gentle as they had been with Marie all those years ago. Silas was looking past Antoine, searching the darkness. Startled, Marie ducked back behind the pillar, heart pounding. Just what had she overheard? When she looked again, Antoine and Silas were gone, the corridor empty.

"A word of advice, Laveau," came a voice from the shadows. Marie whirled to find Silas standing in front of her. Crackling vitality had returned to him, and with it, his usual air of silent contempt, that same look of mocking disdain.

His eyes swept over her tearstained cheeks. "Cry your tears if you must, witch. But outside of these walls, you'd do well to use some of that infamous magic on yourself"—his voice fell soft, strangely gentle—"and turn that bleeding heart of yours to stone."

Silas held her gaze, eyes cutting through the shadows at her. And then he was gone.

Were those the words of an ally or foe? Truthfully, with a man like Silas, she might never know. And there was simply no time. Marie hurried forward into Antoine's chambers.

He was at his great bookshelf, running a finger along the various timeworn tomes, his reading glasses hanging down the bridge of his nose. He took one look at her breathless appearance and made his way to her. "Marie, what is the matter?"

"I am with child, Antoine," Marie said. "Jon's child. I am to have a daughter."

Antoine remained very still, watching her with that same unending patience he had when Marie had first been brought into his quarters as a little girl. He was grayer now, older, but the same.

"Sanite, she . . . warned me of Jon's growing influence on you."

"Jon is a good man," insisted Marie.

Antoine turned away from her, his weathered eyes on the Holy Virgin, who stared down at them both, her marbled eyes completely white and unseeing. "I fear . . . I fear there is no such thing in New Orleans, child. Not even me."

"What exactly is the Song of Three?" Antoine said nothing. His silence told her that he knew. "Did you know this entire time?" she pressed.

"I knew only what the Inquisitors spoke of in whispers," he said finally. "I was a simple priest, Marie. The Inquisition, it was . . . terrible work. Maddening work. You could not always trust the words of those being persecuted. I had hoped that it would not come to pass." He stared into Marie's eyes, into the cold eyes of the past. "When they burned Saloppe at the stake, she spoke of three vessels that would avenge not just her death, but the deaths of all her people. She said that these vessels would form a trinity of power, a triad chosen by the Voodoo gods themselves. The sun, the moon, the star. A union of bloodlines."

The strange mural on the wall. The sun, the moon, and the star. Voodoo's trinity.

"But the child," continued Antoine, "the child would be the sacred conduit, the meeting point at which two vibrant magics flowed. But you know best of all, Marie. Power like this rarely comes without consequence."

"What are you saying, Antoine?" Her voice trembled.

The silence between them seemed to stretch forever. Another second and she would go mad.

"The child would have to die," Antonio de Sedella said at last.

Marie closed her eyes, tears slipping down her cheeks. She wanted to scream.

The Baron's promise, Jon's words at the fire: *I would feel this pain once more, but only once more.* Marie felt her heart twist.

And then she remembered the golden eyes of the snake that bit her. They were Jon's eyes too. She remembered the poison he'd sucked from her veins, the poison he'd made her drink with every sweet kiss and lesson. Those eyes had been trying to tell her something . . . something she'd missed. Jon was a man of practice and principle. He did nothing that had not already been calculated a thousand times over. And then Marie understood. The whole thing had been a stage. A performance before the real thing. Jon was powerful, his magic older than hers. But he was not strong enough for his war. Not *yet*. For that, he would need a conduit to raise his army of zombi.

One last missing piece.

Jon had told her what he intended all along without her realizing. *We must be willing to sacrifice the few to save the many.*

Marie shook her head. "No, I will not let that come to pass. I will *never* allow that." A million thoughts, a million paths before her. Each one leading to the birth and death of her child. Her daughter. "What am I to do? Please, tell me, there must be something—"

"You must keep away from Jon until the child is born, Marie."

"And then?"

"We will baptize the child and look after her together. And you." Father Antoine's eyes dampened with emotion. "You will become the mother you are destined to be. Until then, we must pray fervently. We must pray God forgives us for what we must do."

She should not ask, especially when she could not bear the answer. But ask she did. Because in the end, she would find a way to bear this pain as she had for all the others. For her child, she must. "And Jon?"

"When the time is right, you will use what he has taught you." Antoine took her by the hand as if she were still the same scared little girl who spoke of visions and demons. "But, Marie, you must be sure to strike him first."

CHAPTER TWENTY-ONE

REE

When Ree awoke on the floor in the bayou house, Claudette was bent over her, shaking her back and forth by the shoulders until her teeth rattled.

"What did you learn?" the older witch demanded. "Whatever it was, it was not good. You were screaming like a goat."

Ree said nothing and climbed to her feet, striding over to the water dish filled with lemon balm and rose petals that they used to dampen Marie's brow to keep the fever down. She splashed her face, tried her best to wash away her mother's memories. But they were there, seared into her mind, where they might live forever.

"I know what the Song of Three means now," said Ree. How long had it been since that night she'd heard the spirits' riddle in the bayou? They'd seemed resistant to tell her then, she just couldn't understand why. Would she have even believed them if they had told her what the first Quarter Queen's words had truly meant? What they meant for Ree? Though only a week had passed, Ree could see the stubborn girl she'd been, so foolish and brash, making a game of everything in her path. But this was no game—this was her *life*.

"The Song of Three is just talk," Claudette said. "Fable born out of the Inquisition. A riddle the old folks tell themselves to make meaning out of a dark time."

"No, it *isn't*, Claudette. It's about my parents. It's about me." She faltered. "I . . . I was supposed to die." But Marie had changed that, somehow. She'd changed fate.

Claudette hissed, emerald eyes flashing, and fanned herself with her tarot cards. "'Tis bad juju to suggest such things."

"It is the truth. I saw it for myself. I was born of both their magic." Marie's light and Jon's darkness twined together into some unnamable thing. Into her. "I turned Marcel into a zombi. The Harbinger says a Laveau witch will raise the dead—*don't you see?* It's me, Claudette. I was the thing Jon wanted to use."

"And what would he have done with you?"

Ree wasn't sure of the particulars, or that she even wanted to know. Not entirely. "The loa demanded final sacrifice before they would grant him a rebellion." A sacrifice her father had been willing to make. But not Marie. She felt herself seeded with guilt. She'd always scorned her mother's protections, her ever-watchful eye. But now she knew. If she had known the truth, perhaps their relationship would have been different. But hindsight would do her no favors now.

"But that didn't happen. Your mother saved you. *That* is why she warred with Jon."

Kind as they were, Claudette's words didn't make the truth any easier for Ree to accept. That her own father could come to the decision to sacrifice her. *We must be willing to sacrifice the few to save the many.* To some, that might make him the hero. There was relief in knowing that this other side of her magic was her father's blood at work. That even if it had killed her, he had been willing to use it to save others. A terrible bargain. But New Orleans was full of them.

Her mother took gasping, shallow breaths, her body fragile on the bed. The truth burned Ree's throat: Marie was wasting away. She would be lucky if she lived through the night. Which meant Ree couldn't wait any longer. If she was going to open the Veil, then she must do it now. She stalked to the door but felt a sudden breath of wind push her backward. She whirled to see Claudette staring at her, hands on her hips. How very controlling L'Enchanteresse had become during their time together—some might even say *concerned.*

"And just where are you going?"

"To save my mother!" snapped Ree. "To the city of the fucking dead. That's where Jon hid the spell, Claudette. It's where the Veil magic has been this whole time."

"You can't go just yet."

"And why the hell not?"

"Because of this."

Claudette produced a golden slip of paper affixed with the city's seal, the fleur-de-lis. Ree crooked a finger, and the letter floated into her waiting hand. She read it over:

> *Mayor Felix Corbin*
> *Requests the honor of your presence*
>
> *On Tuesday evening, February 28th*
> *At eight o'clock*
>
> *Théâtre des Lys*
> *New Orleans*
> *1786 Royal Street*

"Then I will not go." She didn't have time for silly celebrations. The magic of Mardi Gras was useless to her tonight.

"Don't be a fool. You can't refuse him. Not after you were caught raising the dead."

"What if it's a trap? You want me to walk directly into it?"

"That is *exactly* what I would have you do, child." She shuffled the shiny silver-and-plum cards with a loud flourish. "You will go to him in a pretty dress. You will drink wine like the rest of the city. You must distract him. Make him believe all the world comes to him. And then, you will slip away while he is preoccupied. Refuse him, and I guarantee he will send officers to every door you've ever walked through in a matter of hours."

Ree had to concede she made a point. But then she looked at her meager dress, which would not do for Corbin's illustrious bal masqué. "I don't have anything to wear."

"Never mind that," Claudette said with a smirk. "Let me work my magic. We shall ask the cards what character you may become."

With a quick flash of her hands, she began shuffling, the golden bangles on her arms tinkling. One card leapt from the bunch, and she turned it over and tapped its glossy surface with a long painted nail. *The High Priestess.*

After Claudette had finished the long task of dressing her, Ree adjusted her mask, checking her reflection in the large gilded looking glass. The irony was not lost on her that this was the mirror Marie had once gazed into while Sanite prepared her for Mardi Gras night, for her fateful meeting with the Conjurer. But it was not her mother she saw. It was the High Priestess who stared back at her now, dark eyes enigmatic beneath the thin slip of golden lace set with tiny diamond specks she'd worn as her mask, the long shimmering black veil that had been carefully picked to accentuate the dark waves of her hair. Claudette had interwoven the gold cloth of her mother's tignon beneath the lace, something that made Ree nervous. The tignon was her mother's. It was *her* crown, after all. But tonight, the piece of fabric was just that—a piece of fabric. It would become the crown only on its chosen successor.

The top of the lace was adorned in a pointed tiara of golden metalwork, the jutting ends fixed with tiny silver stars set at the tips. The gown was sewn in a mixture of copper, gold, and black lace, the shoulders left bare. She could be the Madonna, some gaudy version of the holy mother. *Or,* a dark voice sang at her ear, *you could be as you are meant to. You could be a queen.*

Ree pushed her way through the madness of Mardi Gras. The crowd of revelers had grown thick on this end of Royal Street, people choking her from all sides. She was tempted to use magic to force her way through, but eventually she gave up on the notion entirely. She thought it best to preserve her energy for the ball. She didn't exactly expect Corbin to be up to his best behavior. In fact, she was expecting that she might very well be walking into a trap.

Golden and silver beads fell into the darkened streets from the balconies above, where masked faces jeered down at her, their voices and laughter blending into indistinguishable debauchery.

Light posts glistened where elaborate gold, purple, and green bows had been tied. The gambling parlors, taverns, alehouses, and hotels had all thrown open their doors, the arches well lit in flickering sconces enchanted with purple and gold flames.

The crowd pressed around her, a carousel of faces, each more terrible and beautiful than the last. Sailors and tourists, whores, dancers, magicians, fancy well-to-dos, trumpet-carrying musicians, children, and simple local folks transfigured into vampires and ghouls, phantoms, fairies, and all manner of folktale beasts. Men with horns protruding from their foreheads, masks with long beaks over the noses, white-lacquered disguises, others crafted entirely of plumed feathers. Ree passed lovers locked in searing kisses. Pretty women who'd adorned their bare breasts in jewels and danced along the banquettes. A blond woman sheathed in a glistening white bridal veil, on her knees in an alley, wiping the back of her mouth with her hand. All manner of sin allowed, no pleasure spared. *No saints and no sinners.*

Ree was tempted to snatch a fat piece of beignet from a sweet stand manned by an old fellow donning a feathered disguise, but she thought better of it—the powdered dust would ruin the rouge along her cheeks and lips, the face Claudette had so carefully painted upon her. Ree slid her mask into place and started up the gilded steps that led toward the Théâtre des Lys's double doors, grateful for the disguise. She stepped inside to see the theater had been transformed.

It was a masquerade ball, after all, so she should have expected nothing less than pure transfiguration. Corbin ran his annual bal masqué without fail, sparing no expense. Still, her breath hitched. Shut away from the raucous music and mannerless behavior that had overtaken most of the Quarter's main streets, the theater seemed a city all its own. The floor was a sea of twirling gowns and tinkling laughter. Dignified dandies and refined women with pale-beaded gloves and piles of pearls at their necks, wigs tiered like white-frosted cakes, gowns that moved like La Sirene's water in the candlelight, opulent masks woven with delicate lace and gemstones.

Ree spied endless casks of champagne and honeyed mead. Tables laden with towering king cakes iced in yellow and purple and green as big as her head, their multicolored insides filled with raspberry jam and cream. Steaming pots of spiced coffee that smelled of chicory. Mountains of glistening oysters, scarlet-bellied crabs that had been stewed in butter and garlic, braided sweetbread, little golden dishes of sugared sauces and jams. An old black woman in an apron ladled scalding cupfuls of red jambalaya onto dishes of rice and cornbread.

She spotted Corbin at one end of the chamber, lounging on a long golden settee. She was reminded of the man on the steamboat who'd sanctioned the torture of runaways for his own pleasure and sport. Now here he was, pretending he was the picture of diplomatic grandeur, the Carnival King before his court. Another mask. Another illusion. Ree squared her shoulders, plucked a glass of champagne from a tray beside her, and went to him.

"Marie Laveau the Second," Corbin said as she neared. He stood, brandishing his cup. The scarred half of his face was hidden beneath a shiny copper disguise, the other half left bare. That half was smiling at her. "I don't believe we've ever had the chance to be properly acquainted." They hadn't until now. "I don't think I ever got the chance to thank you for saving my life, sweet girl."

He could hold his praises. It hadn't been to save him, not really, and he knew that. It had been to spare the Voodoos of the consequences Anabelle's killing of the mayor would bring. "You could start by lifting this newest curfew on the Voodoos," said Ree.

"Let us not be hasty. Certain precautions were needed after that day in Congo Square. But your magic was magnificent, I must say. I've seen your mother at work, in glimpses and flashes at her little moonlit rituals in Bayou St. John or the square. But she is so controlled." Corbin waved a gloved hand. "You, on the other hand . . . you showed me pure instinct. Wild power."

"Is that truly what you want in a witch in your city, Mayor?" She'd meant to goad him, but his eyes flashed, and she instantly regretted it.

He'd transformed before her eyes. The man they called the Collector stared back at her, the monster who plucked and preened his careful crop of slaves like treasured dolls, trinkets he could admire and polish then stow away into his war chest. The man who owned Marcel.

"If they are under my control," he murmured. He reached out, stroked a piece of dark hair along her shoulder. "You would be surprised what manner of pleasures and freedoms I allow in my house, Mademoiselle."

"Hmph. I suppose my great-grandmother simply made up her terrible time."

"You are a sassy one." He pursed his lips, thinking on it. "The Vatican has made their intentions known through High Inquisitor Broussard. If a second Inquisition were to come to New Orleans, you would need protection, would you not? Your mother cannot protect you, not from that."

"She has managed well enough," replied Ree stiffly.

"And where is your mother, young child?" He looked about the chamber. "Where is Marie Laveau?"

Did he know? Could he know? It was possible that it had slipped somehow, that talk of Marie's condition had spread from among the Voodoo ranks into the city. And Silas knew, but for whatever reason he hadn't come to collect on her weakness, and she supposed she should give thanks to the loa for that.

"I could protect you from the Vatican," the Collector said. "You would remain unscathed from their Inquisitors. I would see no harm come to a witch who bears my seal."

"Chains," Ree said with a sip of her champagne. "You mean chains."

"Certain precautions, always."

Ree let out a bitter laugh. "Oh, I do believe you are taking precautions, sir. I believe you are scared. There are rumblings, talk of other rebellions in other states. What of Alabama? Georgia? Mississippi? They will hear what that great rule-abiding city of New Orleans has done with their magical-blooded, free or not. And they will be frightened. There are inklings of a civil war on the wind, Mayor."

After what happened with Anabelle, and then her escape, folks might feel bold. Certainly, there was a feeling of anger in the air for the injustices that had gone unanswered for so long. Marcel's hanging had been tinder in the flame, and his resurrection brought notions of Haiti's revolution that New Orleans was not in a position to ignore.

Corbin's face darkened, nostrils flaring. "Be very, *very* careful, little girl, of what you say next."

"I say you're afraid. You wanted my mother, didn't you? But you couldn't have her. She was stronger than you." His eyes flattened, and Ree smirked. "And now you want another weapon to add to your collection. Well, it will never be me."

"I can make it so. Just like *that*"—he snapped his fingers—"you insolent little cunt."

"I don't think you will, Mayor. You see, maybe we let the Inquisition come. And maybe I will be taken, arrested. Tortured even. But you? What would our sweet enterprising governor think of *you*, Felix? You would be the man who allowed all of the city's magic to die on a stake. That would be very, very bad for business." It was she who leaned in now, her voice a silken whisper at his ear. "Press me again, Felix, and I'll turn myself in to Inquisitor Broussard. And if I go, I can promise you, the rest will follow."

There was a faint *crick* as the glass of wine in his hand splintered up the side.

But Ree held her ground. It was a cruel bluff, she knew. A terrible, terrible gambit to make. But it was the only language men like Corbin knew, the only one they feared. If she went down, he would go with her.

Corbin stared dumbfounded, eyes narrowing into his face as he considered the violent possibility she painted in no uncertain terms. "You play a dangerous hand, little girl. But you forget yourself. This entire city is my game. And only I make the cards," he said at last.

Beneath the drawl and bravado, it was clear—she'd just scared the most powerful man in New Orleans. She only hoped it might be enough to buy her the time she desperately needed to save her mother.

Ree turned, heart racing as she snatched another flute of champagne, downed it in one go, then disappeared into the crowd. No sooner had she escaped Corbin than a dark-gloved hand caught hers.

A tall man in a colorful lacquered jester mask cocked his head to the side, long white-blond hair spilling over his shoulders.

"Silas," she hissed.

"Hello, little witch."

Ree made to move past him, to rid herself of him once and for all, but he pulled her firmly into a dance. "Get off of me!"

"Careful, now, people are watching. I don't think you want an audience, my sweet." He leaned in close to her ear. "We wouldn't want them looking too closely, now, would we? Asking too many questions? *Where is the beautiful Marie Laveau, I wonder?*"

Ree froze. He took the opportunity to swiftly pull her into a twirl, and she begrudgingly fell into step with him. She glanced around. No one was watching, everyone was watching. That was the beauty of a masquerade. They could be anyone. Not a Voodoo witch and a Brotherhood alchemist. She was the High Priestess, all-knowing, and he the mad-eyed jester.

"Let me go," she growled.

As if sensing her fear, Silas leaned in. "Do you remember my offer of friendship? Now would be the time I would highly encourage you to reconsider."

But Ree wasn't listening. In the very back of the room, a tall figure in a hooded red robe watched her from behind a black lacquered mask that shone with an eerie stillness under the fall of torchlight. But she knew it was him. Henryk.

Ree said nothing, her mind turning to their last encounter in Antoine's quarters, the fear she'd felt coming face-to-face with the man behind that mask, watching her with such sterile emptiness. Silas silently tracked her gaze. "He's been watching you this entire time."

"He hates me." She didn't know why she said it, only that she did. The champagne had made her dizzy, wild in a way she hadn't allowed herself to feel since before the interrogation.

"The boy does not know hate. Not really." Silas's voice darkened. "I have seen hate, little witch. Seen its true face. And I can tell you that is not the face the Inquisitor wears."

"Are you defending the Inquisition?"

"Listen to me, Marie Laveau the Second, and listen close: You'd do well to form an alliance with the Brotherhood before time runs out. We shall need one another to survive what comes next. Do you think your gods can protect you? Did they? The first time? The First Inquisition peeled the skin from your ancestors' bones. They bleed like the rest of us."

The jester spun her around, the room tilting in a vision of silk and laughter.

"And that's what's coming again to this city. But this time, you must know they will scorch earth. I promise you, sweet, the Brotherhood will not be burned. I trust you to stand on our side."

"The side of victory?"

"No." His voice was cold, all humor vanished. "Survival."

Ree stared into the jester's face, silently turning over his offer in her mind like a coin. She had seen in her mother's memories her brief meetings with Silas, how the alchemist had maneuvered her with the same toying façade. But she couldn't help but see now that something else might live beneath such a mask. Something that scared her to know might be there, the side of him that had intervened aboard that steamboat to spare Marie, to slip Jon the code. But *why*?

"And if I do not?"

"Then I will be forced to change the rules of this game. And I told you once. I play to win." His eyes glimmered from behind the dark hollows of his mask. "Always."

"And what about your piece on the board?"

Silas smirked, eyes flitting to the back of the room, then away. "Needn't you worry, little witch. That piece is already in motion."

The song had ended. The brass band was changing tune. Ree wrenched herself away from him, but as she did, she felt a shock to her hand, the one that Silas had held in his.

A bright flare of light like a stroke of lightning. No, not lightning, she realized. It was fire. Something was burning. She was burning. She was Silas. There was a house on fire, flames greedily eating away at every crevice, every morsel. She kneeled before it, uselessly staring at the flames. Someone was inside. Someone was on fire. Someone, a woman, was desperately screaming for her. For Silas. But she could not move. She could only stare and watch as the fire ate—

Ree was back in the theater, back beneath the twinkling lights of Corbin's ball. People laughed and sang and drank around her. No one was screaming for her. For Silas.

"You are . . . not who you say you are," Ree murmured. The man had two faces. She didn't know more than that. Couldn't even say why she'd said the words. But she knew beyond a shadow of a doubt that they were true.

Silas watched her for a moment. Slowly, he lifted his mask, and she could see him fully at last. He'd shaven the goatee, and the face beneath it was surprisingly youthful. Cold. And he was not laughing now.

But suddenly Silas was smiling again, adjusting his mask back into perfect place. "In this city, no one ever is."

Silas disappeared into the crowd, leaving her alone. Ree whirled, one hand clenching her gown, eyes going to the space along the back wall. But Henryk was nowhere to be seen.

The mausoleum rumbled open, and Ree stepped inside, into the eerie darkness of Jon's tomb. When she'd slipped away from Corbin's ball, she was careful to keep to the shadows, to make sure no one was trailing her. But the truth was, she was rattled. She might have said the worst of the masquerade was facing the mayor himself, the very real threat he now posed to her. But she'd be lying. The worst had been seeing Henryk again, masked and cold. It was a final reminder to her that he was the enemy, and to wish him to be anything less, anything different, was simply a danger she could not risk anymore.

She held out a hand, calling to the fire god. A red-gold flame leapt into her palm, illuminating the mausoleum's darkened depths. Ree stepped forward, holding her burning palm out like a lantern until she came to the painting of herself, her mother, and Jon. A golden sun glowed on her mother's brow, a crooked silver moon on her father's. And on hers, a dark copper star, bright even in the shadows. The words came to her mind at once: *the Song of Three*. The words of the spirits after the demon's Harbinger.

Ree pressed her glowing hand to the mural like she had seen her mother do in her memory. Light spilled along the wall, moving into the pocks and edges that marked the stone until it formed a glowing veve in the shape of a large doorway, revealing the spell her father had hidden inside. In the Old Tongue, it had a single meaning: *Open.*

Ree put an ear to the wall. Something was whispering behind it, pleading to her. And then she heard it. She heard *them*. A hundred, no, a *thousand* voices demanding to be let out. *Open. Open. Open.* Something thudded behind her. Ree whirled to face the darkness. Something was slowly crawling out of it, edging closer to her. She was reminded of the riddle the children chanted on Sundays on their way to mass: *Banish the devil through the door and welcome in six more.*

"Marie Laveau the Second," came a slithering voice from the dark. "Daughter of Jon. Did you like our Harbinger? We've heard you do love a good riddle."

The demon stepped fully from the shadows and into the light of her flame. It took the shape of a man in the barest sense—the body tall and skeletal, but the skin sagged over the bones like withered fruit hanging from a dead tree. The eyes shone like bloodied rubies in the darkness, irises thin like a serpent's. It was the demon who had visited her mother as a child, not an arch-demon. *Snatcher of Gifts.*

Ree took a step back, the flame burning brighter in her hand. If she found it hard to think in the presence of the divine, being so close to the damned was far worse. Fear sunk into her bones like a cold bayou wind, the rotten smell choking her, the glowing eyes that could turn her limbs to stone with a single glance.

"You should be careful onto which doors you knock, little girl," said the demon with a rattling laugh that made her skin crawl. "You never know who might answer."

Death is but a doorway. She didn't have her mother's training. She didn't have a teacher like Jon who'd known how to guard Marie against what evils death might bring. She had only herself.

The demon studied her surprise with barely contained delight. She knew better than to show fear in the face of a demon. But she couldn't help it—they had a special way of coaxing the worst out of you.

"Begone," said Ree. "I will cast you out."

"You should try," it hissed, its tongue flicking from its mouth. "I do love a good game. Don't you, Marie Laveau the Second? We in hell hear you love games. There are many we might show you someday." It moved closer. Something moved at the hem of its dark cloak. Ree froze. A horde of snakes coiled around the demon's legs, hissing at her. "You are your father's daughter. Special, no doubt. But did you think he could ever truly love you? You silly, silly girl. And your mother is the sssssame."

All fear evaporated, fury prickling over Ree's skin. "Don't you dare say her name—"

"You are a tool to them, child. A weapon. A useless weapon, but a weapon all the same. You can't stop what's coming. The Inquisition will return to this city, as the Lord of Chains has decreed, and the streets will run with blood, and we will drink of it. That blood will be on your hands, Marie Laveau the Second, but do not fear." It smiled, that tongue flicking like the thundercrack of a whip. "We shall gladly lick every last drop from them too. *Allow me to show you.*"

The demon seized Ree, and at once she saw a flood of horrendous images before her: *Rows of charred corpses hanging limp on jutting spikes. Nan. Ory. Fabrice. Claudette. Brotherhood. Countless Les Magiques dead. Jeering crowds, faces twisted cruelly as they hurled stones and curses at long processions of heretics being marched to their doom. The black-lacquered faces of Inquisitors watching through twisting dark smoke.*

And through the smoke she saw the most horrifying image of them all—herself.

There she was, Marie Laveau the Second, naked and shackled before a crowd, writhing in the agony of a slow death as she burned on a pyre. And burned. And burned ...

"If you open the Veil and save your mother, you will forfeit your own life," snarled the demon. "*This* is the fate you will damn yourself to. This is what will become of you!"

A horrendous wail tore into the air, the frenzied sound of a thousand animals slaughtered on stone altars for sacrifice, a chorus of torture and long suffering. The sound of the damned. It was Ree. She was screaming. She couldn't take it anymore. But the demon held her firm, holding her in that terrible vision. Its power all-consuming.

A hand seized her by the arm, shaking her. She'd expected claws and horribly scaled flesh, but these hands were oddly warm, and very much alive.

"Come back, Ree," a rough voice commanded. "Come back to me."

Come back to me. Those had been her first words to Henryk Broussard, the words she'd used to coax him back to life. It was Henryk Broussard who spoke them to her now.

But she couldn't come back. It was as if she were split between two places at once, in that terrible vision of sulfur and ash and fire, and now in the tomb with Henryk. She was caught between them, and they both pulled at her, threatening to tear her in two.

Henryk was shaking her fiercely now. "Damn it, Ree! *Wake the hell up!* You're going to die! The demon is possessing you!"

And then his lips were upon hers. It felt like a stroke of lightning had hit her right in the spine, the feeling traveling down through her blood and into her bones. It was torture. It was heaven. She drank from his power greedily, stealing it for her own. Somewhere in the midst of her muddled thoughts, Ree understood what he was doing, what shouldn't be possible. But she felt herself kissing him back, channeling that dark feeling into her body, giving her strength.

Ree's eyes flew open, and the nightmare shriveled away at last. The demon was gone. The tomb was empty, and she was on the ground, kneeling in the darkness. Henryk had folded his arms around her, holding her close, interlacing his hand in hers. Ree's eyes fluttered, sleep creeping over her vision.

"What was that?" she whispered. He'd given her something of his own, enough to fight the demon off. Something an Inquisitor of the Church should never possess. Ree slumped against him, fighting back the weight of darkness tugging at her.

Through the fog, she saw that his eyes were alight. Not gray, but silver.

He smiled. "It was magic, of course."

And then the Inquisitor lifted her into his arms, and she allowed herself to drift away into the blessed quiet of oblivion, far away from the smell of burning flesh and bone.

PART THREE

THE SONG OF THREE

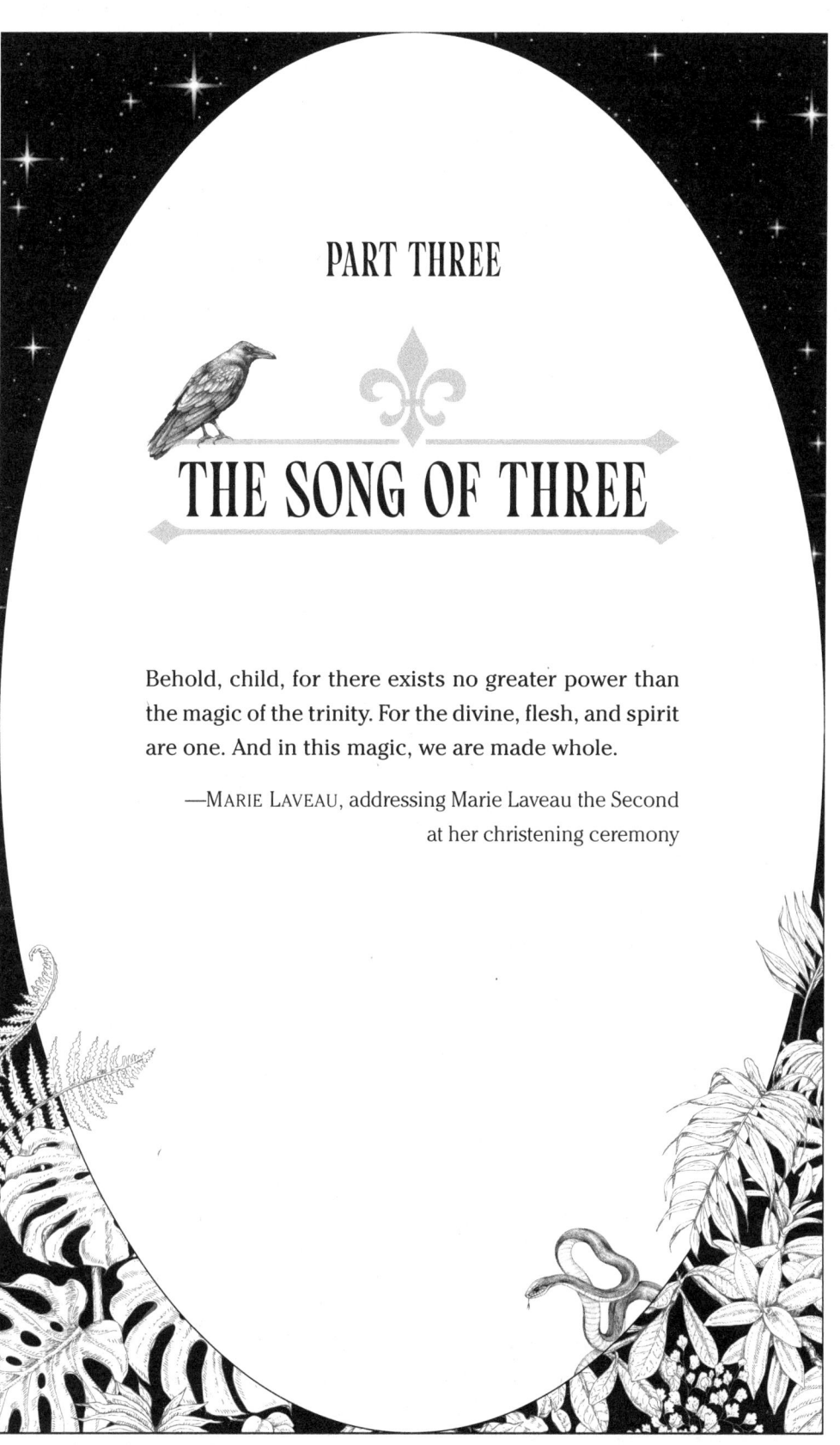

Behold, child, for there exists no greater power than the magic of the trinity. For the divine, flesh, and spirit are one. And in this magic, we are made whole.

—MARIE LAVEAU, addressing Marie Laveau the Second at her christening ceremony

CHAPTER TWENTY-TWO

MARIE

In the long months since Marie had discovered she was with child, she'd done her best to prepare her body. She'd prayed fervently, ate her greens and roots and nourishing soups. She'd warded herself, made the right sacrifices at her ancestral altars. But nothing could prepare her for this.

Marie screamed. The pain itself was alive inside of her, working its way through her innards, past her organs, and against the swollen flesh of her belly. On and on it went.

She panted, her sweat-soaked cotton dress clinging to her skin. And then she pushed. The pain rippled over her in waves, this one threatening to drag her under. She couldn't take much more.

When Marie had been with child before, she'd never carried to term. How many times had she awoken screaming, agonized by the sight of all that blood seeping down her thighs? She'd come close once, right before Jacques's disappearance. He had been the one to wake her that night, the one who carried her to the bath and sponged the blood from between her legs and thighs. Later, he'd held her through the tears and sobs, the grief unending. But when he had gone and left her too, there had been no one to hold her fast, no one to share in her pain.

But not this time. This child would not be like the others, she knew. She would birth her daughter. She must. Grand-mère's old house rattled from the force of the wind. The woods were howling tonight, the spirits were talking. But what were they saying? *Warnings*, Marie thought. *Omens.* Sanite had tried to warn her too, in her own way, just as Antoine had done.

After Antoine's warning, Marie had gone to the only mother she knew—the Quarter Queen. Marie supposed she should have been grateful Sanite had gone with her, for she didn't think she had the strength to face Jon alone.

Jon's mausoleum had rumbled open before them. Marie and Sanite stepped inside, churning red spheres of Ogoun's flame conjured in both of their outstretched hands. Shadows fell across the cold stone walls. A flicker of the mural sliced through the dark: The three of them. A family.

Marie would have her answers—and she would have them now. *Jon!* she called, voice echoing in the hollows of the tomb.

He came at once, in a soft *whoosh* that threw her hair behind her, ruffled the folds of her muslin gown. Marie watched black shadows dart along the wall, a flock of birds descending, heard the brush of their wings in her ear. Jon stepped easily from the darkness.

Hello, love, Jon had said. The Conjurer tipped his hat to Sanite. *Quarter Queen.*

Sanite tutted. *Jon. Tell her the truth. Tell her what you make of the Song of Three, boy.*

His eyes narrowed, his resolve firm. He would not be bent, and he would not break. And why should he? He had survived the worst this world had to offer. *The Song of Three was clear. The child would die before war would begin.*

No, Marie said with a gasp. *I will never allow that. Not for them. Not even for you.*

The Song of Three was wrong. Or Jon was wrong. Maybe both. It mattered not. Marie would not succumb to foolish prophecies. She would fight them all if it came to it. Sanite stood firm at her side, a silent sentinel appraising the shift in power. Her magic rose, moving invisibly along the tomb's walls, those all-seeing eyes washing over them in a cool breath. Had she seen this moment before? Had she known it would all end like this?

The loa told me you would move against me in the end. I had hoped fate could be changed. His eyes cut from Marie to Sanite. *I suppose it cannot.*

Me move against you? You move against us! Your family!

His eyes hardened, bitter gold. *You know nothing of my family! Nothing!*

And there it was. The truth. Or at least all she needed from it.

Marie recoiled, breathless. She took a step back. She had foolishly thought that they might build something new together. Not to replace what he had lost. But to make anew, to endure the way all their kin were taught to in this world—how to heal when the wounds still bled. But she was mistaken. He didn't want a family with her. He didn't even want her.

Jon took a hesitant step toward her, realizing himself. *Marie ... I ...*

Marie's fury split the air. With a flick of her finger, Jon was flung back into the wall, right into his mural. It cracked down the middle, over their daughter's smirking face. The picture of their family ruined. The way he had always intended.

Never touch me again, she said coldly, voice trembling, as she shut away the memories of their first night together, and the many, many long nights after. *Never.*

Jon looked up at her, a cold wetness in his eyes. He didn't fight her. Not now, not when he so easily could have. No. He would wait.

Know this, Conjurer, Marie whispered. *If you should come for this child, I will use every bit of magic in the world to rend you in fucking half, even if it kills me.*

Jon righted himself, adjusted his frock coat. *After everything I have taught you.* He shook his head. *You still haven't learned a thing. You can't stop what the gods have started, Marie. None of us can.*

Marie gritted her teeth, the flame in her hand flaring brighter. She would. Jon's eyes held hers one last time, and in a flurry of wings he was gone.

He is not wrong, said Sanite. Slowly, Marie turned to face her. *Your fates are intertwined, Marie. I had hoped the gods would have been mistaken.*

What are you saying?

Her voice had grown weary now, and she coughed, the sound echoing throughout the dark of the tomb. *You have always known yourself to have a destiny much greater than others.' It is why the others scorn you so. And one day, they will praise you from the same lips that curse you, this I promise. But Jon? He comes from the High Blood in the old land. I tried to rid myself of him many times. And each time, he returns stronger.* Sanite's weary eyes fell to the girl in the middle of the mural. *Together, you would make a child capable of untold magic. The war she will bring is the will of the loa.*

Marie had stilled; her stomach twisted.

I have seen, my dear girl, and I have known, murmured Sanite. *You will be a fearsome queen, Marie. And you will keep peace for a time. But your child? She will bring forth the will of the ancestors. And there will be costs.* She took Marie's hand in hers. *Your daughter will herald the Second Inquisition.* Her eyes fell to Marie's rounded belly. *Which is why you must rid yourself of the child now.*

Marie put a hand to her belly, felt the firmness of her skin, the telltale tremor of magic that was not her own. *What are you saying?* She felt herself growing hysterical.

Sanite nodded, those hazy eyes insisting she see the truth. *I tried to spare you from him. I encouraged you to see him with your own eyes, to see him for what he is: dangerous. He endangers us all. Recklessly risks what little freedom we have left. And I tell you now, Jon will use that child as a sacrifice for his magic. You must stop him now, stop any of this from coming to pass by ridding yourself of the child—*

Enough! Rage flashed red-hot through her. *Danger or not, I will never hand over any child of mine. Not to you. Not to Jon. Not to anyone, do you hear me?*

Not even to the gods, if they demanded so. Marie's own mother had left her, abandoned her to a grandmother ill-equipped to raise a young girl brimming with magic. She would not see her child suffer the same. She'd been angry, so blinded with rage at her mother for leaving her. How could she turn on her child the same way? She would not.

Sanite rasped, her chest rising and falling in shallow breaths. But she was not angry, as Marie expected her to be. Only woefully silent. Tears filled those filmy, all-seeing eyes.

You want me to be as you are, Marie spat. *Loveless and alone.*

No, my child. Sanite shook her head sadly. *I want you to be better.* She reached out with a withered hand.

But Marie had already turned away. *And I will be. A better queen. And a far better mother than you ever were to me. We're done. Goodbye, Sanite.* She could hear the old woman weeping, felt her own heart wrenching at the sound. But she would not look back.

She'd thought the pain of losing Jon then Sanite had been the worst of it in these last months alone. But it was this pain now, the pain of her daughter inching closer to life, that had her screaming.

When the labor first came on, Marie had overturned a table, torn the vials from the shelves as she hunted through her potions and draughts. The pain came in waves, making it hard to think of much else. There was no rest in between the contractions. She felt dizzy, her thoughts muddled and shapeless.

But then she found the willow bark and almost cried from happiness. It was enough to dull the pain so that she might endure it. Another lesson she'd learned from *him*. Marie stuffed it into her mouth and bit down as the next wave worked its way through her body.

Marie had not taken anything that might have lulled her to sleep though. Not when that meant dulling her mind, making her susceptible to her enemies and to . . .

Jon. He was somewhere, skulking about the Quarter, fast under way on his own machinations. In the months since their meeting in his tomb, Marie had kept her distance from him, and he left her alone—so very, very alone. She'd thought of running before the labor had come on, but she was in no condition to travel. The dangers of the road were many, especially for black women. So she had no choice but to endure until after the child was born, and then and only then—Marie swallowed down the lump in her throat—she would be finished with New Orleans at last.

She crawled across the floor to the little brass bed. She was halfway there when another contraction started. She screamed against the willow bark, the noise muffled against its edges. The agony was unending. *Move, Marie,* she thought. *Move now.*

She forced herself to the bed, where, blessedly, she managed to haul herself up onto its sheets. The rest became a fevered blur—wave after wave of blistering agony that made her want to crawl out of her own skin; bucking and writhing against the dampened sheets, sticky from her sweat and tears.

The candlelight flickered. Marie's vision blurred. She froze, eyes pinned on the wall across the room, where two little black girls, slaves perhaps, stood watching, hand in hand. They put their fingers to their lips. *Shhh.* And then they vanished.

In her fevered haze, other things appeared to her. Tricks of the mind. Old Sanite, gray and smiling, rocking on her chair, eyes the white of northern snow. Her grand-mère, *tsk*ing her tongue at Marie's folly. Her mother, turning away again, even now. One face grew into another, then another. The spirits were having their fun. Monsters and devils, the lot of them. Marie prayed. She cursed. But none of it seemed to do a lick of good, not when her body seemed determined to tear itself asunder.

Marie bit down so hard on the bark that she cracked it in half. But none of it mattered. Her daughter must live. The thought burned like fire in her mind, her kindred element. She let it give her life, keep her conscious long enough to finish the labor. She pushed and pushed until at last a wailing cry broke the silence.

Marie reached down and pulled her baby to her breast. All thoughts of spirits and suffering vanished. Because in that moment, staring at her daughter's perfect face, she had found her purpose at last, the reason for it all. The reason she would gladly suffer again, if it came to it.

She was tiny and pale, but her skin held some color, which Marie knew would deepen beautifully in time. Her eyes were dark and filmy, her head mostly absent of hair apart from a few dark curls. She was wild, even then. She was beautiful. Her daughter at last. *Hers.*

Despite her happiness, Marie found herself thinking of her mother again. Although Marguerite Darcantrel had taken off running down that long road to freedom without a look back, sometimes Marie replayed the moment again in her dreams, watching her mother walk backward down that road, back toward her outstretched hand. As a child she wondered what might have come from that moment. What kind of mother she might have had, what kind of mother might have protected her. She would never know. Because she was a mother now, her entire destiny reshaped itself into a single word more powerful than the oldest magic she knew. Freedom was here with her own daughter. Freedom was *this*.

"Marie Laveau, I make this promise to you," Marie cooed to her daughter. "I will never, ever leave nor forsake you. And you will know only freedom. The kind that will allow you to live beautifully and fully until you are an old, old woman who will pass peacefully in her own bed, in her own house, in her own time, because she lived free."

Marie pressed a kiss to her head, sealed the vow into her flesh. A little copper star glowed at the center of her forehead, where Marie's lips had brushed, then vanished. It was the mark of her magic.

It was a promise.

With her daughter swaddled to her back, Marie took to the moonlit roads. She moved as noiselessly as she could, but even after taking a pain tonic, moving in her state meant her breathing was labored, the sound deafening to her own ears. Her eyes darted through the dark, bracing for signs of wolves and men, of spirits lingering amongst the withered trees. But it was empty. She kept on.

She'd given her baby a sleeping tincture, just a few drops to keep her quiet. Crying on the run was a dangerous thing, a danger she simply couldn't afford. But she slept soundly at Marie's back, her little breaths threaded with unspoken magic.

Where the road forked, officers trotted on horseback, patrolling the routes for runaways and thieves. Marie slipped into the brush, careful to keep her baby's head from catching on wayward branches. Finally, they came to a clearing, where blueberries sprang up in bright patches, the damp grass silver against the moonlight.

"Just where do you think you're going?"

Marie's heart fell. Because that was the voice of many black folks' nightmares. The voice of the Brotherhood's Grand Wizard.

Marie turned, eyes narrowing. "What do you want, Gailon?"

Gailon stepped forth, leaning on his staff of aged oak. "As tempting as it might be to regale you with my ambitions, we simply haven't the time, Marie. It is not about what I want at the moment, but what our good mayor intends for you."

"*Corbin*," Marie spat. "You'd work with him? Even if—"

Gailon cut her short with a stilted laugh. "Child, I would work with the devil if it brought me an inch closer to my goals. With you out of the way, the Voodoos would not have a proper successor, would they? Once that old bitch dies, there will be no Quarter Queen to protect them. Our beloved mayor has set his eyes on your child. Corbin wants returned to him what is rightfully his. A Laveau."

"My daughter will be owned by no man," snarled Marie.

"Your hand has been dealt, witch. Come now, and let us make this quick."

"I have no quarrel with you, Gailon." Marie glanced about the darkened field. She counted six alchemists. "Nor with the Brotherhood."

"And truly, we've none with you, Marie Laveau. You are but a means to a very profitable end. Come now, and make this easy. For the both of you."

Fuck that. She would not go quietly. She would not go at all. And she had no intention of making anything remotely easy for a man like Gailon.

At his signal, the alchemists advanced on her.

So be it, Marie thought. She was ready. She had to be.

Two she killed immediately. The fire leapt from her fingers, snaking around their throats like a blazing lasso. And she pulled with all her might until she saw their heads singed from their necks. Gailon swung his staff in a low arc, and weeds shot up from the earth, snatching Marie's ankles. But she was quicker, singeing them with her fire, then casting a spell upon the wind. It came sailing through the dark, her little brace of wind, and struck Gailon in the side. He went flying back and then hit the ground. Marie heaved, panting from the strain. She was still not yet healed, the exhaustion of her labor only a few hours previous. It was no matter. In that moment, her hatred for the Brotherhood burned hotter than any flame she could cast, and through its fury she would gather her strength.

Gailon rose, stalking intently toward her. He made a motion with his hand to his alchemists. *No,* his eyes seemed to say, *this one is mine.*

Because her eyes were trained so closely on Gailon, she did not hear the telltale swing of chains until it was too late. *Snap.* Something heavy closed around Marie's neck. A scream tore its way from her throat and out into the wild of the bayou.

And just like that, her magic vanished. Marie clawed at her neck, but she knew it was useless. *Aurum.* It burned her fingers, but still she pried until her flesh smoked and sizzled.

"Silas," she hissed.

Silas stepped out from behind her, his face smooth as stone. "Hello, Marie."

Marie did not pretend to know a man like Silas Favreau, whose eyes held secrets, his impish smile a book without words. She hadn't known him still when she'd found him that fateful night with Father Antoine, his face marred by some worry. But she had thought she'd glimpsed the face of a man who held remorse, who was capable of change. She was wrong. Now that same face stared coldly down at her, unblinking. Silas crouched beside Marie, and then he was reaching over her, to her baby bundled at her back.

"*No!*" Marie clawed and struck out at him, but he swatted her away, as if she were nothing more than a swamp mosquito. "Silas, no!" She reached for him, but Gailon lifted a hand and spoke a word, and her muscles locked, still as stone.

Silas passed her baby into Gailon's waiting arms. Wild panic and rage made the world spin. He held her a little out from him, as if she were a wondrous novelty, a delightful curiosity he had never seen before. Those harrowing sights she'd glimpsed aboard *La Lune* came flooding back to Marie—those runaway slaves transmuted into beasts, the men in cages made to heel like wild dogs, the experiments all in the name of arcane advancement and craft.

Gailon cradled her daughter in his arms. Marie could no longer talk, but she was screaming on the inside. Her daughter stirred awake with a cry. The tincture had worn off, Marie thought helplessly. Her baby was crying. Marie was crying too, breasts aching with milk, the tears streaking down her face like silver streams to nowhere. She had thought she had known heartbreak before. But that had been only a small, bitter taste.

The Grand Wizard took one last look at Marie, then turned and swept away into the dark. His alchemists followed after him until only Silas remained.

He crouched beside her, staring at her with those impassive eyes. "I told you, didn't I, Marie? I warned you. *Turn your heart to stone.*" He reached out, moving aside a rebellious curl that had tumbled free across her cheek. "And you did not listen."

He put a hand to Marie's furrowed brow, murmuring a spell beneath his breath. And then Marie fell away into the darkness of sleep.

CHAPTER TWENTY-THREE

REE

Ree woke, aching beyond belief, tears streaming down her face from the latest vision of her mother.

The sound of Marie's anguish was unbearable—first the cries of her labor, then her guttural, soul-shaking cries at their separation. She felt every emotion as if it were her own, could still feel the wrenching sob rising in her from her belly, the way it lodged in her throat, a boulder that would not be moved.

She felt like such a fool. Not so long ago, she'd tried to run from this city. Both times, she'd said it was for love. And maybe she was right. For love of *herself*. But not Marie. She'd tried to run too, had tried in vain to escape the beast for them both. But this was a city that had teeth, whose rules were determined to swallow women like them whole at every turn.

She sat up, and a breath of relief coursed through her body. She was in the Laveau hairdressing parlor, lying on the floral violet rug beside the hearth where Marie liked to brew her potions. Although there was a fire burning in the grate, she felt strangely cold, the lingering effects of the demon's presence. Pale light flashed against the shaded windows, the mark of a light show in the sky. Darkened silhouettes drifted by the glass as revelers enjoyed their share of sin, the faint swell of music and laughter drifting in from the streets as the festivities moved along the French Quarter.

"You're awake," a rough voice said.

Henryk leaned against one of the shelves where Marie stocked her infamous butter balm and tins of rouge, his face covered in that wretched black mask. Memories flooded back to her: The demon's voice in her head, its rattling tongue flicking as it spoke of her demise. Henryk's lips against hers. The taste, the feel of his magic intertwining with her own.

"You have magic," Ree said with a gasp. "You're Les Magiques." She remembered at Corbin's ball the way Silas's eyes had gone toward Henryk, briefly, but she had seen. And now she knew. "*You're* Silas's piece on the board."

"I suppose you could say that." Slowly, he slid his Inquisitor mask from his face. His eyes stayed on hers, and she saw in them a flicker of shame. There was a moment of strangled silence between them before he finally said, "I'm a spy, Ree."

"You would work with the Brotherhood?"

He looked tired, his face a pale moon staring back at her in the dark. "Do you think Marie Laveau *hasn't*?" Ree was silent. "They are a necessary means to an end."

"And Antoine? Do you have the good priest's blessing to be a spy?"

"Who do you think molded me, Ree? After the bloodshed of the first Inquisition, he devised a way to prevent that horror from ever reaching New Orleans again, even if it meant he had to break the rules to do so, even if it meant working with someone as awful as the Grand Wizard of the Brotherhood of the White Hand."

What had Silas told her before when he'd offered an alliance? *You will find the dangers in this city require concessions to survive them.*

"How did the Church never suspect you had magical blood?" Eight years he'd been gone. Eight long, cruel years he'd learned the trade of torture and confession, to violently root out heresy from the body.

"They didn't." Henryk's voice turned whisper-soft as he said, "Alchemy doesn't just change one thing into another. It can change the mind, Ree. Bodies. Even blood."

She'd seen as much herself from Marie's memories—flashes of the nightmarish vessel, *La Lune*, the ways in which the Brotherhood had warped time and space itself.

"There is a secret ritual among the Brotherhood's highest order. A transfiguration rite. *Alchemization.* They will perform it on their enemies and even their own."

"Their own?" She should not be so surprised at the Brotherhood's appetite for cruelty, that their hate might turn inward. She was reminded of the stone at the end of Silas's staff, that terrifying beast that consumed itself.

Henryk gave a bitter laugh. "*Especially* on their own. If there are thoughts of defection, if there is a whiff of mutiny, they will be alchemized. No one ever defects from the Brotherhood of the White Hand. No one," he said. Ree thought of Silas's fateful words to her mother in the dark corridor of that cursed steamboat. *There is always a way out.* "Alchemization need not transform minds. It can change *magic* itself. Turn it into something more. Or into nothing at all. It was done on me as a child to keep my magic hidden. Even from me. It would take powerful magic to undo what was done to me, and I believe you did that in the tomb when I tried to save you."

"Why would the Brotherhood alchemize you?" Her breath caught. "Unless you're . . ." She looked at him with eyes anew. ". . . *Brotherhood,* aren't you?"

The truth hung between them, a fragile thing he couldn't bring himself to name. Not right away. "I am Gailon's son, yes."

Gailon, Silas's vile predecessor. She had seen the Brotherhood change men into beasts, transform entire vessels into hellish voids for their own amusement. Why then would it be impossible to consider they might work their strange magic upon their own?

"Make no mistake, he was a cruel, pitiless man," said Henryk. "I didn't mourn him. When my mother didn't want me to become Brotherhood, he had her killed. And after he was killed, Antoine took me in, gave me a chance to make right my father's sins, to atone for his legacy and be a part of a secret reformation of the

Church. It would be a long road, he warned, a dangerous one. But I hadn't cared. Not until, of course, I met you."

Ree stared at him, her fury matched only by her sadness for him, for how much pain they might have avoided causing each other. "You never told me."

"What was I going to tell you? That I was the son of a hateful monster? That I was never going to be a priest like Antoine? That I was going to be an Inquisitor? A *witch-hunter*? Would you have cared for me then?"

Ree was silent. She didn't know the answer to that question. Every line between them was completely muddled now, and she couldn't see straight. She recalled the words Antoine had spoken to her at Marcel's funeral. *You made him believe in more once. Maybe not in magic itself. But in you.* She hadn't believed him then, couldn't much afford to. But now?

"It hardly matters now. You must know a special tribunal is forming as we speak. Some of the most dangerous witch-hunters in the world will be here in one place for the first time in years. We'll never have a chance to move like this again."

"You *wanted* them to come. To draw the Inquisition in."

"Yes."

"And I was the bait." Her mind was spinning.

"Eight years ago, when I began to understand, to really understand what bringing an Inquisition meant, I . . . couldn't do it, Ree. I struggled to . . ." He faltered and did not say more.

"Tell me, Henryk."

I struggled with everything, his gray eyes told her. *With myself. With you.* "You may think the Church is awful, but you've surely seen what the Brotherhood of the White Hand is capable of. It has to be stopped. Eradicated."

"And Silas?" Ree paused. "Will you stop him too?"

"Silas believes his pact with Antoine will save him. He thinks by aligning with the Voodoos, you can kill the Inquisition before it kills you all. But I don't intend to allow the Brotherhood to survive the Inquisition, Ree. I will make sure the Brotherhood is gone for good, and Silas with it."

So, he'd planned on double-crossing the Grand Wizard all along. It was a risk Ree wasn't sure he could afford—none of them could. She had seen the depths the Brotherhood's alchemy might sink to. In many ways, war with the Brotherhood might be far more dangerous than the Church.

"Does Antoine know of your secret plan?"

"Antoine is far too idealistic for his own good. It is better if he doesn't know." He paused. "When I began this path, I didn't care about reforming the Church. Or stopping an Inquisition. Those are Antoine's dreams. I *wanted* the Brotherhood destroyed, the one thing I hated most. But then I met you. And everything changed. And I understood that if the Church destroyed magic, that would mean destroying—"

"Me," she finished. "Is that why you asked me to leave with you eight years ago?" When he didn't answer, Ree cursed. "Henryk, answer me, damn it!"

"Because I knew what I would become! What I would be made to do to *you*," he said brokenly. "And the truth is, I couldn't do that because I was in love with you. And I've been in love with you since the moment I opened my eyes and saw your wicked little face. And I might be—" He stopped himself. *I might be in love with you still.*

"I—I don't know if I can believe you." She thought back to the interrogation. "You've hurt me." But he had also saved her, hadn't he? In those small, discreet ways she could see now. Suggesting she save Anabelle from the burning pyre, protecting her from Marcel's undead form. The demon. Even when he had questioned her, he'd tried to get her to give up her mother to save her own life.

"I know. And for that I am sorrier than you'll ever know." The look of pain on his face told her this was the truth. But it did not matter. Apologies would not change where they were now. Maybe nothing would. "You became a complication in my plan, Ree. And I didn't know how to finish this while keeping you safe at the same time."

"I can keep myself safe."

"Is that what you were doing in that tomb? I saw you on your knees, eyes rolled back, screaming into the darkness. Was that your idea of *safe*?" He needn't be so sharp, so cruel, but she could tell the sight of her in that moment had rattled him too. "When I touched you . . . when I kissed you . . . I saw it too." His eyes found hers. "I saw how this ends for you, Ree."

With her on a burning pyre. Just like the first Quarter Queen. History repeating itself in a vicious wheel of time.

"Demons lie." Ree got to her feet and strode over to the shelf where her mother kept the poisons and hexing powders. She leaned against it, resisted the urge to shatter everything. She hated feeling trapped, cornered. So many truths. And so many lies. Spoken in the short span of a few days after not seeing each other for years. It was maddening. How she *felt* for him was maddening.

"Are you willing to take that chance? If you open the Veil, you would be opening the door to death, and you wouldn't just be bringing back Marie Laveau. You would be bringing back Jon, and all of the dead too. That is what the Harbinger meant. Do you understand that now?" Henryk was on his feet now too. "And if you do that, I can guarantee that the Inquisition would make it their mission to have you tortured and executed."

Outside, the music had stopped briefly. The silence that stretched between them was somehow louder, more urgent than the note of any trumpet.

"And what would you have me do?" she asked finally.

She could see in his eyes the same impossible bargain he'd tried to make during their interrogation. "Let her go, Ree. Let Marie go this time. And live your life, not your mother's. *Yours.* Choose your own freedom."

Ree turned away from him and gripped the shelf with both hands.

This time. She knew his eyes had turned to the past, to the moment she'd left him on that bridge alone. She'd thought of what might have come from that day a thousand times but could never quite see the future. Now she could, with bittersweet clarity. She could see them sailing off across the blue expanse of the Mississippi, to somewhere, anywhere else. And they would have found it, whatever it was, because they would have had each other. They would have been happy. And they would have been, most important, free from the golden cage of New Orleans at last.

But that day had not come. Ree was certain of her decision, and

Henryk would not sway her from it. But she would have this night, if she would have nothing else. Ree peeled the gown from her body, let it slide uselessly to the floor in a glittering puddle. She remained in the silken slip that she'd worn beneath.

Henryk had taken a step toward her, then froze. It looked as if she'd caught him deliberating on his next words but then—by the startled look in his eyes—she'd snatched the words clean from his mouth. Ree watched his eyes slowly lower over the contours of her body, the roundness of her hips in the candlelight.

"Are you going to stand there and be a statue, Inquisitor?" Her mouth quirked into a smile. "Or are you going to spend the night with me?"

That was all it took. He crossed the room, taking Ree into his arms. His lips found hers, then trailed greedily along her shoulders, her neck, the tender space beneath her ears. There was that overpowering scent of myrrh again, that smell of anointing that had no place between them. It was an oil for holy rituals. Surely, they would join together in a ritual tonight. But it would not be holy. *No saints and no sinners.*

"It is not morning yet," she whispered against his lips. Was that a reminder to herself? A warning to him? In the morning, things would be different. *They* would be different. But for now? Her eyes snatched hungrily at the shape of him in the candlelight. For now, she would indulge herself this one pleasure.

"No," he agreed softly. "It is not."

"Fornication would be . . . forbidden in the Vatican, yes?"

"Yes." He cast a toying glance about the chamber draped in red silks and incense, then lifted her by the waist as if she weighed nothing. "But we are not in the Vatican."

He carried her over to the soft rug near the fireplace, their intertwined reflections caught in a long mirror edged in golden scrollwork and vines that was hung beside the mantel.

He tore the slip from her shoulders, leaving her in only her thin stripping of undergarments. She ripped off his own clothes, buttons popping. She greedily drank in every inch of his bare skin. He was hardened with muscle, the firelight dancing on the sculpted lines of his chest, the soft sprinkle of auburn hair trailing down to the thick evidence of his desire for her. Her heart hammered in her ribs, and she licked her lips. His eyes followed the movement, dark. Hungry.

She pulled the veil and Marie's golden cloth from her hair, and they slipped from her bare shoulders like dark water as she shook out her unruly curls. Claudette had softened her coils into looser waves for the night—it could never be truly straightened, least of all in the frustrating perpetual Louisiana damp—and her hair fell over her breasts and down to her belly in wild ringlets.

Her fingers slid into his hair; it was normally the most beautiful shade of russet brown, a deep chestnut with a hint of red wine. But now it shone black in the mix of shadow and candlelight that bathed the room, almost as dark as hers.

Softly, he kissed her neck, suckling until she felt a shiver trail up her spine.

"Show me," he murmured, teeth against her throat. "Show me where I hurt you, princess."

Henryk pulled back, staring at her with a look that was as amorous as it was repentant. *Go on. Show me.*

She could start with her wrists, which that horrifying chair had squeezed and squeezed until she felt less than human. The same hand he had cruelly twisted in that cell when he'd left that coin for her. He'd been wearing a disguise then, she understood now. But that hadn't made her pain, her sadness any less real. Fine. She would show him. Ree took his hand and slowly dragged it down from her neck to her chest, right over her beating heart. He had hurt her plenty. But he had hurt her there most of all.

"Ree, I—"

Ree pressed a finger to his lips and moved his hand lower, to cup one of her breasts, so full in his hand. Her nipple peaked under his worshipful caress, her blood roaring in her veins. She reached again for his hair, fingers slowly feeling into its thick dampness, then pulled his Inquisitor mask back down. She reached into her hair, pulling the thin scrap of fabric back over her eyes. They could hide behind the faceless disguises, pretend that this was another part of the long, uneasy game they'd been playing since his return.

It was better this way. She would not have to see his face, and she would not be forced to remember the look of pleasure and rapture, the look that might break her heart in the end. Theirs would be a truce of the body, a temporary pact that would break like a spell at morning's first light. She wanted to hold on to that spell as long as fate allowed.

They twisted and turned until she was astride him. The music from the streets flared, smothering the hiss she released as she lowered herself over the hard length of him and started into a slow, steady rhythm. Ree's eyes turned up to the mirror, where she could see her reflection: her body rising glistening and damp, her hair wild and undone, through the twin holes in the mask her eyes completely white, flooded with the force of her magic. She turned her face back to his, allowed him to see her as the witch that she was. Ran her hands up his muscled arms and around the Inquisitor's throat. She squeezed softly, then harder, eliciting a moan from Henryk, a feral sound trapped in the back of his throat. So tortured he was, gazing up at her through his lashes, his eyes half lidded with desire. No more lies between them. No more games.

She was in love with him.

She had only ever been in love with him. *Only* him. She had never allowed herself to admit that small truth, not even to herself. It was better that way, she told herself. Better to bury herself with the others, all the others. They had been flirtations, distractions she'd entertained herself with, anything to deflect from the ever-present ache in her chest. She made a game of love. With all the others. With Anabelle. So reckless. Careless. And now she would have this moment—she would have him—if she could have him only once. They were on borrowed time. Tomorrow, in the pale wash of dawn, she might think better of such choices. But not now. All she had was right now. She had him, and that was enough.

So long as Ree drew breath, she decided then, she would not turn her heart to stone. Even if it hurt her, ruined her. Because maybe, just maybe, it might heal her too in the end.

"Ree," he said with a gasp in her ear. He did not—could not—say more. But it was fine by her. His touch was confession enough.

Faster and faster she moved, winding her hips until he released a stifled sound of pleasure, a soft hissing through his teeth, and flipped her over. She stared up into his masked face, the cruel dark contours of the disguise, her body arching into his, music swelling to its crescendo. The fire in the grate sizzled and hissed, overflowing with the building magic of her passion until, at last, it was extinguished in a single, distinct snap as Ree let out a final cry of pleasure into the dark.

After, they lay against the rug, facing each other. Bursts of gold lights in the sky shone between the lace curtains of the parlor's windows. The Brotherhood had spared no expense, no magic, for their annual light show. After a moment, the lights faded, the room dark again. She knew daylight was hours away. New Orleans would celebrate even then—the night would not stop. But it would for them. The sun would soon rise, and their spell would be broken.

Henryk's gaze fastened to hers as if he might never let go. But something behind his eyes had died. And she knew whatever had been between them for these few blissful hours, whatever lovely feeling had blossomed, it was now dead too. Her hand cradled his cheek, felt the coarse stubble along his jaw. "I think I preferred when you hated me."

"I confess to hating many things. But you?" His eyes searched hers, silently willing her to understand what he could not fully say. "You, Marie Laveau the Second, could never be one of them."

"I'm sorry," she murmured. And she was. She truly was.

His lips brushed her knuckles, feather-soft. "For what?"

"For not joining you that day on the bridge. I wanted to be my own woman. And yet, when the time came for me to choose, I—"

"You chose Marie," he said quietly. "Some part of you will always choose Marie." Bitter. *Over me. Over yourself.* Words he did not dare say. And yet she heard them, as loud as the light show that colored the night sky outside. Was she foolish to think one night of passion might fix whatever had broken between them?

Her mother had chosen love. And she had been sorry for it in the end, hadn't she? Jacques. Jon. Both men had made her pay dearly in different ways. But she'd chosen Ree too. Maybe her mother's story had taught her something, after all. Love was the strange and fickle thing that could break you in half. Love was unwieldy, transformative. And, quite possibly, the only magic in the world that could make you whole again. If you let it.

"I'm terrified, Marie." He said her full name, soft like a hushed prayer. "I'd be lying if I said I wasn't terrified of losing myself. But the thing that scares me more is the thought that I might lose you again too."

She rested her hand upon his cheek, committing to memory the curve of his face in the dark, the cool gleam of his eyes searching hers. "Whatever we may be, we will face it together." That much she could say. That much she could promise him.

Ree rose to her feet and stepped back into the slip she'd worn beneath her gown. She tied her hair in the golden tignon to keep it out of her face, then went to the hearth to start a pot of water to boil for tea. She could make some at the stove in the back room, but then she would miss the generous view of Henryk as he stood, bare in the slant of moonlight that fell through the apothecary's windows, and began to dress with languid slowness. As if they had all night before them. The thought made her eyes prickle.

When he was dressed again, he joined her at the hearth, planting a sleepy kiss on her bare shoulder. When the kettle started to whistle, she brought him a cup, and together they shared their tea in easy silence. Henryk watched her, a soft grin on his lips. She knew what he was thinking, what he could not bring himself to say. They were not a witch or an Inquisitor in that moment. They were simply two people sharing a cup of tea, a quiet moment in the dark.

When Ree brought the cup to her lips, another scent rose up from its hazy cloud. Something bitter—*foxglove.*

The cup shattered in Ree's hand.

And before she could scream, Henryk shoved her hard across the room. She was hurled backward and hit the shelf lined with Marie's brews and talismans. Bottles and vials exploded, potions and decanters spilling around her in a glistening mess, broken glass puncturing her skin. The dizzying perfume of countless herbs and concoctions rose from the floorboards, overwhelming her vision in a dense cloud.

Ree looked up to see a dark-robed figure drifting in from the dark, a curl of silvery smoke tangling around it.

Silas.

When the smoke dispersed, she could see the Grand Wizard

standing directly in front of the door, in the only path to the apothecary's exit. The alchemist had Henryk by the hair with one hand and his glowing staff in the other. He wrenched Henryk's head upward, showing her his bludgeoned face.

"No!" yelled Ree as she sprang to her feet. Henryk's gray eyes remained locked onto hers, the eyes that begged her silently to run. Silas jabbed the end of his staff into Henryk's neck, drawing a thin line of blood. Ree stopped cold.

"Do it," Silas hissed, "and I'll turn every bit of him to stone. And then"—his eyes narrowed—"I'll break him. And nothing, and I mean nothing, will put him together again." His lips quirked as if to say, *Not even you, little witch.*

She didn't doubt that he would. She would put nothing past the Grand Wizard.

But still she said, "You wouldn't." Her voice shook. "You can't kill him. I know that he's your so-called piece on the board you and Antoine made. Another part to your little game."

It was a desperate play on what little knowledge she had.

"Well," Silas said with a sneer, "the rules just changed."

"You fucking bastard." Marie was wrong. Her mother was wrong. There was nothing good left in this man, if there had ever been any at all. He was a living shell, worse and more pitiful a creature than any zombi.

She felt another power surging through her. A vibrant anger she could not stamp down to ash. It wanted to be let out, to burn free.

And yet, the spell died on Ree's lips. She lowered her hands. "Goddamn you."

"I warned you to make an alliance, little girl. But you did not listen."

She was reminded of the words he'd spoken to Marie when he'd betrayed her in that moonlit glade. *I told you, didn't I, Marie? I warned you. Turn your heart to stone. And you did not listen.*

Music started up again, louder, as a second procession of dancers and revelers made its way down the thick of Royal Street. Silas pointed his staff at her.

"*Mutatio,*" he whispered.

Her throat began to close—it was as if someone had stuffed hot wool inside her mouth, crushing her magic down to dust on her tongue. The tissue inside her mouth had begun to sew itself up. Ree screamed, but only a dry sob escaped. Outside, the notes swelled, rising to meet her pain, her cries swallowed beneath the maddening music of a city whose song would never die.

CHAPTER TWENTY-FOUR

MARIE

It was Marie's worst fear come alive—to be shackled. No, to be *owned*. And that was exactly what she was now, wasn't she? The iron manacle hanging from her neck was proof.

They'd fitted her with a collar heavy enough for an ox, with enough aurum for at least three men. *Like a dog,* Marie thought. *Like a fucking dog.*

Marie flexed her fingers, the flesh still burned and reddened from where she'd touched the aurum. They'd left them unbound. She'd half expected to have woken up in the Brotherhood's dungeons, or one of their laboratories. But she'd been promised to someone else—the hangman. She looked around, her cell a small, lightless thing. This was the jailhouse. When she'd first started making her rounds as a plague nurse some years ago, she'd made it a habit to stop here, to treat the worst of the city's victims, those cutpurses and murderers and cons. Not even Sanite had understood. *Why bother, when they are already dead?* But Marie had only smiled. *Because being dead and being doomed are not the same.*

But now she felt herself doubting those words. How naïve she'd been, so eager to please, so sure of her own power and gifts. But her brief glimpse of motherhood had shown her different. Without her daughter, she would be as good as walking death on two legs. If she survived this whole ordeal and her baby didn't? Well, death and doom would be one and the same now.

Footsteps clattered along in the darkness, drawing near. Marie sat up, forced herself to gather some semblance of courage. *Turn your heart to stone.* Light flooded her cell, and suddenly Marie was staring at three leering police officers.

"My, my, look here, the great Marie Laveau saddled like a horse." The officer let out a whooping laugh, his men joining in.

Marie swallowed down the sting of humiliation. Her pride would not help her tonight. "Are you always so eager to see a woman in chains?"

His eyebrows rose. "You'd be surprised, Laveau. My momma always said don't go askin' questions if you ain't prepared for the answers. And you"—his eyes flickered over Marie's dirtied frame—"surely don't want the answer to that."

"What have I done? Tell me, what is my crime?" she demanded. "Will there at least be a trial?"

"No time for all that. So, I'd reckon no. There's an insurrection waging in the streets. The good folks of New Orleans are eager to have order restored. Everything back to the way it was." The officer sneered, having taken her silence for surrender. "I'll see you at dawn, witch." He turned and left, his men following, except for one. The officer lingered behind, holding on to the bars of her cell with both hands.

"They say you're the next Quarter Queen." The man pressed his face against the bars of her cell. "You think yourself a queen, do you? And what do you rule, exactly? A bunch of juju negroes already owned by another?"

Marie turned to face him, considering him in the weak light of the lantern that swayed in his hand. She knew what he wanted—it was what Corbin wanted, what they *all* wanted from her in some way or another. They wanted her magic. No, not the garden variety of spells or hexes she could cast with a single breath. They wanted her real craft, her power, her innermost light. Marie smirked. Well, they could keep wanting. That she would never give.

"If you are a queen, then where is your crown, your majesty? Is that dirty little rag on your head supposed to be it?" He laughed at her, eyes flickering dismissively to the cloth tignon on her head. Her simple cloth of rough cotton was certainly not the golden crown of the Quarter Queen, but Marie was not one to be mocked.

She watched him silently. Something about her gaze must have unnerved him, for his laughter soon quieted. He spat into her cell. "You'll hang by dawn, Laveau. And after, you're going to hell, witch."

She very well might, this was true. But it wouldn't be for her magic.

Moonlight fell through the little box of a window, casting silver puddles onto the floor of Marie's cell. Her magic was as good as dead with the aurum around her neck.

There was one last hope, one last ritual she could try. Conduction. Different from the kind Jon had used in his ritual, this was gentler magic, the magic born of the natural tether between mother and child, a magic that didn't require an ounce of her own, magic not even aurum could stop. Marie cast a silent prayer to her saints and closed her eyes.

Marie, she called into the darkness. *Marie* ...

And when she opened her eyes, she was in a different room altogether. The world was mostly formless and blurry, but there were shapes drifting into view. Faces, Marie supposed. Which could mean only one thing ...

She was seeing with her daughter's eyes. Gailon's face floated into view, and a surge of anger burst forth in Marie's chest. The connection wobbled. The world went dark. Marie took a breath and held the connection steady. The time for retribution would come. But now she couldn't stop the fear. She could handle this cell, these men, but the thought of her little baby facing the very same ...

Marie's stomach lurched. Gailon was facing her, which meant he was facing her daughter. Something flickered overhead—his staff. Dark green light glowed from the end of it. He took aim, pointing it directly at her ...

Something moved behind Gailon. Marie gasped. She saw the knife first, the quick flash of silver, then saw the blood spray the air. Then Gailon's dark eyes, impossibly wide, still bright with stupid surprise as he fell away.

Silas stepped forward, quickly pocketing the knife. Cries filled the chamber. Her daughter was crying. And then Silas's face swam before hers as he picked her daughter up and rocked her from side to side.

Marie, he said quietly, speaking directly into her daughter's ear. *I can feel you here, witch. Listen closely. There's going to be a man. Perhaps you've already met him. I can control him, but only to an extent. He is going to have a set of keys in his pocket. What happens in that cell I cannot control. Do you understand?*

It was not as if she could respond. The connection flickered. A spark of hope flared in Marie's chest. Perhaps all was not lost yet.

Good, he said at last, the ghost of a smirk on his lips. *I thought that you might.*

Marie opened her eyes. She was back within her cell. Even in the silence, she could hear her baby crying. Marie stilled, shutting her eyes to the darkness. Worrying would not help her now. Like it or not, she needed to trust Silas to do his part. So, she sat very still. And she waited.

Later, Marie heard the thud of footsteps leading to her cell, the telltale jangle of keys. The click of the lock rang in the air, and the door to her cell groaned open.

"Hello, witch," the guard crooned. He smiled, flashing stained teeth.

Marie sat up, staring at him with slow regard. "Come to take your fun, I suppose?" Her gaze flickered over his smile, the eagerness of his body. She lowered her voice to a soft coo. "Then *take* it."

He stepped closer. "Where is your magic?" he taunted, his breath the sourness of whiskey and stale tobacco. The stench turned her stomach. "Where are your spells and hexes, witch?"

"Come closer," said Marie, "and I will gladly show you."

Marie did not dare move, not even when he was suddenly upon her, his hands roving greedily along her body. The guard pushed her flat on her back with enough force that she gasped. What did it matter? She was without her magic, not a witch any longer, just a woman now. He struck her in the face, then planted a drunken kiss along her shoulder.

Marie squirmed, her hair coming undone from its tignon. His hands squeezed along her waist, over her breasts.

Marie reached for the cloth at her head, the material slipping between her fingers.

"Little witch," he crooned into her neck, fingers hastily working at getting his trousers undone.

Marie touched his throat, the gesture almost tender. He smiled drunkenly, his expression glazed with pleasure. And then he gasped, eyes bulging as Marie coiled her tignon around his neck. He reached out, clawing blindly for her. But Marie held fast and squeezed and squeezed, even when she felt him going slack against her. The guard flopped and flailed like a cold fish in her hands, but she stayed fastened upon him, viperlike, watching as the light slowly ebbed from his eyes.

He stilled, dropping upon her like a heavy stone. Marie rolled his body from her and heaved herself to her knees. She was frozen like that for a long moment, rooted to the spot, her body coated in sweat, her breathing ragged. But then the cry of another prisoner in the distance startled her into action. She quickly patted along the guard's chest, over his shirt, and then his trouser pockets. Finally, her hands closed around the keys. She brought trembling hands to her neck, to the little space at the back of the collar, and fit the key inside. The collar unlocked with a *click*, clattering to the dirtied stone.

Marie climbed to her feet. She cracked her neck, her magic flowing back to her in a warm rush, banishing the soreness from her bones. She looked ahead and saw the barest speckle of light in the distance. *There.* There was her path forward.

Marie spared one last look to the man at her feet, those eyes staring up at her wide and unseeing. "There," she spat, "there's your fucking magic."

Marie found him soon enough. When she made her way through the jailhouse's back door, she saw a man turn into an alleyway just across the street, saw the familiar flash of dark spangled robes. She quickly followed, crossing the empty cobblestoned road and slipping into the alley.

He stood with one hand clutching a wicker bassinet, the other Gailon's staff. She might have laughed under less dire circumstances—the alchemist had certainly wasted no time.

"Silas," she said quietly. She couldn't forget that the last time they'd met, he'd seen fit to collar her.

"Marie," he said. There was a smirk in his voice. His eyes fell over her battered form. A muscle in the side of his jaw ticked. "You look like hell."

She did laugh now. "I'm Catholic. Everything's hell."

He looked different. The blue of his eyes was darker, nearly black. His reddish-gold hair had lost its luster—it was a paler hue, edging closer to light wheat. Not quite the snowy-white hair of the Brotherhood's ascended. *Not yet.* Marie stopped cold. He was changing. *Ascending,* the Brotherhood of the White Hand called it—those last sacred rites into the upper echelons of their mysterious ranks. But she did not care. Because there in that wicker basket was her daughter, sleeping soundly, with no recollection of this entire hellish ordeal that had befallen them both.

Before she could remember her wits, she pulled the alchemist into a fierce embrace.

"Thank you," she murmured into the crook of his neck.

"*Don't,*" Silas grunted. "Let me go, Marie." His voice was strange. This was a warning.

She let him go at once, remembering her senses. She reached for the bassinet, but Silas held it back. "First, you must give me something that I want, witch."

"Are you so depraved of spirit you would use a child as a bargaining chip?"

His eyes flashed. "I might use anything as a bargaining chip, Marie. Anything."

"What is your price?"

"Simple enough. You will tether a piece of your power to mine."

"That would be . . . illegal."

"Everything I've done tonight has been illegal, Marie. Let us not worry about the rules now."

"And what would you do with it?" She had seen what the Brotherhood did in their experiments, though she had no proof. Stealing black folks' magic for their own purposes in secret transmutation rituals.

"You are an important piece of my game, Marie Laveau. But we must finish playing first. Ours will be a pact of alchemical equilibrium. If you hurt me, you hurt yourself."

A matter of insurance then. She should have known. "If I refuse?"

"You will have wished Corbin had taken her. Do you agree?"

Marie was at a loss. Silas had the advantage, and she could not take on both him and Jon. Her eyes fell to her daughter, sleeping soundly. There was nothing she would not do for her. Nothing. Slowly, she nodded.

"Very well. Hold out your hand." Silas placed his wrist over hers, then tapped the stone end of his staff at the intersection where their flesh met. "*Omnes aequales iure.*" *All are equal in law.*

The end of his staff glowed. An emerald ring shaped like a snake formed around their skin. She recognized the symbol. It was the same as the end of his staff—the mythical ouroboros, the beast who devoured itself. Marie felt a searing pressure form between their wrists, constricting like rope, then nothing. The light vanished, the pact sealed.

Silas removed his staff and passed the bassinet to her without touching her.

"They can never know," he said quietly. "Do not confuse my convenience for anything else. That would be a mistake."

She did not like this man, could hardly stand his presence, but still she found herself saying, "You've saved my daughter, Silas. That is more than I can say for her father."

It was the curse of her faith. Always searching for the goodness in the hearts of men where there lived none. First Jacques, then Jon, and now a Brotherhood alchemist. *But you know why, Marie,* sang a dark voice. Because if there existed some speckle of goodness in them, then surely there was still some in her.

"Jon and I share one commonality, and one commonality only," said Silas. "We are both men who seek means to ends. And make no mistake, saving your child served my own."

"And what are those ends, Silas? Do you intend to become the Grand Wizard now?" Gailon had made a great Grand Wizard as far as the Brotherhood of the White Hand's requirements went. A sharp mind. Immense magical talent. A scholar's taste for advancement at whatever cost, and cold-as-ice regard for those who dared interfere. But Silas? Shrewd. Calculating. With a sickle-thin smile—unreadable and completely unpredictable. Whatever kind of leader Gailon had been, Silas would exceed him in strides, even Marie knew.

He considered her in the moonlight, searching her face for a moment, weighing, perhaps, how much to disclose when he'd already divulged too much. "I told you, what I intend to play is a very dangerous game, Marie Laveau. A long game with far-reaching consequences. You'd do well to stay out of my way. Are we clear?"

It was as much warning as a man such as he could give. He turned, drawing up his great staff.

She snatched his wrist. Silas turned, eyebrows raised. "Silas, if you do this, if you mean to become the Grand Wizard, you will become Gailon. Is that truly what you want?"

A moment of hesitation bristled between them. She could see now that this was the same man she had glimpsed all those months before in the cathedral's dark halls with Father Antoine. Deeply and utterly conflicted. Finally, Silas drew his hand away.

"I should think that for whatever man or monster Gailon was," Silas murmured at last, a strange note in his voice, "I am far worse."

Silas turned away, leaving her there alone, frozen in the moonlight, as he passed into the oily heat of the night. Somewhere in the distance, a scream echoed. Marie stared down at her sleeping daughter, thinking. Flashes of the night she'd met Jon came back to her. Their dance. His fateful words to her. *War I will have, and war I will win.* She had not known then what he was truly capable of, what he had intended for her all along. *But if you had, Marie?* a small voice asked her. *Would you have done things differently? Might you have loved him all the same?* The truth was, she didn't know. She had sought Jon for her own selfish purposes, and he had sought her for his. There were so many things she should have done, so many she hoped she still might do when this was all finished. But now she had a different purpose that drove her, a glorious destiny that she held in her arms, hers alone. Her daughter.

Marie wound her tignon around her head, fastening it into a secure knot atop her hair. More screams broke the quiet. Surely, somewhere in the Quarter, Jon was waiting, carefully considering her next move as if this were all some elaborate dance between them. And perhaps it *was*. Perhaps the night of the ball, when they'd met again, their dance had never quite finished, and they had been locked into some maddening spiral ever since. But now Marie was done. She would meet Jon again as enemies. No truces. No lies. No love. With her sleeping daughter in her arms, Marie took a step forward into the darkness.

If it was war that Jon the Conjurer wanted so badly, then it was war that he would have.

The crows were watching her.

As Marie ran through the French Quarter's tangled streets, she could hear them somehow louder than the screams, squawking at her back. Admittedly she'd never cared for the little black birds—crows were exceptionally unforgiving creatures, never forgot a face who'd wronged them, could hold a grudge like nobody's business. And she needed that—to forget the faces of those who'd wronged her, and even those she'd wronged in turn. She needed forgiveness too for what she'd done—her eyes found the path forward—and for what she was about to do.

Marie turned a corner onto Bourbon Street, bassinet in hand, then came to a breathless halt, eyes darting through the chaos. But she was too late. It had already begun.

Dust choked the air, blanketing the long road ahead in white. A shrieking crowd came surging from the white smoke, faces dusted in debris, stumbling blindly for shelter. The sharp tang of aurum stained the air, burning Marie's throat and eyes. Her ears rang, thundering with the charge of hooves over stone as the police rode in, brandishing their rifles and batons into the crowd. Her gaze drifted, lingering over the wreckage—the dead littered the street in droves, facedown in their own ruin, black flies buzzing over their pale corpses. Teeth rotten. Plague-ridden. Distant cannon fire rattled the ground, like thunder trapped beneath Marie's feet, rumbling through the cobblestones, shaking the very foundation of the city until she thought it might tilt right over.

A little colored girl came stumbling from the dust, cotton dress stained in red, a tattered violet ribbon hanging from her coiled hair. Another *boom* sounded, lifting the girl high into the air. Marie flung out a hand, using Bade's wind to steady the girl midair. Marie lowered the girl back onto the ground, where she stood shaking. She stared at Marie for a moment, wide eyes streaked with red, irrevocably haunted, before vanishing into the crowd, passing through the smoke like a ghost. Marie plunged deeper into the wreckage, trying to shake the image of those haunted eyes from her mind.

She'd been jailed for less than one night and already Jon had turned the city in on itself, the whole of New Orleans spinning and spinning into mayhem like one of those paper disks performers on Royal Street would twirl on a string, the colorful little pictures moving into one maddening blur.

A hand seized her ankle, sharp fingernails digging into her flesh. "Priestess!" Marie looked down to find a white man gasping at her feet, black bile spilling between his teeth and down his lips. His nails dug in harder, achingly desperate. "Spare me, *please.*" It was Monsieur Garnier, an indigo merchant who'd made his fortune on a plantation down Bayou Road. A big white house hedged in apple orchards and rolling purple fields. Pleasant enough. The slaves called it *l'abattoir*—the slaughterhouse.

Black dots blossomed in her vision. Marie coldly shook him off, hurrying off into the chaos. More bodies in the streets, and the damp, decomposed stench of stewing garbage and rancid flesh. Marie had no pity for these men, the same men who watched her through narrowed eyes, day by day, wishing she were under their own lock and key, where she might perform her magic for their own sick amusement and profit. But it was what came after that scared her—war. *Aren't you already in it?*

There was no time to think—her daughter would wake soon. She needed to get her to safety, and the rest she would sort out after.

The hiss of magic hung in the air, the stench of old spellwork clinging to the humidity. In the distance she could see the water rising—the deep blue banks of the Mississippi swelling into the darkened horizon. The tide-turners were locking down the docks and channels—no one would be allowed to escape this madness, and certainly no reinforcements would be permitted in. The thought struck her, a wave of horror rising in her chest. *There is no one coming.* There was only her.

She passed a group of kindlers, young boys who shot fire into the air from their fingers like rifles. They cavorted around the body of a small merchant man who lay facedown, swimming in his own blood. Their former owner, perhaps.

One of the boys extended a flaming hand to her, his smile stretched into his eyes. "Dance with us!"

"We're free," they sang and sang at her back. "*We're free!*"

Dozens of corpses littered the road—men, women, small children, their little bodies angled oddly beneath their parents, who'd done their best to shield them. This was the cost of rebellion.

The truth was, she would have gladly paid it. But not with her daughter's life.

Marie might have reigned by Jon's side, or he by hers. She harbored no fantasies about her power in this city or her golden throne. It was an illusion—the best one she'd ever cast. And for all her magic and wiles, the only power she had was the power they *allowed* her. Nothing more. And nothing less. Because that was the way of things in New Orleans, the way things had always been. Those were the rules. *But what if they weren't?*

Marie swept the thought from her mind.

Father Antoine met her in the courtyard of Place d'Armes, the St. Louis Cathedral casting its steepled shadow over them. Marie passed him the bassinet. Her eyes lingered over her daughter, over the same brown skin, the glossy dark crown of her head. Even now, she was her twin in every way. *Marie Laveau.* The child would be her namesake, the only part of her legacy worth keeping.

"Take her. Keep her far away from the sanctuary. Do you understand?" When Antoine said nothing, Marie rattled the old man by the shoulders. "*Do you understand?*"

This drew a stilted nod from Father Antoine. Marie relaxed. Her daughter would be safe at last. Even if it came to the worst, Antoine would see to it that her daughter was raised with principle, with kindness, and perhaps, if she was lucky, with love.

"What do you intend to do, Marie?"

"Stop him, of course."

Antoine's eyes fell to the infant resting in his arms. A telling silence settled between them. "Will you kill him?"

Marie kept her face calm, steadfast in her choice. "It is better that you do not know."

"Then may God forgive you, Marie Laveau." He put a wilted hand on Marie's shoulder, just as he had done when Marie had been a wayward child looking to her teacher to tell her right from wrong. Perhaps she'd never stopped being that little girl. Perhaps she never would. "And may you, one day, forgive yourself," said Antoine. He crossed the air over her forehead, the only protection he could give her.

Père Antoine took her daughter and crossed over the threshold back into the road, vanishing into the flickering torchlight. Marie watched him go, staring into the shadows long after the priest's footsteps had faded on the cold stone. But there was no time for fear. Not when she'd need every ounce of courage to face the monster waiting for her inside. *A monster of your own making.* She'd set Jon on this path the minute she'd decided to use him for her own selfish gain. And maybe, just maybe, he'd been using her the whole time too. Perhaps they both deserved what was coming to them. The voices of the ancestors, the spirits of the dead, whispered at her ear. Taunting, heckling. Warning. But there was only one voice she heard now, rising above the rest. *I told you.* Marie laid a hand over her heart, hammering in her chest. *Turn your heart to stone.*

She raised a hand, and the cathedral door flung open at her silent command. Candlelight spilled out from within, golden and warm, almost welcoming.

Marie took a breath and stepped inside.

It was as if she'd walked into a dream. No—a *memory.* It was the night Jacques disappeared. They'd had a fight. A bad one this time. They were always bad, by all accounts, but today was worse because Jacques was actually leaving. He had business up north in Baton Rouge and wouldn't be expected back for a week.

He wanted her to come with him. And she knew why. There was talk of a coup against the governor, whisper among the slaves of a rebellion yet to come.

You're going to cause a riot! she had yelled at his back. *You endanger us all.*

It was those words that angered him so, brought him back from the door and made him whirl around to face her, green eyes alight with strange magic.

I endanger us? Surely you meant the white men at the market who shoved that old black lady down in the middle of the road? Surely you meant that danger, mon amour?

Marie froze. She had not. He knew what she had meant. He was mocking her.

The danger does not live in this house. It lives in the rules, Marie. The rules you don't dare work to change.

How can I? I am not the Quarter Queen, and—

Not yet. But Sanite will be gone one day, and just like that—he snapped his fingers, illustrating his point—*you will have her crown. Tell me, Marie Laveau. What kind of queen will you be then?* Jacques sighed, turned those green eyes up to the ceiling as he ran a hand over his brow. *You have all the magic in the world, Marie. And look at you...so tame. So afraid. So disgustingly content with being less than you are.*

And maybe you've never been enough. Marie bit back the words she did not dare say. So instead, she said, *What do you want me to do? Break the rules? They will kill me! Kill us both!* She was breathing heavy now, cheeks red with shame and anger. But she saw in his face the look of absolute resolve. He was ready for that. He would die if he had to. If it came down to it. *Tell me what you want me to do with my magic!*

Use it. Those green eyes held hers, defeated. She didn't know this would be the last time. *For something more than yourself.*

Her husband turned and left, leaving Marie in the doorway, watching as he disappeared down the dark of the road.

Marie's eyes prickled. She reached out, into the darkness, into anything, for something to hold on to. But the dream wobbled, the memory finished. Just what was Jon trying to get her to see?

But for all his magic, Marie had learned his ways. He would not pry inside of her head without costs. Her magic bucked against his, twisting the shape of the memory until the picture changed. That warm dream took on a new life.

She was now in a crowd, drowning in a swell of bodies, the air thick with screams and the crack of gunfire. She was standing in the middle of a riot. This was not the cloistered heat of New Orleans. A man streaked by her, a rifle strung over his shoulder, green eyes barely registering her presence.

She stilled. For it was her husband.

It played as if time had slowed itself to a crawl: Jacques taking aim . . . the glint of a baton in an officer's hands . . . the spray of blood that choked the air, splattering all those faces who watched as it struck his skull . . . the crack of the baton as it came down again . . . and again . . . and again . . . Jacques reaching out blindly to someone she could not see, blood thick and gurgling on his lips . . .

Marie screamed, but it was no use. She was a passenger here. An empty vessel.

The world spun, as if in reverse.

Marie was now staring with Jacques's eyes. At a man in a tall hat who watched impassively from the crowd. Still as stone. The stench of death heavy on him.

It was Jon.

A hand on her shoulder. Marie looked up, saw the familiar withered face before hers. Sanite Dede. She looked older than Marie remembered, but her skin was glowing faintly, the deep brown flecked with sunlight. Her eyes were completely white, filled with the force of her magic. *Take control, Marie,* she commanded. *Take back what is yours. Get on your feet.*

The memory shattered into a thousand glowing pieces that swirled in the air. Sanite was standing over her, magic pouring from her in waves that pulsed in the air, as if it were breathing.

"Get on your feet, Marie," the real Sanite commanded. Those filmy eyes were still looking ahead, her teeth clenched, her long dark braids writhing slowly around her glowing face like coiled snakes.

Marie's vision slowly cleared. She was on her knees in the cathedral's sanctuary, rasping for air. She reminded herself that the pain of losing her loved ones couldn't hurt her anymore. She'd already lost them once. And somehow, in her unending grief, she'd lost herself too.

She didn't know how, she didn't know why, but she knew Jon was responsible for Jacques's death. How could it be that one man was the source of her joy and the architect of her greatest misery?

Marie cast her eyes at Sanite, the woman she'd rejected, who wanted her to get rid of her pregnancy. But Sanite was here. She'd come back. She'd come back for *her*. It was more than her own mother had done for her. "Sanite, I'm—"

"*Silence!*" Sanite's nails dug into Marie's shoulder, and in one heave, she wrenched her up by the collar of her dress to her feet. "I said on your feet, Marie. Prepare yourself." She hissed toward the darkness, "Get out of her head, Jon."

Tap. Tap. Tap.

Someone was walking toward them from the shadows.

A flock of crows took flight, a swarm of black drifting high above into the cathedral's rafters. Jon stood in their place, top hat in his hands. "Now, why would I do that?"

The air quivered, shuddering, the illusion shriveling around him into little glowing particles. Once she'd seen him for what he truly was, she couldn't stop seeing through him, his games, those terrible, terrible lessons.

"Jon."

"Hello, Marie." His eyes slid to the old woman in front of her. "And Sanite, my dear, dear Quarter Queen." His lips drew into a sneer, that old history between them conjured again. He took a sobering look around the sanctuary, lips pressed into a thin, displeased line. "The ever-devout Marie Laveau. I've always thought you served too many gods."

His gaze flickered up to the crucifix that hung before them—Christ's head weary and bent, tilting his crown of thorns. Beside it, the statue of the holy Madonna cradled her swaddled baby. But Marie saw only a frightened mother, scared for her child, of what might become of him if he were to fulfill his destiny, what the others might do to him if he did, or worse yet, if he did not.

"Tell me, does this one care for you?" Jon taunted. "Will he lend his power now if you ask him so?"

Marie remained silent. She could not say. She knew only that in the end she didn't need a powerful god to work miracles for her. She could work miracles herself through Voodoo. And terrible curses too. In the end, she just needed a god that might forgive her for both.

It was Sanite who spoke now. "I'm going to set things right, Jon."

"Set things right," he echoed. A small smile touched his lips. "Tell me, Quarter Queen, do you like things the way they are now?" His eyes went to Marie. "Do *you*, beloved? Because the rest of our kind sure as hell don't."

Marie shut her eyes, hating herself. Some part of her did, she could admit that. Power. The freedom she wielded was not lost on her. But Jon's alternative was not the only path, was it? There had to be another way. There simply had to be.

"You are going to hurt our daughter." Marie sucked in a rattling breath. "*Our daughter,* Jon."

"I've hurt plenty on this path. And I'll hurt plenty more before the end of it."

And I will hurt you again if it makes you stronger.

"And Jacques? Did you hurt him too?"

"I do as I am bid, Marie. I serve only—"

So that was it then—he had caused her husband's death, somehow. When Jacques had said he would join the revolution, she had no idea that it was *Jon's*. And when she had sought him for help for the magic to bring him back, the Conjurer had always known that he was going to make a fool of her. Oh, what a fucking fool for love she'd been.

"You serve only yourself!" Marie hissed.

"You would know a thing or two about that, now, wouldn't you, Marie?"

A low, bitter laugh worked its way from her throat. Despite it all, he had still found a way to hold her to blame. Equals, she supposed, to the end. "Tell me something. Was our child always meant to be the sacrifice?"

His dark eyes fastened on her, unflinching in their honesty. *No lies,* they'd promised each other at the beginning of this. "Yes."

It surprised her to hear the pain in his voice, that he was still capable of it. If only it were truly that simple. And maybe for a man like Jon it was. Maybe he'd lost the part of himself that could distinguish his own evil from another long ago in a forgotten lifetime, and the Jon she'd gotten was merely the cold husk, bitter and stripped of all feeling.

"Give me the child, Marie," said Jon. "And I will do it quickly."

"I won't let you sacrifice her, Jon. I won't." How easy it was to cast aside his own family. How easy it had been for her own mother.

"Better me"—his eyes moved to the windows, to the chaos outside—"than *them*."

Did he not know she would kill them all? Him. The Brotherhood. Even this church, her beloved sanctuary. She'd see the whole fucking city burned to ash, the earth scorched to dust, before she'd allow *them* to have her child.

"What about our family, Jon—"

"*What about my family?*" Jon bellowed. "My wife? My sons? My—my . . . *daughter.*" His voice cracked, his face splitting with soul-consuming despair. "I have lost everything on this long, long road of death and misery. *Everything!* The gods demand sacrifice of us all. And to this rule you are no exception, Marie!"

Marie knew he had lost everything. And still it was not enough to sway her. How could it be? They had a child of their own, flesh and blood, as real and true as the gods they both served.

Sanite stepped into his path.

"Out of the way, old woman." His eyes flashed. "We've done our dance."

"No." Power radiated from the Quarter Queen in searing waves. "I don't think we've quite finished, young man."

Marie realized then that Sanite had been stalling. The air stirred, constricting itself back and forth as she pulled the water from it. The water La Sirene blessed her with for her vision, the same water that had baptized Marie, cleansed her of her sins. Marie coughed. She felt Sanite pull it from her too, from her hair, her skin, the tears that had caught on her lashes, even the fountain of holy water that was erected near the cathedral's doorway. La Sirene's wrath became the Quarter Queen's wrath, and in one terrible burst of magic, it exploded.

Dark water surged forth from the air, swirling around Sanite in a dreadful hurricane that surged higher and higher, reaching even the cathedral's rafters, until Sanite thrust her arms forth and those dark waters engulfed everything, even Marie. There was hardly any time to hold her breath. She sank along with Jon, plunged into the cold water of the priestess's destruction. But Sanite would not let her drown. Sanite, still caught in that wind of swirling tide, flung an arm out, and the water goddess mimicked her, moving to encase only Jon in a sphere of churning water.

He thrashed and thrashed inside, but now Sanite was constricting her hand into a fist. The sphere of water grew smaller and smaller. She was going to crush him as a hurricane might.

Sanite smiled. But then something darted along the rafters—a streak of black—and Aram came shooting out from the dark, directly for Sanite. His beak found purchase against her left eye, and she howled from the pain. He might have gone for the other too, but Marie called Ogoun's fire into her hand and thrust it at him. The crow screeched, taking off toward Jon.

Marie whirled, realizing the water had dispersed. The floor was soaked but empty. It had been only a diversion.

Jon clicked his teeth from behind her. Marie spun, saw that he was leaning against a pillar, his clothes and skin sodden, mouth set into a furious line. "Still, you do not learn, Marie." His golden eyes went flat black. "Shall I teach you, beloved?"

Jon the Conjurer broke apart into a thousand screeching crows. The birds flew around her in a storm of whirling darkness, clawing into her flesh as they circled in a flurry so black Marie thought she had gone blind. The crows were screaming at her, viciously taunting her weakness until she had no choice but to cover her ears from the madness. It was too much. Something was clawing at her face, at her eyes. Marie squeezed them shut. But the Conjurer meant only to mock her, to demonstrate that the limits of his dark magic knew no bounds.

The murder of crows broke apart. Marie opened her eyes. Jon was crouched over Sanite, a small blade in his hands. "I'm going to give you one last chance, Marie. *One*. Give the child now, or . . ." He balanced the knife in his hand like a wand. "I finish what I started with your precious Quarter Queen many years ago."

Furious, Marie stepped forward, tears in her eyes, a bolt of fire flickering to life in her hand. But Sanite gave the barest shake of her head. Marie closed her fingers, crushing the flame.

"So be it." Then Jon ran the blade along Sanite's throat, blood spurting from the neat little line he'd carved, spraying along the blade's silver handle, his hands and face.

"*No!*" Marie howled, lurching forward. But it was too late. She thrust out a hand, and Jon was flung to the far end of the hall. She wailed for Sanite, Ogoun's fire spilling from her mouth, pouring out over the stone until it had formed a flaming wall.

Marie knelt by her queen. The old woman was lying on her side against the stone, the blood from the knife wound along her neck and from her torn eye seeping into the cracks.

Sanite gurgled and gurgled, choking furiously as she tried to speak, her one good eye on Marie. It was completely white, still filled with that terrible all-seeing magic, even as the life faded from her.

"You will look, Marie Laveau, and you will never find. What . . . you seek . . ." Sanite gasped, blood spurting from her lips. She pulled the golden cloth from her hair and placed it in Marie's hand with trembling fingers. "Does not lay outside of you, but *within*. As above, so below. So within, so without."

That eye hung on Marie's face for a moment longer, and then it was rolling up into the socket, unseeing. Sanite fell slack until Marie was holding only her golden cloth. Marie stared at it for one painful moment, realizing what Sanite intended for her to do, then slowly tied it upon her head. At once, she felt all of Sanite's strength, that terrible wrath, her many faults, the few virtues—all of it flowed into Marie. She felt the tignon change and transform until it became a crown, as Sanite had intended.

The fire parted. Jon stepped through. Marie was still kneeling when he approached her. But she had the strength of the Quarter Queen within her now. And she understood, at last, Sanite's final lesson. Not Jon's.

As above, so below. So within, so without.

Marie was shaking. Jon held his hand out to her, just as he had during their second fateful meeting, at the masquerade. She'd wanted so desperately to learn his secret magic, his tricks. And learn she did.

"Join me, Marie." One last chance. She stared at his hand . . .

She took it.

"What a righteous queen you are." He'd meant it as a taunt, another cruelty to seed into her spirit.

"No." Marie slowly lifted her head to face him, tears stinging her eyes. "A mother."

By the time Jon realized what was happening, Marie already had the aurum collar in place. It burned her bare hands, but she ignored the pain, that same blistering ache, and closed it around Jon's wrist with a *snap*.

Jon let out a howl, stumbling back in disbelief. She knew what wearing those chains again meant to him, what it would cost him.

She slowly rose to her feet. "I am sorry, Jon." And it was the truth. She *was* sorry.

Jon watched her, his golden eyes wide. It was the first time she'd ever seen him truly afraid. Marie supposed she should be thankful. He'd taught her pain could be useful, that it could be anchored to make one's magic stronger.

"Take this off," Jon demanded shakily. Not a monster, she realized, but simply a man broken by his own pain. "*Marie.*"

She ignored him. The truth was she didn't need to taunt him with illusions of the past, trickeries of power. No, she didn't need any of that, not when she had the real thing.

Power surged through her in a furious burst of light. The ground shattered, cracks traveling along the stone. She knew what lay beneath. But did Jon? Her magic began to carve itself into the stone, into the veve shaped like a doorway, a flickering veil. Something older, something powerfully ancient coursed through her veins, pulled from the dark well of the earth itself. The air split, then circled around her in a furious gale. She was on the threshold of death. She felt the soft caress of its hand reaching from the great beyond, reaching for her.

Horror slowly filled Jon's face. After all, Marie had sought at first to learn the secrets of the Veil for Jacques. Not for *him*. Jon was a man of contingencies. So, with Father Antoine's blessing, she'd been forced to make her own.

"I would have joined you, Jon." Marie's magic intensified. "But not at the cost of my daughter. You would kill her. And that's just not something I'm willing to forgive."

Marie felt herself floating, higher and higher until she hovered over the bloodied stone, until Jon kneeled directly beneath her, frozen.

She began the forbidden incantation, drawing upon her magic. It came to her, rippling over her body—her eyes, forearms, glowing fingertips. Finally, she dropped to the ground, her magic flowing from her in throbbing waves, her dark hair scattering behind her.

"Marie . . ." Fear edged his voice now. "*What have you done?*"

Unbidden magic crackled with her fury and despair. "Everything you taught me."

Marie slammed a blood-soaked hand into the ground, into the sacred markings. It began to glow with a pulsing violet light.

"Open," she whispered in the Old Tongue.

There came from the silence a dull creaking sound, the groan of an old gate being swung open.

The door to the Veil opened before Marie Laveau at last.

Darkness seeped into the sanctuary, a whisper at her ear. *You've opened the door, Marie Laveau,* it said. *Now, come see who answers.*

It was death. And Marie Laveau knew death well. She'd felt it all around her since she was a child. She'd glimpsed it in the eyes of chained men and women, saw it looming over those poor souls in their sickbeds drawing their final, fevered breaths, watched hopelessly as it followed her husband like a shadow when he turned to leave her one last time.

So when death came to her now, she held out her hand, greeting it like an old friend.

"*No!*" Jon screamed. "What have you done?"

That was when the world went white.

A blinding light flooded the sanctuary. Marie squeezed her eyes shut. When she opened them again, a towering black door had appeared before her. Silver light glowed around the edges like moonlight had seeped into its old cracks. The door was covered in a long tattered white curtain that swayed softly. The blood drained from Marie's face as her eyes remained fixed on that pale shroud and the glowing door behind it. *The Veil.*

There were voices whispering from behind it. Whispering to *her.*

Marie slowly rose to her feet. Jon shouted for her, but Marie could not hear him. It was as if the sound had been bled from the room except for the voices from behind the door. Marie drifted toward that strange glowing light.

Someone else was calling for her now—someone from behind the door.

Come, Marie, it said.

She'd know that voice anywhere—even after the long, lonely years she'd spent without it, she'd know it in a heartbeat. Because it was the voice of her mother.

Come back to me, her mother begged, *and we can be together again.*

As she drew closer, she could hear other voices too—Grand-mère, Sanite Dede. And Jacques. Her once beloved. He called to her, a caressing whisper at her ear. *Join me.*

Marie could hear something else, some faint echo in the distance—someone was crying. It was her daughter. From somewhere in the cathedral, her daughter was crying for her. Marie clung to that blessed sound, anchored herself to it. Her daughter. Her reason for it all. She could not leave her. Not now—not ever. Marie stopped, reason flooding back to her. This was an illusion, another trick. The Veil had no power over her—she was the one who had summoned it; she was the one who had opened this door. And it was hers to close if she wanted.

A dark laugh sounded from behind that tattered white veil. The door opened, and a figure stepped from it, limned in silvery light. Papa Legba stood before her, glittering copper scales in hand. Lord of the Crossroads, keeper of keys, He Who Stands at the Beginning and the End.

"Marie Laveau," Papa drawled slowly, something like a smile playing on his lips. "You would dare to open the sacred doorway to the dead?"

"I would."

Those red eyes flashed. Not with anger, but with intrigue. "And so you have. Make your petition known to the Lord of the Crossroads. Whose soul is it that you require from me?"

What might she say? That she wanted to know what had become of her husband? That after the long, terribly lonely years, this was what she had long sought after? And here it was before her now, tauntingly real. It was said that those foolish enough to dabble in Veil magic were looking for their lost loved ones, to bring back the souls of the dead. But never had she heard of anyone offering the *living*.

Marie slowly looked to Jon, unbidden tears in her eyes. "I do not seek to take a soul. I only seek to *offer* one before you, Papa Legba."

Jon stared numbly, frozen with incomprehension. Marie grimaced as she watched the white veil billow softly over the cold stone. He did not yet understand. But he would.

Papa's red eyes crinkled at the corners, pleasantly bemused. "I have long watched you, Marie Laveau. I know you to be steadfast in your retributions. Vindictive, even. But this?" His withered lips curved. "This is truly diabolical. Are you sure, priestess?"

Marie was silent. It was this . . . or . . . She shut her eyes. She could not bear the alternative. If she killed him, Jon would be no more. At least this way, she could spare herself the act, and some part of him might still live on.

"Well . . . ?" A dangerous edge to Papa's voice now. The loa did not linger in the land of the living long. "Answer properly, witch."

Finally, she brought herself to nod. "Yes."

Marie turned to face Jon, lifting her hands. They were shaking. She hadn't even realized she'd been crying until she tried to speak.

"I—" Marie stopped.

Jon's eyes found hers. For a moment he searched her face,

snatching at the details of her features for his own. What was it she saw there, reflected in their gold depths? Pain? Love? She might never know.

The knot in her throat widened, her tongue like cold lead in her mouth. And yet she spoke anyway, voice quivering, heart stammering. *Turn your heart to stone.* She found the words at last. "I banish you, Jonathan, from this world," Marie said, tears slipping down her cheeks. "I cast you out."

Papa Legba nodded, the deal done. "And so it shall be. A soul for a soul." The scales in his gnarled hands tipped, weighing just a little heavier.

Jon opened his mouth to speak, then suddenly froze. The skin around his face stretched oddly, as if a thousand invisible hands were prying into his flesh. And they *were*. The spirits from the other side pulled and pulled at Papa Legba's command, dragging Jon toward that strange silvery light.

As Jon's thrashing body grew closer to the black door, it opened a little wider, waiting. Jon fought, but he was not strong enough to defy Papa's command. No one was. The Lord of the Crossroads's word was final.

"Marie! Please. *Marie!*" Jon yelled, voice curdled with dread. And he kept on calling for her. *Marie. Marie. Marie.* On and on, her name rang through the cathedral's halls, a dull echo in her ear. Marie could not bear to look. And yet . . . she did.

The dead clawed viciously into Jon's flesh, into his face, arms, hauling him across the stone to the tattered white veil. It drew apart, silently welcoming him. Jon dug his fingers into the ground until his fingernails snapped and broke, rebellious to the end. His eyes found hers, blood seeping from his mouth as he made a strange gurgling sound. Marie realized he was trying to speak.

"I . . ." Jon's eyes shone, mouth gaping, teeth wet with his own blood. ". . . *love you.*"

And then he was gone, dragged down into that silvery light. The white veil drew closed, the glowing door shut behind it. The blinding light returned, flooding the room until the whole of it was swallowed in its white glare. Marie shut her eyes, and when she opened them again, she was alone. The voices of the dead were gone. And she knew with a wave of sadness that they would never trouble her again.

Marie stood frozen, Jon's voice still ringing in her ears. *I love you.* And even as she thought it might be a trick, one last way to deceive her, she knew it was not. *No lies,* they had promised each other, after all.

With tears spilling down her face, Marie raised her eyes to the ceiling, to the god she could not see. She screamed, a sound of bone-deep ache, twisting remorse, sin that needed to work its way out of her like a sickness. God did not answer. She was alone. Only the crows were listening. They were silent, staring from the rafters. But even as they flew away, one by one, high into the dark—she knew.

The crows would not forgive.

CHAPTER TWENTY-FIVE

REE

Black spots danced in Ree's vision when she came to. A burlap sack covered her head, veiling the world. The ground was cold beneath her, sodden with damp. The back of her head pulsed with a dull, throbbing ache. She must have fallen after Silas attacked her, hit her head. She tried to move—no use. Her arms were twisted behind her, her wrists tightly bound. With aurum, she suspected from the metallic stench of her own flesh burning. Magic would be of no use then. She was out of cards, and the game was done. Saints, she was well and truly fucked.

Then it hit her—a soul-splintering crack in her chest, fissuring right down the middle. Something in her snapped, broken, as bits of Marie's memories rushed in, flooding her mind in fragments of sight and sound: *Her mother standing in St. Louis Cathedral ... great fire in her hand, Jon descending from the air, a flock of black birds surrounding him ... Marie shoving her hand to the ground, invoking the sacred opening ritual of the Veil ...*

One last memory flared—blinding and final. *Marie cradling Ree as a baby, the little glowing star on Ree's brow, the soft press of her kiss against it, sealing it with love and magic.* The image fizzled, then slowly faded from view, a little boat pushed out into a sea of nothingness, on the path of no return. Her mother's memories had reached their end. And she knew why. Marie was dying. Oh, gods, Marie Laveau was dying. She'd sent those memories in one final bid to Ree, and here she was too slow, too late—out of time.

The sack was ripped from Ree's head, light returning to her world as a voice sneered her name: "Marie Laveau the Second."

Her vision adjusted—she was in a darkened field, kneeling among swaying sugarcane, the stalks turned shriveled and pale against the moonlight. Mayor Felix Corbin stood before her, leaning on his fleur-de-lis cane, countless of the city's policemen proudly flanking him. Behind him stood the shadow of a towering, galleried white house. It was as her mother's memories had shown her. The great chateau, the palace where he'd long lived as a king, a man who'd built the riches of his court from sugarcane and blood.

"I hope you will forgive the circumstance of our meeting, Mademoiselle. But I'm afraid the matter is urgent."

Now, as her eyes adjusted to the light, she found Henryk kneeling across from her, bound and gagged. To her horror, there were the others: Claudette, Nan, Ory, Fabrice.

"My apologies," said Ree.

Corbin smiled at her, delighted. "You do have your mother's tongue." He twirled his cane. Her eyes darted to the hunting rifle at his shoulder. From the toxic smell, she was sure that it was loaded with aurum bullets.

"Why am I here?"

"Tell her, Silas."

The smell of foxglove overwhelmed Ree. Silas stepped out from the shadowed corner of the fields. Ree watched him, her blood boiling. The Grand Wizard's eyes were blank. Ree had seen her mother captured by the Brotherhood, betrayed by Silas, only to be saved by him in the end. He had saved Ree too, hadn't he? She remembered the bayou, the snatchers. *Hello again, little witch.* Now she understood what the alchemist had meant. But the Grand Wizard couldn't be trusted, not completely, since he'd forced her mother into a bargain she couldn't refuse. That was why he'd known about Marie's condition; they were tethered by some strange force of equilibrium.

"The mayor is a very generous man, little witch," Silas said. "He intends to offer us all a deal. You see, when the Inquisition begins their tribunal, they will leave no magical stone unturned. I highly doubt they will be satisfied with just your arrest and execution. They will want the Brotherhood too. Let us consider the source." He turned to Henryk, took the gag from his mouth. "Is this true, Inquisitor?"

Henryk's eyes narrowed into furious slits. "Fuck you."

Silas only laughed, the sound of dry leaves underfoot. "Charming."

Henryk turned to Ree, a rippling storm in his eyes—fury, longing, something tender and secret and only for her. They'd had one night. And maybe that would be enough. "Ree, say nothing. Agree to nothing."

"I don't have time for this—" Corbin seized Ree by the chin, examining her in the light as if she were a gemstone. "Join me, witch. This will be your only offer. If you don't, think of what will happen to your lover."

"Touch her, and I'll fucking kill you," the Inquisitor snarled.

"Is that so?"

And then Corbin backhanded her, hard enough that her teeth dug into her tongue, her vision dimmed. The force of his hand left her jaw aching and the metallic taste of blood in her mouth, but Ree said nothing, choosing instead to glare at him. "I find that some deals require a delicate balance of pressure," Corbin said. "Tell me, was that enough?"

She spat blood onto the ground, eyes glinting. "Not nearly."

Silas watched, leaning on his great staff. His face as impassive as cool stone.

Corbin stalked over to Henryk, wrenched him up by the hair to face him. "You will find that I can be very persuasive, Inquisitor Broussard. Now, I will ask of you both one last time: Join me and avoid the persecution of the Inquisition. Refuse me and I throw you both to the wolves of the Inquisitors. You know what they do to traitors, hm, boy? Surely much worse than they do to heretics and witches." He whirled, eyes scanning the rest. "Maybe your lover's blood is not enough? Perhaps I should sweeten the deal, hm?"

Down the line of captives he went, skimming the fleur-de-lis end of his cane along their backs. He was going to pick. Saints, he was going to pick one of them to die. Who among them would break first? Ree's eyes darted to Claudette. Not her—she would never break. The fierce set of her jaw told Ree that. Nan—no. Not quickly, at least. But Ory would. Fabrice. Their blood would be on her hands. But she couldn't save them, could she? She was not the Quarter Queen, and she had no grand magic left.

"It kills you, doesn't it? To not have any real magic of your own," said Ree. "You're so pathetic that you've got to devise a way to steal someone else's. No wonder the Brotherhood didn't want your sorry ass!"

A weak attempt at stalling, she knew. Delaying the inevitable. Already, she could feel her mother fading with every second that passed, her shallow breaths playing in Ree's ears. She could *feel* her. Slipping away, minute by minute.

Corbin's smirk faltered, like chipped glass. He knew what she was doing. But he held the knife of the advantage now, and he was doing his damn best to twist it where it hurt. "I reckon what I did to that boy, that stupid piece of shit I hung in that square 'til he was cold and gray"—his eyes narrowed down into his face, and Ree thought she might be sick. *Marcel*—"I reckon I'll do worse to you, you fucking witch. But first, I'll enjoy breaking you."

"No!" Henryk bucked and twisted, but Corbin only shoved the dirtied rag back into his mouth, then jabbed the end of his fleur-de-lis cane into his side, and Ree heard his ribs give a sickening snap. He shoved Henryk onto his side, now screaming through the gag. But the sound came out all wrong—the wild, panicked sound of an animal.

Corbin turned to Silas. "Cut off her hand. Let us see how pretty she is then."

Silas bent over Ree, his hand tracing down her arm to her manacled wrists. He gave them an agonizing twist. Ree gasped from the pain, terror gripping her throat, but said nothing. She would not give him the satisfaction.

"Well, get on with it then," said Corbin.

But Silas had gone strangely still. "You were right about one thing, Felix. I am here to make a deal. Just not with *you*." He turned glittering eyes on Ree. "What are friends for, little witch?"

The manacles fell away from her wrists.

Shock left her speechless as she realized what he'd done. When he'd twisted her wrist, the alchemist must have quietly undone the lock. Ree understood at last the arrangement he was proposing.

Slowly, they both turned to look back at Corbin.

"What are you doing?" Corbin demanded, fear lacing his voice.

Silas cast a sidelong look at Ree. "Clearing the board."

Swearing, Corbin jabbed a finger at Ree and Silas. "Fucking kill them!"

"*Mutatio,*" Silas yelled, slamming his staff down as the police fired. A thin green barrier formed in the air in front of Ree, bullets ricocheting, the fire returned upon Corbin's men. Screams whistled in the air as bullets flew, some striking the house, some the men. Corbin squealed; he'd taken a hit in the side. Blood spewed between his fleshy fingers.

Silas quickly turned to Ree, one hand still holding up the green barrier between them and the police. It would not hold for long. "Perhaps now this will convince you of my loyalty."

It had been a trick. A dirty, rotten trick. She remembered Corbin's ball, the way she'd glimpsed that moment of fire and horror; the only thing she was sure of was that he was not who he said he was, that he was a man with two faces, and she never knew which she was looking at.

"You stupid sons of bitches think you can mutiny? Against me?" Corbin spat, eyes wild and blue in the moonlight. His fear betrayed him. "I have my men!"

Silas sneered. "And I have more."

Darkness spread out from the center of his eyes, seeping like spilled ink until the whole of the white spaces were filled. The pupils at the center shone as pale as bone. He tapped his staff once on the ground, sending a vibration of pressure out, a wind that shook the stalks and the trees. Dozens of Brotherhood alchemists stepped out from the cane fields. They made for a frightening picture—a line of dark-robed white men with silver hair that blanketed their shoulders like freshly fallen snow, their faces obscured by long hoods.

Even through her shock, Ree registered the advantage. Their

numbers outweighed Corbin's now. The odds had turned. Henryk and Claudette watched the alchemists, their faces uneasy. It was the worst kind of deal, but it was the only one left on the table. An alliance was made.

Reading her surprise, Silas said, "It needed to look convincing. To get past his defenses. *Kill* him, Ree. And then there will only be one enemy left."

The Inquisition. If only it were that simple. The Grand Wizard had no idea that the last enemy would not be the Church. It would be the Brotherhood of the White Hand. But not today.

Ree turned furious eyes on Corbin, who was cowering before her, inching along like a worm seeking soil. She would kill him, yes. But first? First, she would save her mother.

Ree slammed her hand into the ground, allowing the spell of the Veil to leak from her and into the earth, just the way her mother's vision had shown her. Pulsing violet light spread from her fingertips, weaving across the dirt and into the sacred veve of opening.

"Open," she commanded.

From the silence came a dull creaking sound, the groan of an old gate swinging open ...

The whole of the sugarcane fields filled with a blinding white light. Ree was forced to shield her eyes with the back of her hand until the light receded and in its place stood a towering black door that was covered in a long white curtain. The Veil.

Despite the sticky heat of the night, Ree felt the air chill. It was the hand of death, reaching out from beyond the grave, sowing a bone-deep cold as its shadow passed over them all.

Ree glanced around her. The wind had frozen through the stalks, the people around her rigid where they stood, mannequins propped into position. Time itself held its breath, and she was sure, somewhere in the very heart of the French Quarter, that the hands turning upon the face of St. Louis Cathedral's great clock had stilled into place. The bells would not toll. Only Ree moved and breathed, untouched by the presence of the divine. He was here.

The Veil stirred gently as if someone were moving behind it, their shadow slowly drawing closer. The black shadow was too tall, too narrow to be human. A withered brown hand reached to part the curtain. In her sudden fright, Ree half expected some kind of dark creature to step through, a horrendous monster. But it was only an old man who hobbled out from behind the Veil and into the mortal realm.

He leaned on a cane with one gnarled hand, a pair of copper scales in the other. The only sign of vitality he held was in the eyes: They glowed like red rubies out from the dark, smoldering furnace of his face, betraying his true divine nature.

"Marie Laveau," the Lord of the Crossroads said. And with a smile he added, "The Second."

"Hello, Papa."

CHAPTER TWENTY-SIX

MARIE

When Marie emerged from the Dreadwood, Papa Legba was waiting for her. He leaned on his cane with one hand, drumming his fingers along the head, his shining copper scales in the other. She might have mistaken him for one of those old fellows on the corners in the Quarter, heckling passersby for a bit of coin and drink. But he was no old man—he was an old god, an immortal capable of untold magic. She would not allow herself to so easily be deceived by another man wearing a mask.

"You are too late, Marie. Fate has been set in motion."

Too late? Marie drew in a breath. Flickering shadows danced behind Papa, shapeless against the gray mist. All those wandering souls. Marie suppressed a shiver—she wanted out of this strange realm.

"I told you, Marie Laveau, that you would complete my Trial of Spirit. But I never said you'd be the *only* one." He paused, testing the silence. "There is another, is there not?"

Marie went very still, terror flooding her belly like cold water. "What have you done to my daughter?"

"No, what have *you* done, Marie?" he said. "Did you think that it is the will of the loa to see their people subjugated? Suffering endlessly? You intervened where you shouldn't have. You stopped Jon's rebellion. So now there will simply have to be another."

A wave of panic seized Marie. She put a hand to her stomach, steadying the painful lurches. Saints, she was going to be sick. "He was going to sacrifice our child. I couldn't just—"

"Did you ever think that request of sacrifice might have been a test? That the consequences of your actions and the Conjurer's might have fortified you both in ways you can't yet comprehend?" Papa's eyes flashed, molten red in the dark. Marie fell silent, that familiar aching heat crawling over her skin. He could snatch her soul from her body with only a thought. What hope did she have to stand against his divinity? "There will be a war, Marie Laveau. A reckoning. And the gods need their vessels to make it so. But you are far too righteous, Marie. The sun eclipsed by its own light. Jon is far too blinded by his own darkness." Papa Legba turned red eyes to the sickle moon above. "Eventually, even the moon is consumed by the night. But the star? The star hangs between the two in perfect symmetry."

"*No.*" Marie froze, a look of horror slowly dawning on her face. It was as Jon had promised. The foretold Song of Three.

Papa Legba's smile stretched as he looked down at the swaying scales in his hand. It was then that Marie noticed a sun and a moon on each side of the scales, and a little golden star hanging in the middle. The scales stopped moving, perfectly balanced at last.

"The gods have chosen you three as our intended trinity. And war you will bring us."

Marie fell to her knees. She allowed the tears she'd held back for years to finally, finally come. Her body was racked with the ache of guilt and shame for her part in this, for her sins, but also with the pain she'd endured in turn. She might serve these loa, she might even lay down her life for them. But she would not give her daughter's. She would not.

"I will do anything. Anything. But spare my daughter. Please. I beg of you."

"You beg for nothing, Marie Laveau. You, who have been given the gift of freedom." Papa Legba shook his head, those red eyes dimmed. "And that freedom will cost you."

Papa Legba vanished, leaving Marie utterly alone in this world of darkness and smoke and spirit. Marie did not know how long she waited like that, kneeling and alone, hot tears in her eyes. She could scream, and still nothing might sate the hopelessness she felt.

Had it all been for nothing? Would it have always led to this?

Marie bent her head and wept.

"Come now, Marie. I taught you better than that."

A hand appeared in front of her. And Marie slowly looked up into the face of Jon the Conjurer. She stared, frozen, tears in her lashes, remembering his last words, the words she heard in her heart and in her nightmares every night. At every mass, in every dark room. *I love you.*

"I've been waiting for you," Jon murmured. His eyes, rich gold, softened.

His face, scarcely touched by time. She wondered how he saw her all these years later. Was it vanity? Some semblance of old feeling? Time had changed her—creased her brow in faint lines, threaded the dark of her hair with strands of gray—and most days she thought for the worse. But here now, with him again, she felt as if she were twenty all over again. Young. Powerful. A terrifying illusion.

"You would take my hand again, Jon?" she asked quietly. "After everything I've done? After all this time?"

His answer made her breath hitch. "I would take your hand always, Marie. Always." His hand was still before her, as it had been many years ago during their dance. "Now, come. I have much to still teach you. And there is still so much you might learn."

Marie considered his eyes, the peculiar eyes of a harvest moon, the eyes that told her everything with one look: that he had not forgotten her sin, nor his own. The eyes that said that he might love her still, that after all this time apart, he had never stopped. She would not ask for his forgiveness. But for their daughter's sake, she might ask for his help.

And very slowly, she took Jon's hand once more.

CHAPTER TWENTY-SEVEN

REE

The world was still frozen around them, cocooned in the Lord of the Crossroads's power.

Ree beheld Papa Legba. He Who Stands at the Beginning and the End. If she were at one of his altars, she might offer poured rum and pale slices of coconut flesh. A pipe and tobacco. Simple gifts. But she was not at his altar. She was at his sacred doorway, a door many whispered should never be opened.

"You have called. And I have come," said Legba.

A strange light touched his eyes. If Ree hadn't the sense to know that these loa—these spirit-gods of different names—were so unabashedly inhuman, she might have mistaken him for simply a very old man. But an old man he was not. His eyes glowed with enough heat that her skin ached.

"You wanted me to come, didn't you? Why?"

"This was a lesson, child. And you have been a very, very difficult child to teach," explained the elder loa.

"I don't understand."

A sudden whisper at her ear that made her hair stand on end. *Oh, but you will.*

Then Papa Legba was gone.

In the darkness he still spoke, his voice coming from different directions all at once. *You were born with your mother's life in you. Your father's gift for death. You are the balance. You are the door. And we command the dead to walk through it. But the loa are kind, and so we allow choice. You must choose the road you seek.*

"Did you allow my mother to choose? Or my father?" she called to the dark.

She turned on her heel to find the loa was standing behind her, silently appraising her. Her heart leapt into her throat—she might never get used to seeing gods made flesh. *Dangerous,* a small voice inside of her screamed. He could end her with a thought.

"Yes, in a way. Marie Laveau and the Conjurer chose their fates for different ends. One for love. And the other for revenge. The sun and the moon." And she was the star. At last, maybe, she was beginning to understand. "You will be our vessel for war. This was the will of the loa before your birth, before the union of your mother and your father. Such was decreed by the first Quarter Queen, the agreement with death she struck on the pyre, and it was so. You will finish her work, and you will avenge. But only if you accept."

Saloppe had burned on a stake. Had the loa allowed that? Had all of this suffering truly been the will of the gods? Had they simply stirred a war with Marie and Jon and all the sorrow in between to fulfill their own selfish whims?

"We loa do not control the mortal world," Legba answered, easily reading her thoughts. "We can only guide what already exists, manipulating the threads man has woven. We desire only to cleanse the mess mortals have foolishly made. You must see this, yes?"

New Orleans. The city was broken long before the loa. The Voodoo gods and spirits did not call for chains and misery. This was not their sin.

"Bring Marie back. Papa, *please.*" She was not her mother. She was not used to making such requests before the loa, less sure of how to make herself humble before their divinity.

"Bring back one. You bring back *all.*" Legba made a tutting noise with his tongue, an elder admonishing a wayward babe at his knee. "Choose now, and choose wisely. You open this door, and there may be no closing it. If you do not, you will go on living as you are.

But your kin will die. If you *should* open it, the will of the loa comes again, and we will bring war. And that war will cost you, Marie."

She saw the horrifying vision of herself twisting on a burning pyre, just as the first Quarter Queen had done. She still heard the demon's words, the rattling of its tongue as it proclaimed, *If you open the Veil and save your mother, you will forfeit your own life. This is the fate you will damn yourself to. This is what will become of you!*

A vision? Or a lie? She couldn't be sure. It was an impossible choice. Here she was, stranded in the twilight between the lies of demons and the promises of deities older than the ground she stood on. These weren't kind odds. But she was a betting woman, after all. And this was a risk she was willing to take, even if it was against her own life. She would take it for her mother.

"Do you accept the will of the loa, child?" asked Papa Legba.

"I do," she said finally.

"Then it is so." The loa turned back to the Veil and started toward its strange glowing light, the scales in his hand shifting.

"Can fate be changed?" Ree called to his back.

The Lord of the Crossroads stopped in his tracks. It was bold of her to call to a spirit-god who'd already made his proclamations, some might say foolish. Ree felt the wind shift, her heart frozen in her chest.

But the old gatekeeper only turned and smiled, his bright red eyes crinkling amiably at the corners. "You must ask yourself, child: Do you have the power to change it?"

And in one blinding flash of light, he was gone. The door closed.

The sound came rushing back, and with it, the sweet, earthen smell of the fields, the humidity dewing on her skin. The world moved again. The stillness shattered, breaking apart into chaos. Ree spun around—Silas was beside her, still holding the ward in place against Corbin's men as if he hadn't moved at all.

Ree felt something crawling inside her, something dark welling to the surface. She could still feel the power of the Veil on her—around her—pressing in. It was in her veins now.

She rushed to Henryk's side and quickly undid the manacles binding his arms. Claudette made a noise, cutting green eyes at Ree. *I am still here.* When Ree pried the aurum from her, she was surprised when the older witch snatched her into her arms. "You little brat," Claudette gasped into her shoulder, Ree surprised at her turn of emotion. "You nearly died." They all had. But the danger was not over yet.

The roar of a cannon broke the quiet, hurling iron-shot through the night that slammed directly into the alchemist's ward, its surface flaring with static and light. The force of the blow swept dust and dirt from the ground, tossing their hair into the wind. The other alchemists raised their glowing staffs, projecting them toward the ward, fortifying its hold.

But the cannon had still struck its target—the air. The searing sting of aurum clung to the wind now, weakening their magic. Another shot like this and they may very well be in trouble. Corbin had come prepared.

"Behind me, quickly!" snarled Silas. "Prepare yourself."

The Brotherhood and the Voodoos, standing side by side, tethered in uncertain truce. One side with their glowing staffs raised, the other calling down the fury and magic of the spirits. The air was charged with the force of their differing magic, the cold light of transmutation joined with the conjured old lightning of Sogbo, loa of storms, and Bade's fierce blow of wind fused into one crackling breath.

Ree stood between them, close beside Henryk, heart thudding in her ears, each beat keeping pace with the cannon fire. Another terrible burst of cannon shot shook the sky, this one landing with force. The ward broke apart, bit by bit, dissolving into shards of smoking green light.

The blow tossed them back. Ree flew through the dark, landed with a thud in the sugarcane. She scrambled to her feet, saw the chaos rippling around her—Corbin's men advancing, spells and bullets charging the night, mingling in a mess of smoke and fire.

Ree's eyes snapped to Corbin. After everything—after the pain he'd caused the women in her line, her friends, the city—she would have him.

She took a step toward Corbin, who dragged himself to his feet, one hand clutching his bleeding side. She halted. Something began to pull at her. She could feel it all around her, calling to her, demanding she let whatever it was inside. It was as if there was a door open in the darkest part of her mind, a thousand hands clamoring against it, prying it open with rotten fingers from the other side. *Let us in*, a voice whispered in her ear. *Let us in and we will save you.*

And that tall black door opened just a little for her.

She could feel that sweet sensation of life and death moving across the grounds, calling to her, drifting like a spirit. It was tethered to her—*in* her. Some of Corbin's dead slaves would not be buried. New Orleans was the city of water, after all—in the air, in the skies, even in the ground. Any graves dug into the soil were likely to be flooded by rain, with the corpses rushing back to the surface, moldered skin drenched in dark, pulpy earth and wriggling worms. But she could feel their souls tugging at her from the city of the dead, from the many unmarked graves in the wood.

We are many. And we are coming, voices sang to her from the dark.

All that death. It wanted to come back. *Through* her.

Come, she beckoned at last.

And that black door within her heart finally opened wide.

Ree convulsed. Henryk grabbed her, folded her into his arms. He shook her. "Ree! *Ree!*"

But it was too late. The dead were rising now; the deal was done. And there was nothing anyone could do to stop it.

The smoke began to thin, revealing a long line of soot-covered bodies slowly trudging toward her. They were slaves. Or they had been, when they were *alive*. Now their dark skin shone with a grayish cast in the moonlight, some puckered with seeping wounds, others marred with decayed gashes along their arms and stomachs. Tattered cotton dress hung from some of the decayed bodies, while others were half naked. Different as they were, they all held the same glassy look in their eyes—violet light burned in their irises, a strange cold fire. Ree knew what they were now, these creatures of old folktales.

They were the undead, the unholy resurrected, damned to walk the earth barren of all soul, hungering for life and flesh. They were zombi.

Do you understand now, child? Legba called from the dark. *It always comes back.* She did—she finally understood why her magic had always felt so different from her mother's, why the spirits taunted her, nudging her path away from her mother's and into the shadows. She was never meant for her mother's light. Because *this* was her power. This was her birthright.

The convulsing passed through her, one last terrible wave of cold, before it finally subsided. Henryk pulled Ree to her feet as they watched the undead creep out from the mist. Corbin turned tail and ran, leaving his men in his wake.

She bolted after him but was seized by the wrist.

"Don't," Henryk warned when she turned to face him. "Let him go, Ree."

Didn't he see that there was no letting him go? They'd already come too far to not finish this dance. If by some miracle they survived the night, it would be Corbin's word against theirs. Corbin and his men would have to die. Mutiny was already here.

"I'm not asking."

"You don't have a choice." Ree snatched her wrist back. "Let me finish this."

"Let me help you."

"You want to help me? Help *them.*" She nodded toward the Voodoos. They had been there when Corbin had announced him a traitor. By now they would know he was a spy. If they were going to work together beyond tonight and stop the Inquisition, then he would need to prove his worth now, prove that he was more than the monster behind the mask.

Show me you're different.

She could tell from his expression that she was winning this argument. But who knew winning could feel so awful? If discovered, they would all be charged and hung in the square before dawn. Her hand rose to cup his cheek, her thumb gently wiping the blood from the side of his mouth. "I'll find you," she swore softly. *I promise you: This time, I will find you again.*

It wasn't a promise she could afford to make. And yet she pulled him to her, crushing her lips to his. In many ways, it felt like the first time they had met, when she had breathed life into his cold body. Or maybe it was like their second kiss, when he had kissed her this time and had poured his magic into her weakened body and brought her back from the edge of darkness. When they broke apart, she kept her eyes on his, drinking in the details of his face. Just in case it might be her last chance.

Then she turned and ran. A bullet grazed her cheek. She whirled to find one of Corbin's men falling to the ground, turned completely to stone. Silas lowered his staff, his expression seeming to say, *You take care of our mutual friend, and the Brotherhood will take care of the rest.* Ree nodded. Silas held her eyes one last time, then disappeared into the smoke.

She followed Corbin's trail of blood up through the house.

The air in the house constricted her as Ree made her way through the dark of the parlor. Every inch of it full of tumultuous memory. The house creaked and groaned, calling for her to see and hear its pain. The pain of her grandmother. Of her mother before her. Marcel's agony. It followed her like a shadow at her heels, all the way up the winding staircase and into the dark mouth of the hall.

Ree spotted a door ajar at the end of the hall. She crept toward it. She was in no condition to keep going. First the encounter with the demon in Jon's tomb, then opening the Veil—it had cost her something, had drained her of power. She sorely needed rest. How long could she go on like this? She set her eyes on the darkness beyond the door where Corbin waited and gritted her teeth.

Slowly, Ree crept into the room. The air changed, and she stepped aside as Corbin went for her throat. She was faster, and she'd been expecting his violence. Ree grabbed him by the collar of his shirt, then, using the magic of Ogoun's iron-clad strength, forced him to the ground. She followed him, snatching his face toward the light. Fury lit her veins on fire.

Corbin's face swam beneath hers, his eyes a bright hungry blue in the dark, the pupils dilated, enlivened in a way that made him appear mad. "You will give yourself to me, you fucking cunt. Or I will give you the pain of a very slow and public death."

"Like how you killed my friend," she gritted out. "Not a chance."

"No." Corbin smiled, red in his teeth. "*You* killed your friend. They told me you gave him the vial. If that's true, then you might as well have hanged him up yourself."

"To punish an overseer who nearly murdered him!" Ree twisted his arms into the floor over his head. But he was laughing still. Why wouldn't he stop?

"*You killed him*," he repeated. "And you can't live with it, can you?"

Ree saw Marcel swinging from that rope, his body limned in cold sunlight. Other horrors too, that she had pretended not to see: The bruises along Anabelle's shoulders, the ones from rough men and paying clients. Anabelle turned on her side, silently crying so that Ree would not hear. But Ree had heard. The countless other little black and colored girls with flowers in their hair and collars on their necks. Ree held out her hands, raised them high, right over Corbin's smiling, bloodied face . . .

All she had to do was press down and bludgeon him with her bare hands. No magic. And he would be done.

"You go on and bash my head in, love," he taunted. "But when you're done, you make sure to take those chains, raise them in the air just like that, and bash your pretty little head in too." His blue eyes were alive. Wild. "Bash and bash until there is nothing but blood and brains left on this fucking floor because, make no mistake, you are as wicked as me! You're as much *complicit* as me, as your mother who sat idly by for years!"

He was right. Ree hesitated.

And that was her mistake.

Corbin brought his cane up with vicious precision, striking Ree directly in the temple. She staggered backward, then hit the ground, her vision blurring.

Corbin seized her by the ankle, then began to drag her across the room, toward the balcony outside that was splintered from cannon fire, the railing broken in half. Corbin wrenched her painfully by the hair, forcing her to see the dead clamoring below. More had come. They seemed to be trudging directly for the chateau, for Corbin himself.

"Call those demons back!" he bellowed into her face. Corbin began shaking her, back and forth. "Stop them!" he cried.

Ree shook her head, laughing. She couldn't. Even if she knew how, she wouldn't. She could feel them pulling on her life force, tugging greedily for her as an anchor. She couldn't stop them. It was too much now. She felt herself growing weaker with every breath. The truth was, she wouldn't last much longer. Perhaps the demon had lied. Perhaps she'd always been hurtling toward death, down Legba's long crossroads toward Baron Samedi, and maybe she would never make it to the pyre. Maybe this was how it was meant to happen. Here, like this. At least she would die with the satisfaction that a monster like Corbin might come with her.

"You wanted a Laveau's magic? Well, now you can have it," said Ree, warm blood on her tongue.

He didn't seem to understand that her magic was beyond his control because it was beyond hers now. He twisted Ree to face him, looked down at her, confused for a split second by her words.

Ree slammed her face into his, felt the bone of his nose crushing against her skin, blood spurting hot between them. He staggered backward, startled by the force, then teetered on the ledge. For one split second, it looked as if he might fall, but he caught himself on the slice of broken railing, dangling like a piece of rotten fruit against the night.

Ree stood over him, the hiss of the wind stinging her face, lifting the dark fall of her hair at her shoulders. Strange that such a large man should look so small now.

Staring down at him, she felt it—that thread of fate taking shape, sewing along the air, drawing a new line in the world. One choice, this choice, would change everything. Why had her mother not killed this man? Because one choice would have set off a chain reaction of other choices, consequences, deaths. Maybe she was ready to face them. Someone had to.

Ree raised a hand in the air, using Bade's wind to lift Corbin, his life force throbbing against her palm as she held him in the crackling grasp of her magic. Her power constricted, an unseen manacle tightening around his throat.

"Careful, little girl." Corbin's voice rose, trembling with fear. The iron groaned. "Mutiny has a price. You break these rules, you're as good as dead." His face split with rage, eyes streaked with panic. "You hear me, witch? As good as *dead*!"

One last appeal. He needn't have. His fate was set. All of theirs were now.

"Respectfully, Felix." A wicked smile pulled at Ree's lips. "Fuck the rules."

She made a dropping motion with her hand. And Felix Corbin plunged through the air, right over the balcony from his big house, free-falling through the starlit night and down into the dark, gaping mouth of the damned that waited for him below.

Ree watched the zombi crash over him in a crushing wave, swelling around him. His flailing limbs poked the air, twisted white thorns. The undead seized him with snarling mouths. They tore the flesh from his bones as easily as peeling a rind. In the end, they tore him down to nothing at all.

Corbin was dead. The mutiny done. But now the game had changed and set itself anew. There would be consequences. And as sure as the sun would rise, there would be a reckoning. Another sound rose above the screams, the gnashing teeth, the crackling of magic and transmutation spells being hurled into the night. Papa Legba's laugh danced on the wind, rustling in the sugarcane, a voice only Ree could hear. *Well done, Quarter Queen.*

Something changed. She felt the pull of the world below, the invisible currents of fate rustling around her. She recalled her question to Papa Legba: Could one change fate? *You must ask yourself, child: Do you have the power to change it?*

Ree grinned. Yes, she thought she might, after all. Maybe they all did.

Fate stitched around her, unseen hands reaching from the cosmos, rearranging the light of the stars. She felt it inside the marrow of her bones—deeper than that, down in the dark well of her spirit. It was the dance of the ancestors awakening inside her. The stir of the old gods finding their way through her blood. This was the magic of ordainment, the raw, blistering power of magic bending shape, changing hands, the anointing of a queen finally being crowned.

Below, the crowd stared up at her, an awestruck silence permeating the dark. The few Voodoos knelt. The Brotherhood stilled, alchemical sigils surrounding their pale shining heads like halos. She spotted the white circle of Henryk's face below as he saw her with new eyes. Ree turned, saw her reflection in the looking glass that hung inside the room. Her mother's golden cloth had spun itself into a new shape. A glowing fleur-de-lis crown.

She was the Quarter Queen, like her mother before her. Now and into the long hereafter.

Outside, the world had changed shape. What was left of Corbin's grounds burned, the sugarcane fields transformed into a gruesome battlefield littered with slain men and curling smoke. Ree stumbled forward through the oily stench of alchemy and aurum, blood and gunpowder. She put a hand to her chest where she felt a deep shudder at her touch. There was something inside of her, something terrible that was trying its best to tear its way out. It was the magic of the Veil, she realized. Some part of it was still working its way through her, a violent deluge of a thousand cold hands clawing up from the darkness of her heart.

It was the zombi. They were *using* her. Stealing her life force to keep crossing back over. And they would not stop, Ree realized. She could not stop them. This was not the magic her mother had taught her. This was her father's magic. And he was not here.

The ground tilted beneath her, and Ree fell, rushing to meet it—

A hand seized her from the dark, holding her up in a viselike grip.

Marie Laveau stared down at her. The widowed queen. The priestess. Her mother. Her eyes were so white they were silver, a wholly unnatural power circling around her in pulsing waves. A sun veve glowed at the center of her forehead.

"You will not die, daughter. So long as I draw breath," she said, "I expressly forbid it."

Marie helped Ree to her feet. Her eyes flitted over Ree, the crown on her head, and Marie smiled, tears flowing from her white eyes.

Wordlessly, Ree took her by the hand. She felt the magic flow between them, easy now in a way it had never been before. She knew that whatever would come, they would face it together.

Arm in arm, Marie and Ree stepped into the chaos. But something was wrong. Very, very wrong. That dark feeling inside Ree was too much. It was clawing at her now. The voices behind the door were getting louder and louder, multiplying by the second. More undead were demanding to be let out.

Spells whizzed past her head as she and Marie made their way across the grounds. Voodoos and Brotherhood holding back Corbin's men. Zombi trudged forward, shuffling in silence through the smoke. Ree felt them calling for her, reaching for her with rotted hands. An army of soulless creatures, listlessly awaiting her command. *Let us out,* the dead demanded, over and over again. Too many dead to count. Vast and terrifying in their numbers.

Ree shoved her hands to her ears. With a start of horror, she realized they were bleeding. *She* was bleeding. From her eyes. Her mouth. Her nose. The life was bleeding out of her. Because they were taking it. That black door inside of her was pounding. She couldn't let them all in, not at once. She wasn't her father. And this wasn't the magic she was raised to know.

But we know you, Marie Laveau the Second, those voices said, a sonorous thunder. *Give to us, Quarter Queen. Bring us back.*

Ree was scarcely aware of her surroundings: There were men firing at them, a zigzag of color and sound all around them. Then a flash of searing green light as a giant serpent appeared before Ree and Marie, moving in a maddening whirl in the air. She realized it was Silas's mark, the ouroboros, moving in a pinwheel of static in front of them, a shield of light.

Then Ree was falling, down into the plantation's damp earth, then farther below, into the darkness of that long corridor inside. Her mother's face was swimming above hers in the moonlight. She could hear someone screaming. It was her. It was Marie. They both were screaming. The pain was agonizing, unending, and she felt her body betray her—convulsing, writhing on the ground as a serpent might. And still her mother was screaming.

Marie tried to heal her, tried every spell, every prayer, every bit of knowledge she could think of. But, in all her power, this was not a wound she knew how to mend.

Ree let out another scream—an unnaturally loud, high keening sound. Another wave of dead rose. She could feel them clawing, a tidal wave. She was glad Henryk was not here to see her like this, a malevolent thing, twisting away in the dark.

Ree was dimly aware that her mother had taken her in her arms, cradling her like when she was a child. Her mother held her close, rocked her back and forth, swaying from the weight of her own grief.

"*No!*" A broken chorus Marie kept repeating over and over.

Ree could feel death upon her, a hovering dark presence that was now pressing down on her, blanketing her vision, her every thought with the promise of oblivion. Of sweet nothingness. She just needed to accept its offer. And there would be relief at last.

Her only regret was in not keeping her promise to Henryk. She knew now that she would not find him again, and that when this terrible night had long passed, when the magic of Mardi Gras had finally waned, he would go to that bridge, and he would wait for her. And she would not come to him. The thought made her cry, and then she began to choke. She fought to hold on to that promise, on to that spark of life that still existed in her spirit.

"Maman," Ree choked through the blood that was quickly filling her mouth. "I don't want to . . . I don't want to die . . ."

"Shhhh now, ma petite bébé . . ." Marie cooed. *Ma petite bébé.* What she called Ree when she was young, when she would hold her in her arms after a bad dream. Her little baby.

It had been easier to be brave before. But here, cradled in the safety of her mother's arms, she felt like she was eight years old again, facing down a long, scary road she could not walk alone. Marie's tears fell hot on her face as she rocked her in her arms, her lips still moving between every prayer, every curse, every bit of life-sustaining magic she knew. But in the end, it seemed, the great Marie Laveau did not know enough.

The world darkened. Ree reached up, touched her mother's face one last time. If she had to die, what better place than in her mother's arms? There was something about that that made her smile some. She would end as she began.

But there was singing. And it was coming closer and closer.

It was Aram. She was not used to this sound, this strange new crow-song. It was a melody she had never heard before but still faintly recognized. He was calling. But he wasn't calling to her. He was calling to *someone else*.

Ree's vision blurred, but she could just make out, through the horde of undead, the blanket of smoke, the red-orange flare of fire that kindled across the dark grounds, a man in a tall dark hat walking toward her.

Toward Marie. Toward them both.

Baron Samedi, she thought. The Lord of Death was coming to take her at last. At least the pain would end, the door would close with her. But it was not Baron Samedi who crouched over her, who held her in his arms. The baron's eyes were dark and sinking, beautifully inhuman. No, this man's eyes were golden, bright with strange, old magic. It was not Baron Samedi who whispered in her ear.

It was Jon the Conjurer. It was her father.

It was her father whom she felt now, lifting her from that cold dark place. Her father who whispered a word of healing. This was a magic he was well suited to, the dark magic of death, the delicate balance it held with life. And she felt that balance shift inside her, felt all the pain and sadness slowly begin to ebb away like a bad dream. The scales righted.

"Get up, daughter." There was a smile in his voice, and the pain had gone from her. She was healing. The voices were whispering to her again, singing faintly from the dark. A Song of Three. "For a queen never, *ever* kneels."

EPILOGUE

MARIE

One Week Later

Marie followed the smell of alchemy, the strange scent of metal and magic that made her skin crawl. There was a hint of foxglove too, the bitter smell of a trickster. She walked deeper into the Dreadwood, but its gnarled arms did not scare her now. Spirits called softly at her ear, beckoning for her to stay awhile. But she could not.

She had to return to her daughter. Now her queen. It was a paradox she was still getting used to. Her mind turned to New Orleans, to the Quarter, as it had done in the days since her return from the Veil. Communication with the other Voodoos had been sparse, only a quick letter with Claudette, who'd taken the Voodoos underground within the city as best she could while they waited for the fallout from Corbin's death to pass. News of the undead uprising had already spread like wildfire in the city, although Jon had made sure to lay the zombi to rest deep within the Dreadwood for safekeeping. Such power, Jon had warned, they would need to soon call upon.

Now Marie ventured farther into the haunted wood, past glowing yellow eyes and sharp teeth that showed from the dark. She'd faced down demons. Death. Her own past. There was nothing in these woods to fear now, least of all the alchemist who was somewhere in her midst, playing a game.

"Show yourself, alchemist," Marie shouted. "Silas!"

There was a distinct *whoosh*, the softness of footfalls over dried leaves, and she turned to see Silas leaning against a withered tree, his white staff hanging over his shoulder, his spill of pale hair trailing to his waist.

"Hello, priestess."

In the week since she'd been pulled back from the Veil, life had seemed to move faster, the days shorter than she remembered. She felt as if she'd aged an eternity in that shrouded world of death and twilight. But Silas looked as if he *had* aged. Something was wrong. "I'm quite busy at the moment."

His lips quirked. "So it seems."

A moment of silence between them. His dark blue eyes drifted curiously in the direction that led to Jon's hut. "How is she?"

"My daughter," said Marie, her tone protective, "is mending."

It was the truth. It had taken two days for her to regain consciousness, but when she had, Marie had nearly wept for an entire day. She'd done so privately, as it would do no good for Ree to see her like that, less so for Jon. Her heart constricted at the thought of the Conjurer, the man she'd been forced to share a house with for days on end. Her eyes raised to the withered canopy above, to the glimpses of fading sunlight. They hadn't killed each other yet. But there was still time.

"She needs longer to recover. Her wounds . . ." She closed her eyes, unable to think of that night when death had tried its best to take her daughter from her again. "She just needs a little more time."

"There is none left, Marie. We're out of time."

Marie met his eyes. He was not toying with her. He was being serious, more serious than she had ever seen him. "But the Inquisition—"

"No, Marie. You misunderstand. The Second Holy Inquisition . . ." He turned toward the edge of the wood that led out to the eastern bayou and, beyond that, the golden arms of New Orleans. ". . . has already begun."

Marie thought they might have more time. Surely after news of

Corbin's death reached the governor, there was a chance martial law might have been declared in fear of further mutiny. That may have bought them some time. The governor's influence could supersede that of the Church. It was a slim bet.

"The tribunal has formed, and they've made their decision clear: Marie Laveau the Second is to be tried for charges of heresy and necromancy. They've formally called for her arrest this morning."

"And?" She could tell that there was more. Saints, there was always more.

His lips quirked into a sneer. "Inquisitor Broussard is to be the one to arrest her."

The matter of Henryk Broussard was a complication she couldn't work out quite yet. When Silas had told her in their meeting before of how the boy was his and Antoine's spy, she'd been skeptical at best. Fearful at worst. Her daughter had loved this strange boy. And she suspected, after everything she'd heard Ree recount about the time Marie was in the Veil, that he might love her too. Love could be a fickle thing. A strange thing that could be twisted. But perhaps Broussard was a hidden advantage in this whole matter. Perhaps he might be their only hope.

Marie stared down at the gem-flecked dragon at the end of the Grand Wizard's staff. The serpent coiled in upon itself. She knew it to be a mark of ancient alchemy, but she'd always thought it was a warning of some kind, although of what she could not say.

"Can I count on the Brotherhood to hold up their end of the deal?" Marie asked quietly. It was foolish to make deals with devils, she knew, but she was out of options. Taking on the Church would be a truly complicated matter, no matter her faith.

It would be a war.

"So long as those paths align," he said simply.

"And when they do not?"

"Are you sure you want the answer to that question, Marie?" When the Grand Wizard spoke again, there was a strange note to his tone, a suggestion of danger to come. "Let us fight one war at a time."

Marie held his eyes. She understood now that Silas Favreau was a man frustratingly intent on speaking in riddles, even if she made no effort to solve them. It was his armor. What he was truly hiding beneath, she could not say. Nor did she want to find out. And yet . . .

She must know. "Whose side are you on, Silas, *truly*?"

Silas took a step into the twilight, into that portion of the land that swirled with dusk and shadow. He cast a look over his shoulder, the barest hint of a smile.

"My own."

Marie closed her eyes, offered a small prayer to her saints. There might not be any saving his soul in the end, she knew. Just as there might not be a way to save hers. She felt another feather-soft *whoosh*, the stir of the wind in her hair and in the trees, then opened her eyes.

He was gone.

When Marie returned to Jon's hut, she found Ree was still sleeping, Jon sitting at her side. Ree's little black bird, Aram, was perched on Jon's shoulder. She'd always hated that little bird, that piece of Jon that she could never be rid of. Maybe that hate had never really been for Aram. Maybe it had always been for herself, the part of her that had still longed for the Conjurer.

Sosie was perched on a shelf, watching the little bird with unblinking eyes. An air of hostility charged between the two familiars. Marie might have laughed, had her mood not been so soured. They were a house full of uneasy truces all around, it seemed.

She kept her face coolly impassive as she swept into the room and took the seat on the opposite side of Ree's bed. But inside? She wasn't quite sure what to make of this, the three of them, a makeshift family again. It hurt because it was happening now, after all this time, and it hurt more to know that it might never happen again. If Silas's words were any indication, there was danger waiting in the city now, waiting for them.

They couldn't stay in the bayou. They couldn't hide forever. She was aware of Jon's gaze on her, but he didn't say a word. He knew her well enough to know that something had changed. When she looked up, their eyes met. His were gentle and tawny in the cool dusk. The exact way they had looked in her nightmares, and sometimes in the sweeter dreams too. The Veil had frozen his features in place, as beautifully preserved as amber and bone. But his eyes.

They had changed some, she realized. They were far wiser now, the magic behind them churning with complicated possibility.

"You would work with the Brotherhood, Marie?" Jon asked quietly.

"I might work with the devil if I thought it would save my child."

"*Our* child."

Marie pursed her lips but said nothing. She'd learned in the last few days to hold her tongue, no matter the urge she had to yell and scream. How easy it was for him to acknowledge this familial bond. How easy it might be for Marie to remind him that he had nearly thrown it away for bloodshed, orders of the gods be damned. The truth was, she didn't just want to fight with Jon; she had wanted him to fight *for* them. She had thought herself steadfast in her faith, but even she would do away with her devotion if it meant she might hurt her daughter. Why was it so easy for Jon to put his faith before his family?

But his eyes told her that it was not easy at all. That the dark work of death and sacrifice had changed him in ways she could not comprehend.

"Yes," Marie said. "Our child, Jon. And today the Inquisition has called for her arrest. How long do you think we can hide here in the shadows?"

He stared at Ree's face for a long time, and she wondered if he might be seeing the child he had lost before. The daughter the Lord of Death had claimed for his own.

That the loa might have demanded her daughter's death as a necessary sacrifice frightened her. It frightened her more how easily Jon might have obeyed. But hadn't God tested Abraham the very same? Hadn't he commanded him to sacrifice his own child, his son Isaac, on an altar? Why could she so readily accept this story and not Jon's? *Because Isaac was not your child. Because you are selfish, Marie.*

"We are not hiding, Marie," Jon said finally. He was staring down at Ree, some notion working behind his eyes' golden depths. "We are preparing."

Suddenly Ree took her hand. Marie knew she had been listening. But there was no point in hiding things from her now. *No lies.* It had been her promise to Jon, but now she could see it in where she had gone so wrong with Ree. If only she had not kept so many secrets, maybe they might have avoided where they were now.

Marie cast a look over her daughter, her beautifully reckless and rebellious daughter, and wondered why she had ever tried to stamp that out of her, to correct the nature that God had intended. Whatever Ree was, for all her faults, for all her differences from Marie, she was what the loa intended, what they all needed. Rebellion was in her blood. And now—Marie squeezed the hand that was in hers, laid a kiss against her damp brow—rebellion had somehow found its way into her too.

"No fighting," Ree said as she sat up. "For fuck's sake, I can't take any more fighting."

The corners of Jon's eyes crinkled at Ree's coarseness. He would get used to it in time.

"There will be no fighting. Not between us," Jon said, voice darkening. "This is a time for learning."

A smile had worked its way onto Ree's lips. She was trying and failing to put on a brave face, to undo the damage of what she'd nearly done to herself by calling on the dead. There were hollows beneath her eyelids, and perhaps deeper scars Marie could not see. But she was the Quarter Queen now. And she would come to understand that it was a position that demanded sin as much as it gave blessings.

"Come," Jon said as he rose to his feet. "Let me show you."

Ree hesitated. And rightfully so. Here was her father, the man who had tried to kill her.

But he was also the very same man who had cast death's shadow from her body, had showed her how to control this strange magic within her when no one else could. Not even Marie.

"You . . ." Her voice trembled; she was unable to say more.

Jon reached out, grasping her hand in his. For all Ree's weariness, she did not pull away.

"I know," he finally murmured. "After what happened to me, to my family . . . I craved revenge. War." Old, unspeakable pain ignited behind those golden eyes, a flame that might never be fully stamped out. "And I still do. Badly. I threw myself to the gods and made myself a weapon to their will. I'm not sorry for that. Not one bit. But those things I wanted? I never should have wanted them more than I wanted *you*. My flesh and blood. My daughter." His gaze flitted to Marie, who watched, stone-faced. *Go on,* she silently urged. *Finish the story.* "I don't deserve your forgiveness. But I would—I *will*—spend a thousand lifetimes kneeled at your altar begging for it, if you could try, Marie Laveau the Second."

Slowly, Ree managed a faint nod, lips trembling. So, there was grace in her yet, more than Marie had ever been capable of, despite her prayers to her many saints and to God.

Marie glanced away, tears stinging her eyes. All this time, selfishly, she had thought that her daughter had needed only her mother. But fate was a cruel mistress. She'd only ever been able to give half of herself, always more queen than mother, always more secrets than the honesty Ree deserved. And the plain truth was, Ree didn't need just her mother, nor just her father. She needed both. She needed a family. Marie recalled Jon's mural in the tomb with stinging clarity. A picture of what might have been. And yet, what might still be.

Gently, Jon helped Ree from the bed, then carried her outside into the cool of the bayou. Marie quietly followed, trailing in their shadow, her mind turned to the past. How many times had she walked this path out into the wilderness, hand in hand with Jon? How strange and beautiful it was now to see the story repeat itself.

Outside, Jon drew three symbols into the ground. The sun. The moon. The star. He drew a line, weaving them together. They made a veve that Marie had never seen before, a shape of magic that began to pulse with life anew.

"Our magic is stronger together," said Jon. "I can promise you this: Divided we will fail. And they will pick us off one by one. But together? Together we would be . . ." His lips rose into something like a smile. ". . . limitless."

Jon held out his hand to Ree. She slowly took it, timid in her own way, unsure still of what to make of the Conjurer, the man of myth and lore and death who was her father.

Jon turned to Marie. He held out his hand, waiting.

She thought of Corbin's ball when he had done the same, then again in the Veil. Both had been invitations to more, to step into a destiny greater than she might know. She had taken it then. Marie caught his eyes and, despite everything—the pain between them, the misery, the love that might yet still exist—he winked.

Marie felt her heart stammer, that same spark of old feeling that she had not allowed herself to acknowledge for twenty-five long years. Her heart, the thing of stone. Turning like gears set to a miserable clockwork. Against her better wishes, it was coming alive again. She held Jon's gaze a moment longer. Maybe, just maybe, it had never truly died.

Marie took the Conjurer's hand once more, a smile playing at her lips.

She felt herself lifting from the ground. The three of them rose higher and higher, golden light threaded among them, binding them into a circle of three over the sun, moon, and star veve. Their magic thrummed through their fingertips, jumping between each of them, sparking to life like flames on a wick. As the seconds passed, she saw the color return to Ree's cheeks, the bruises recede, the hollows in her eyes slowly fill.

Marie heard a rustling in the trees, the whisper of the ancestors and the spirits and the gods, a stirring in the wind that sounded of faint singing. Marie closed her eyes, relishing in the glory of the moment.

It was a new feeling, a safety she thought she might never find. In this trinity, she was sure that the deep wounds of the past would heal, their sins and shames forgiven, and in its magic, they might finally be made whole.

HISTORICAL NOTE

Sosie, the name of Marie's beloved snake in this story, means "double" in French.

I found this name as an appropriate metaphor for the parallels between Marie and Ree and the world they inhabited. The events of this book are an alternate history that exists within a heightened "second reality" just askew of the real nineteenth-century New Orleans. Represented in a fantastical context, this is a world that is both horrifically like the one we know and one we do not.

The real-life Marie Laveau was in fact a long-reigning Voodoo Queen in New Orleans who, after the disappearance of her husband, Jacques Paris, was regarded as the Widow Paris. Much of what we know about her life remains frustratingly vague—*veiled,* if you will. I like to imagine that's exactly the way a woman like Marie intended. Marie Laveau II (stylized Marie Laveau the Second within this book for more dramatic flair) was not called Ree and was entirely an invention of my own, to distinguish her from her mother and to give her more of her own sense of character. It is true that Marie had other children, but none were more infamous than Marie II, often regarded as being more "wicked" than her mother. Readers will find a mix of my own historical research and imaginings of what Marie's and Ree's inner emotional worlds must have looked like. I was most drawn to exploring what a sense of power must have meant for a Voodoo Queen like Marie Laveau, and how she must have negotiated this in a world hellbent on taking it from her and all her kind. *That* was the story I endeavored to tell here.

The title *The Quarter Queen* is an invention of my own, made up of the real-life epithet for Marie as the "Voodoo Queen" and the iconic part of New Orleans known as the French Quarter, where she dwelled. The intent behind the title is to go beyond the trappings of an honorific and to interrogate the politics and spiritual significance of what carrying such a mantel might mean in a world so factionally divided by racial and magical lines. Figures such as Sanite Dede and Marie Saloppe did actually exist, and were prominent Voodoo Queens in the city. Thought by many to be teachers for a young and enterprising Marie Laveau, the order in which they are the Quarter Queens in this novel has been intentionally switched for plot purposes. John Bayou (or Dr. John)—thought by some to be a Voodoo practitioner or king of renowned abilities, a contemporary of Marie Laveau's, and in some instances, one of her early teachers and mentors in the craft—existed. There were also the folkloric figures High John and John the Conqueror, characters in black folklore who came to represent trickery and resistance and revolution in a time when enslaved peoples shared stories orally. So, *TQQ*'s version of Jon the Conjurer (spelled differently here with intention to reflect this new take) is an amalgamation of such characters into one mythic but broken man whose sense of revolution has cost him dearly.

The Brotherhood of the White Hand is a fantasy representation of more fraternal occult orders that existed within the time, such as the Freemasons. It should be noted the real Father Antoine died in 1829. For the purposes of this novel, he is alive and well—a creative divergence taken to serve the fictional history of a Second Holy Inquisition. It should be noted that while the Spanish Crown (with papal approval) did in fact bring inquisitions to their colonies, one such never reached New Orleans. Allegedly. What we do know is that the real Father Antoine, before becoming a much-venerated figure of the local community, had ties to the Inquisition and perhaps sought to bring one to New Orleans. Thus, the historical events within the world of *The Quarter Queen* sprang from two questions: What if an inquisition *had* happened in New Orleans? and What might be the dangers if it happened *again*?

Fictional locations such as the House of Flowers and the Bridal Bridge are made up of my childhood memories of New Orleans and a more fantastical sense of wonder. The Haitian Revolution absolutely influenced politics within the city of New Orleans as well as its hold upon the slave trade. The word *zombi* can trace its origins to Vodun and Voodoo, having existed within the creole tradition well before Hollywood got its hands on it. There are no malevolent steamboats in the city that I can recall. Readers will find reference to the Code Noir, which existed and was used to govern the lives of enslaved peoples. Slavery itself caused very real traumas: forced miscegenation, sexual violence, and beating and commodification of enslaved peoples and the separation of their families.

But do you know what else must have existed within this world? Joy, persistence, and enduring faith. I have found that history is a mix of both. Dear readers, if you take anything from this story, let it be the notion that the real bloodied past of this country can be frightening. But this fear, like any monster in fantasy, can only be overcome once properly confronted. As all those who are Catholic might say: Amen. But as Marie Laveau might close a prayer—*ase*.

ACKNOWLEDGMENTS

To anyone who still doubts it—magic very much exists. I know because I've been blessed enough to experience it firsthand with these special people in my life who've shown me grace and unending support.

To my darling agent, Emma Kapson, one of the very first believers in this book and its ability to be so much more in the end—a world, a force, a love letter to my creole roots. You are magic. You are my Quarter Queen. To the rest of my team and family at Verve, who championed this book deal and who tirelessly work behind the scenes to bring the rest of my stories to life: Liz Parker, Noah Ballard, Isaiah Williams, and Manal Hammad.

To the editor of my dreams: Natalie Hallak, you are a vision and a literary tour de force. I knew from our first meeting that this would be a match made in heaven. How you were able to alchemize and distill so many different elements into such pivotal moments for this story is simply beyond me. What we were able to accomplish together is simply a spell I never want to break. Here's to many more stories together.

My Ballantine family: To Ivanka Perez, who saw every iteration of this novel with unblinking focus and was a stalwart help in ushering this story into its final form. To my copy editor, Laura Dragonette, you are the best and a lifesaver! To my production editor, Jocelyn

Kiker, thank you for keeping this book together and on schedule! To Sophia Chunn, the *amazing* artist who created a simply enchanted cover for this moody little book. And to the rest of the team at Ballantine and Random House, thank you for believing in this book and bringing the Laveau legacy to life.

My family: To my maman, Gail, the woman whose story inspired this take on Marie Laveau, and to my stepfather, Lamar, for always having my back. To my amazing sisters, Kiana, Lila, Robyn, and Dana, who put up with hours on end of my absences when I disappeared for what must have seemed like an endless carousel of Zoom meetings and writing sessions.

My closest friends: To Nick, my partner in crime and mischief and movies, who kept me sane through many a creative-development call turned venting session. Thank you to Steve, one of my dearest friends, for first believing in me as a storyteller at one of the rawest points in my life. To Jake, who gave such sage notes for *TQQ* when this was just a television pilot that would soon turn into a whole lot more. Shout-out to Kelly Asher for being the very first person to inquire about pre-ordering this book. It meant the world to me. To Ryan Cunningham, who supported me as a writer so many times. To Nikki Coble for being such a great friend (even when I took a vow of silence to go away to write).

To the team of execs who championed this world and story through its different iterations: Geoffroy Faugerolas, Donnita Shaw, and Spencer Janes. To the writing and literature teachers over the years who inspired me to never give up and keep going: Bob Pope, Eric Wasserman, Dr. Jon Miller, Dr. Sheldon Wrice, Dr. Mary Biddinger, Alexi Zentner, Jaimee Wriston Colbert, Dr. Mary Grace Albanese, and Tom and Larry O'Neil. To my friends in BU's English Department, Donna and Colleen, whose cherished advice and guidance as a grad student and teacher helped me through many a tough day. Also, this book very much was written (and edited) to Sleep Token's "Rain" and "Dark Signs" as well as Sace6's "Limerence" on constant repeat.

And to you, dear readers. Thank you for making all this worth it in the end. May you find the magic in your life beyond these pages and never, ever let it go.

ABOUT THE AUTHOR

KAYLA HARDY is a mythology expert and multi-hyphenate author and screenwriter of Louisiana Creole descent. She earned a doctorate in English, specializing in creative writing and African American literature, from Binghamton University. Hardy is an adjunct professor at Binghamton University and an accomplished scholar of Black folklore, mythology, and Voodoo. *The Quarter Queen* is her first novel.

kaylahardy.com
Instagram: @ohkaylago

ABOUT THE TYPE

This book was set in Cheltenham, a typeface created in 1896 by a distinguished American architect, Bertram Grosvenor Goodhue (1869–1924), and produced at the Cheltenham Press in New York in 1902 by Ingalls Kimball, who suggested that the face be called Cheltenham. It was designed with long ascenders and short descenders as a result of legibility studies indicating that the eye identifies letters by scanning their tops. The Mergenthaler Linotype Company put the typeface on machine in 1906, and Cheltenham has maintained its popularity for more than a century.